THE TALISMAN

VOLUME 1: THE ROAD OF TRIALS

STEPHEN KING and PETER STRAUB

THE TALISMAN

VOLUME 1: THE ROAD OF TRIALS

Adapted by ROBIN FURTH

Artwork by TONY SHASTEEN

Colors by NEI RUFFINO & JD METTLER

Lettering by BILL TORTOLINI

BALLANTINE BOOKS
NEW YORK

The Talisman: The Road of Trials is a work of fiction. Names, characters, places, and incidents are the products of the authors' imaginations or are used fictitiously. Any resemblance to actual events, locales, or persons, living or dead, is entirely coincidental.

Published in the United States by Del Rey, an imprint of The Random House Publishing Group, a division of Random House, Inc., New York.

ISBN 978-0-345-51798-2

Printed in the United States of America on acid-free paper

www.delreybooks.com

9 8 7 6 5 4 3 2 1

First Edition

Welcome to the Territories

The opening chapter of this graphic novel
is a never-before-told prequel to *The Talisman*.
In it we discover the dual lives of Jack's father, Philip
Sawyer: one that he lives with his family
in the world as we know it, and the other in a
mysterious land known as the Territories.

And don't miss the back of this book, which
contains all-new material about the making of
The Talisman graphic novel!

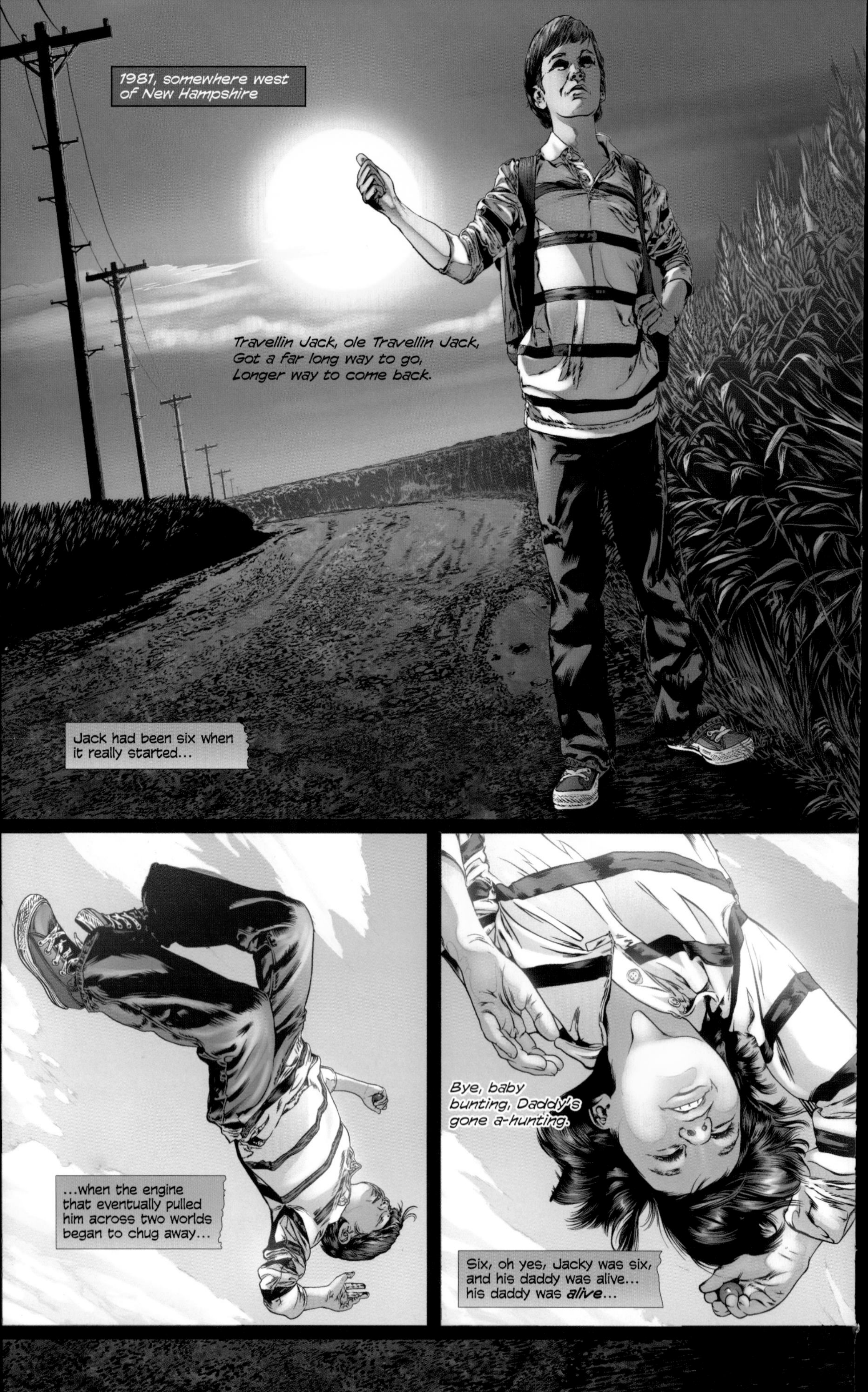
1981, somewhere west of New Hampshire
Travellin Jack, ole Travellin Jack, Got a far long way to go, Longer way to come back.
Jack had been six when it really started...
...when the engine that eventually pulled him across two worlds began to chug away...
Bye, baby bunting, Daddy's gone a-hunting.
Six, oh yes, Jacky was six, and his daddy was alive... his daddy was *alive*...

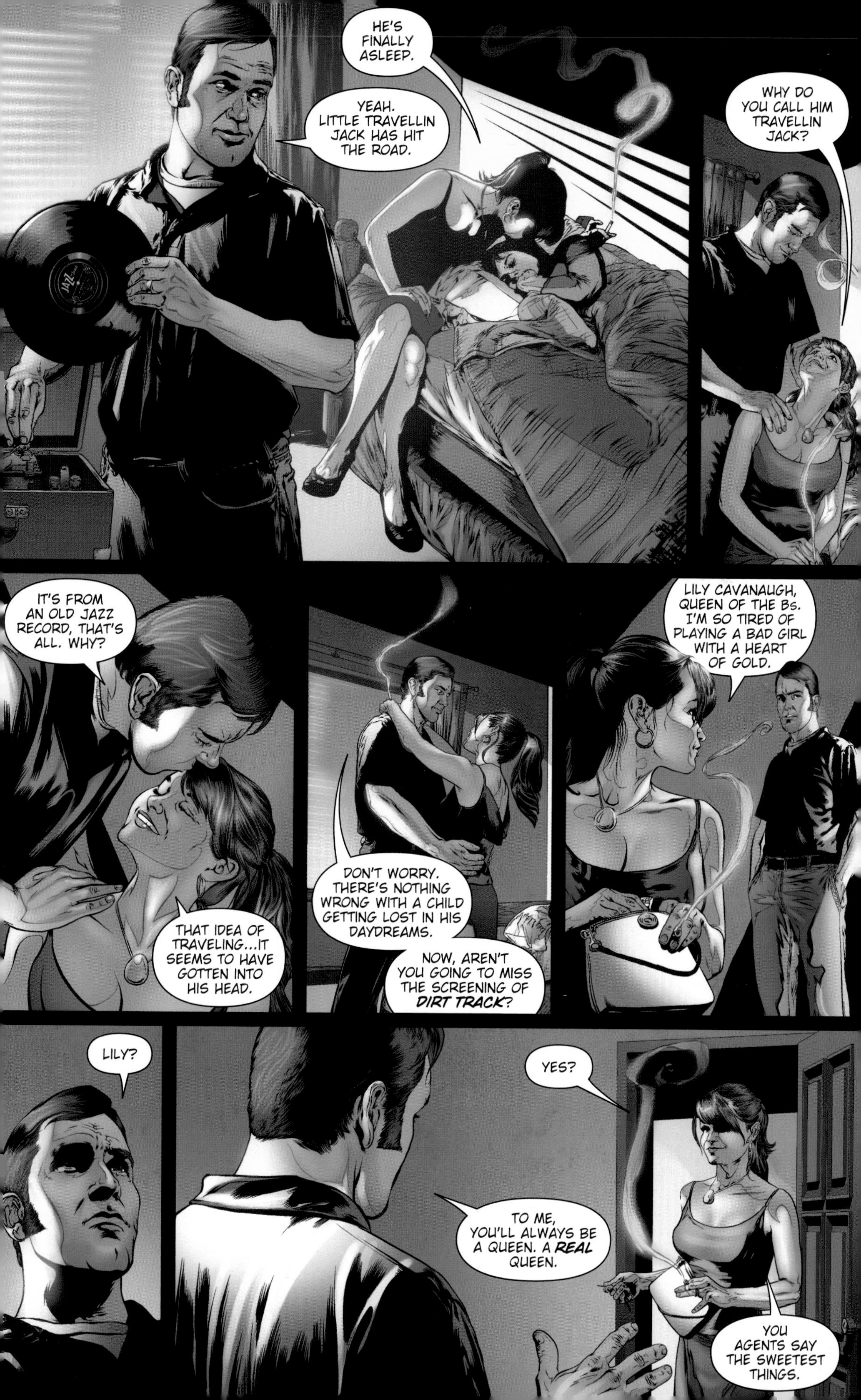
HE'S FINALLY ASLEEP.
YEAH. LITTLE TRAVELLIN JACK HAS HIT THE ROAD.
WHY DO YOU CALL HIM TRAVELLIN JACK?
IT'S FROM AN OLD JAZZ RECORD, THAT'S ALL. WHY?
THAT IDEA OF TRAVELING...IT SEEMS TO HAVE GOTTEN INTO HIS HEAD.
DON'T WORRY. THERE'S NOTHING WRONG WITH A CHILD GETTING LOST IN HIS DAYDREAMS.
NOW, AREN'T YOU GOING TO MISS THE SCREENING OF *DIRT TRACK*?
LILY CAVANAUGH, QUEEN OF THE Bs. I'M SO TIRED OF PLAYING A BAD GIRL WITH A HEART OF GOLD.
LILY?
YES?
TO ME, YOU'LL ALWAYS BE A QUEEN. A ***REAL*** QUEEN.
YOU AGENTS SAY THE SWEETEST THINGS.

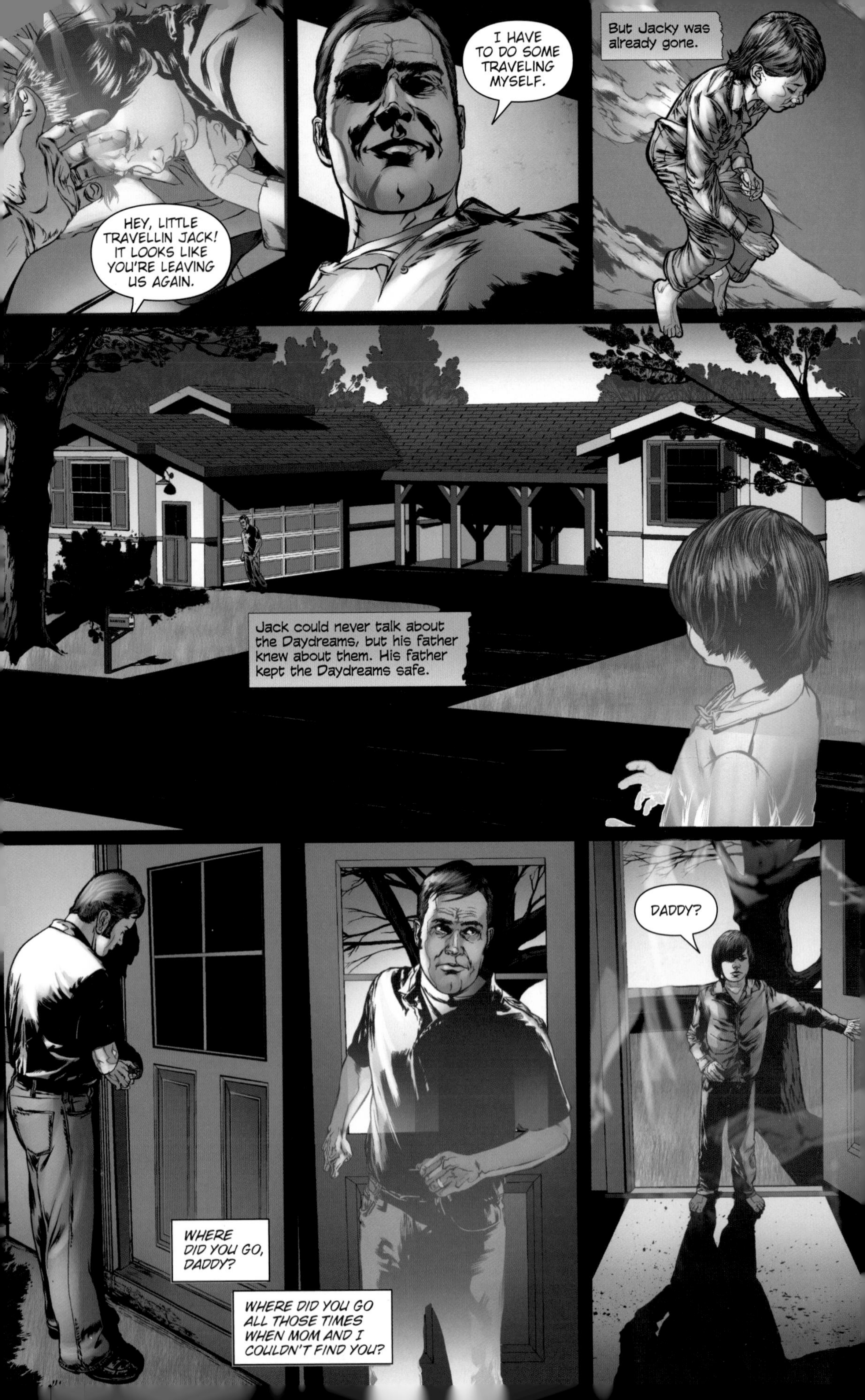
HEY, LITTLE TRAVELLIN JACK! IT LOOKS LIKE YOU'RE LEAVING US AGAIN.
I HAVE TO DO SOME TRAVELING MYSELF.
But Jacky was already gone.
Jack could never talk about the Daydreams, but his father knew about them. His father kept the Daydreams safe.
WHERE DID YOU GO, DADDY?
WHERE DID YOU GO ALL THOSE TIMES WHEN MOM AND I COULDN'T FIND YOU?
DADDY?

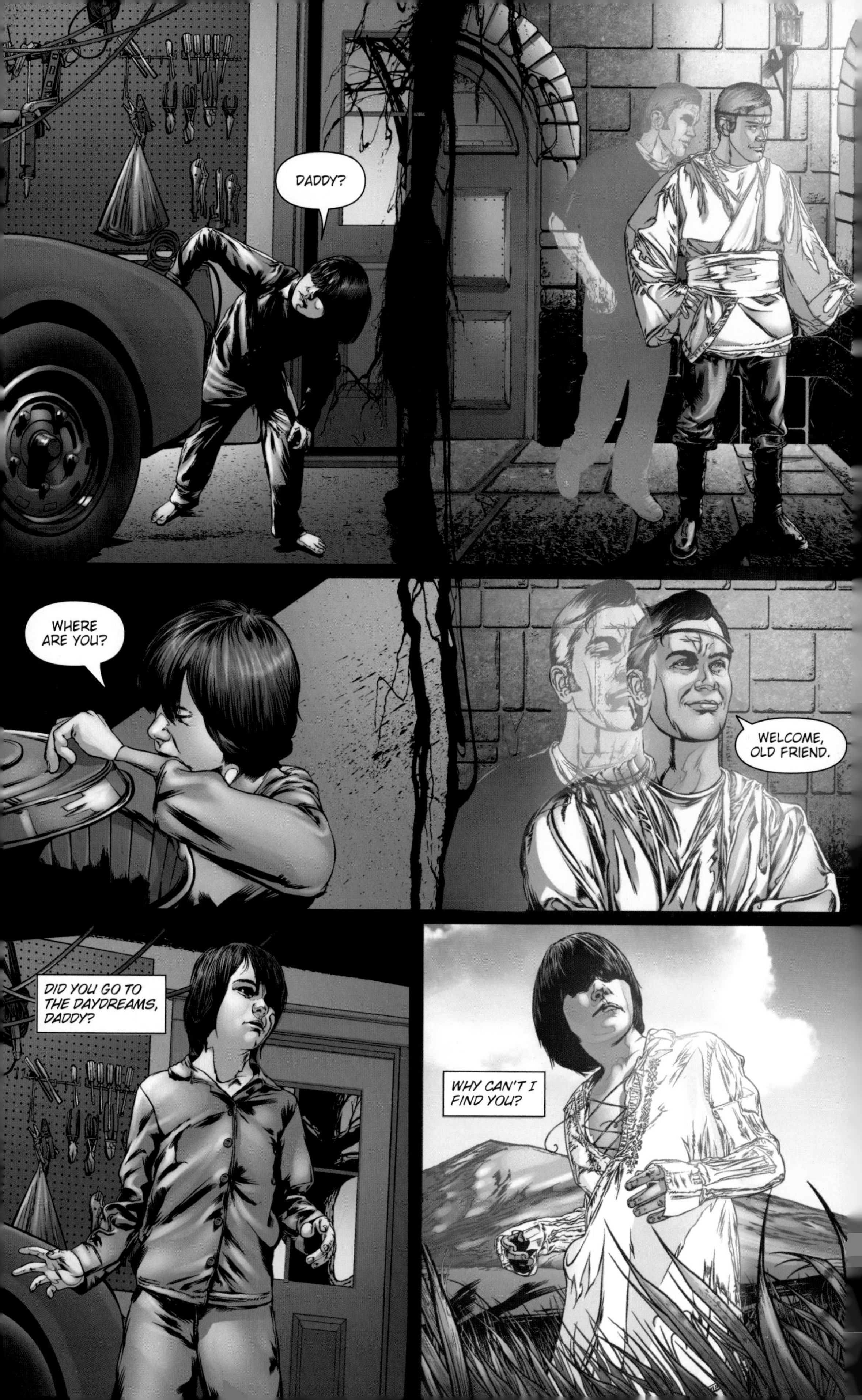
DADDY?
WHERE ARE YOU?
WELCOME, OLD FRIEND.
DID YOU GO TO THE DAYDREAMS, DADDY?
WHY CAN'T I FIND YOU?

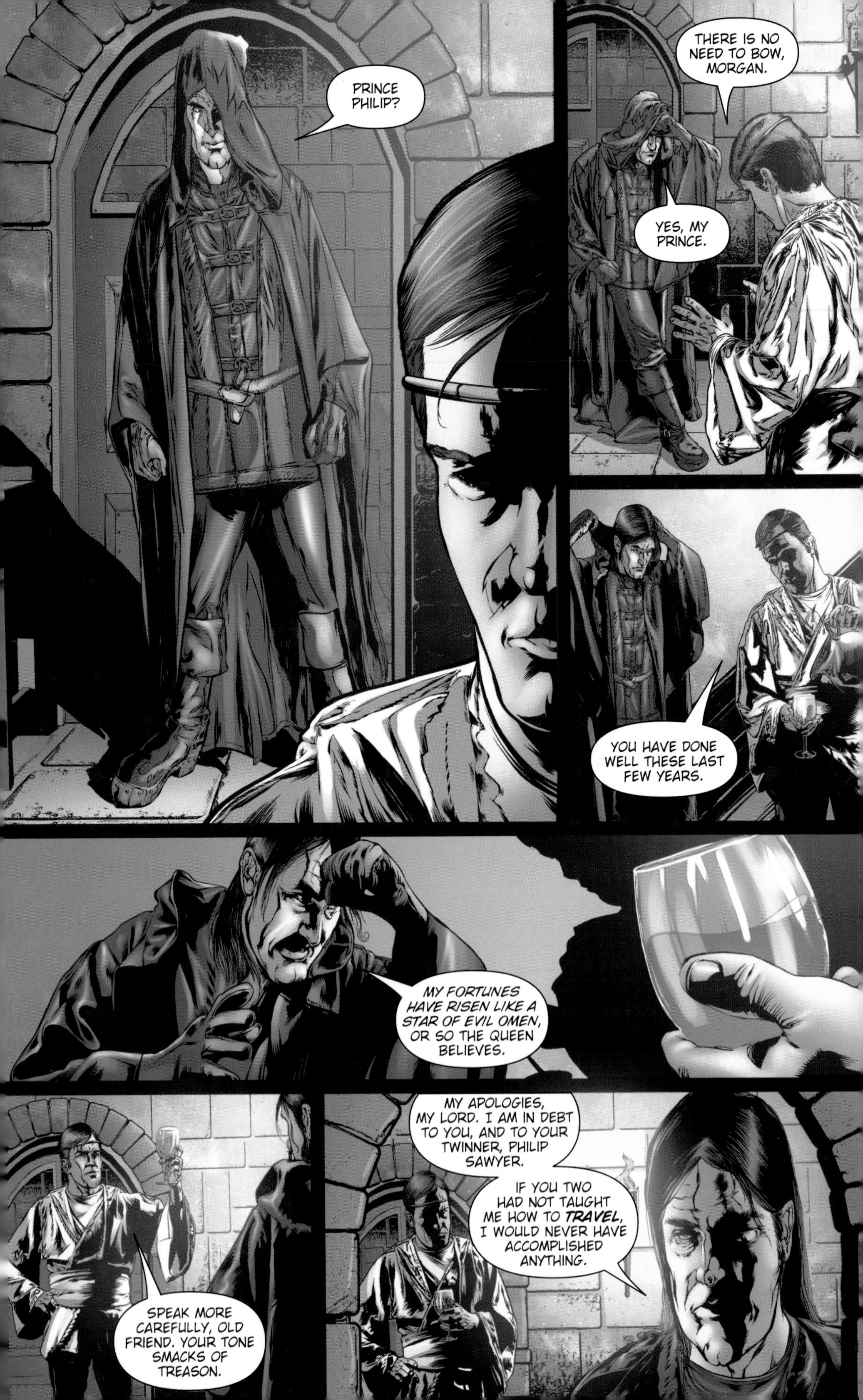
PRINCE PHILIP?
THERE IS NO NEED TO BOW, MORGAN.
YES, MY PRINCE.
YOU HAVE DONE WELL THESE LAST FEW YEARS.
MY FORTUNES HAVE RISEN LIKE A STAR OF EVIL OMEN, OR SO THE QUEEN BELIEVES.
SPEAK MORE CAREFULLY, OLD FRIEND. YOUR TONE SMACKS OF TREASON.
MY APOLOGIES, MY LORD. I AM IN DEBT TO YOU, AND TO YOUR TWINNER, PHILIP SAWYER.
IF YOU TWO HAD NOT TAUGHT ME HOW TO ***TRAVEL***, I WOULD NEVER HAVE ACCOMPLISHED ANYTHING.

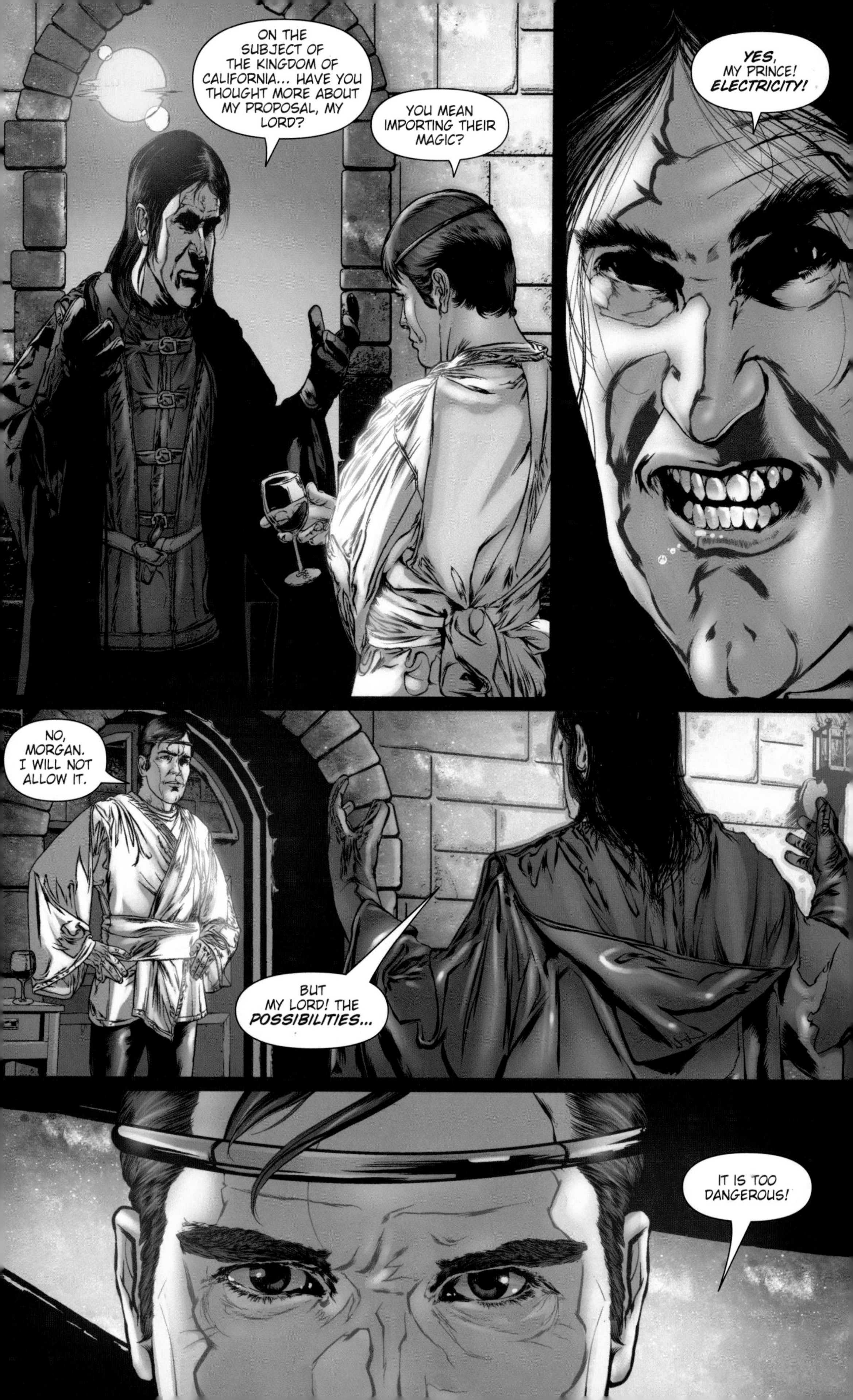
ON THE SUBJECT OF THE KINGDOM OF CALIFORNIA... HAVE YOU THOUGHT MORE ABOUT MY PROPOSAL, MY LORD?
YOU MEAN IMPORTING THEIR MAGIC?
YES, MY PRINCE! *ELECTRICITY!*
NO, MORGAN. I WILL NOT ALLOW IT.
BUT MY LORD! THE *POSSIBILITIES...*
IT IS TOO DANGEROUS!

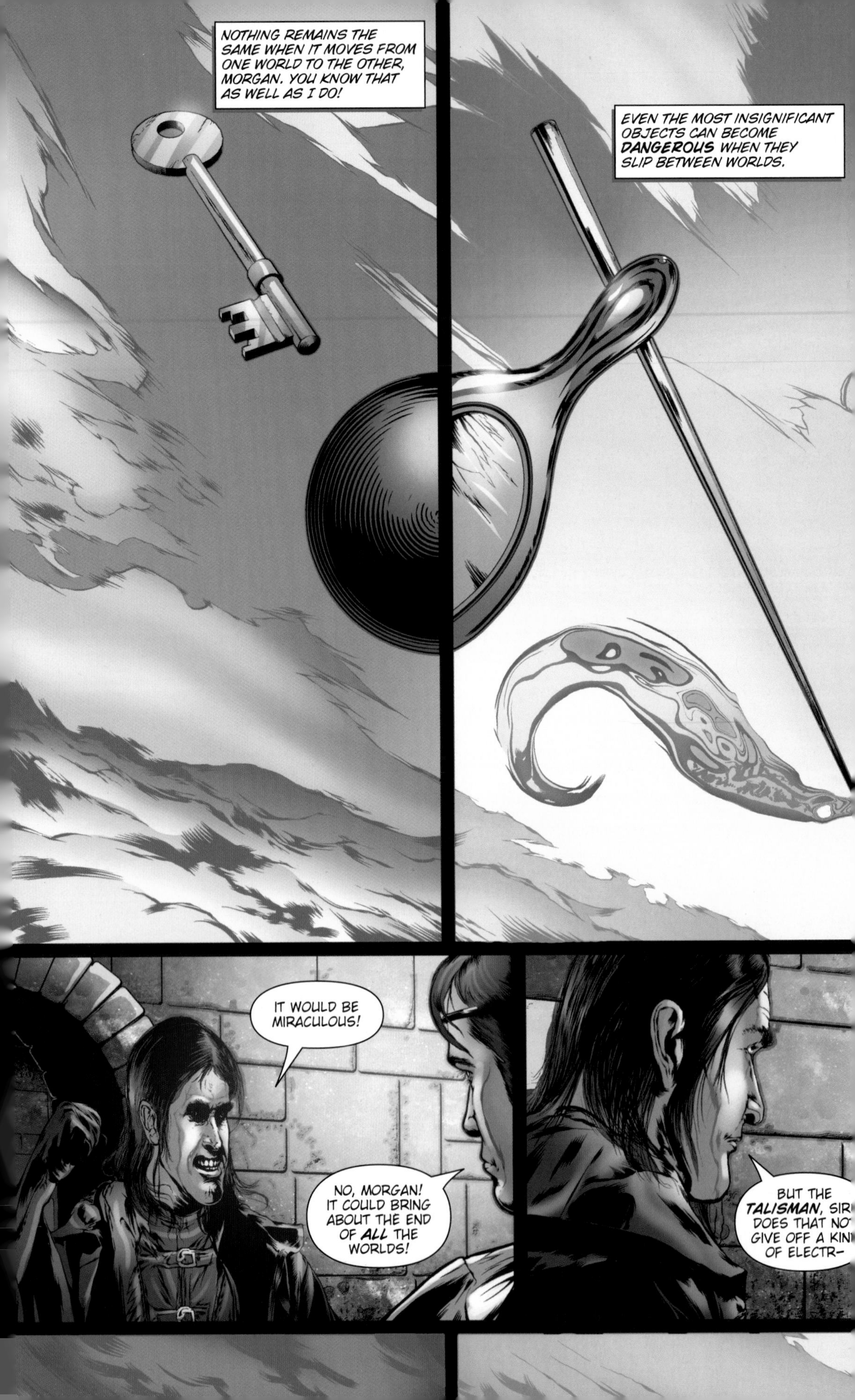
NOTHING REMAINS THE SAME WHEN IT MOVES FROM ONE WORLD TO THE OTHER, MORGAN. YOU KNOW THAT AS WELL AS I DO!
EVEN THE MOST INSIGNIFICANT OBJECTS CAN BECOME **DANGEROUS** WHEN THEY SLIP BETWEEN WORLDS.
IT WOULD BE MIRACULOUS!
NO, MORGAN! IT COULD BRING ABOUT THE END OF ***ALL*** THE WORLDS!
BUT THE ***TALISMAN***, SIR
DOES THAT NO
GIVE OFF A KIN
OF ELECTR–

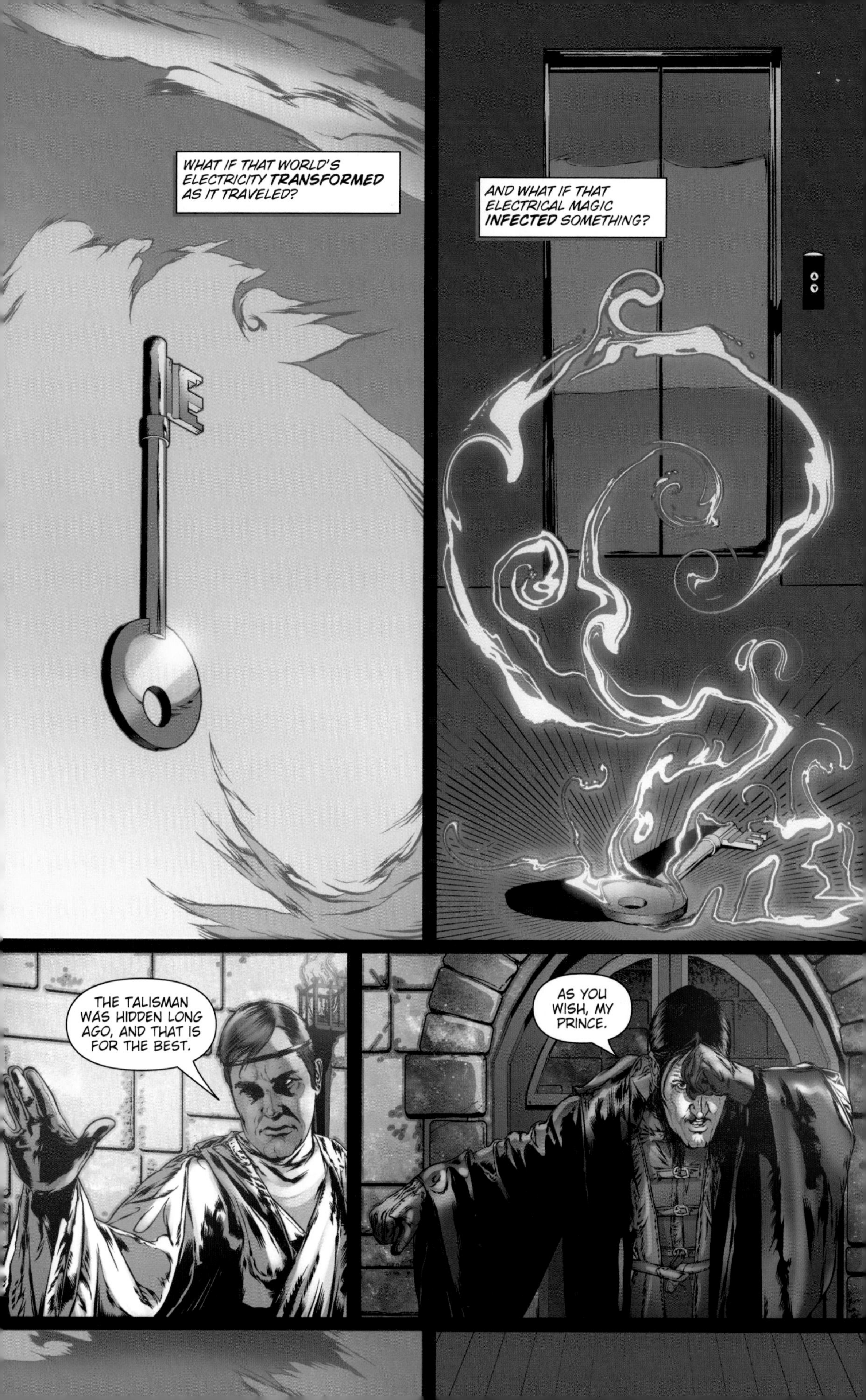
WHAT IF THAT WORLD'S ELECTRICITY TRANSFORMED AS IT TRAVELED?
AND WHAT IF THAT ELECTRICAL MAGIC INFECTED SOMETHING?
THE TALISMAN WAS HIDDEN LONG AGO, AND THAT IS FOR THE BEST.
AS YOU WISH, MY PRINCE.

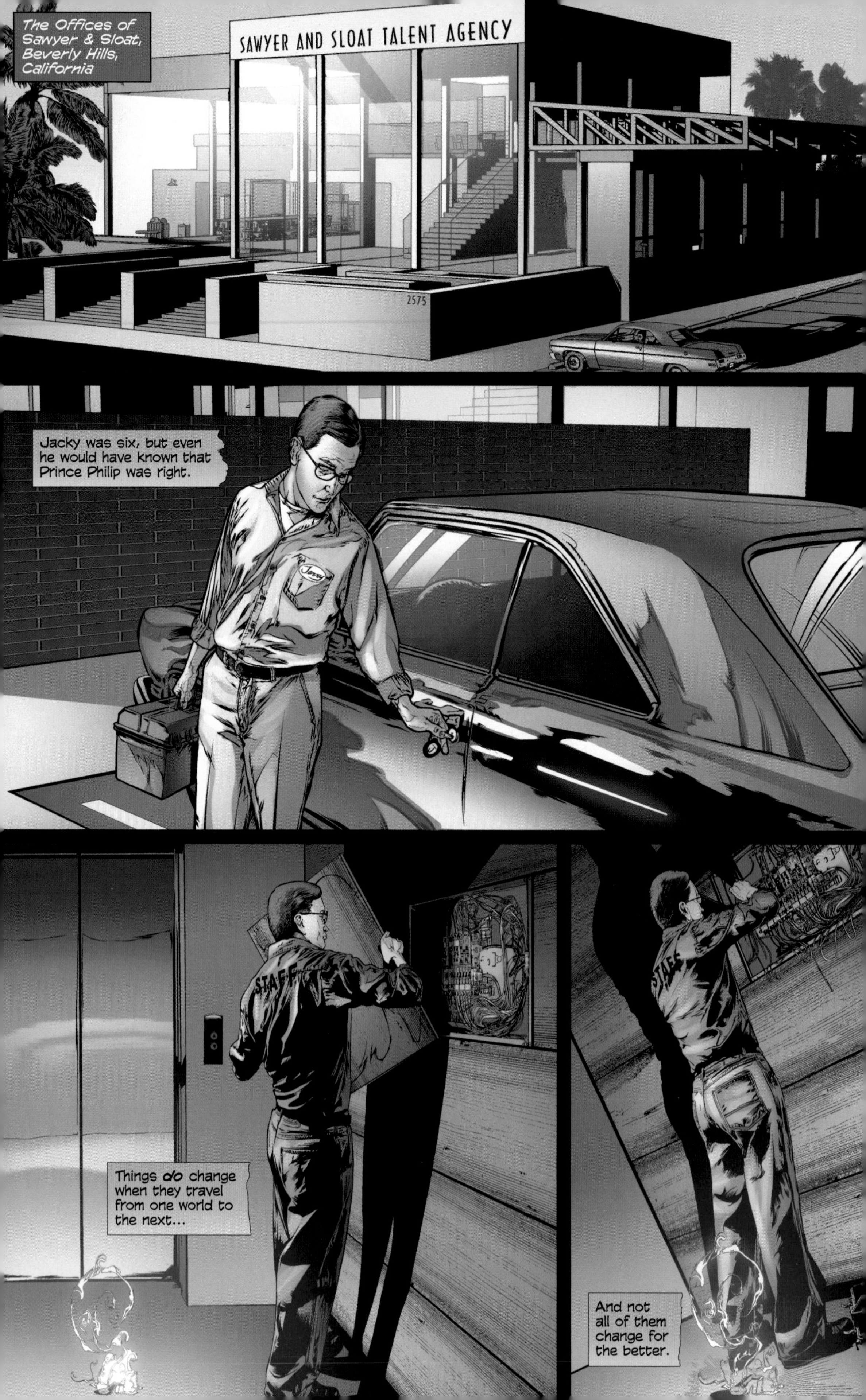

The Offices of Sawyer & Sloat, Beverly Hills, California
SAWYER AND SLOAT TALENT AGENCY
2575
Jacky was six, but even he would have known that Prince Philip was right.
Jerry
STAFF
Things *do* change when they travel from one world to the next...
STAFF
And not all of them change for the better.

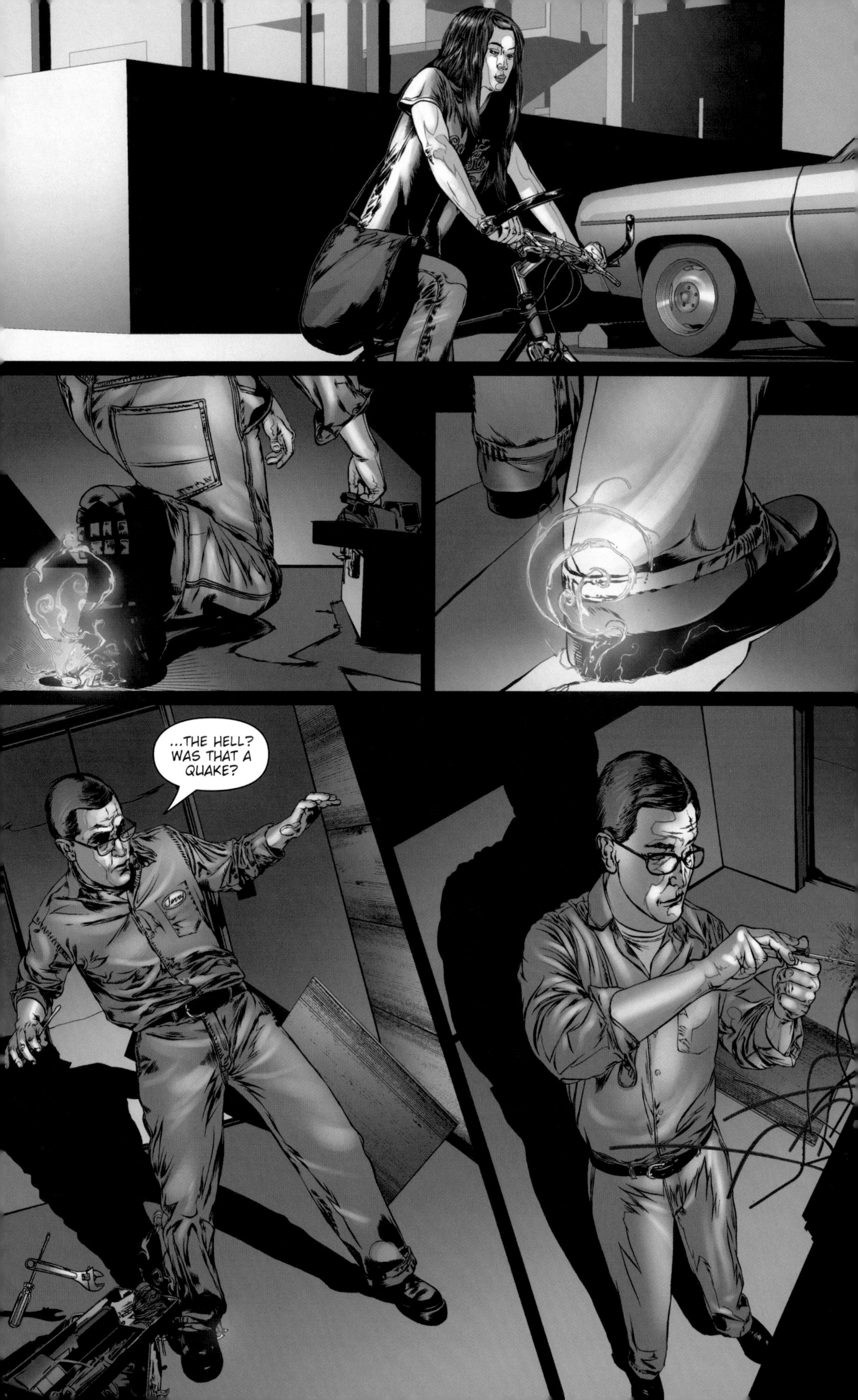
...THE HELL? WAS THAT A QUAKE?

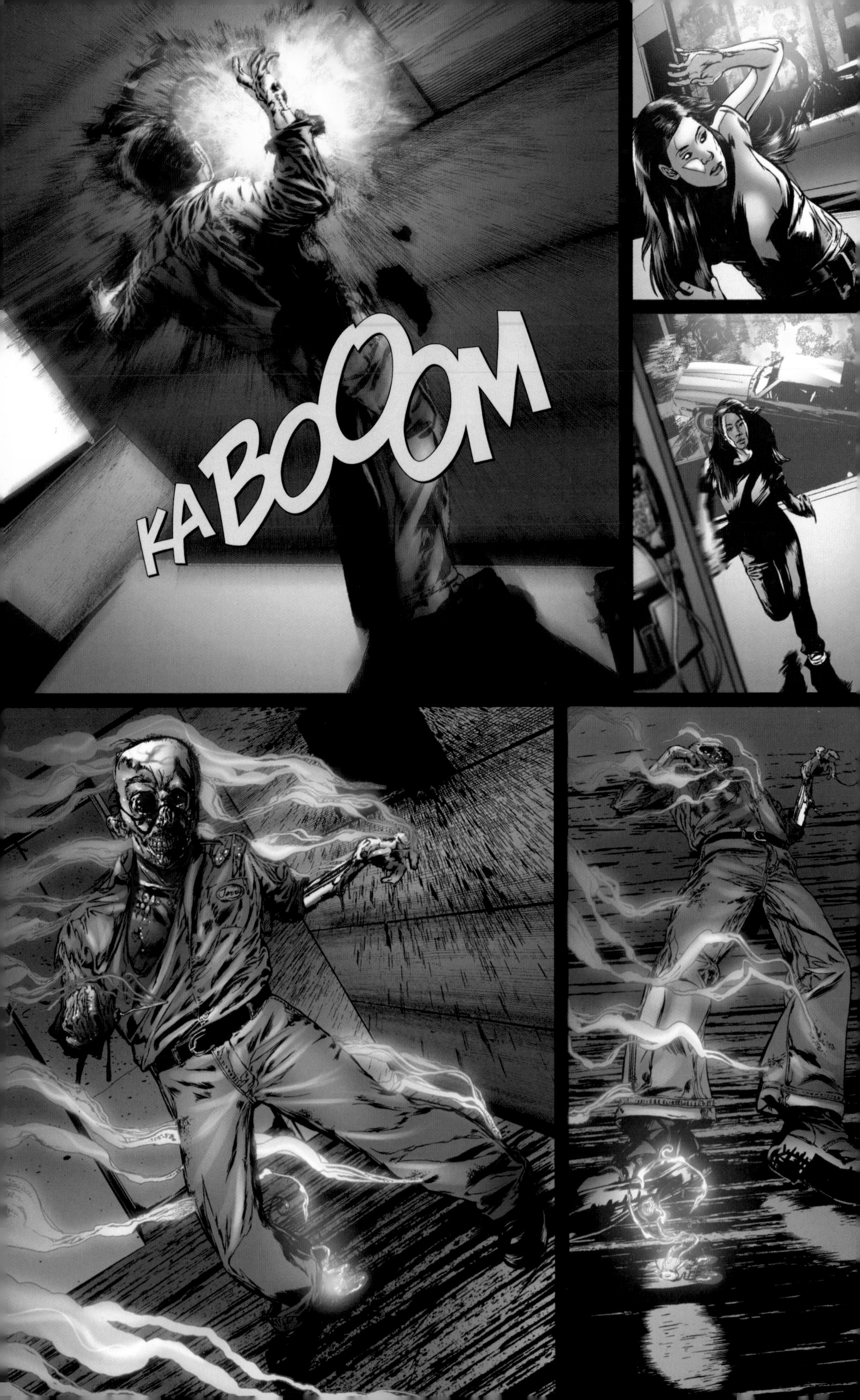
KABOOOM

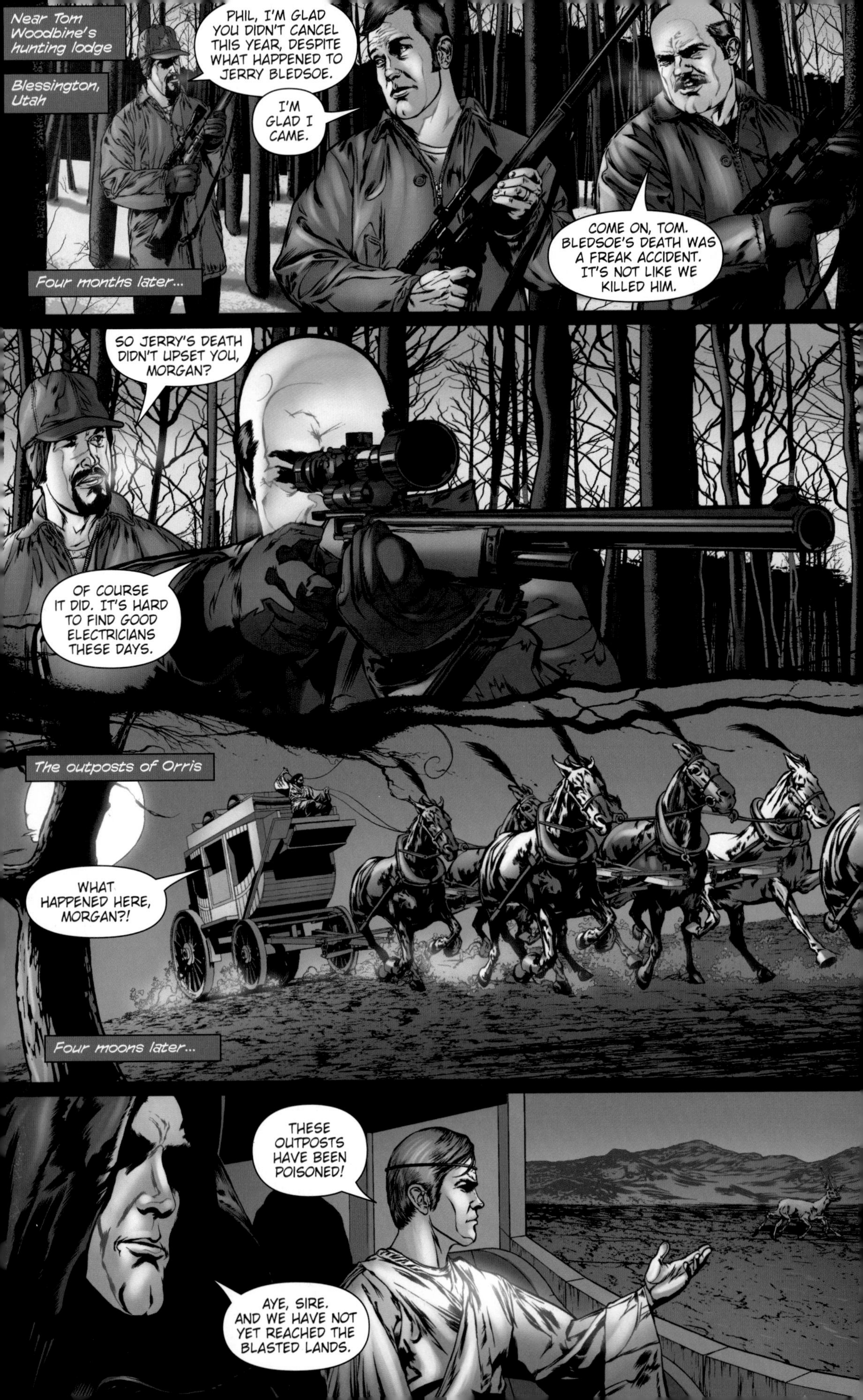
Near Tom Woodbine's hunting lodge
Blessington, Utah
PHIL, I'M GLAD YOU DIDN'T CANCEL THIS YEAR, DESPITE WHAT HAPPENED TO JERRY BLEDSOE.
I'M GLAD I CAME.
COME ON, TOM. BLEDSOE'S DEATH WAS A FREAK ACCIDENT. IT'S NOT LIKE WE KILLED HIM.
Four months later...
SO JERRY'S DEATH DIDN'T UPSET YOU, MORGAN?
OF COURSE IT DID. IT'S HARD TO FIND GOOD ELECTRICIANS THESE DAYS.
The outposts of Orris
WHAT HAPPENED HERE, MORGAN?!
Four moons later...
THESE OUTPOSTS HAVE BEEN POISONED!
AYE, SIRE. AND WE HAVE NOT YET REACHED THE BLASTED LANDS.

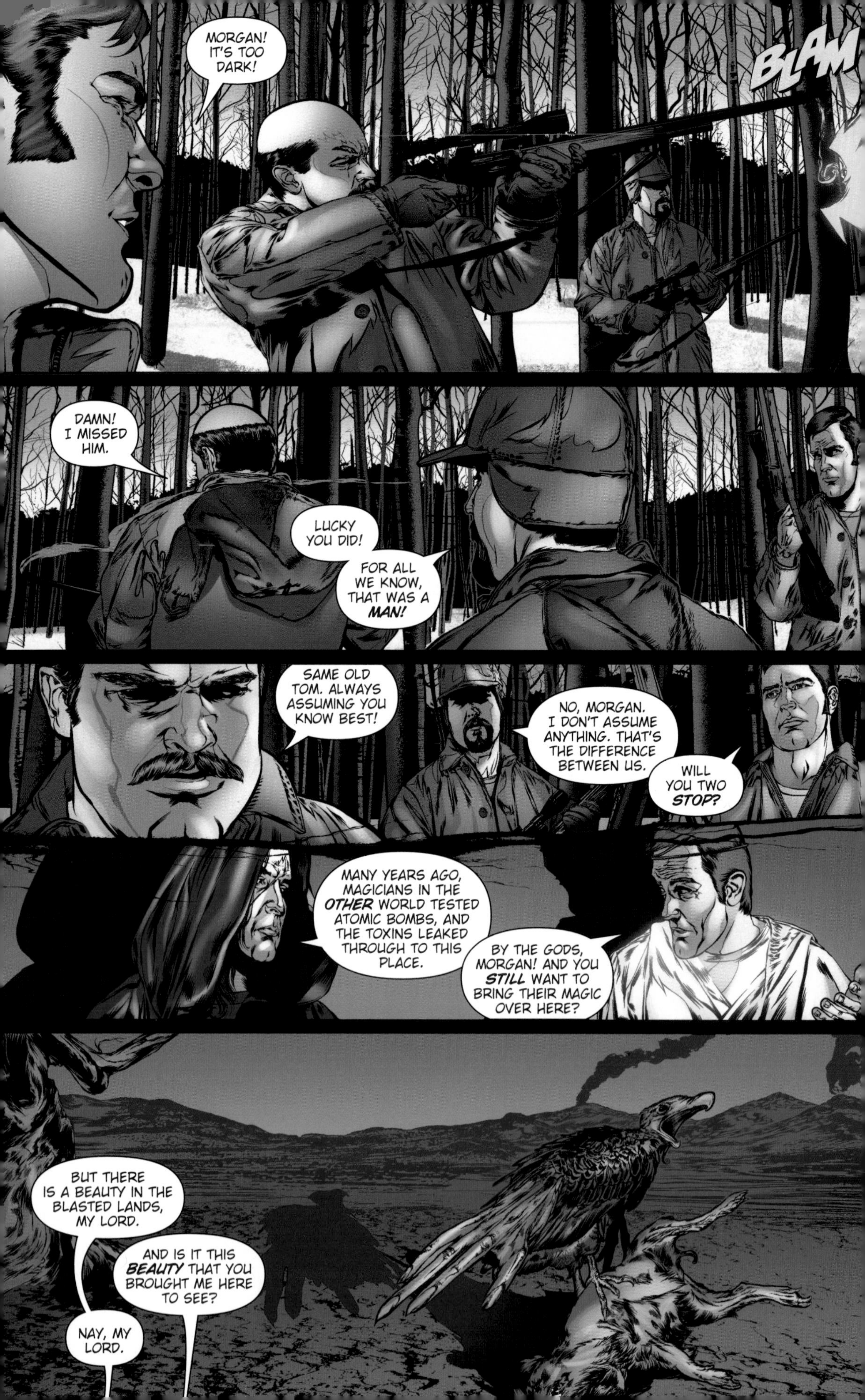
MORGAN! IT'S TOO DARK!
BLAM
DAMN! I MISSED HIM.
LUCKY YOU DID!
FOR ALL WE KNOW, THAT WAS A *MAN!*
SAME OLD TOM. ALWAYS ASSUMING YOU KNOW BEST!
NO, MORGAN. I DON'T ASSUME ANYTHING. THAT'S THE DIFFERENCE BETWEEN US.
WILL YOU TWO *STOP?*
MANY YEARS AGO, MAGICIANS IN THE *OTHER* WORLD TESTED ATOMIC BOMBS, AND THE TOXINS LEAKED THROUGH TO THIS PLACE.
BY THE GODS, MORGAN! AND YOU *STILL* WANT TO BRING THEIR MAGIC OVER HERE?
BUT THERE IS A BEAUTY IN THE BLASTED LANDS, MY LORD.
AND IS IT THIS *BEAUTY* THAT YOU BROUGHT ME HERE TO SEE?
NAY, MY LORD.

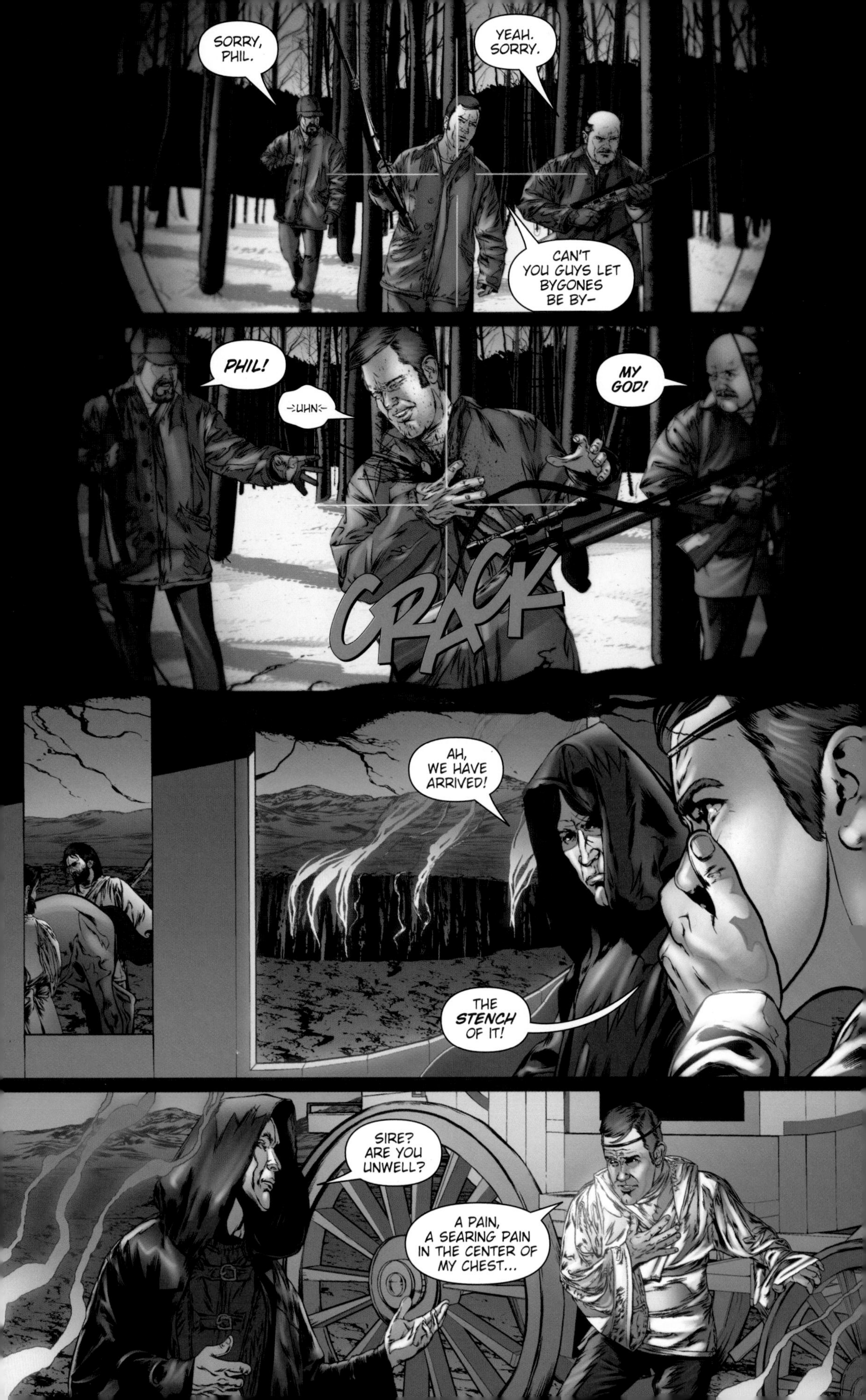
SORRY, PHIL.
YEAH. SORRY.
CAN'T YOU GUYS LET BYGONES BE BY–
PHIL!
UHN
MY GOD!
CRACK
AH, WE HAVE ARRIVED!
THE STENCH OF IT!
SIRE? ARE YOU UNWELL?
A PAIN, A SEARING PAIN IN THE CENTER OF MY CHEST...

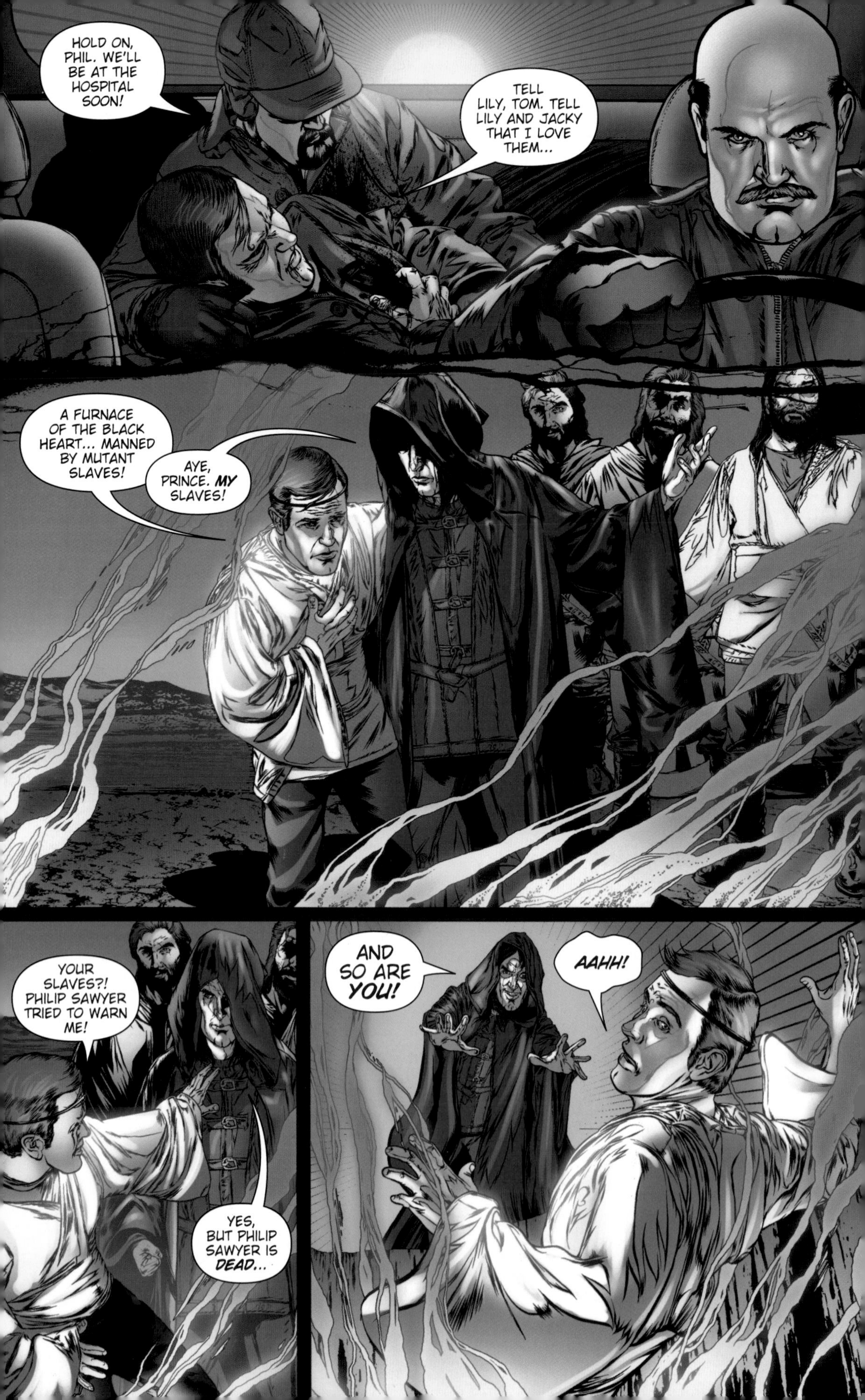
HOLD ON, PHIL. WE'LL BE AT THE HOSPITAL SOON!
TELL LILY, TOM. TELL LILY AND JACKY THAT I LOVE THEM...
A FURNACE OF THE BLACK HEART... MANNED BY MUTANT SLAVES!
AYE, PRINCE. MY SLAVES!
YOUR SLAVES?! PHILIP SAWYER TRIED TO WARN ME!
YES, BUT PHILIP SAWYER IS DEAD...
AND SO ARE YOU!
AAHH!

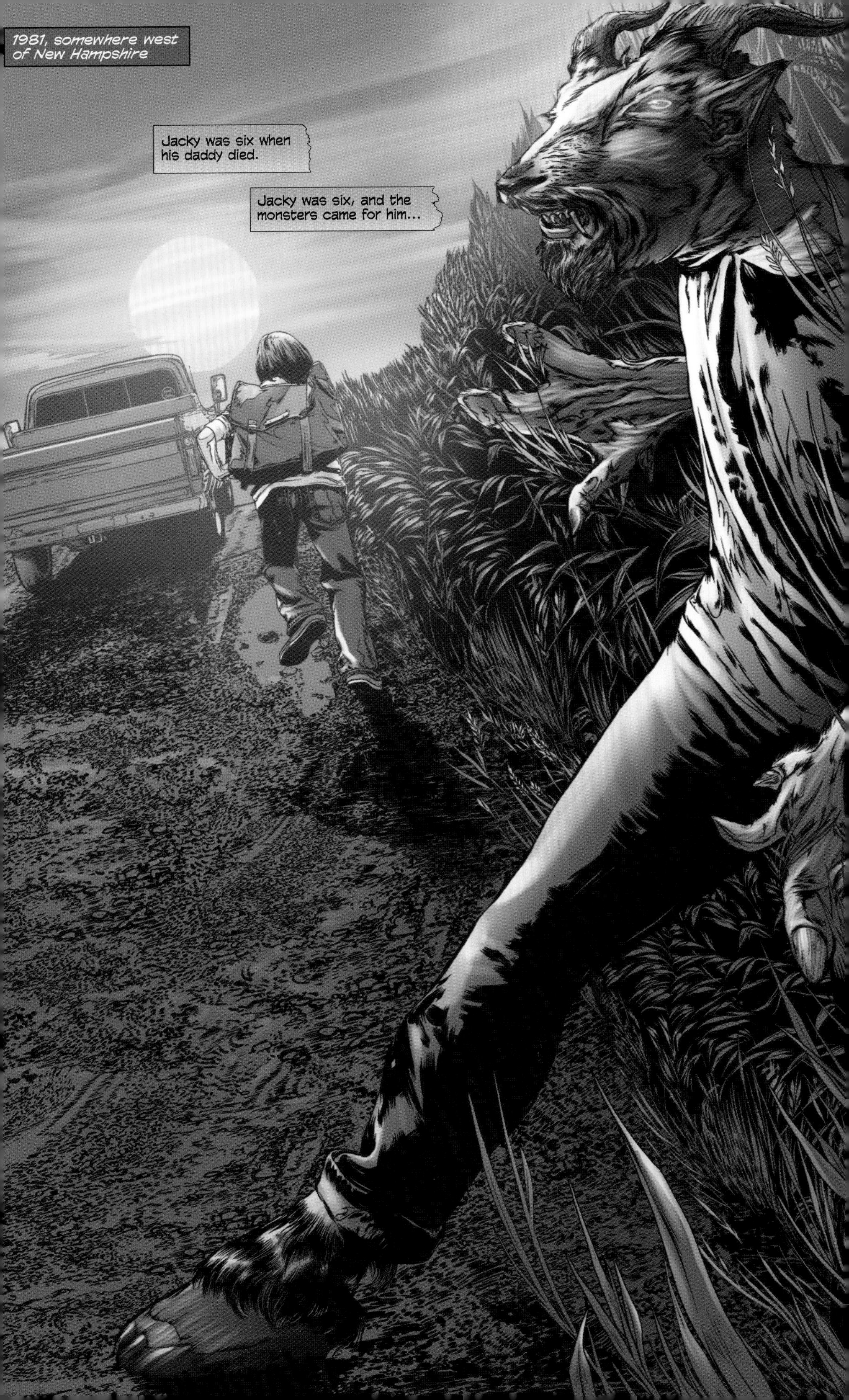
1981, somewhere west of New Hampshire
Jacky was six when his daddy died.
Jacky was six, and the monsters came for him...

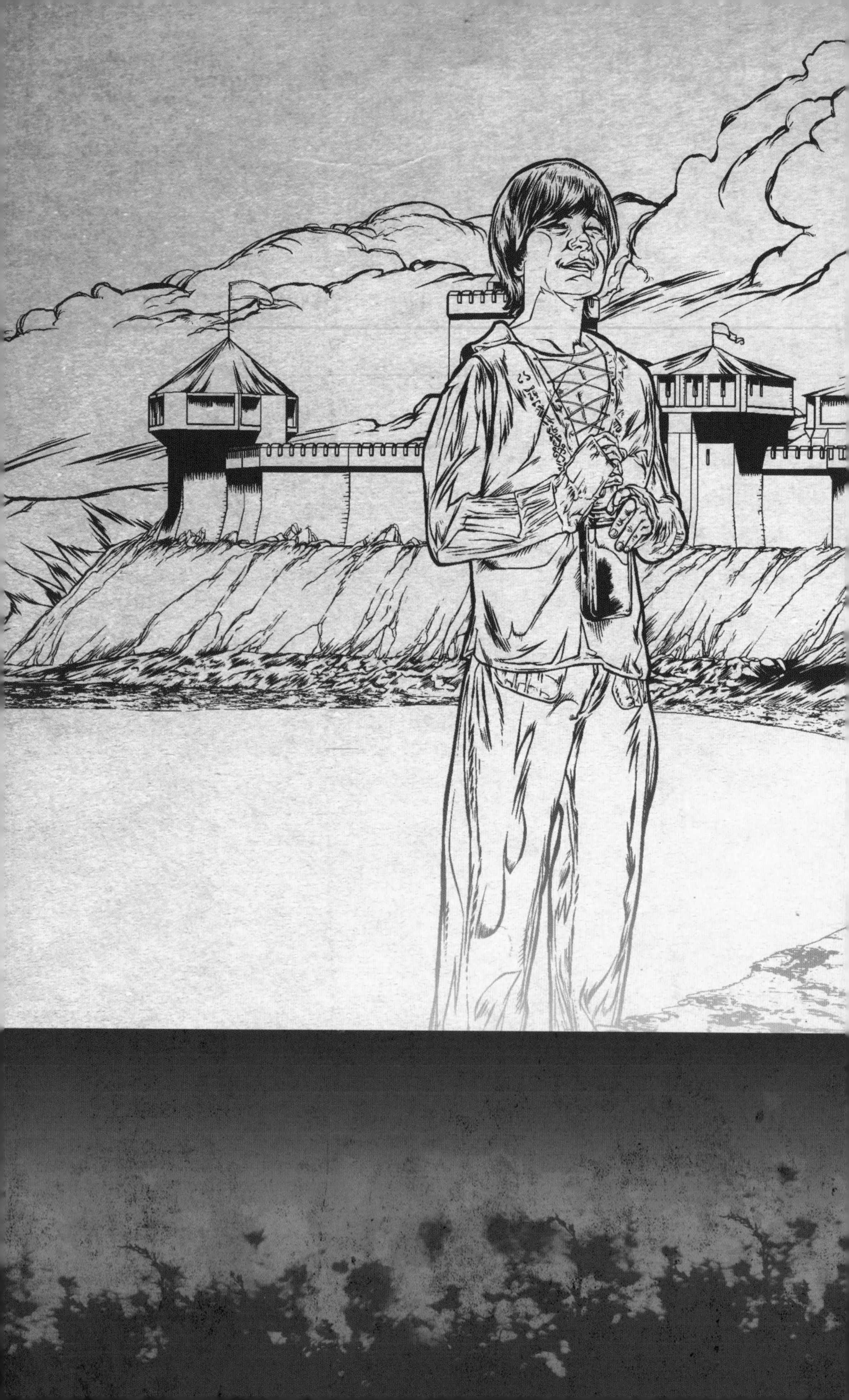

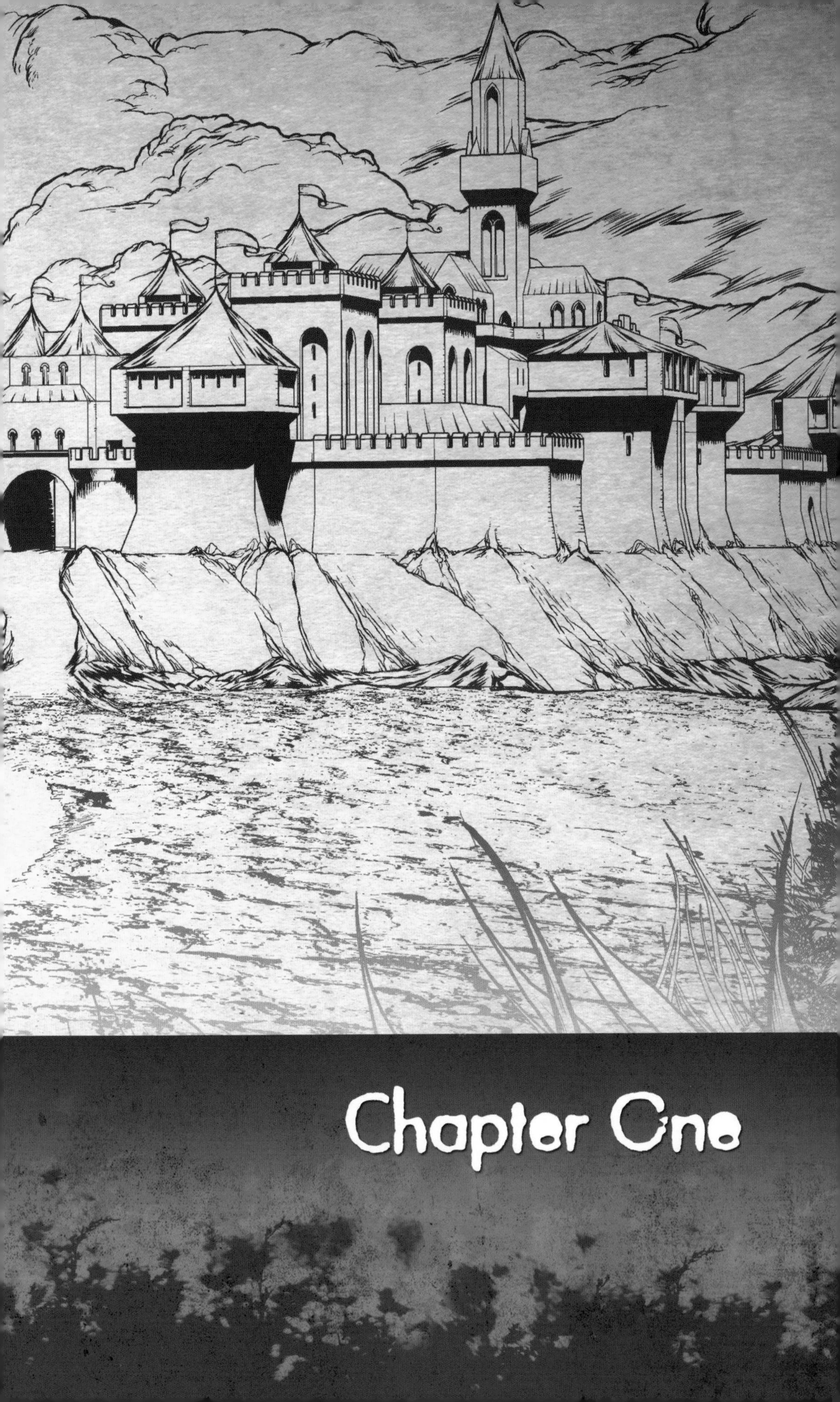

Chapter One

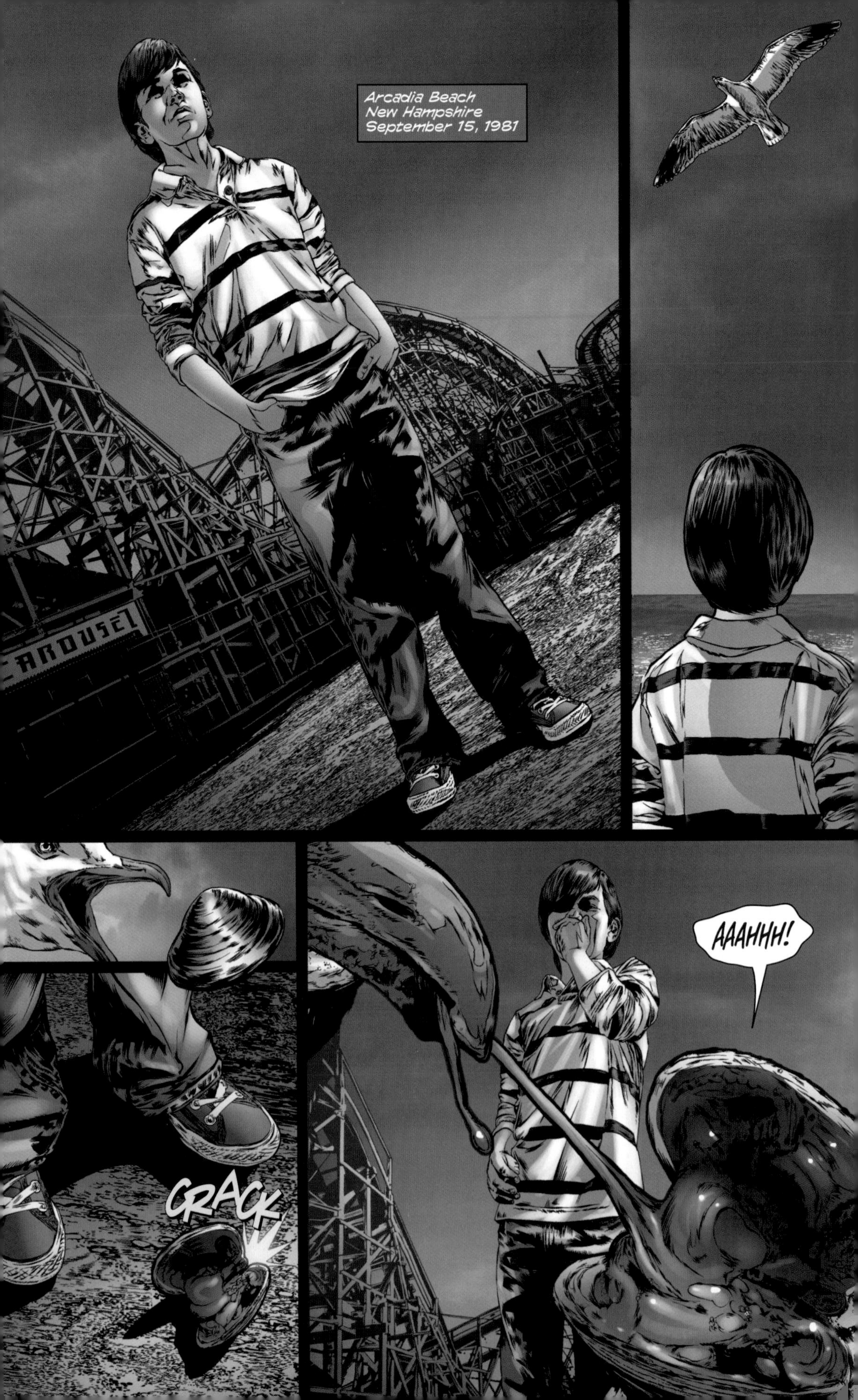

Arcadia Beach
New Hampshire
September 15, 1981
CAROUSEL
CRACK
AAAHHH!

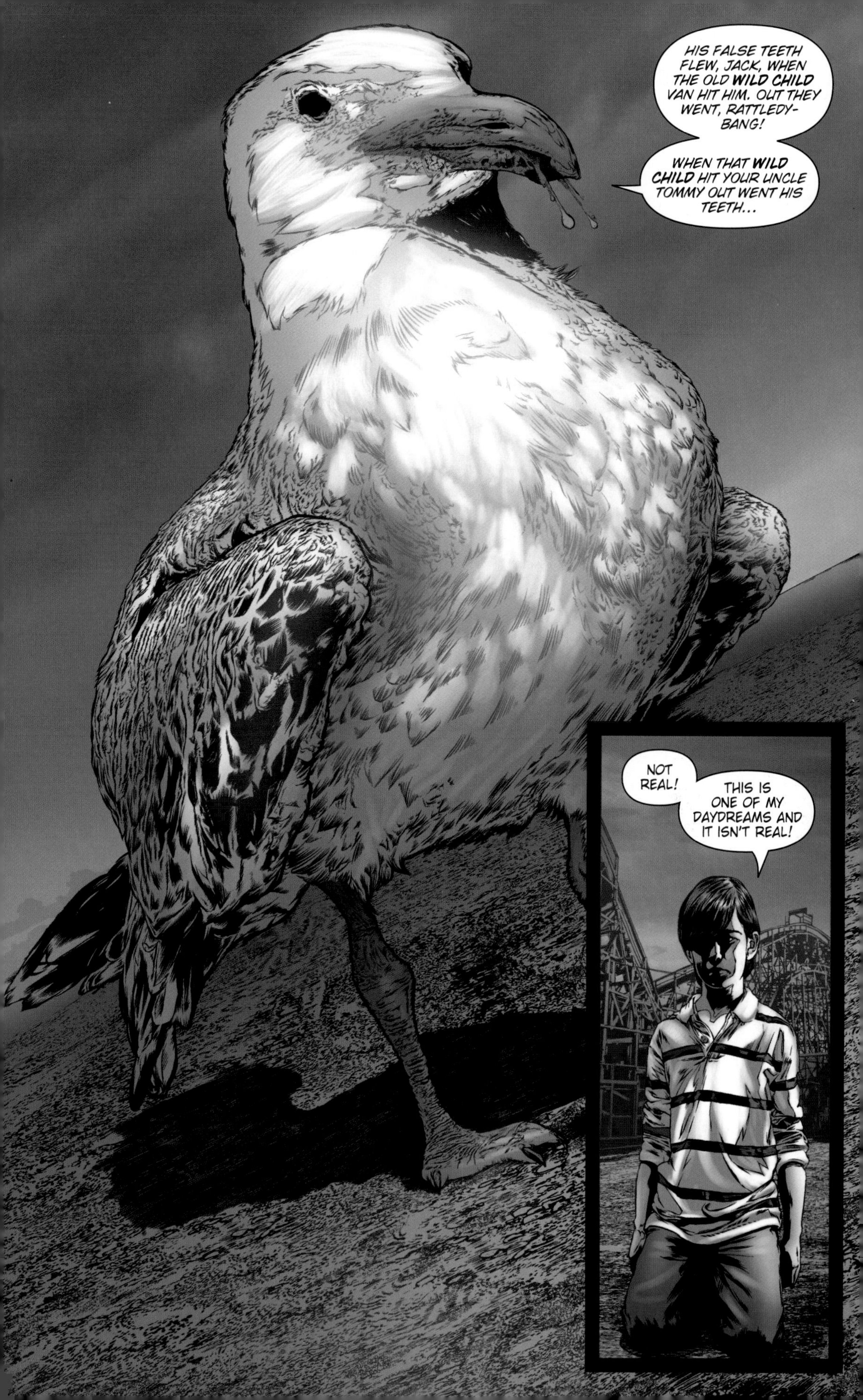
HIS FALSE TEETH FLEW, JACK, WHEN THE OLD WILD CHILD VAN HIT HIM. OUT THEY WENT, RATTLEDY-BANG!
WHEN THAT WILD CHILD HIT YOUR UNCLE TOMMY OUT WENT HIS TEETH...
NOT REAL!
THIS IS ONE OF MY DAYDREAMS AND IT ISN'T REAL!

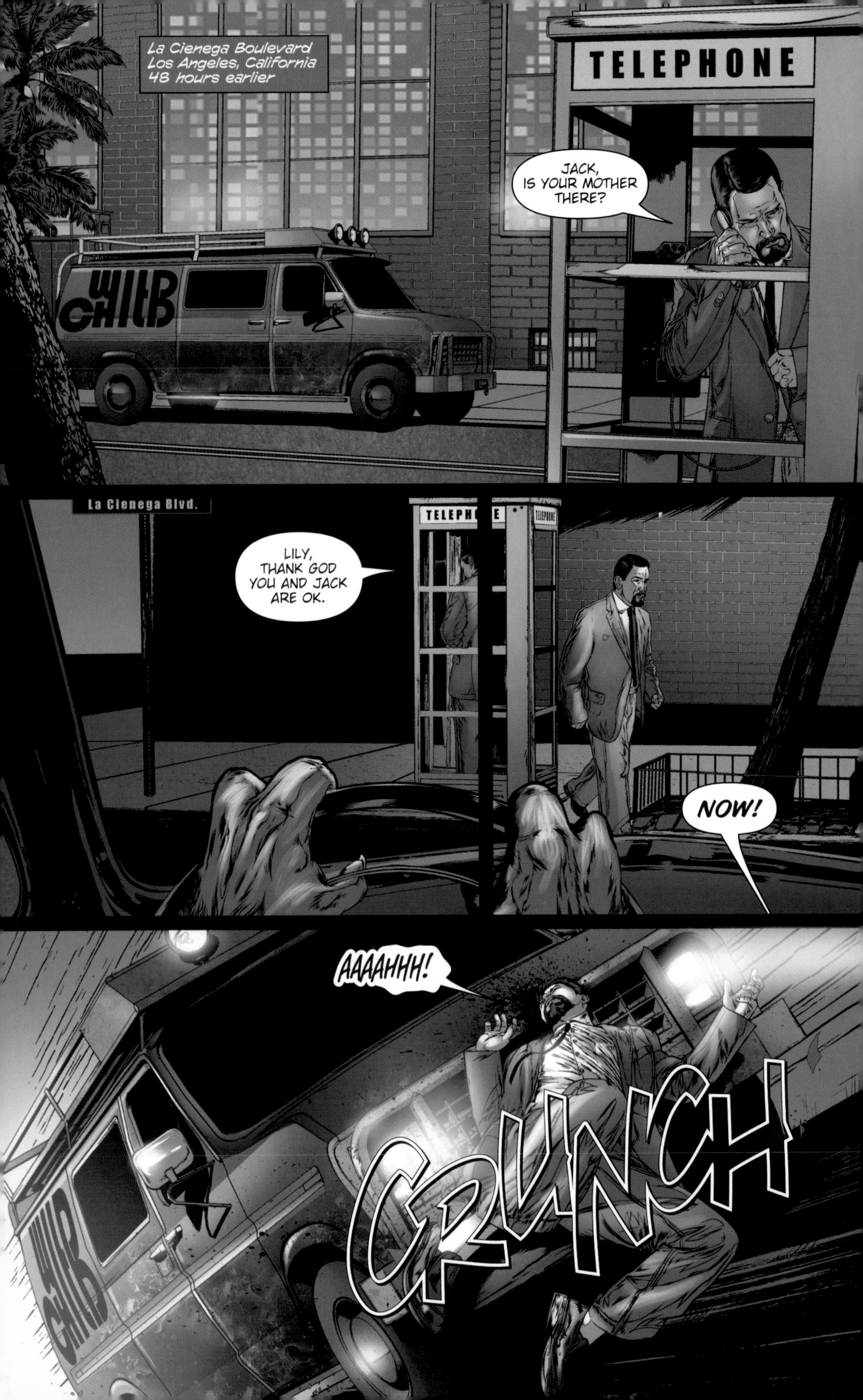
La Cienega Boulevard
Los Angeles, California
48 hours earlier
TELEPHONE
JACK, IS YOUR MOTHER THERE?
La Cienega Blvd.
LILY, THANK GOD YOU AND JACK ARE OK.
NOW!
AAAAHHH!
CRUNCH

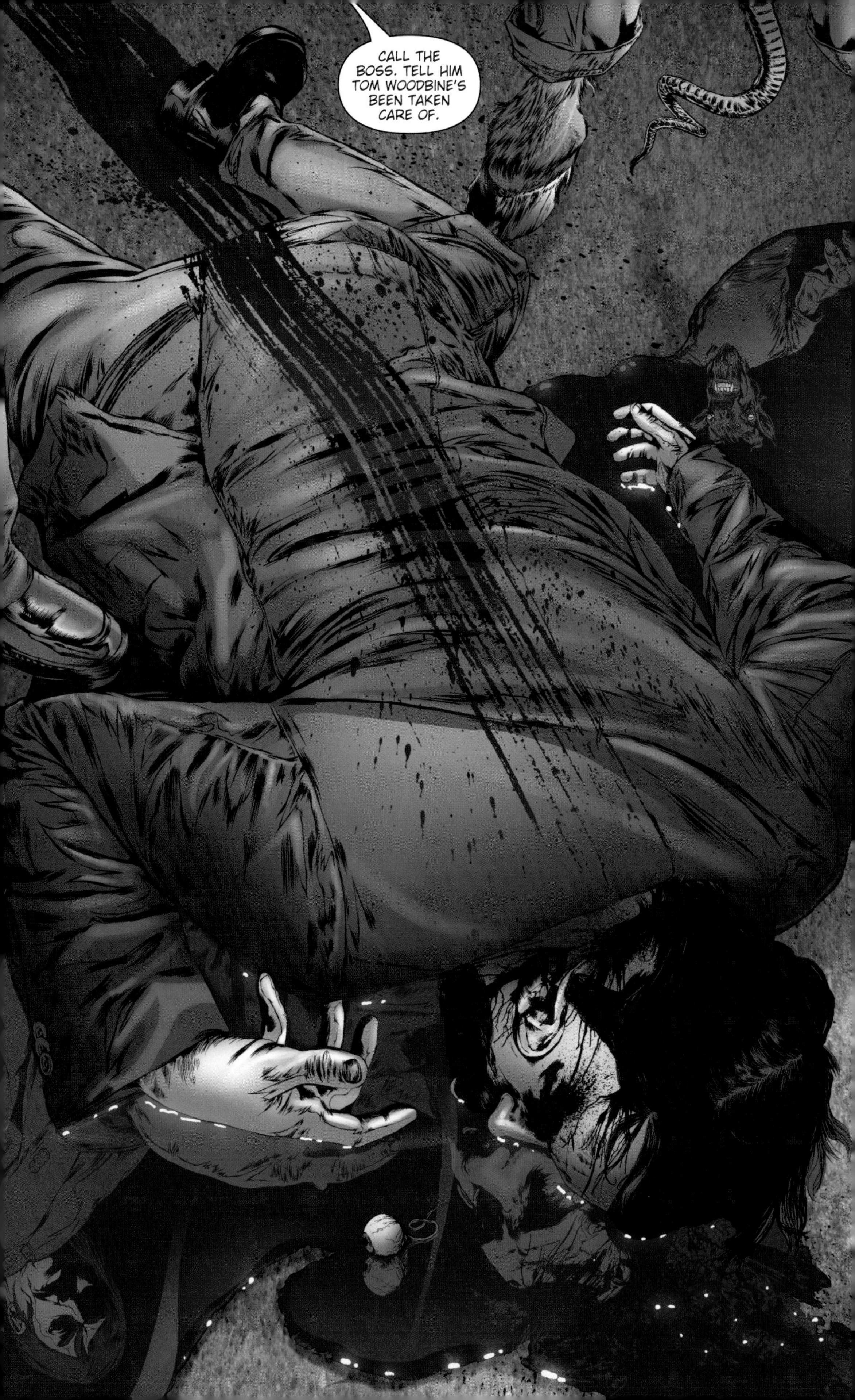
CALL THE BOSS. TELL HIM TOM WOODBINE'S BEEN TAKEN CARE OF.

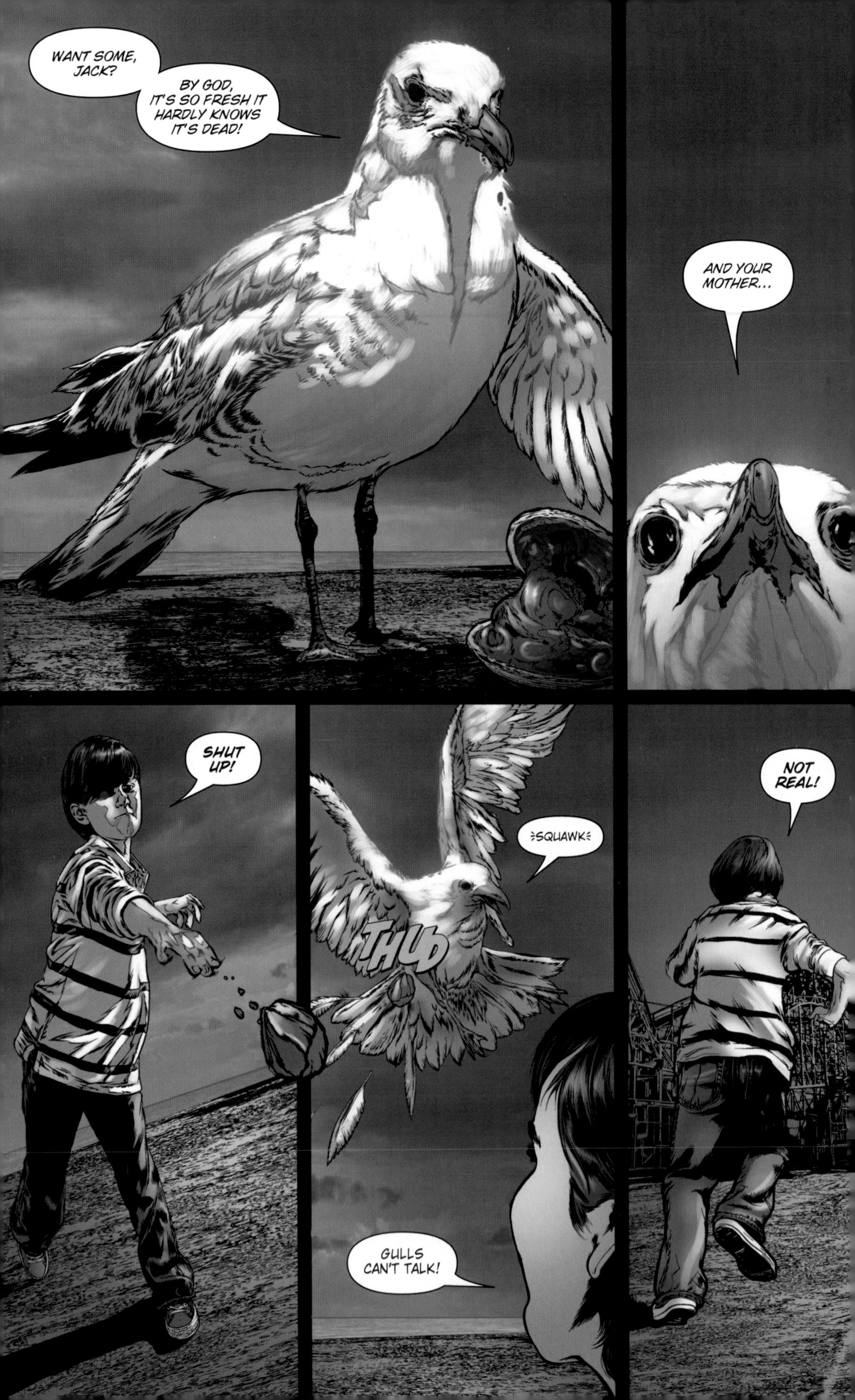
WANT SOME, JACK?
BY GOD, IT'S SO FRESH IT HARDLY KNOWS IT'S DEAD!
AND YOUR MOTHER...
SHUT UP!
SQUAWK
THUD
GULLS CAN'T TALK!
NOT REAL!

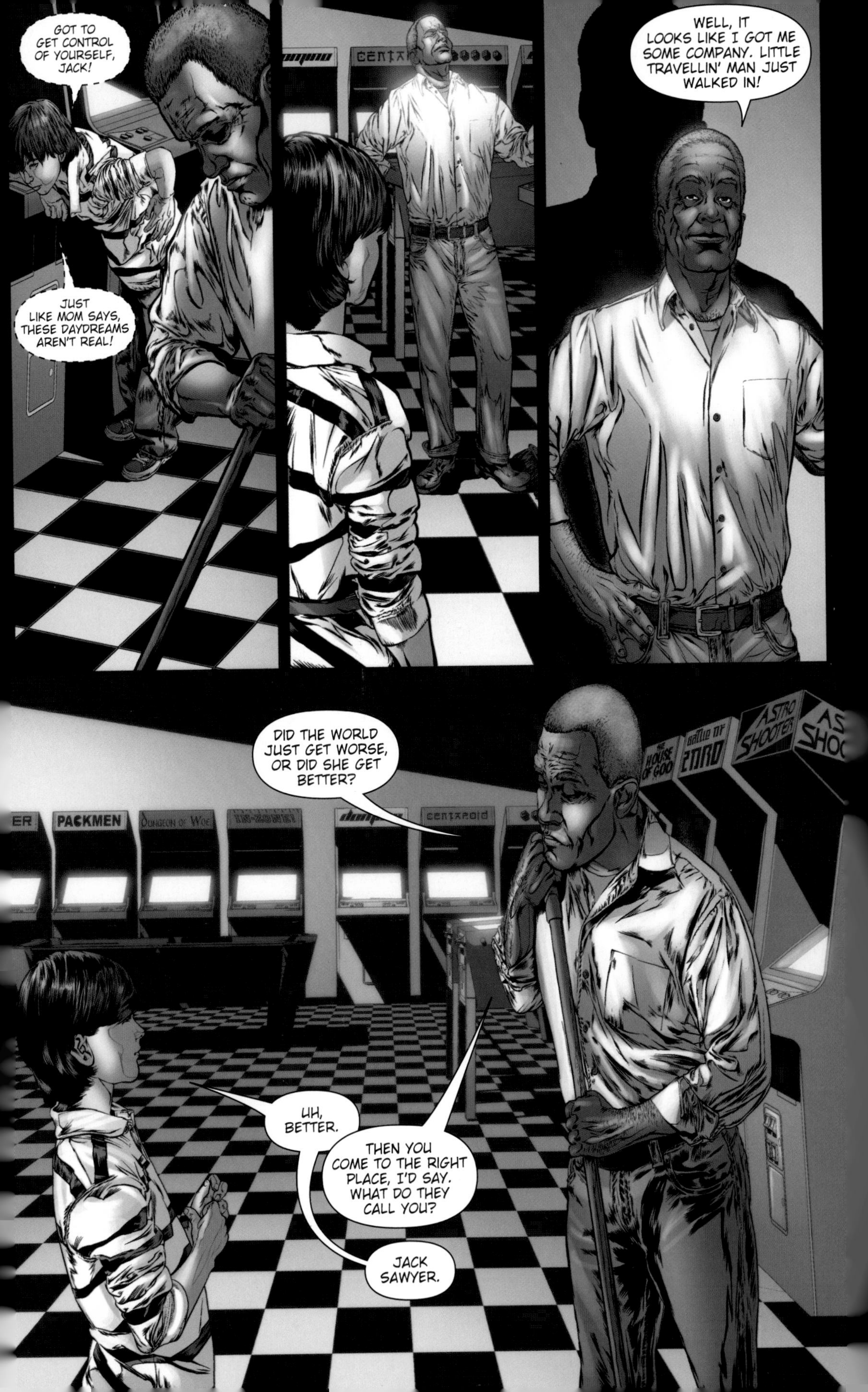
GOT TO GET CONTROL OF YOURSELF, JACK!
JUST LIKE MOM SAYS, THESE DAYDREAMS AREN'T REAL!
WELL, IT LOOKS LIKE I GOT ME SOME COMPANY. LITTLE TRAVELLIN' MAN JUST WALKED IN!
DID THE WORLD JUST GET WORSE, OR DID SHE GET BETTER?
UH, BETTER.
THEN YOU COME TO THE RIGHT PLACE, I'D SAY. WHAT DO THEY CALL YOU?
JACK SAWYER.

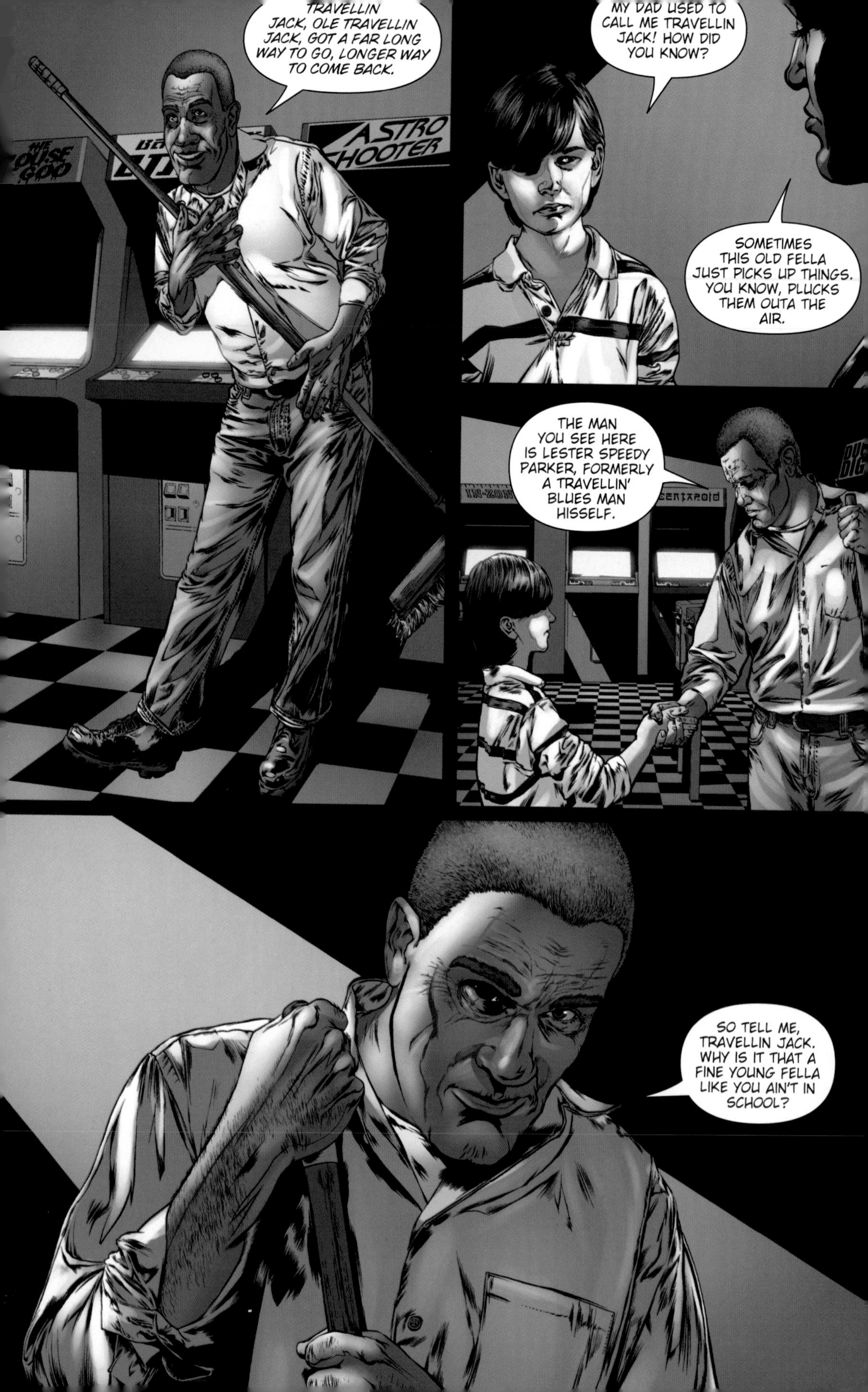
TRAVELLIN JACK, OLE TRAVELLIN JACK, GOT A FAR LONG WAY TO GO, LONGER WAY TO COME BACK.
ASTRO SHOOTER
MY DAD USED TO CALL ME TRAVELLIN JACK! HOW DID YOU KNOW?
SOMETIMES THIS OLD FELLA JUST PICKS UP THINGS. YOU KNOW, PLUCKS THEM OUTA THE AIR.
THE MAN YOU SEE HERE IS LESTER SPEEDY PARKER, FORMERLY A TRAVELLIN' BLUES MAN HISSELF.
SO TELL ME, TRAVELLIN JACK. WHY IS IT THAT A FINE YOUNG FELLA LIKE YOU AIN'T IN SCHOOL?

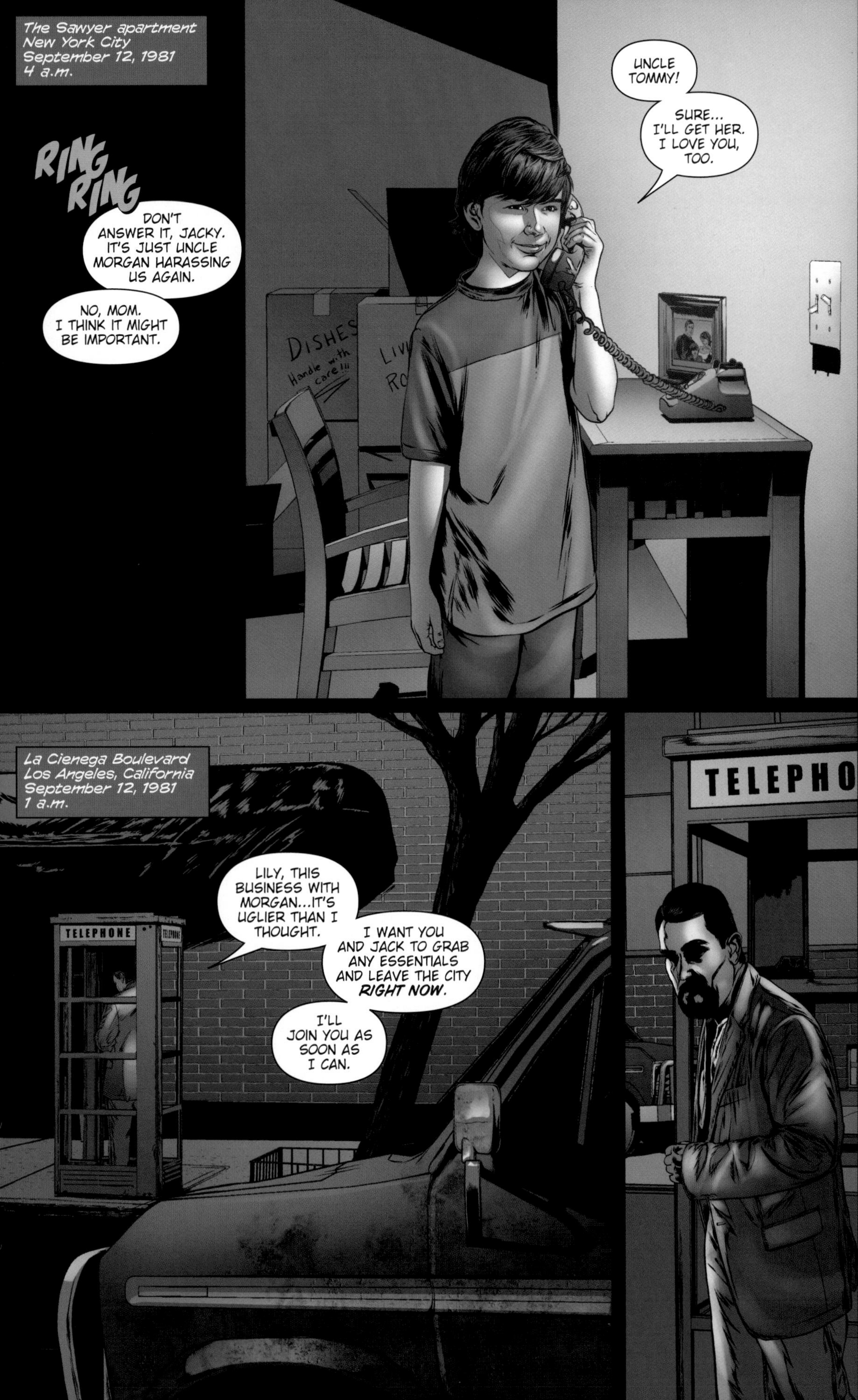
The Sawyer apartment
New York City
September 12, 1981
4 a.m.
RING RING
DON'T ANSWER IT, JACKY. IT'S JUST UNCLE MORGAN HARASSING US AGAIN.
NO, MOM. I THINK IT MIGHT BE IMPORTANT.
UNCLE TOMMY!
SURE... I'LL GET HER. I LOVE YOU, TOO.
DISHES
Handle with care!!!
La Cienega Boulevard
Los Angeles, California
September 12, 1981
1 a.m.
TELEPHONE
LILY, THIS BUSINESS WITH MORGAN...IT'S UGLIER THAN I THOUGHT.
I WANT YOU AND JACK TO GRAB ANY ESSENTIALS AND LEAVE THE CITY ***RIGHT NOW***.
I'LL JOIN YOU AS SOON AS I CAN.
TELEPHO

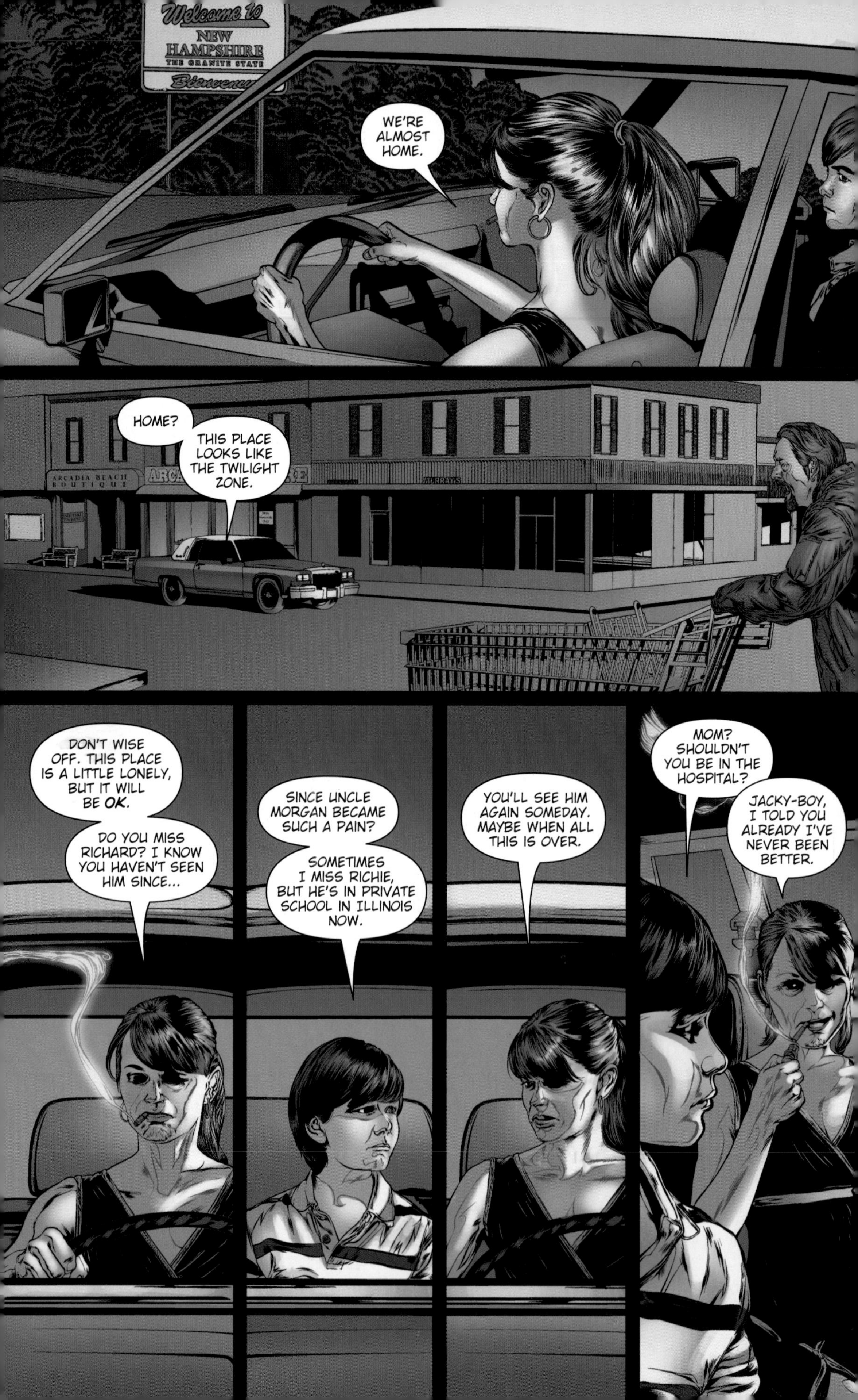
Welcome to
NEW HAMPSHIRE
THE GRANITE STATE
WE'RE ALMOST HOME.
ARCADIA BEACH BOUTIQUE
MURRAYS
HOME?
THIS PLACE LOOKS LIKE THE TWILIGHT ZONE.
DON'T WISE OFF. THIS PLACE IS A LITTLE LONELY, BUT IT WILL BE ***OK***.
DO YOU MISS RICHARD? I KNOW YOU HAVEN'T SEEN HIM SINCE...
SINCE UNCLE MORGAN BECAME SUCH A PAIN?
SOMETIMES I MISS RICHIE, BUT HE'S IN PRIVATE SCHOOL IN ILLINOIS NOW.
YOU'LL SEE HIM AGAIN SOMEDAY. MAYBE WHEN ALL THIS IS OVER.
MOM? SHOULDN'T YOU BE IN THE HOSPITAL?
JACKY-BOY, I TOLD YOU ALREADY I'VE NEVER BEEN BETTER.

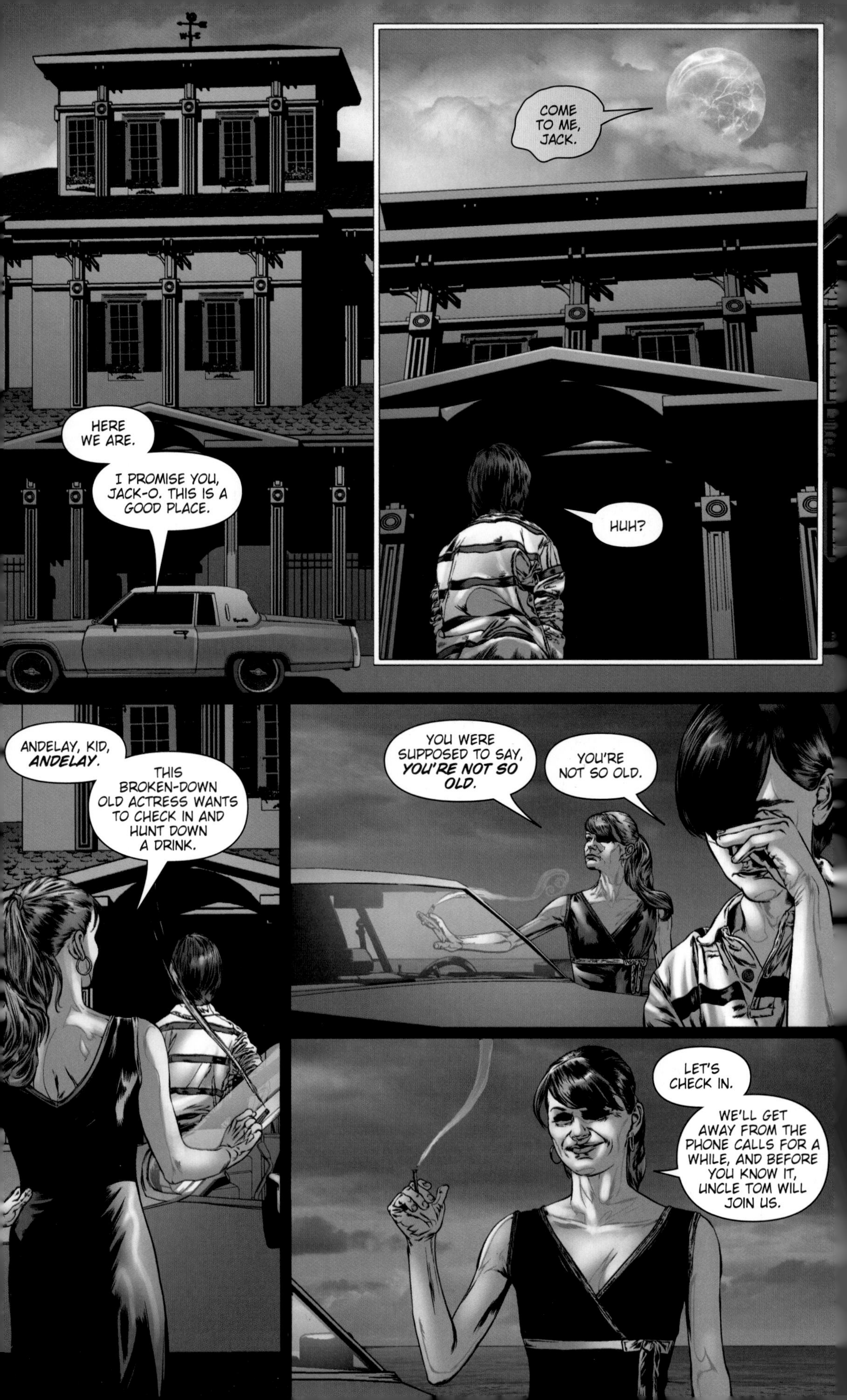
HERE WE ARE.
I PROMISE YOU, JACK-O. THIS IS A GOOD PLACE.
COME TO ME, JACK.
HUH?
ANDELAY, KID, **ANDELAY**.
THIS BROKEN-DOWN OLD ACTRESS WANTS TO CHECK IN AND HUNT DOWN A DRINK.
YOU WERE SUPPOSED TO SAY, ***YOU'RE NOT SO OLD***.
YOU'RE NOT SO OLD.
LET'S CHECK IN.
WE'LL GET AWAY FROM THE PHONE CALLS FOR A WHILE, AND BEFORE YOU KNOW IT, UNCLE TOM WILL JOIN US.

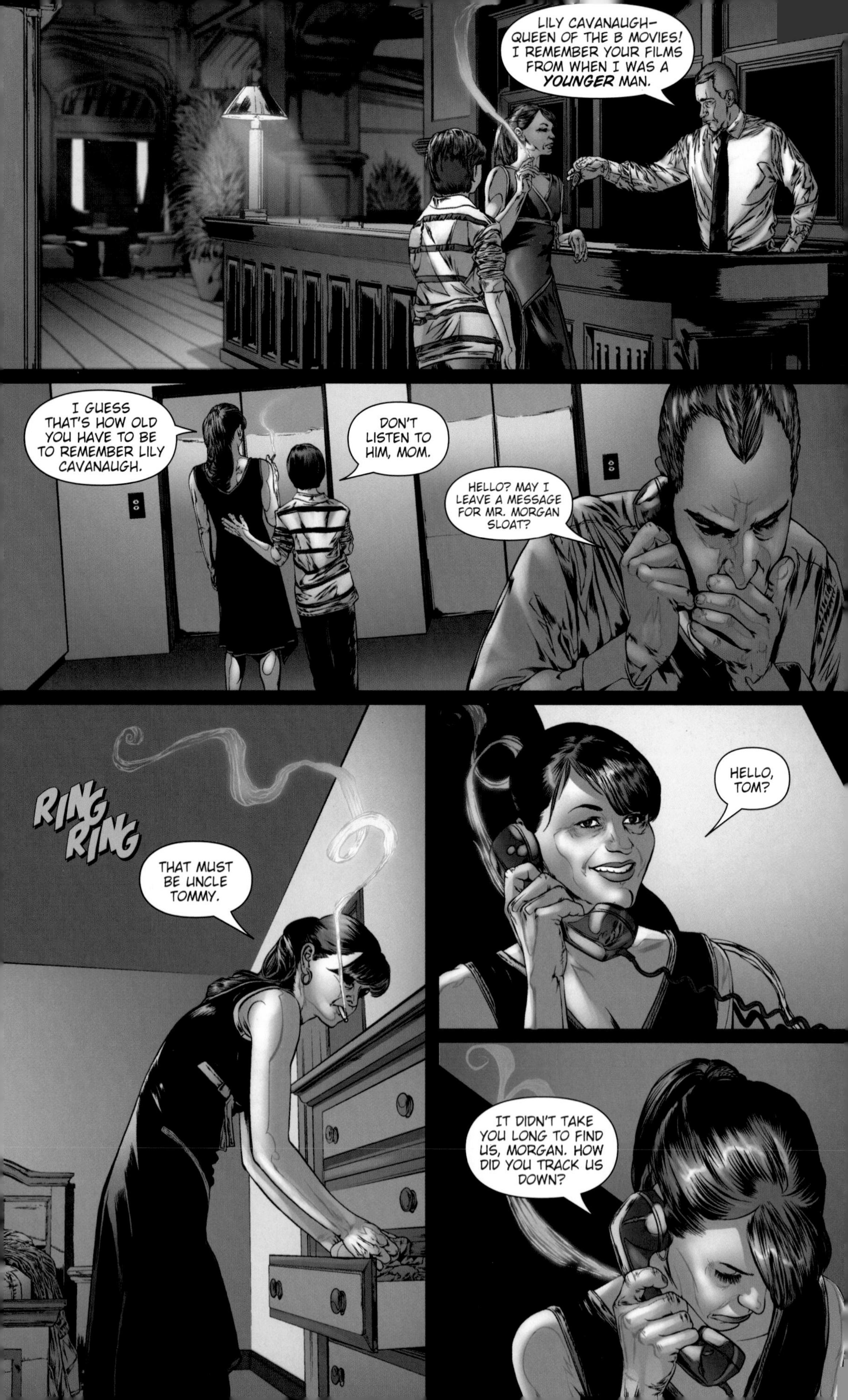
LILY CAVANAUGH—QUEEN OF THE B MOVIES! I REMEMBER YOUR FILMS FROM WHEN I WAS A *YOUNGER* MAN.
I GUESS THAT'S HOW OLD YOU HAVE TO BE TO REMEMBER LILY CAVANAUGH.
DON'T LISTEN TO HIM, MOM.
HELLO? MAY I LEAVE A MESSAGE FOR MR. MORGAN SLOAT?
RING RING
THAT MUST BE UNCLE TOMMY.
HELLO, TOM?
IT DIDN'T TAKE YOU LONG TO FIND US, MORGAN. HOW DID YOU TRACK US DOWN?

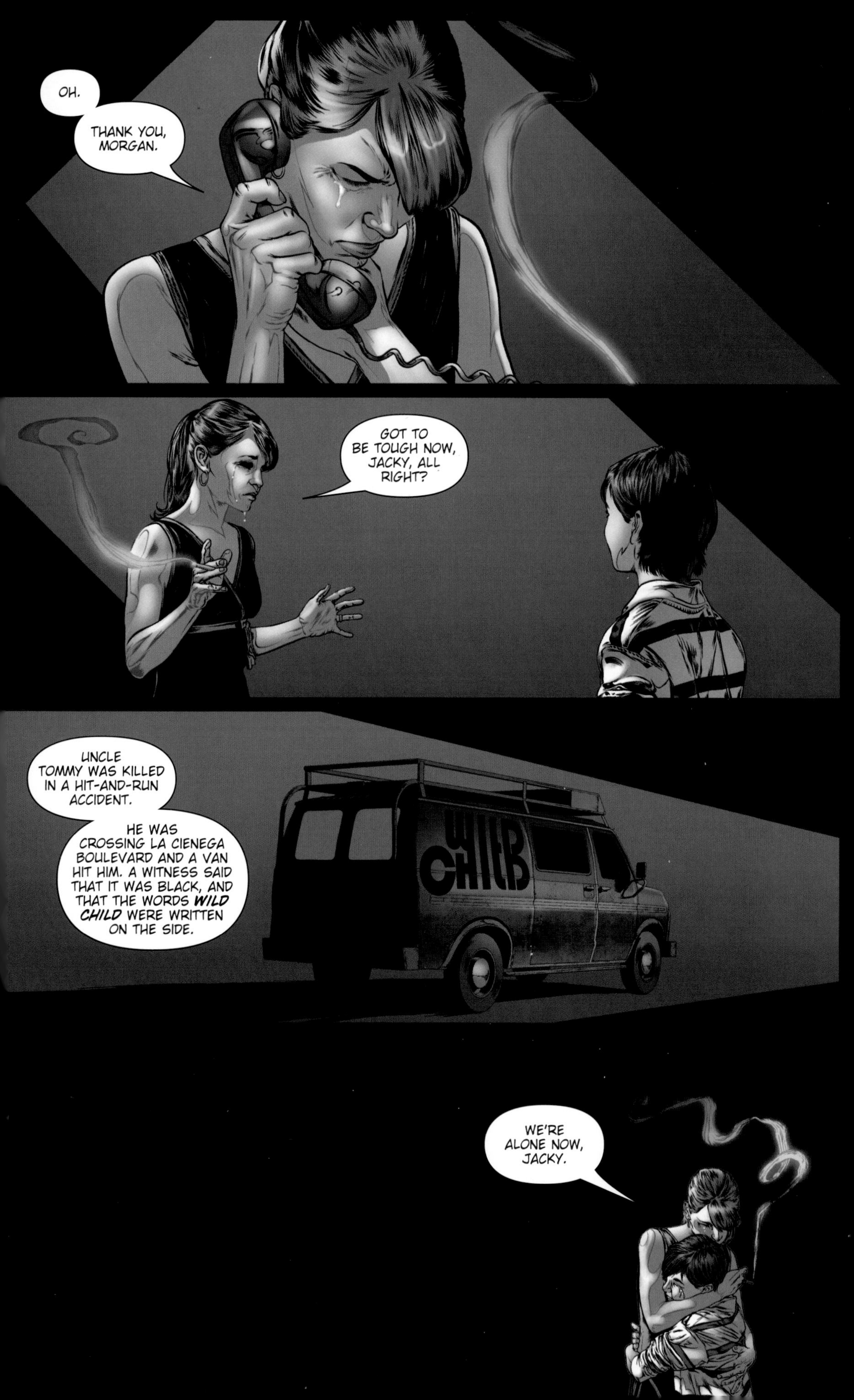
OH.
THANK YOU, MORGAN.
GOT TO BE TOUGH NOW, JACKY, ALL RIGHT?
UNCLE TOMMY WAS KILLED IN A HIT-AND-RUN ACCIDENT.
HE WAS CROSSING LA CIENEGA BOULEVARD AND A VAN HIT HIM. A WITNESS SAID THAT IT WAS BLACK, AND THAT THE WORDS ***WILD CHILD*** WERE WRITTEN ON THE SIDE.
WE'RE ALONE NOW, JACKY.

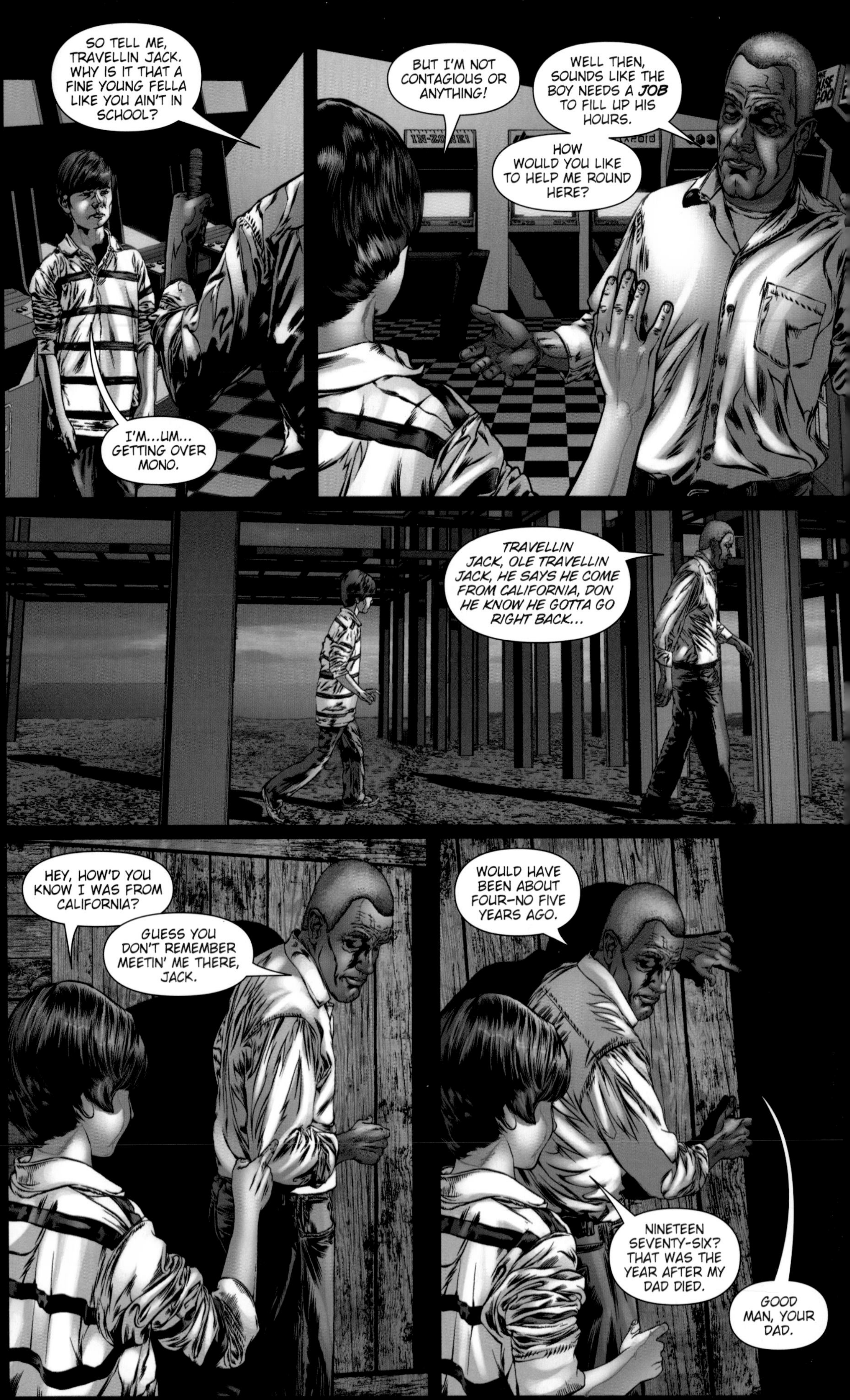
SO TELL ME, TRAVELLIN JACK. WHY IS IT THAT A FINE YOUNG FELLA LIKE YOU AIN'T IN SCHOOL?
I'M...UM... GETTING OVER MONO.
BUT I'M NOT CONTAGIOUS OR ANYTHING!
WELL THEN, SOUNDS LIKE THE BOY NEEDS A JOB TO FILL UP HIS HOURS.
HOW WOULD YOU LIKE TO HELP ME ROUND HERE?
IN-ZONE!
TRAVELLIN JACK, OLE TRAVELLIN JACK, HE SAYS HE COME FROM CALIFORNIA, DON HE KNOW HE GOTTA GO RIGHT BACK...
HEY, HOW'D YOU KNOW I WAS FROM CALIFORNIA?
GUESS YOU DON'T REMEMBER MEETIN' ME THERE, JACK.
WOULD HAVE BEEN ABOUT FOUR-NO FIVE YEARS AGO.
NINETEEN SEVENTY-SIX? THAT WAS THE YEAR AFTER MY DAD DIED.
GOOD MAN, YOUR DAD.

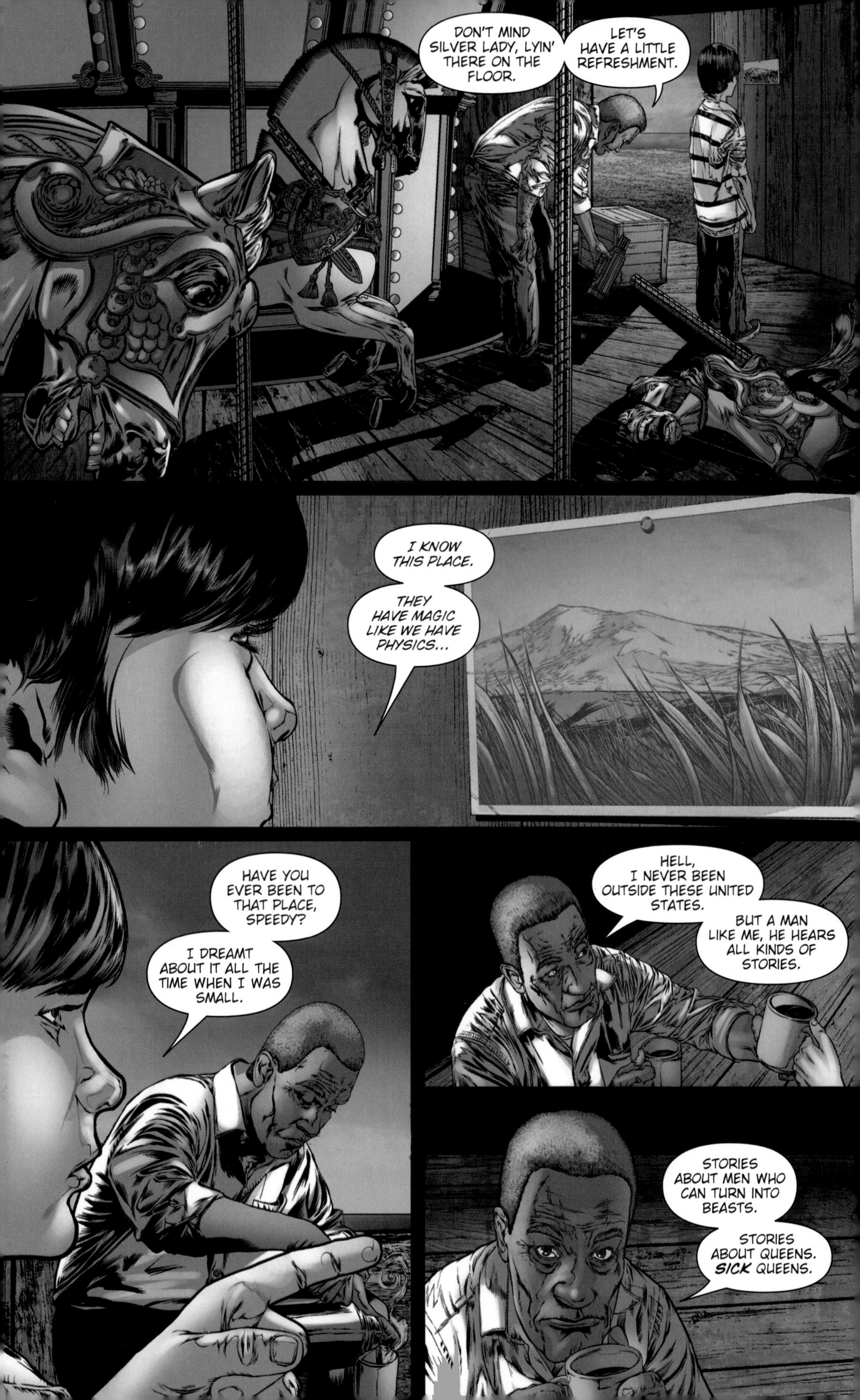

DON'T MIND SILVER LADY, LYIN' THERE ON THE FLOOR.
LET'S HAVE A LITTLE REFRESHMENT.
I KNOW THIS PLACE.
THEY HAVE MAGIC LIKE WE HAVE PHYSICS...
HAVE YOU EVER BEEN TO THAT PLACE, SPEEDY?
I DREAMT ABOUT IT ALL THE TIME WHEN I WAS SMALL.
HELL, I NEVER BEEN OUTSIDE THESE UNITED STATES.
BUT A MAN LIKE ME, HE HEARS ALL KINDS OF STORIES.
STORIES ABOUT MEN WHO CAN TURN INTO BEASTS.
STORIES ABOUT QUEENS. SICK QUEENS.

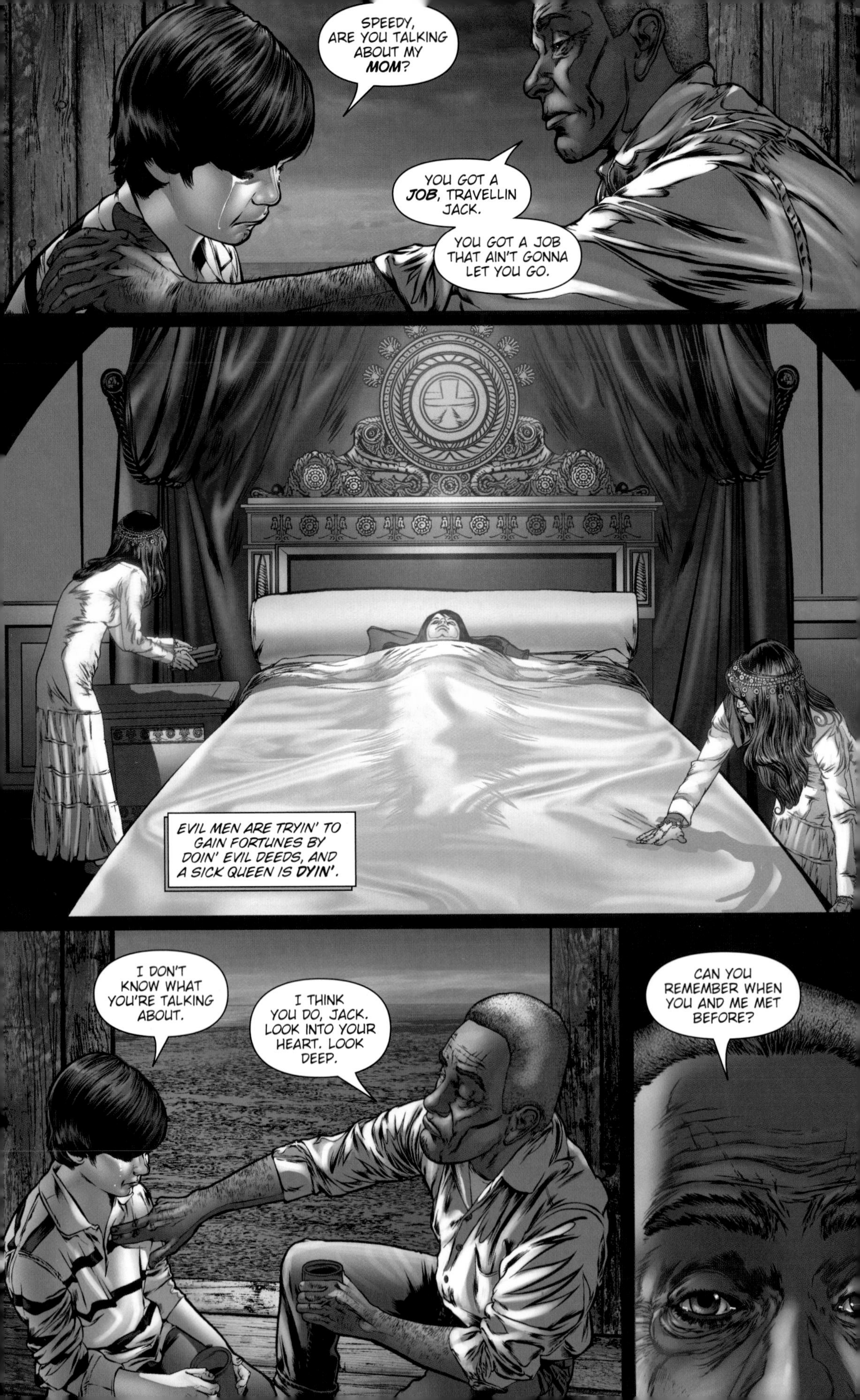
SPEEDY, ARE YOU TALKING ABOUT MY **MOM**?
YOU GOT A **JOB**, TRAVELLIN JACK.
YOU GOT A JOB THAT AIN'T GONNA LET YOU GO.
EVIL MEN ARE TRYIN' TO GAIN FORTUNES BY DOIN' EVIL DEEDS, AND A SICK QUEEN IS **DYIN'**.
I DON'T KNOW WHAT YOU'RE TALKING ABOUT.
I THINK YOU DO, JACK. LOOK INTO YOUR HEART. LOOK DEEP.
CAN YOU REMEMBER WHEN YOU AND ME MET BEFORE?

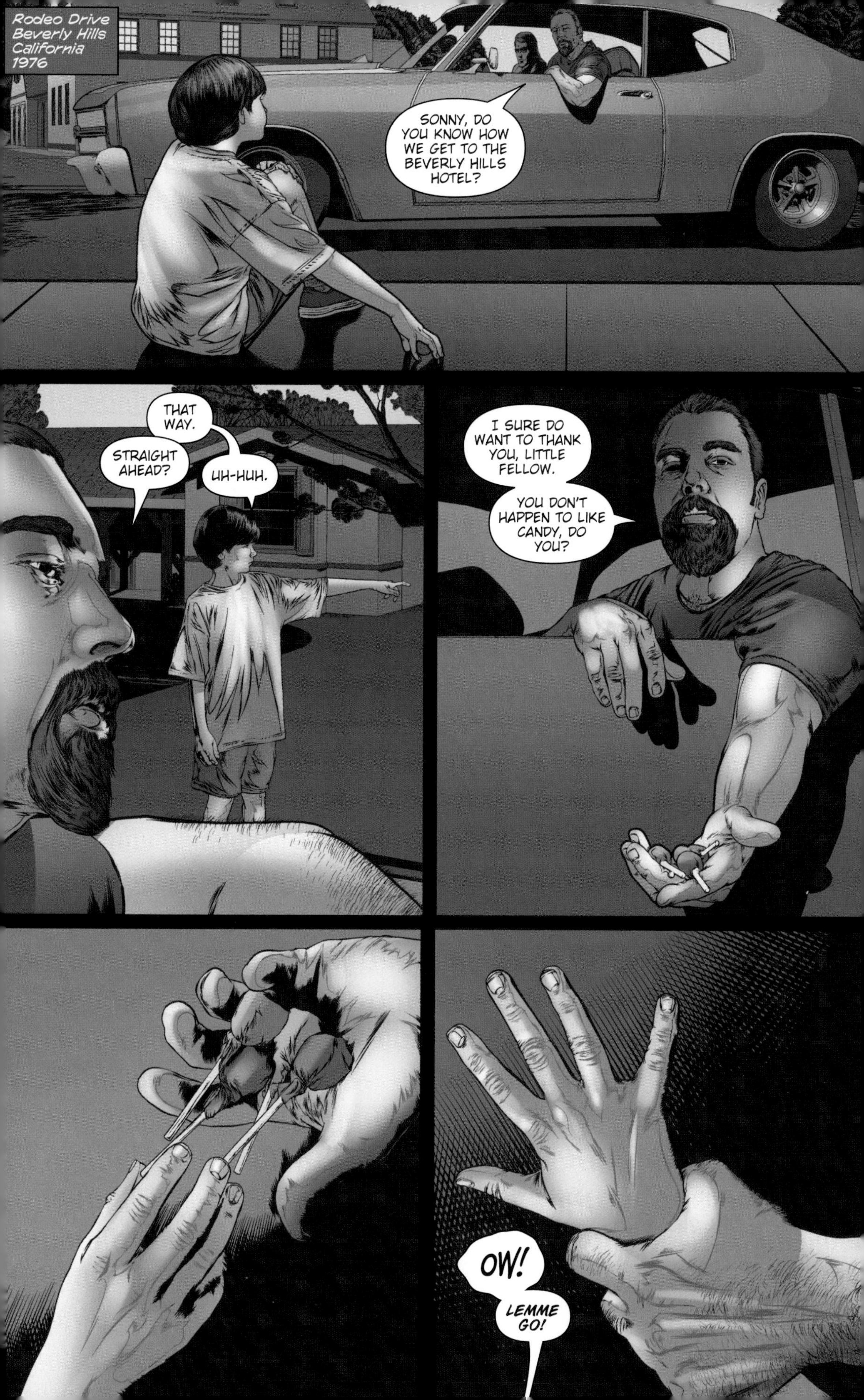
Rodeo Drive Beverly Hills California 1976
SONNY, DO YOU KNOW HOW WE GET TO THE BEVERLY HILLS HOTEL?
THAT WAY.
STRAIGHT AHEAD?
UH-HUH.
I SURE DO WANT TO THANK YOU, LITTLE FELLOW.
YOU DON'T HAPPEN TO LIKE CANDY, DO YOU?
OW!
LEMME GO!

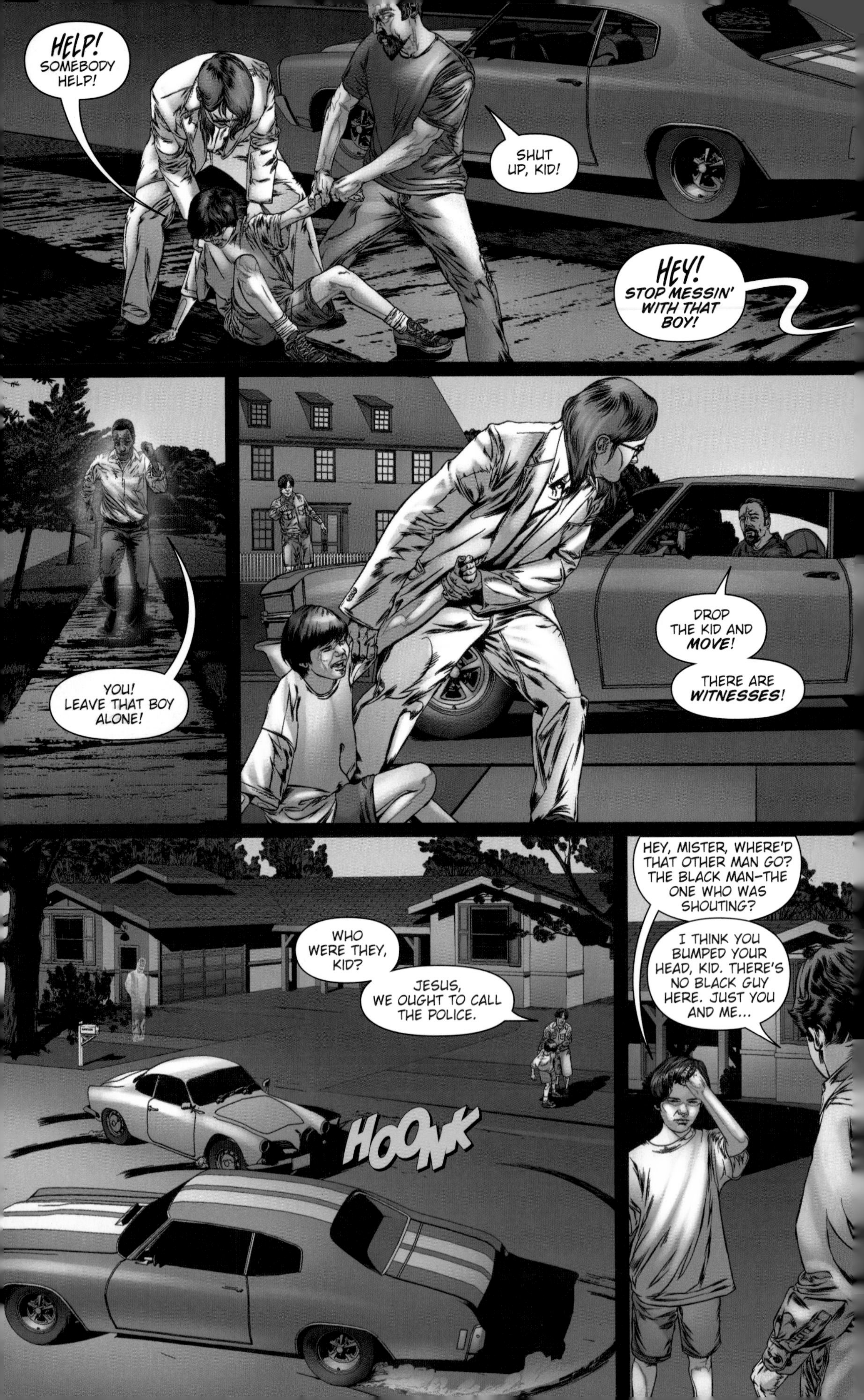
HELP! SOMEBODY HELP!
SHUT UP, KID!
HEY! STOP MESSIN' WITH THAT BOY!
YOU! LEAVE THAT BOY ALONE!
DROP THE KID AND MOVE!
THERE ARE WITNESSES!
WHO WERE THEY, KID?
JESUS, WE OUGHT TO CALL THE POLICE.
HOONK
HEY, MISTER, WHERE'D THAT OTHER MAN GO? THE BLACK MAN—THE ONE WHO WAS SHOUTING?
I THINK YOU BUMPED YOUR HEAD, KID. THERE'S NO BLACK GUY HERE. JUST YOU AND ME...

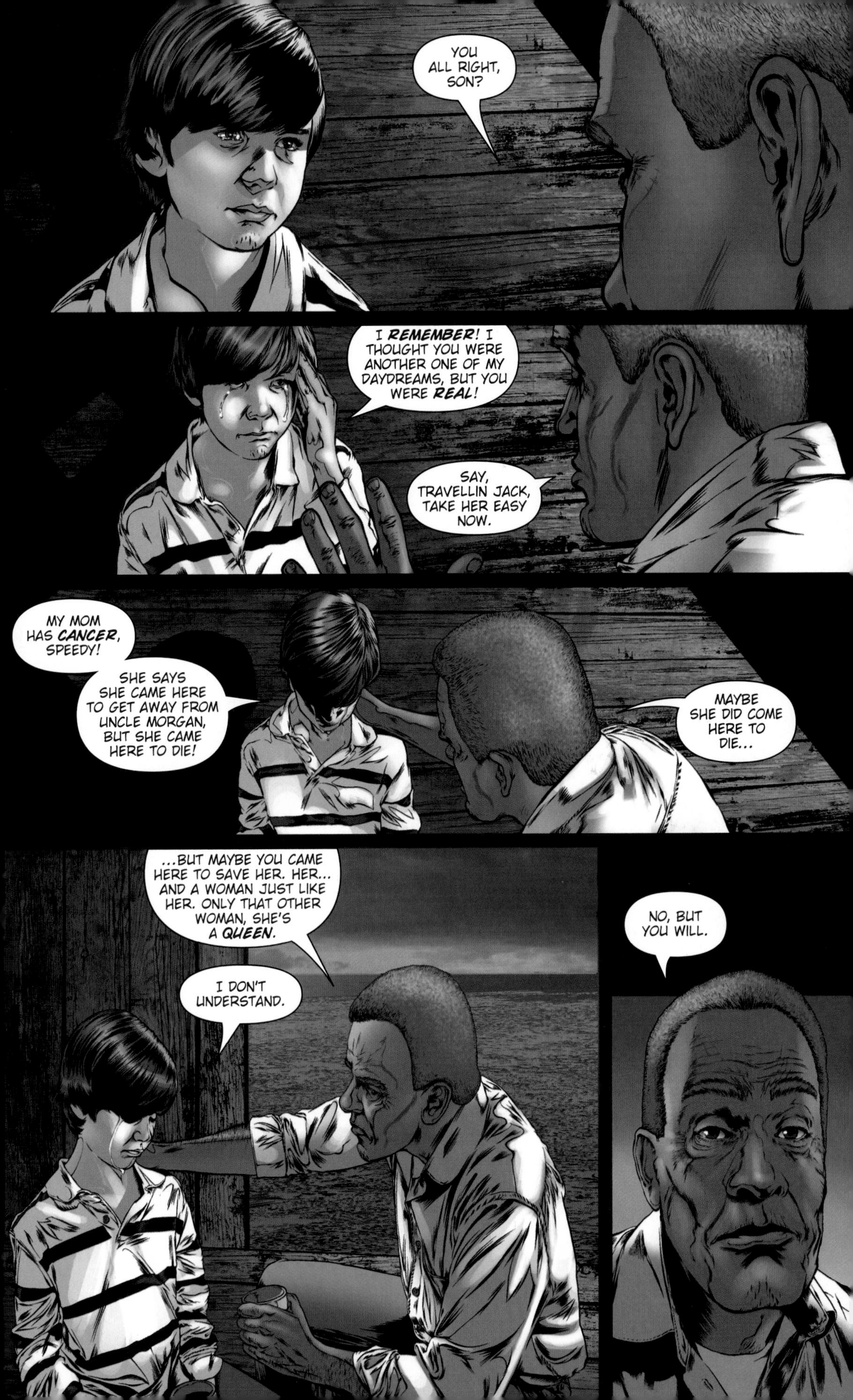
YOU ALL RIGHT, SON?
I REMEMBER! I THOUGHT YOU WERE ANOTHER ONE OF MY DAYDREAMS, BUT YOU WERE REAL!
SAY, TRAVELLIN JACK, TAKE HER EASY NOW.
MY MOM HAS CANCER, SPEEDY!
SHE SAYS SHE CAME HERE TO GET AWAY FROM UNCLE MORGAN, BUT SHE CAME HERE TO DIE!
MAYBE SHE DID COME HERE TO DIE...
...BUT MAYBE YOU CAME HERE TO SAVE HER. HER... AND A WOMAN JUST LIKE HER. ONLY THAT OTHER WOMAN, SHE'S A QUEEN.
I DON'T UNDERSTAND.
NO, BUT YOU WILL.

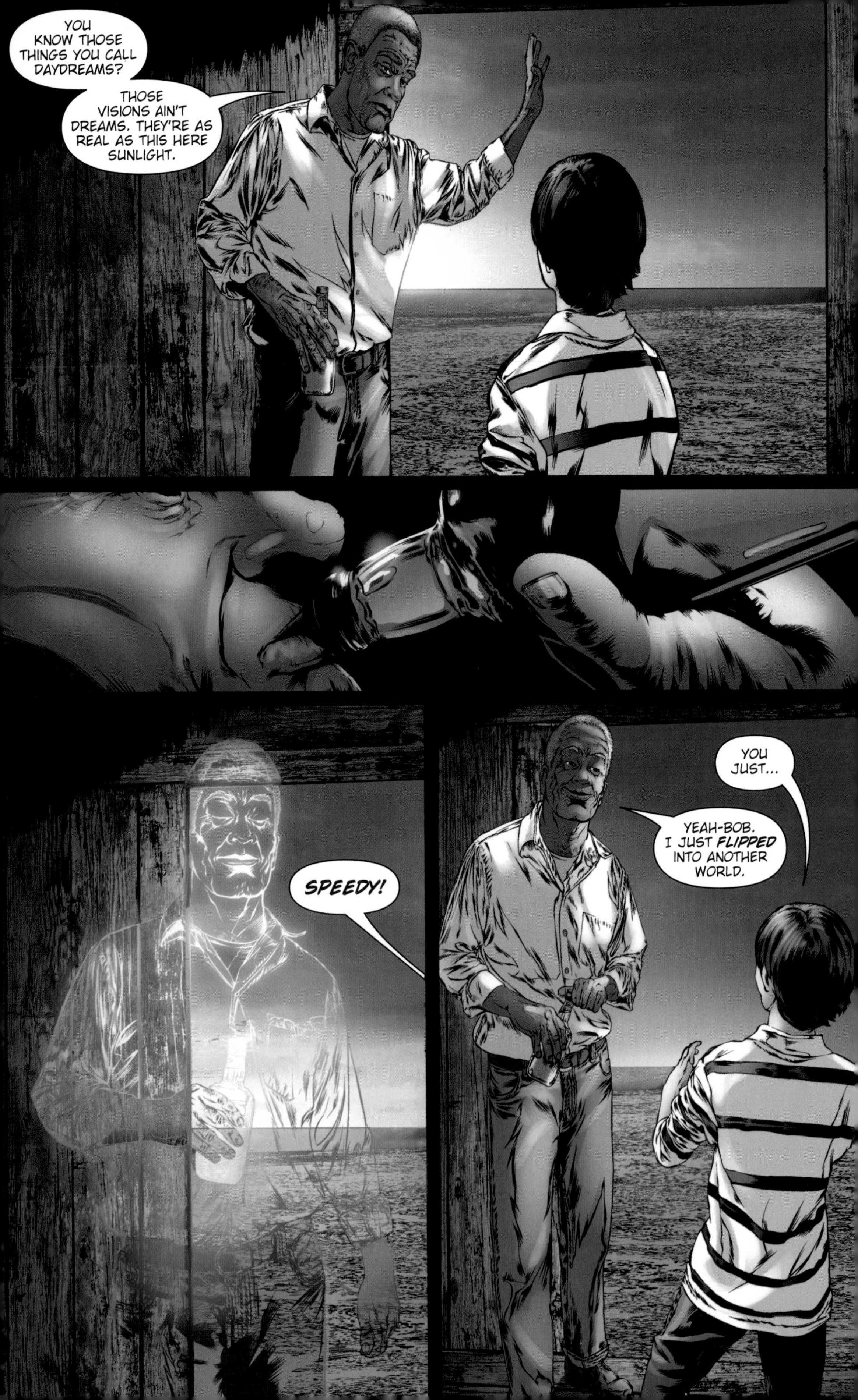
YOU KNOW THOSE THINGS YOU CALL DAYDREAMS?
THOSE VISIONS AIN'T DREAMS. THEY'RE AS REAL AS THIS HERE SUNLIGHT.
SPEEDY!
YOU JUST...
YEAH-BOB. I JUST *FLIPPED* INTO ANOTHER WORLD.

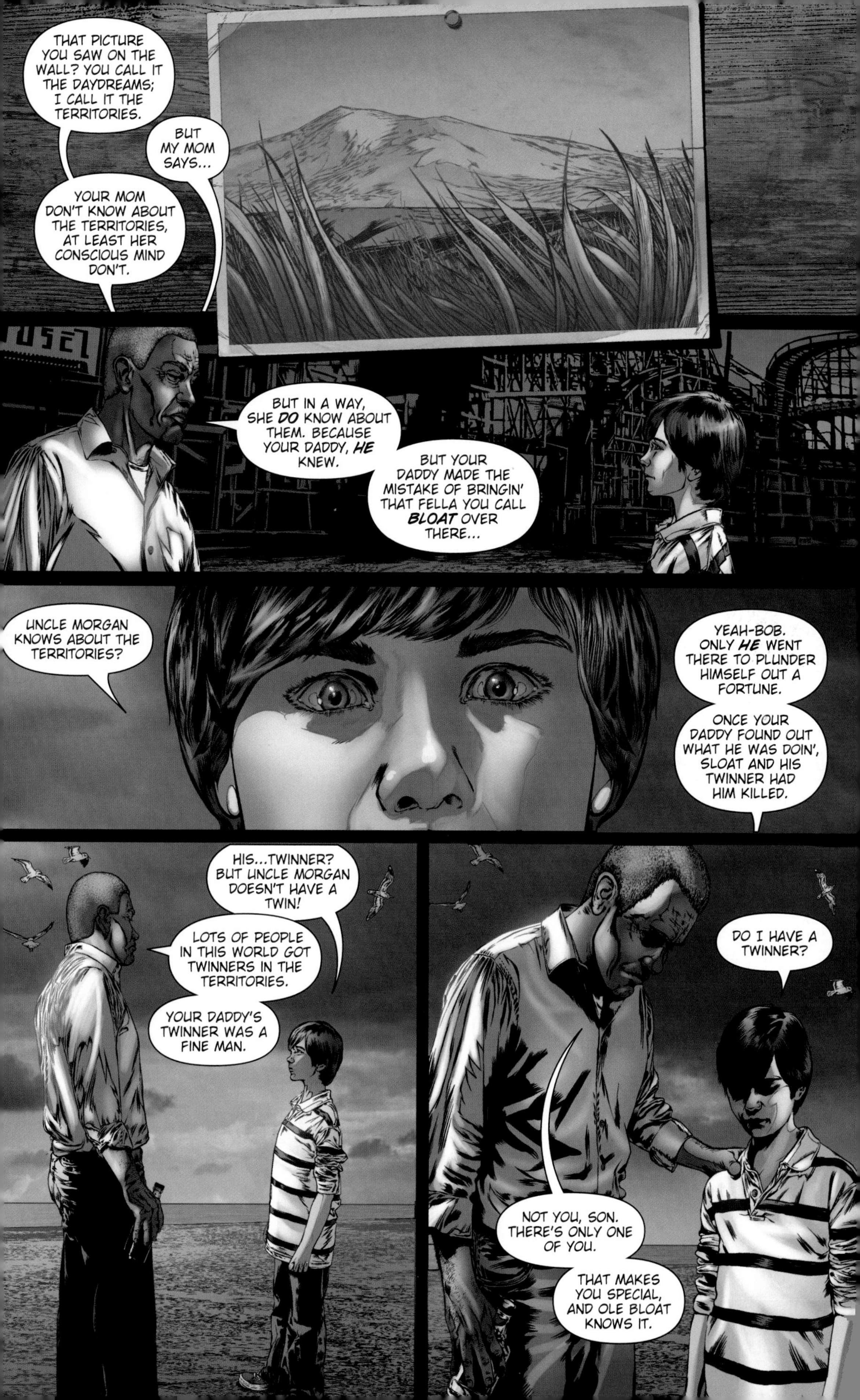

THAT PICTURE YOU SAW ON THE WALL? YOU CALL IT THE DAYDREAMS; I CALL IT THE TERRITORIES.
BUT MY MOM SAYS...
YOUR MOM DON'T KNOW ABOUT THE TERRITORIES, AT LEAST HER CONSCIOUS MIND DON'T.
BUT IN A WAY, SHE **DO** KNOW ABOUT THEM. BECAUSE YOUR DADDY, **HE** KNEW.
BUT YOUR DADDY MADE THE MISTAKE OF BRINGIN' THAT FELLA YOU CALL **BLOAT** OVER THERE...
UNCLE MORGAN KNOWS ABOUT THE TERRITORIES?
YEAH-BOB. ONLY **HE** WENT THERE TO PLUNDER HIMSELF OUT A FORTUNE.
ONCE YOUR DADDY FOUND OUT WHAT HE WAS DOIN', SLOAT AND HIS TWINNER HAD HIM KILLED.
HIS...TWINNER? BUT UNCLE MORGAN DOESN'T HAVE A TWIN!
LOTS OF PEOPLE IN THIS WORLD GOT TWINNERS IN THE TERRITORIES.
YOUR DADDY'S TWINNER WAS A FINE MAN.
DO I HAVE A TWINNER?
NOT YOU, SON. THERE'S ONLY ONE OF YOU.
THAT MAKES YOU SPECIAL, AND OLE BLOAT KNOWS IT.

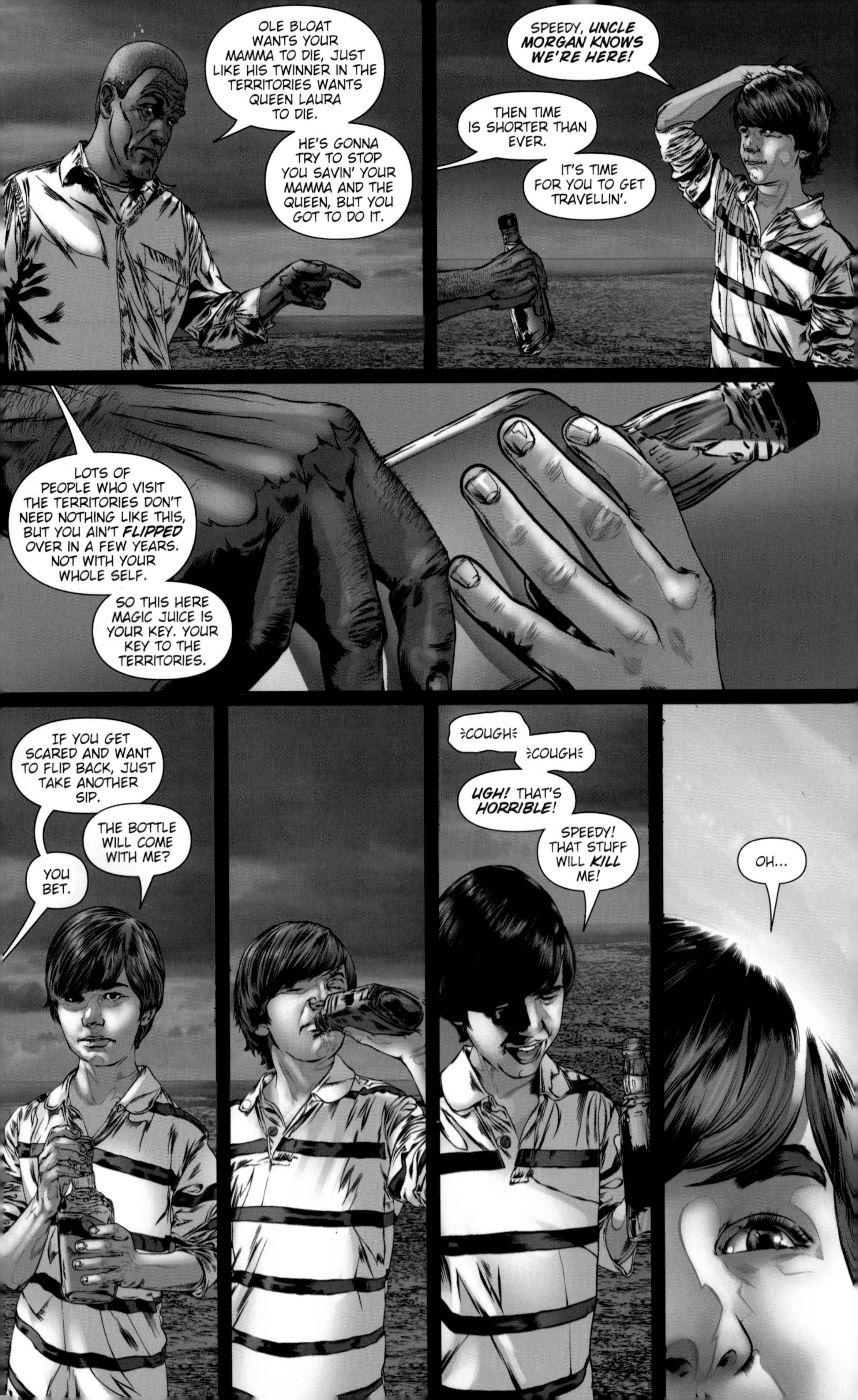
OLE BLOAT WANTS YOUR MAMMA TO DIE, JUST LIKE HIS TWINNER IN THE TERRITORIES WANTS QUEEN LAURA TO DIE.
HE'S GONNA TRY TO STOP YOU SAVIN' YOUR MAMMA AND THE QUEEN, BUT YOU GOT TO DO IT.
SPEEDY, ***UNCLE MORGAN KNOWS WE'RE HERE!***
THEN TIME IS SHORTER THAN EVER.
IT'S TIME FOR YOU TO GET TRAVELLIN'.
LOTS OF PEOPLE WHO VISIT THE TERRITORIES DON'T NEED NOTHING LIKE THIS, BUT YOU AIN'T ***FLIPPED*** OVER IN A FEW YEARS. NOT WITH YOUR WHOLE SELF.
SO THIS HERE MAGIC JUICE IS YOUR KEY. YOUR KEY TO THE TERRITORIES.
IF YOU GET SCARED AND WANT TO FLIP BACK, JUST TAKE ANOTHER SIP.
THE BOTTLE WILL COME WITH ME?
YOU BET.
≷COUGH≶
≷COUGH≶
UGH! THAT'S ***HORRIBLE***!
SPEEDY! THAT STUFF WILL ***KILL*** ME!
OH...

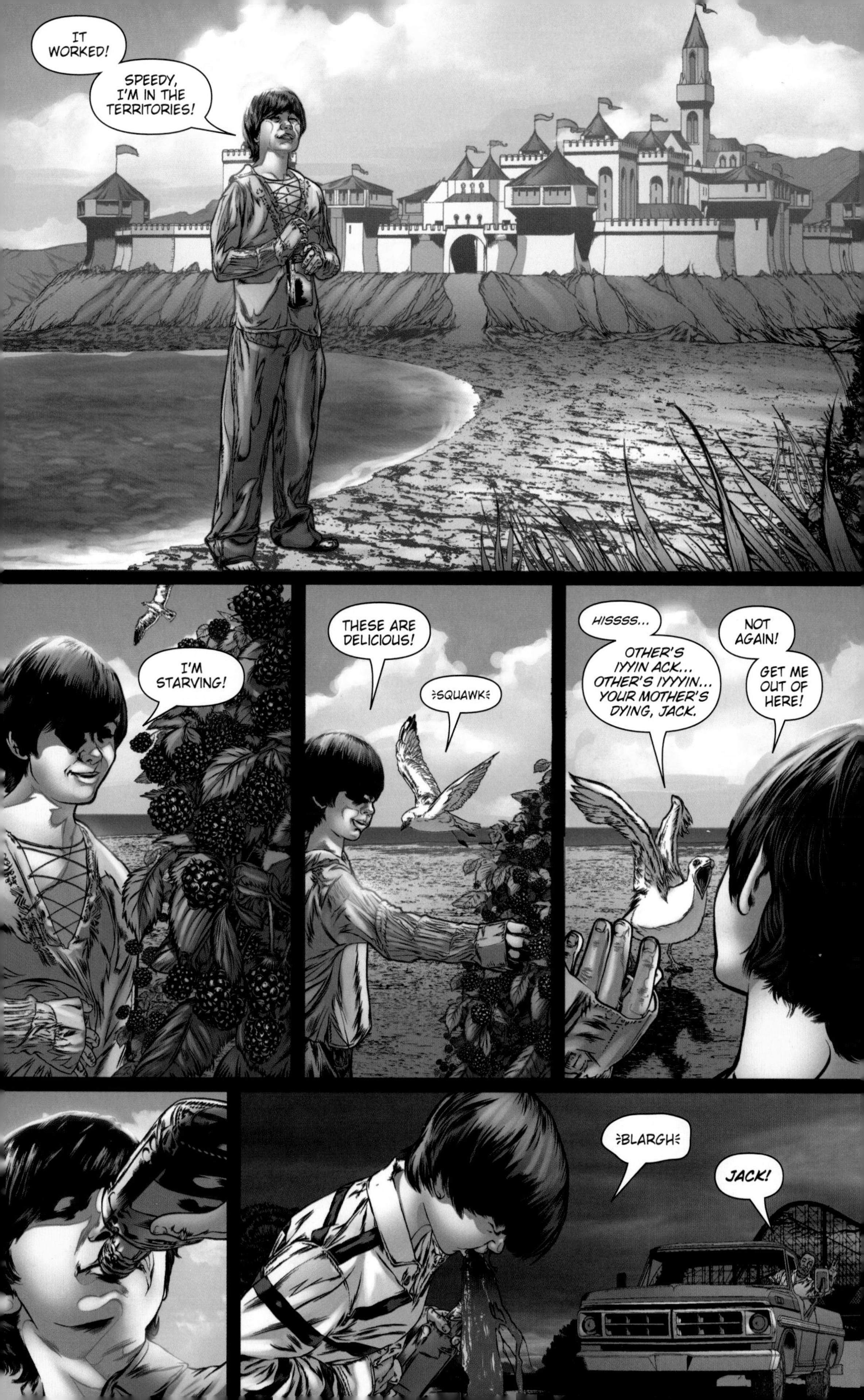
IT WORKED!
SPEEDY, I'M IN THE TERRITORIES!
I'M STARVING!
THESE ARE DELICIOUS!
SQUAWK
HISSSS...
OTHER'S IYYIN ACK... OTHER'S IYYYIN... YOUR MOTHER'S DYING, JACK.
NOT AGAIN!
GET ME OUT OF HERE!
BLARGH
JACK!

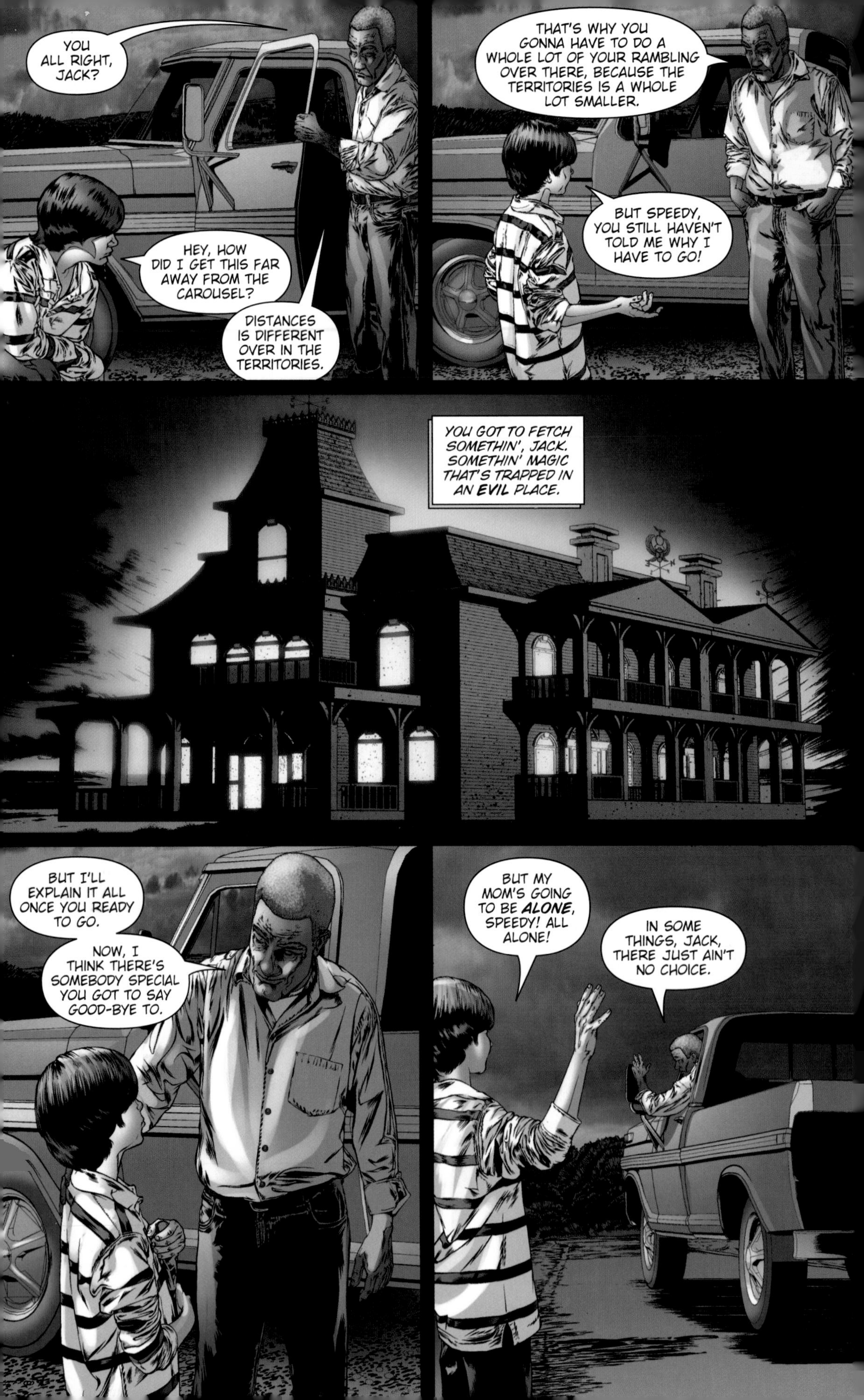

YOU ALL RIGHT, JACK?
HEY, HOW DID I GET THIS FAR AWAY FROM THE CAROUSEL?
DISTANCES IS DIFFERENT OVER IN THE TERRITORIES.
THAT'S WHY YOU GONNA HAVE TO DO A WHOLE LOT OF YOUR RAMBLING OVER THERE, BECAUSE THE TERRITORIES IS A WHOLE LOT SMALLER.
BUT SPEEDY, YOU STILL HAVEN'T TOLD ME WHY I HAVE TO GO!
YOU GOT TO FETCH SOMETHIN', JACK. SOMETHIN' MAGIC THAT'S TRAPPED IN AN EVIL PLACE.
BUT I'LL EXPLAIN IT ALL ONCE YOU READY TO GO.
NOW, I THINK THERE'S SOMEBODY SPECIAL YOU GOT TO SAY GOOD-BYE TO.
BUT MY MOM'S GOING TO BE ALONE, SPEEDY! ALL ALONE!
IN SOME THINGS, JACK, THERE JUST AIN'T NO CHOICE.

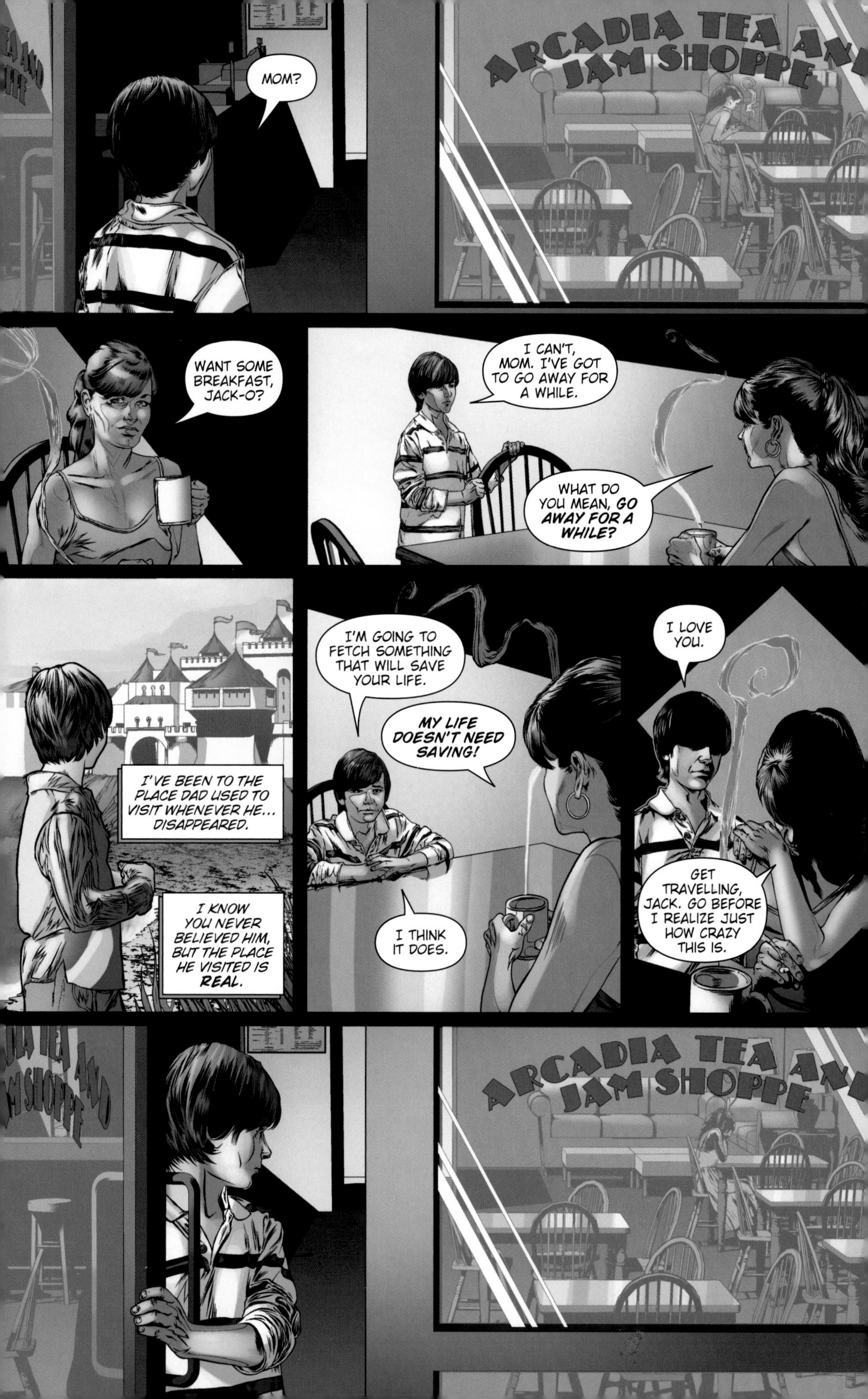
MOM?
ARCADIA TEA AND JAM SHOPPE
WANT SOME BREAKFAST, JACK-O?
I CAN'T, MOM. I'VE GOT TO GO AWAY FOR A WHILE.
WHAT DO YOU MEAN, ***GO AWAY FOR A WHILE?***
I'VE BEEN TO THE PLACE DAD USED TO VISIT WHENEVER HE... DISAPPEARED.
I KNOW YOU NEVER BELIEVED HIM, BUT THE PLACE HE VISITED IS ***REAL.***
I'M GOING TO FETCH SOMETHING THAT WILL SAVE YOUR LIFE.
MY LIFE DOESN'T NEED SAVING!
I THINK IT DOES.
I LOVE YOU.
GET TRAVELLING, JACK. GO BEFORE I REALIZE JUST HOW CRAZY THIS IS.
ARCADIA TEA AND JAM SHOPPE

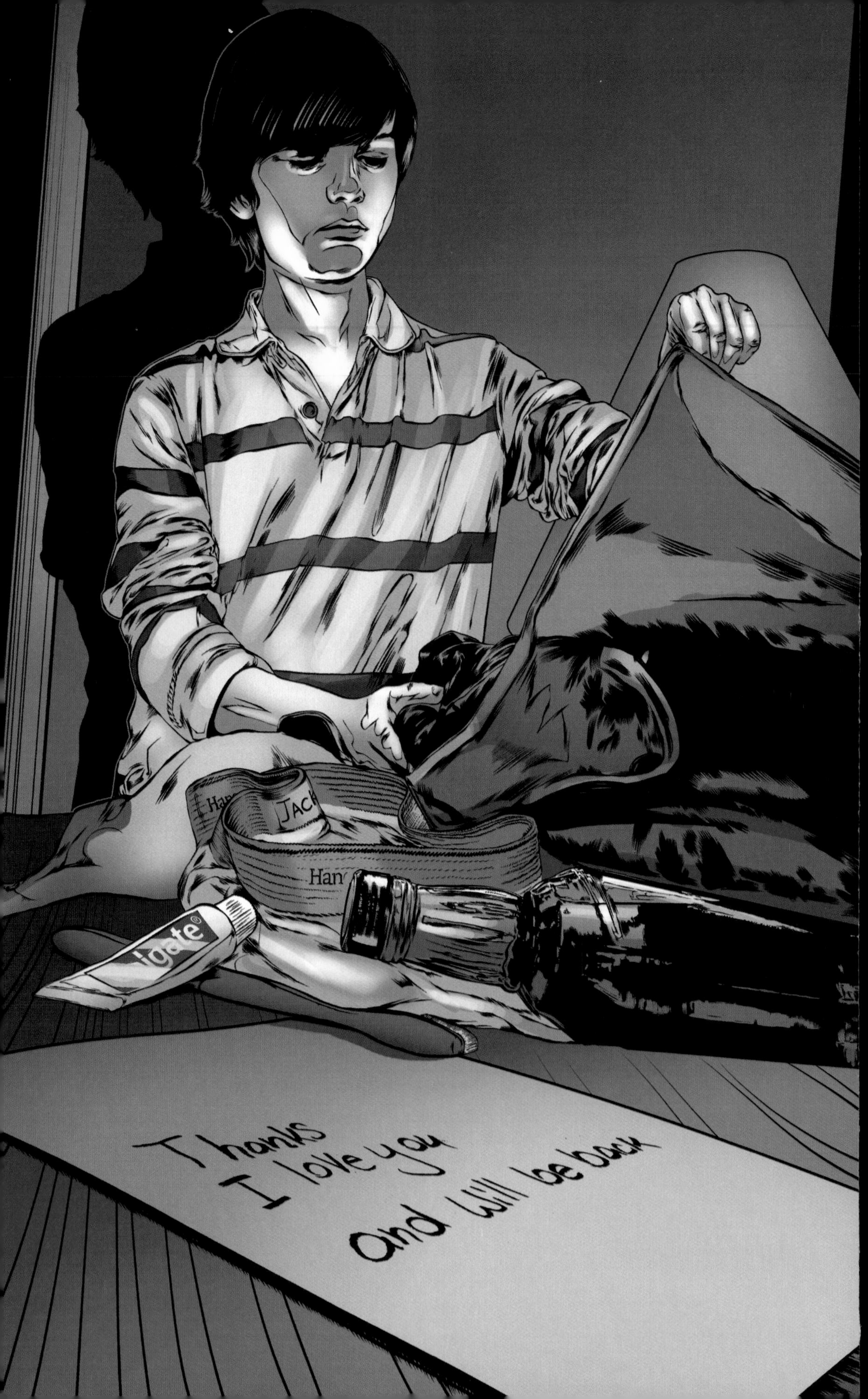

JACK
Thanks
I love you
and will be back

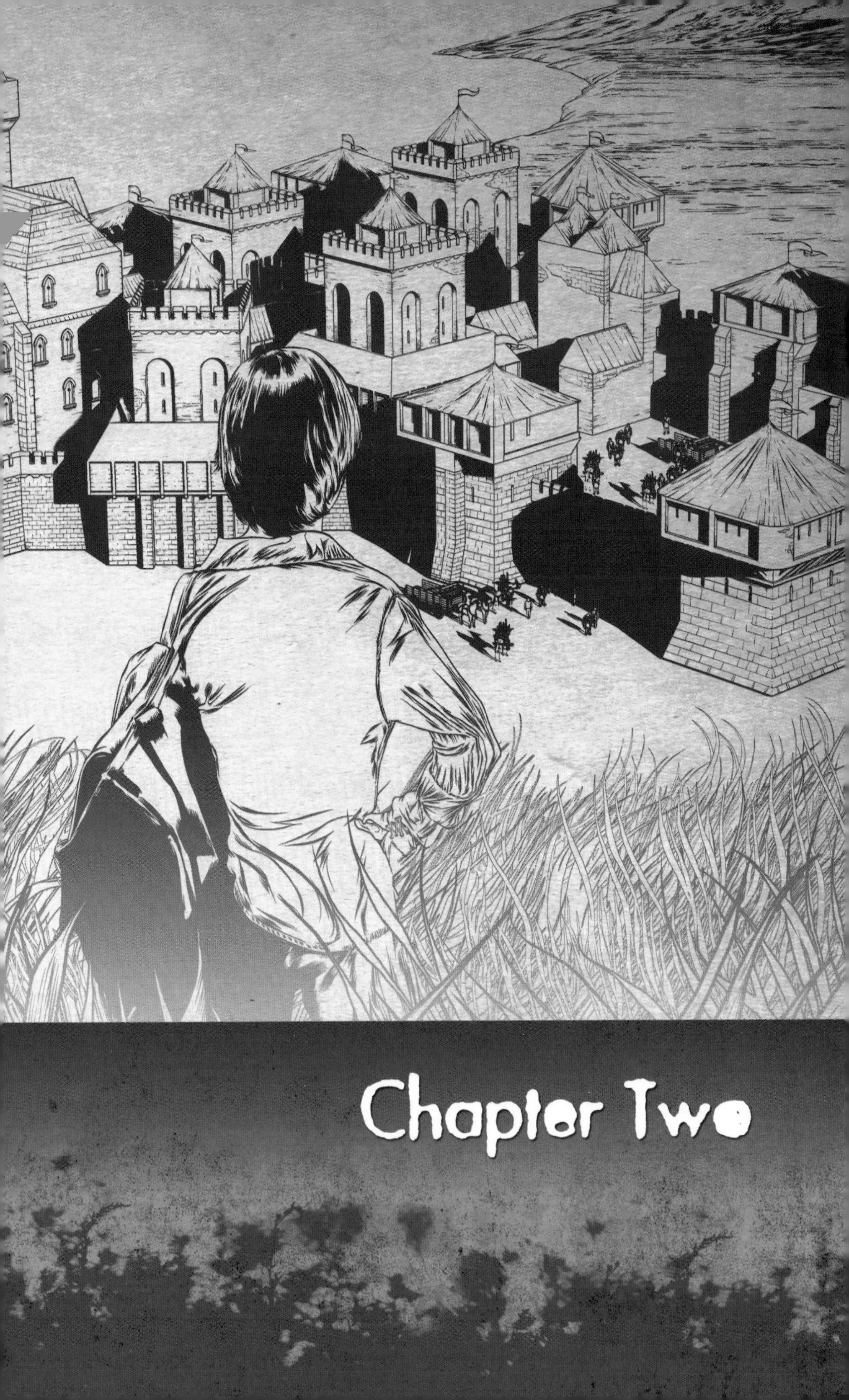

Chapter Two

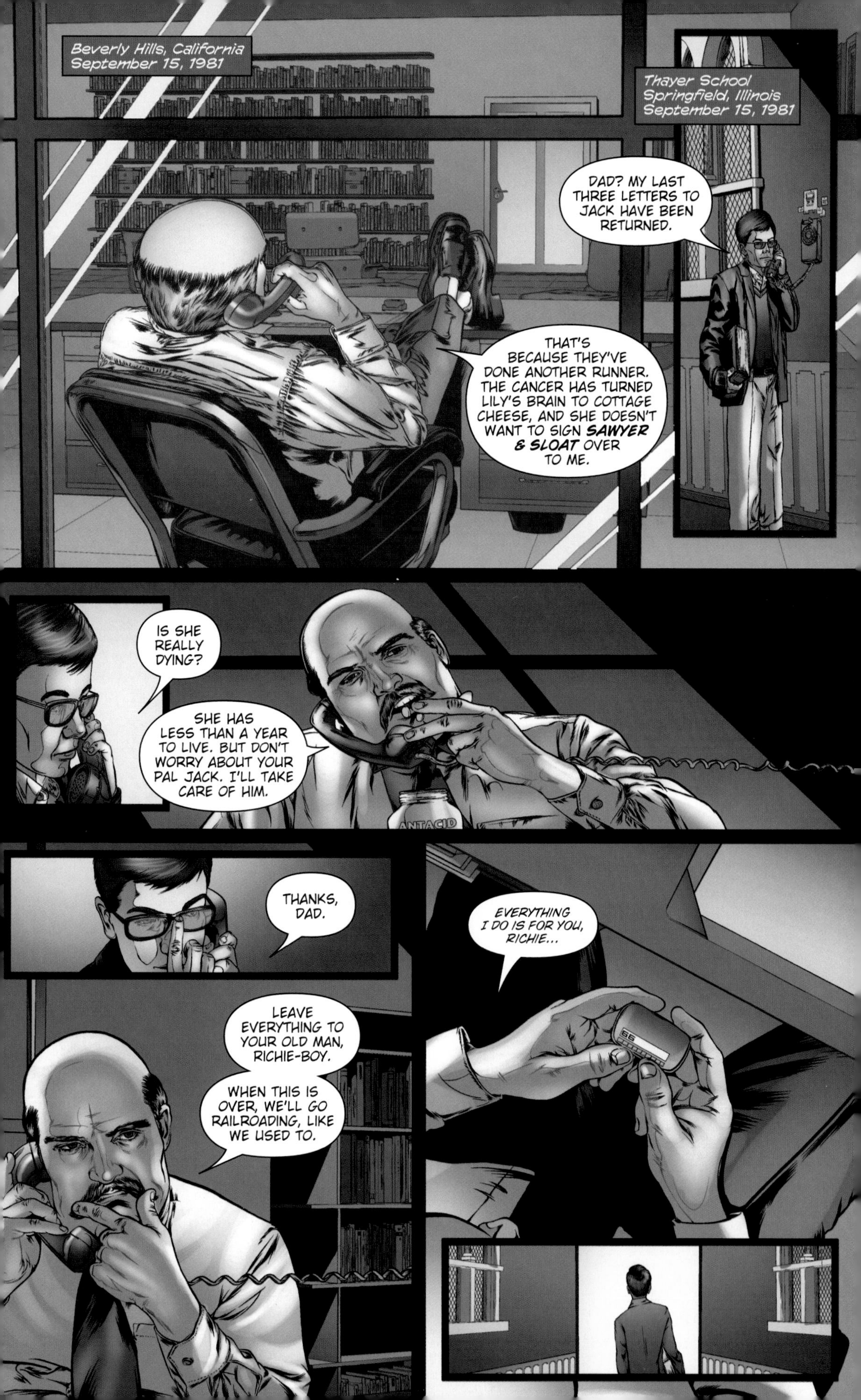
Beverly Hills, California
September 15, 1981
Thayer School
Springfield, Illinois
September 15, 1981
DAD? MY LAST THREE LETTERS TO JACK HAVE BEEN RETURNED.
THAT'S BECAUSE THEY'VE DONE ANOTHER RUNNER. THE CANCER HAS TURNED LILY'S BRAIN TO COTTAGE CHEESE, AND SHE DOESN'T WANT TO SIGN SAWYER & SLOAT OVER TO ME.
IS SHE REALLY DYING?
SHE HAS LESS THAN A YEAR TO LIVE. BUT DON'T WORRY ABOUT YOUR PAL JACK. I'LL TAKE CARE OF HIM.
ANTACID
THANKS, DAD.
LEAVE EVERYTHING TO YOUR OLD MAN, RICHIE-BOY.
WHEN THIS IS OVER, WE'LL GO RAILROADING, LIKE WE USED TO.
EVERYTHING I DO IS FOR YOU, RICHIE...

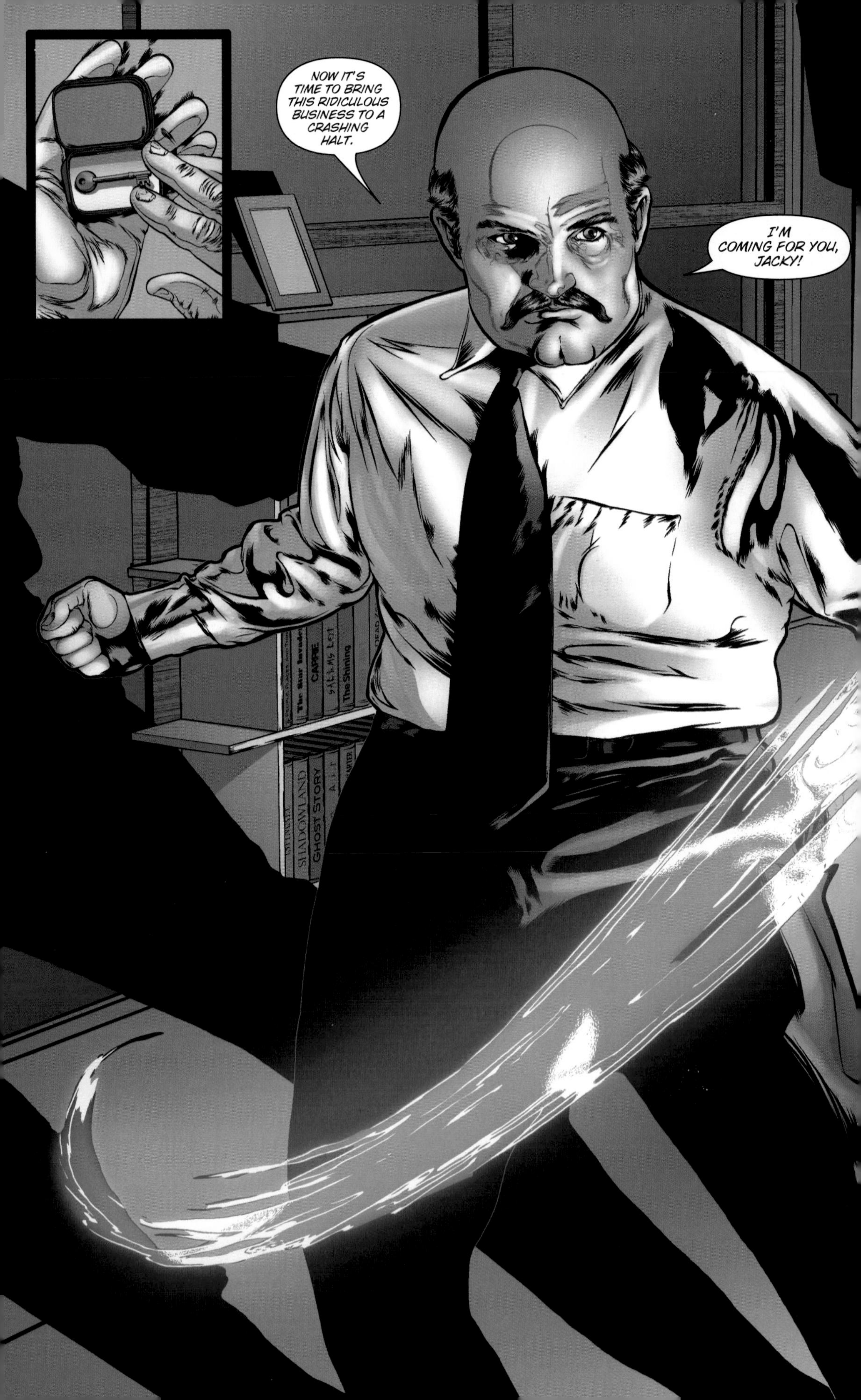
NOW IT'S TIME TO BRING THIS RIDICULOUS BUSINESS TO A CRASHING HALT.
I'M COMING FOR YOU, JACKY!
The Star Invaders
CARRIE
The Shining
SHADOWLAND
GHOST STORY

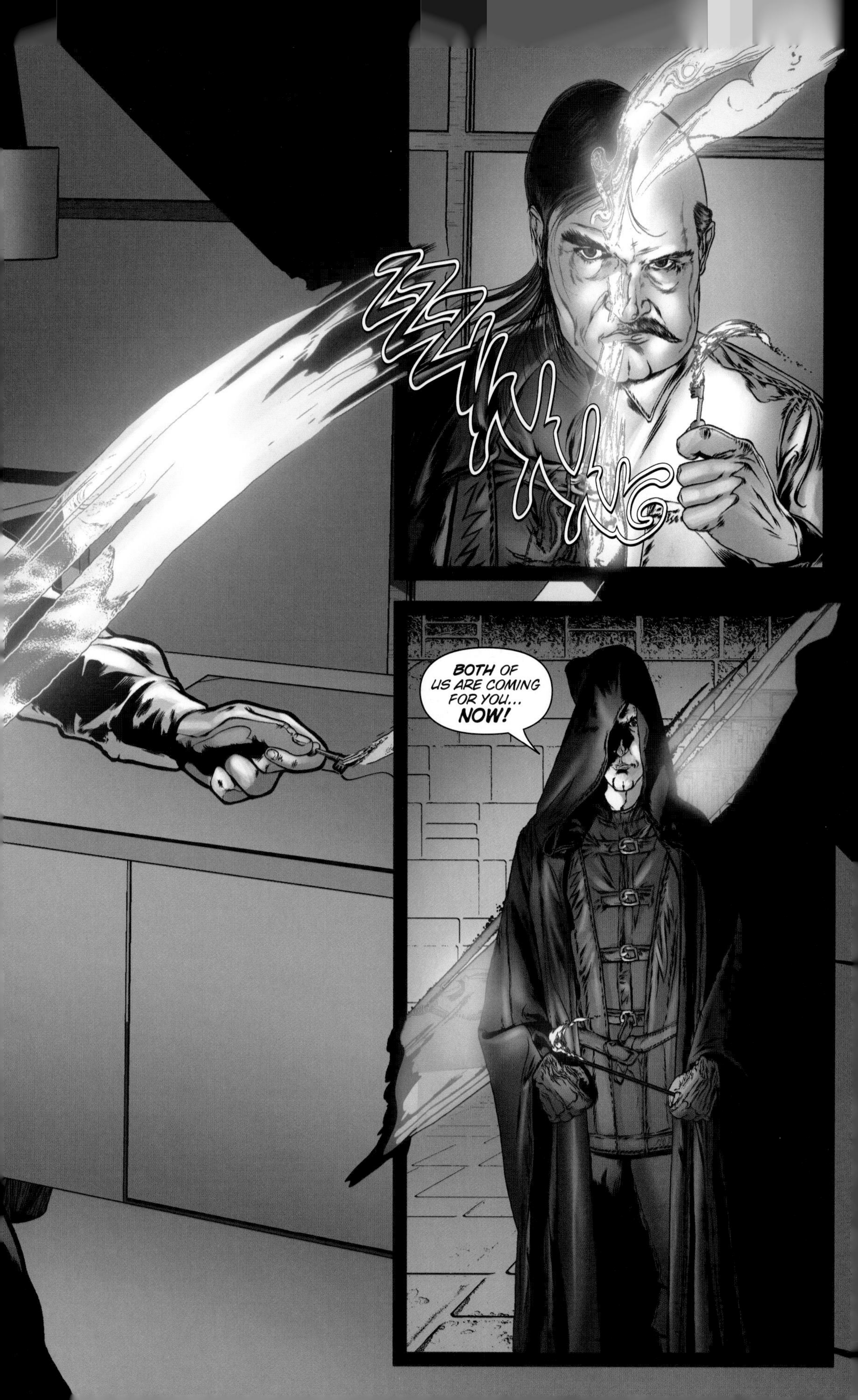
ZZZWHANG
BOTH OF US ARE COMING FOR YOU... NOW!

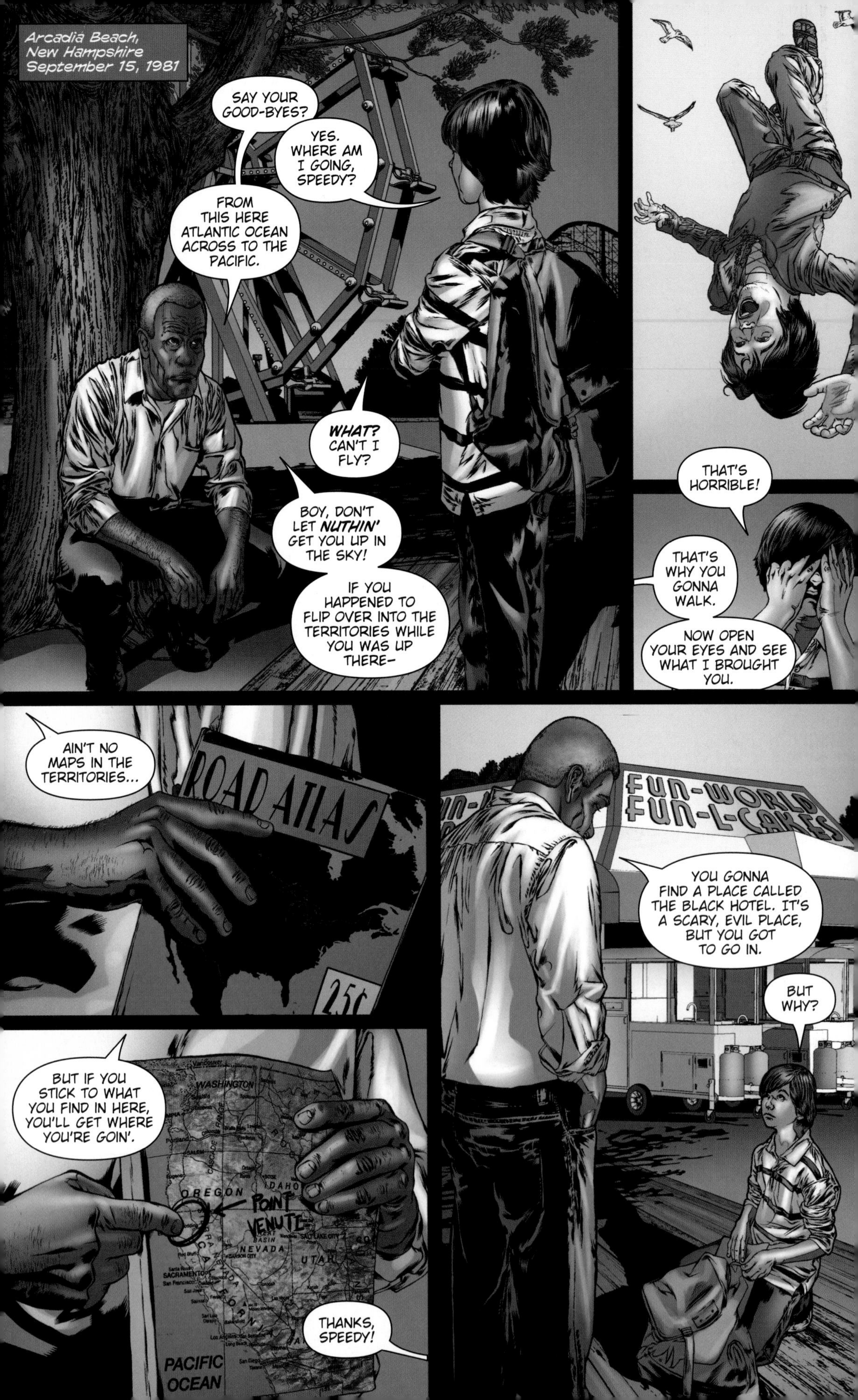

Arcadia Beach, New Hampshire September 15, 1981
SAY YOUR GOOD-BYES?
YES. WHERE AM I GOING, SPEEDY?
FROM THIS HERE ATLANTIC OCEAN ACROSS TO THE PACIFIC.
WHAT? CAN'T I FLY?
BOY, DON'T LET NUTHIN' GET YOU UP IN THE SKY!
IF YOU HAPPENED TO FLIP OVER INTO THE TERRITORIES WHILE YOU WAS UP THERE–
THAT'S HORRIBLE!
THAT'S WHY YOU GONNA WALK.
NOW OPEN YOUR EYES AND SEE WHAT I BROUGHT YOU.
AIN'T NO MAPS IN THE TERRITORIES...
ROAD ATLAS
25¢
BUT IF YOU STICK TO WHAT YOU FIND IN HERE, YOU'LL GET WHERE YOU'RE GOIN'.
WASHINGTON
OREGON
IDAHO
POINT VENUTI
NEVADA
UTAH
SACRAMENTO
PACIFIC OCEAN
THANKS, SPEEDY!
FUN-WORLD FUN-L-CAKES
YOU GONNA FIND A PLACE CALLED THE BLACK HOTEL. IT'S A SCARY, EVIL PLACE, BUT YOU GOT TO GO IN.
BUT WHY?

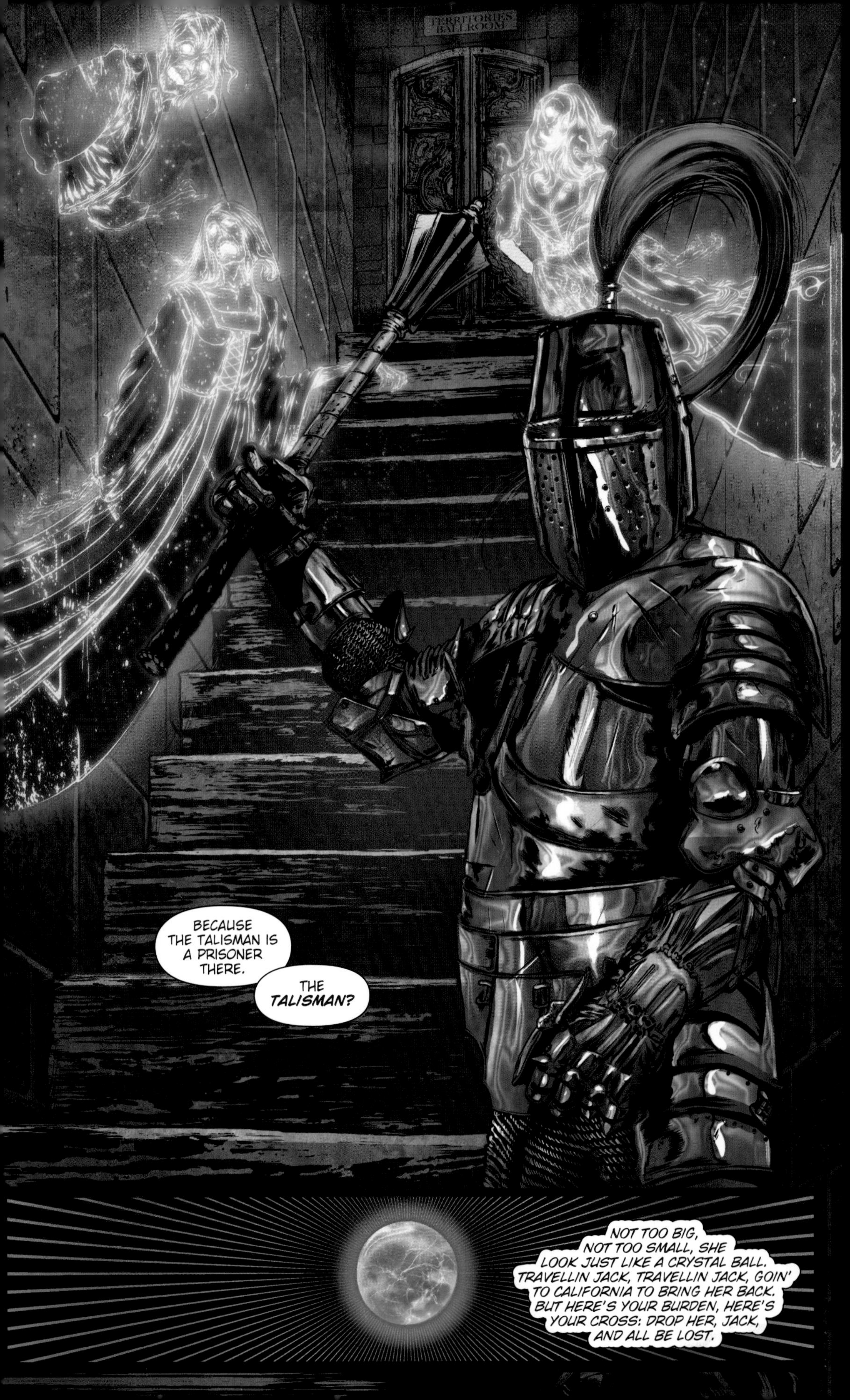
TERRITORIES BALLROOM
BECAUSE THE TALISMAN IS A PRISONER THERE.
THE *TALISMAN?*
NOT TOO BIG, NOT TOO SMALL, SHE LOOK JUST LIKE A CRYSTAL BALL. TRAVELLIN JACK, TRAVELLIN JACK, GOIN' TO CALIFORNIA TO BRING HER BACK. BUT HERE'S YOUR BURDEN, HERE'S YOUR CROSS: DROP HER, JACK, AND ALL BE LOST.

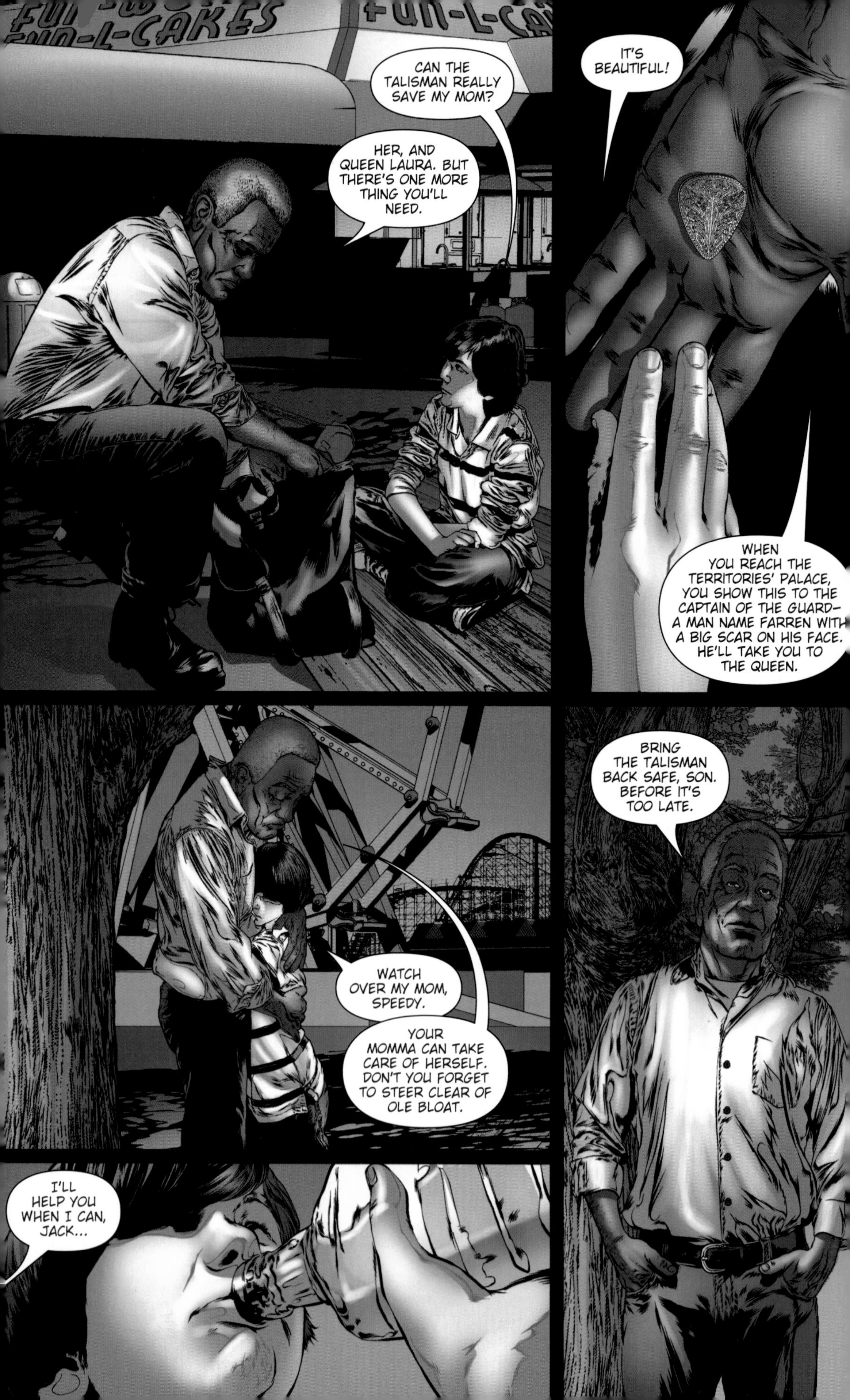
FUN-L-CAKES
FUN-L-CAKES
CAN THE TALISMAN REALLY SAVE MY MOM?
HER, AND QUEEN LAURA. BUT THERE'S ONE MORE THING YOU'LL NEED.
IT'S BEAUTIFUL!
WHEN YOU REACH THE TERRITORIES' PALACE, YOU SHOW THIS TO THE CAPTAIN OF THE GUARD– A MAN NAME FARREN WITH A BIG SCAR ON HIS FACE. HE'LL TAKE YOU TO THE QUEEN.
WATCH OVER MY MOM, SPEEDY.
YOUR MOMMA CAN TAKE CARE OF HERSELF. DON'T YOU FORGET TO STEER CLEAR OF OLE BLOAT.
I'LL HELP YOU WHEN I CAN, JACK...
BRING THE TALISMAN BACK SAFE, SON. BEFORE IT'S TOO LATE.

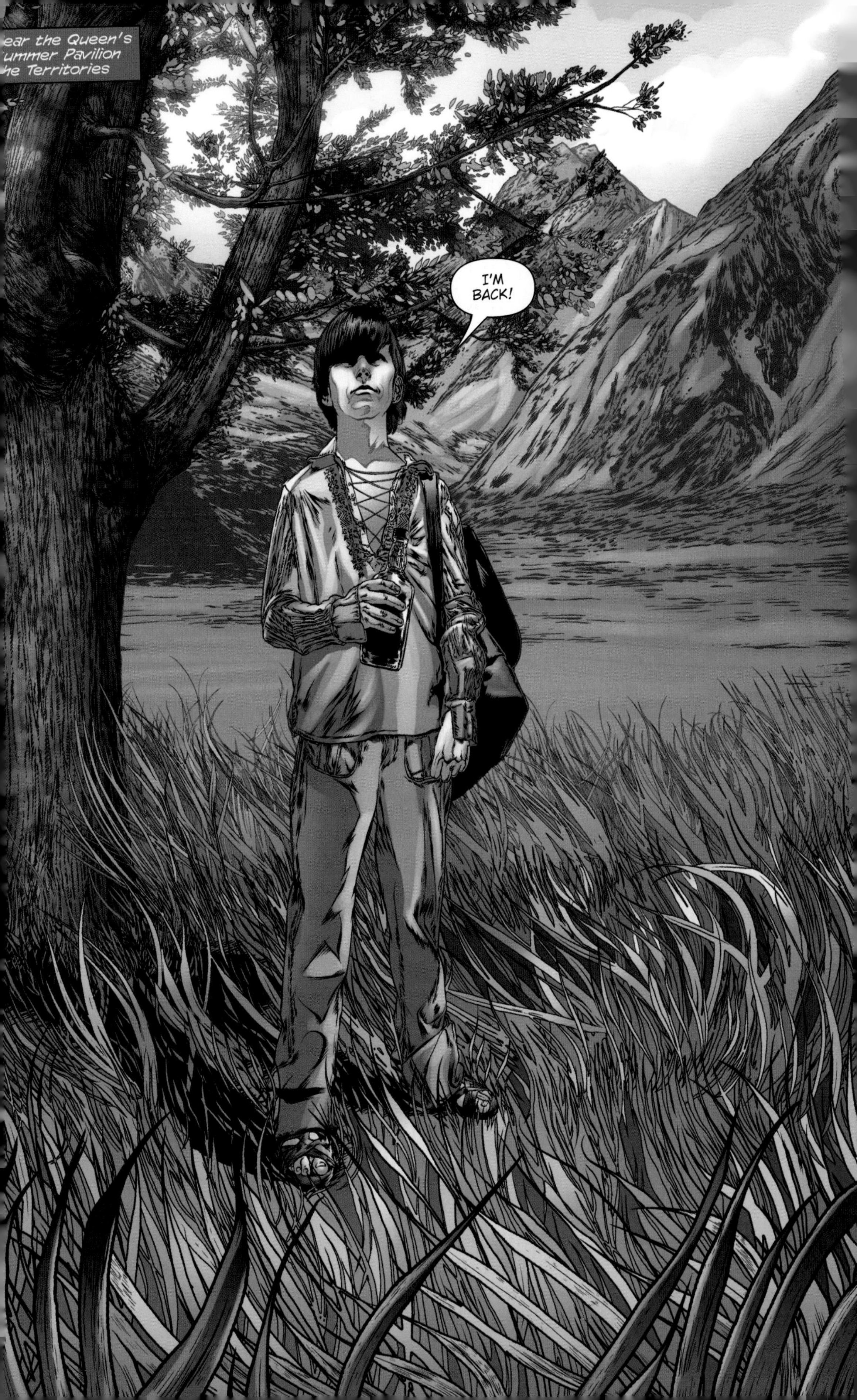
ear the Queen's
ummer Pavilion
he Territories
I'M BACK!

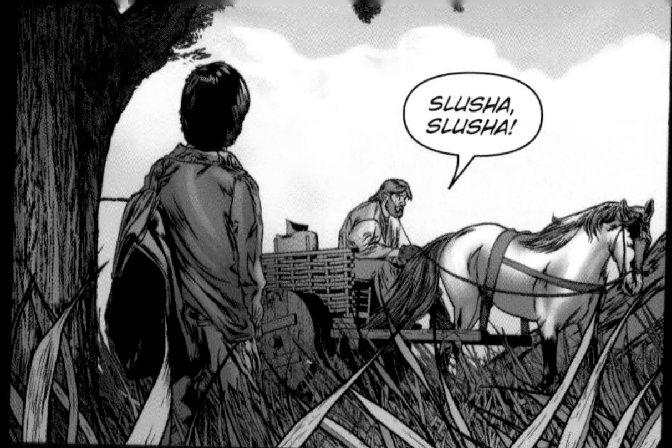
SLUSHA, SLUSHA!

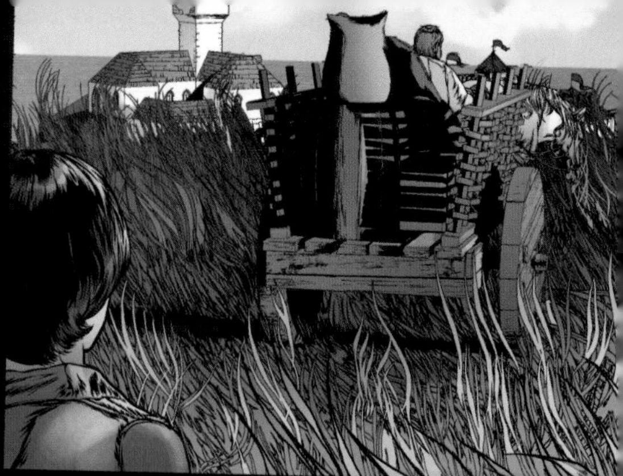

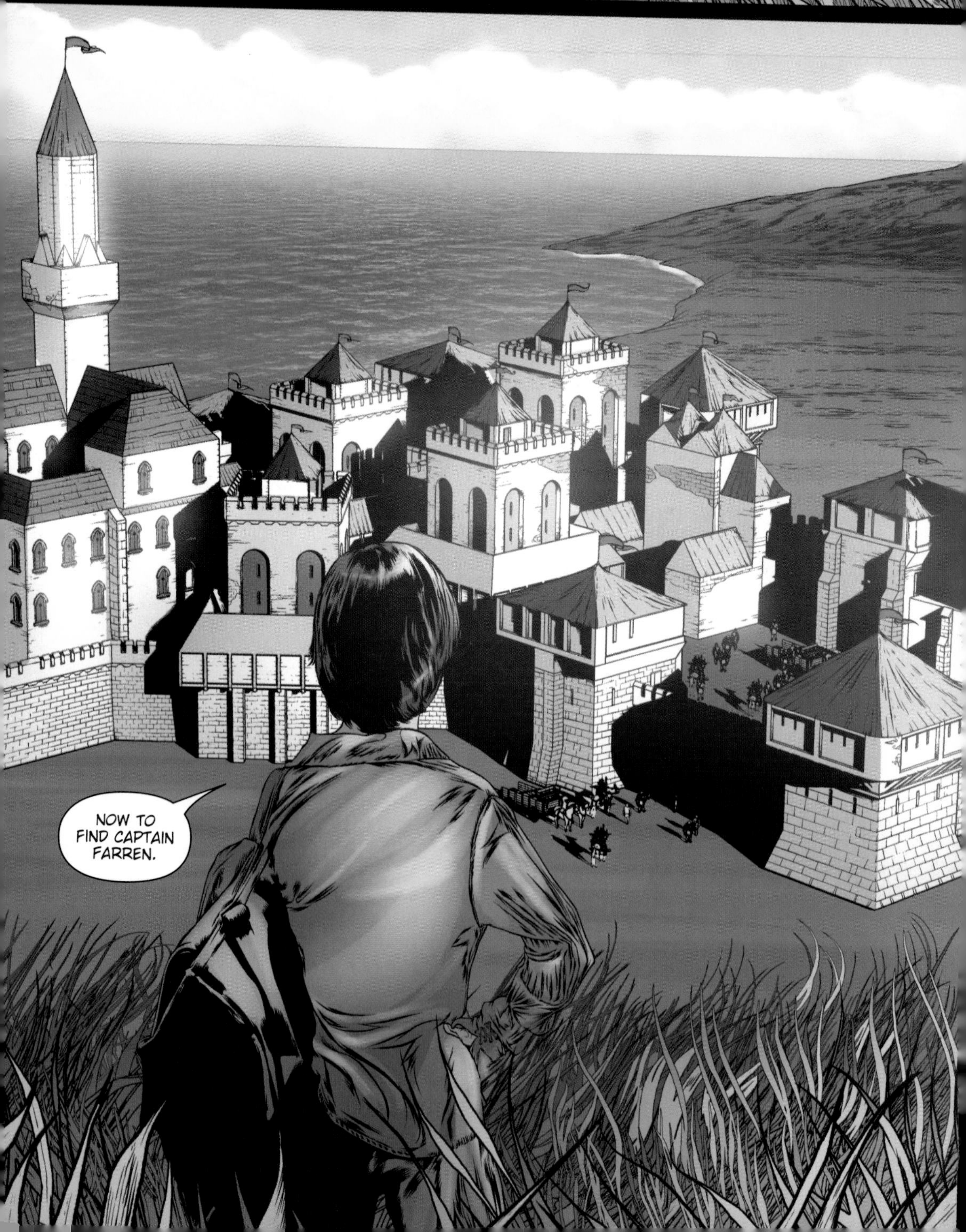
NOW TO FIND CAPTAIN FARREN.

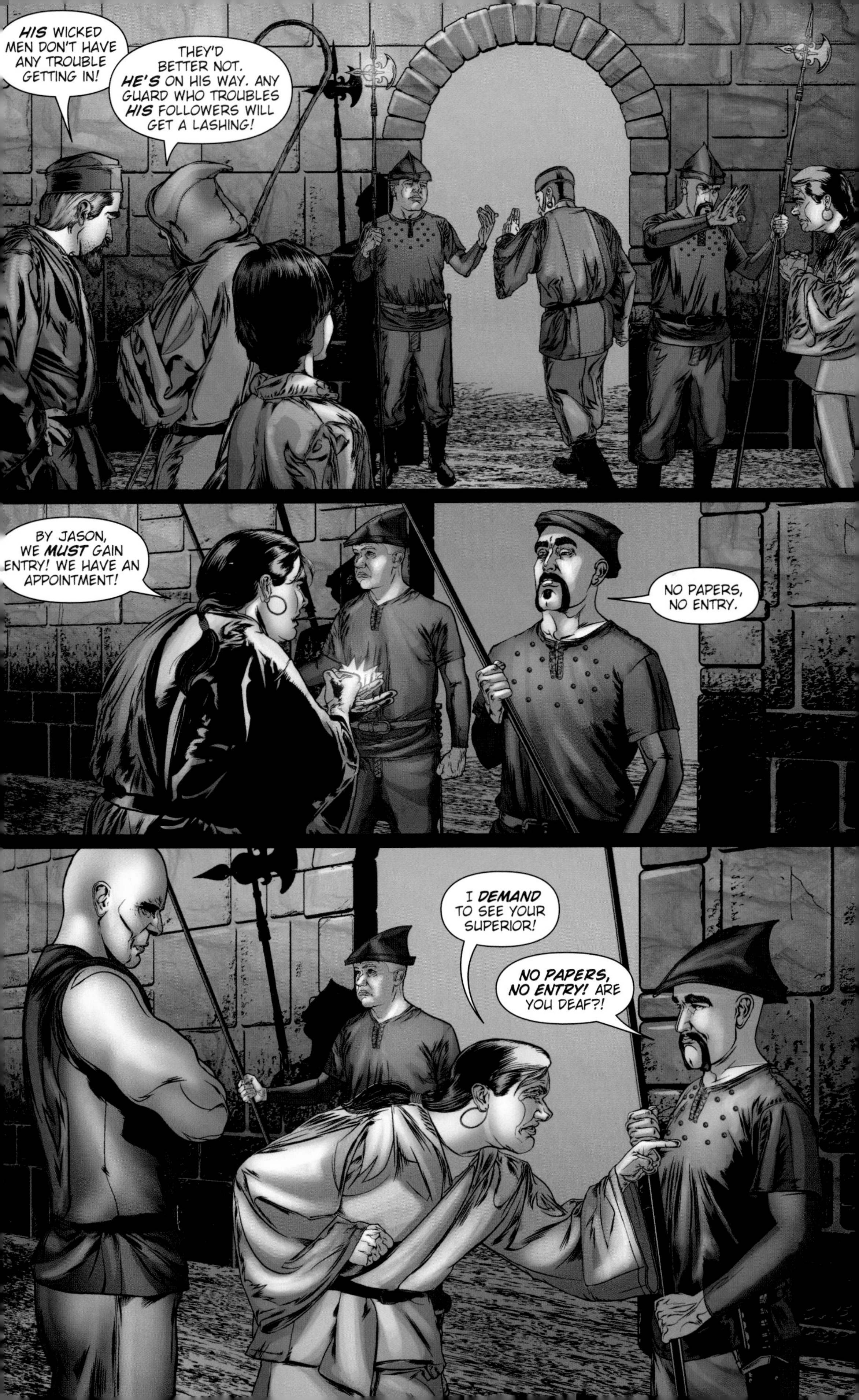
HIS WICKED MEN DON'T HAVE ANY TROUBLE GETTING IN!
THEY'D BETTER NOT. HE'S ON HIS WAY. ANY GUARD WHO TROUBLES HIS FOLLOWERS WILL GET A LASHING!
BY JASON, WE MUST GAIN ENTRY! WE HAVE AN APPOINTMENT!
NO PAPERS, NO ENTRY.
I DEMAND TO SEE YOUR SUPERIOR!
NO PAPERS, NO ENTRY! ARE YOU DEAF?!

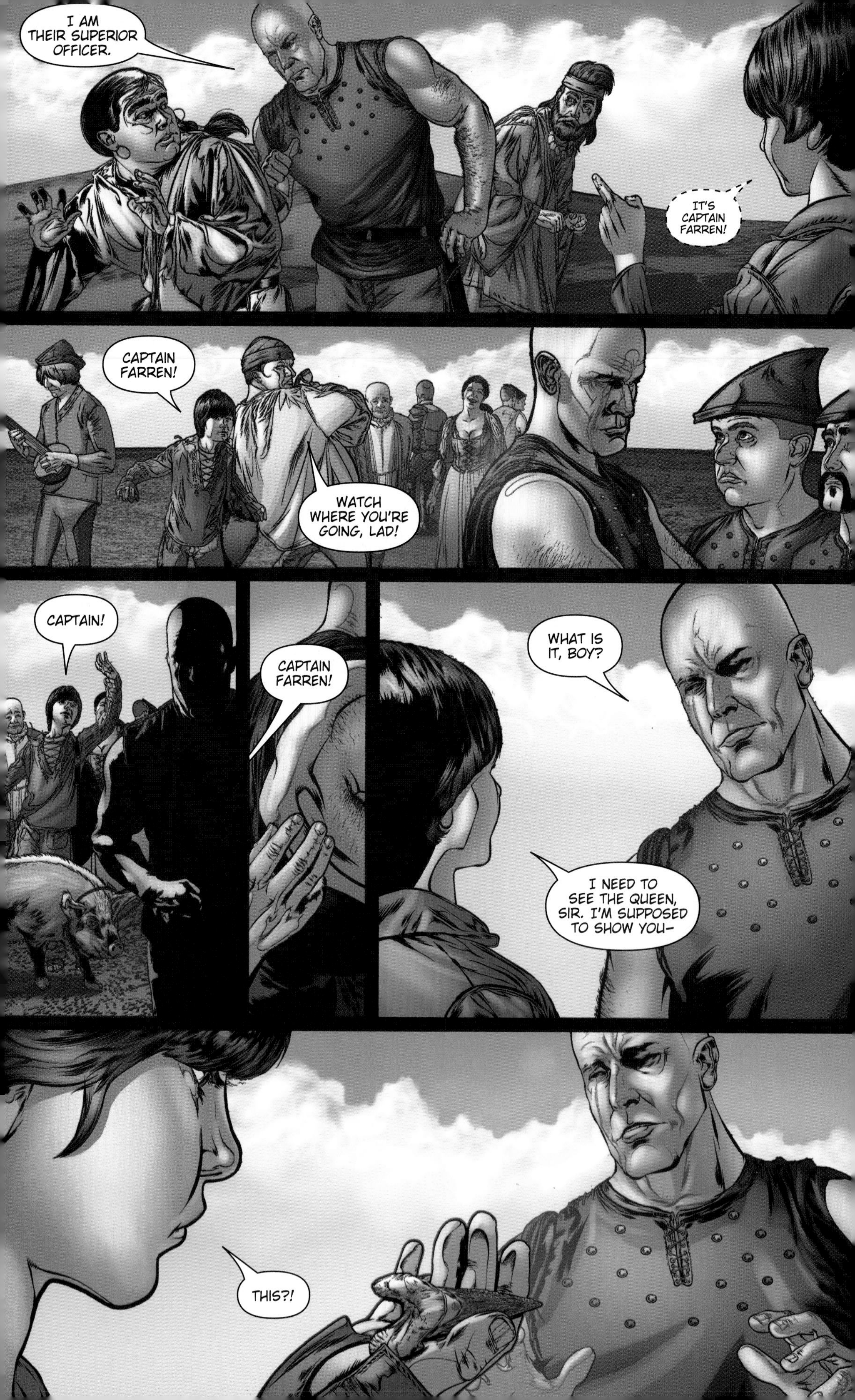
I AM THEIR SUPERIOR OFFICER.
IT'S CAPTAIN FARREN!
CAPTAIN FARREN!
WATCH WHERE YOU'RE GOING, LAD!
CAPTAIN!
CAPTAIN FARREN!
WHAT IS IT, BOY?
I NEED TO SEE THE QUEEN, SIR. I'M SUPPOSED TO SHOW YOU–
THIS?!

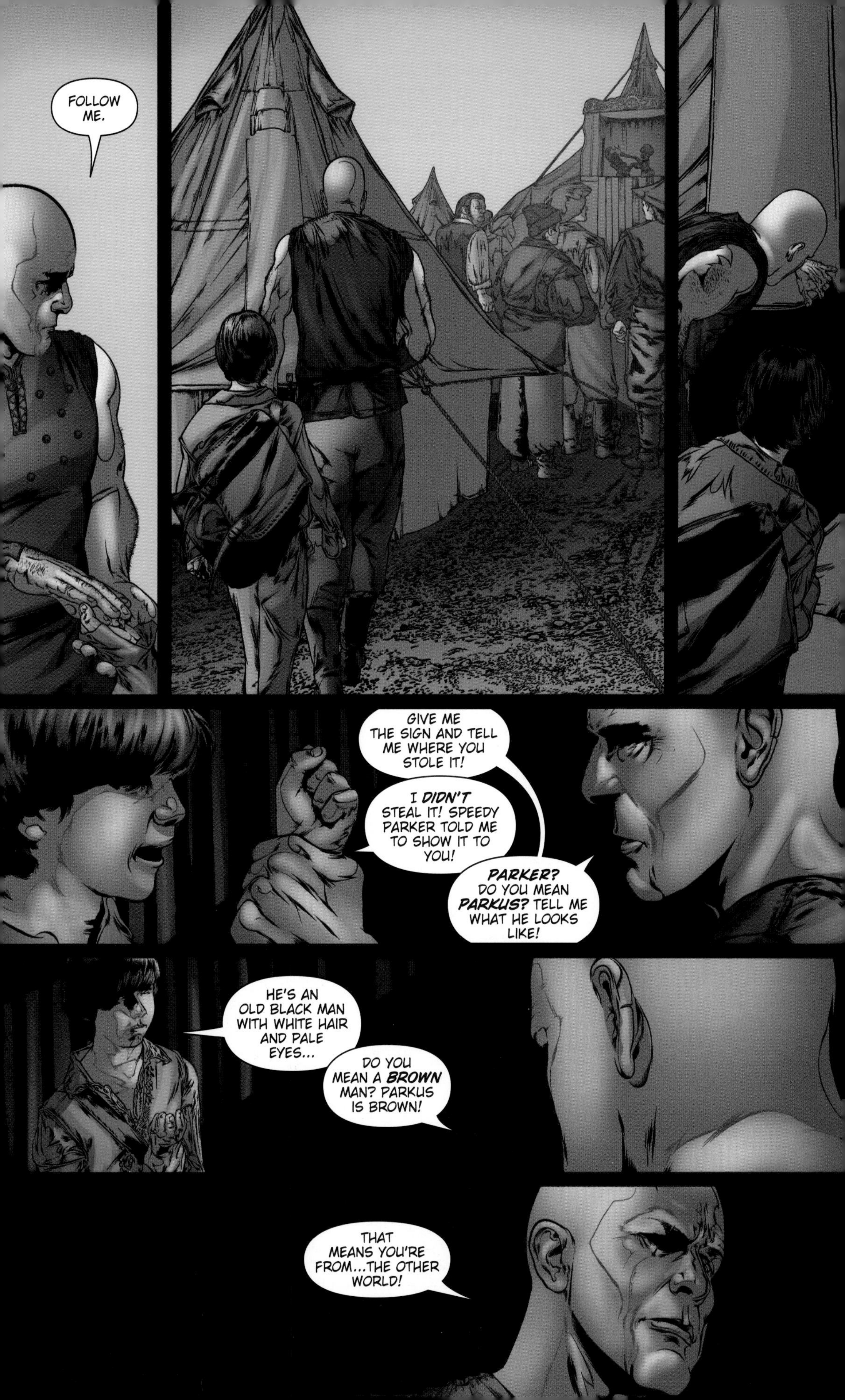
FOLLOW ME.
GIVE ME THE SIGN AND TELL ME WHERE YOU STOLE IT!
I DIDN'T STEAL IT! SPEEDY PARKER TOLD ME TO SHOW IT TO YOU!
PARKER? DO YOU MEAN PARKUS? TELL ME WHAT HE LOOKS LIKE!
HE'S AN OLD BLACK MAN WITH WHITE HAIR AND PALE EYES...
DO YOU MEAN A BROWN MAN? PARKUS IS BROWN!
THAT MEANS YOU'RE FROM...THE OTHER WORLD!

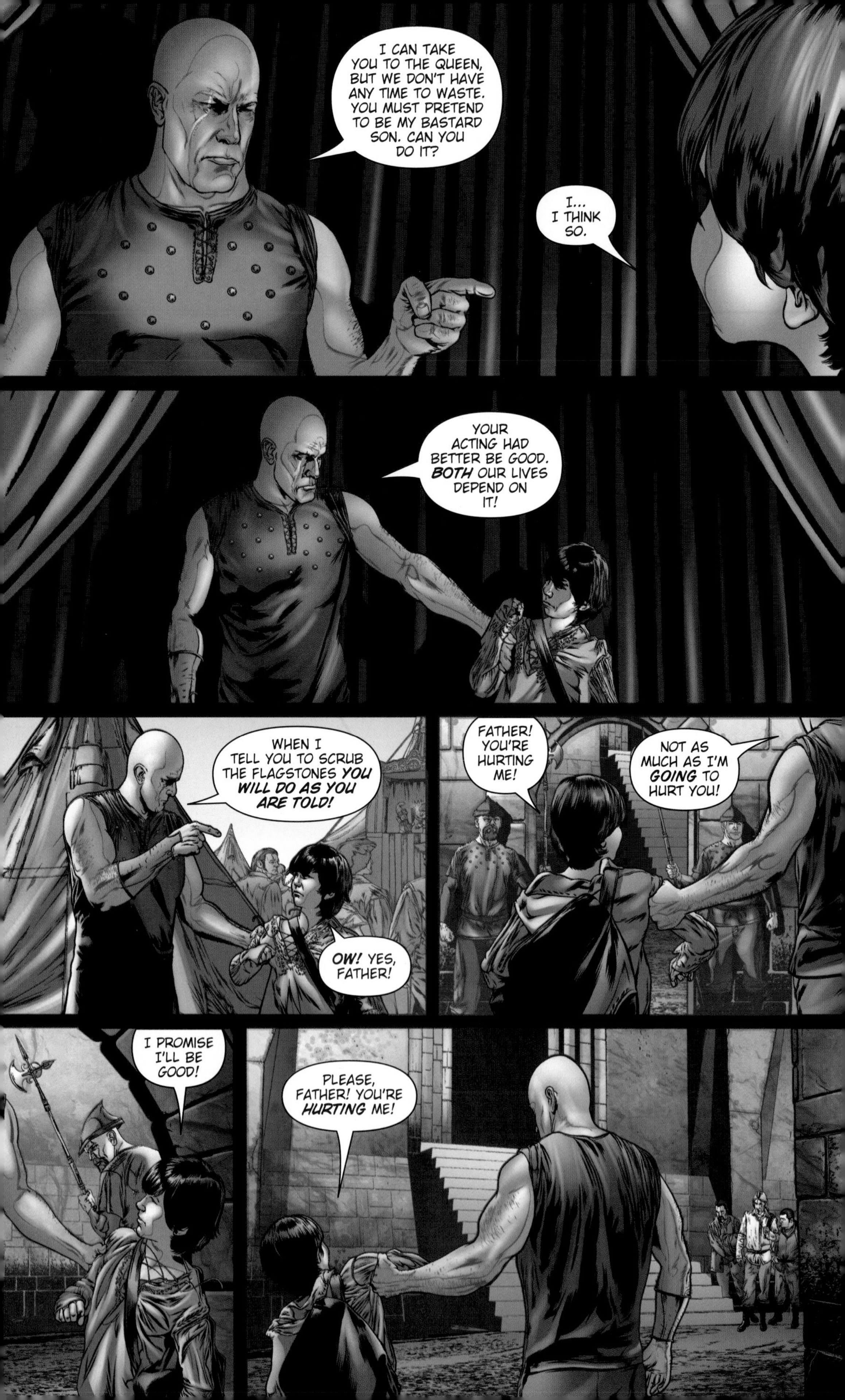
I CAN TAKE YOU TO THE QUEEN, BUT WE DON'T HAVE ANY TIME TO WASTE. YOU MUST PRETEND TO BE MY BASTARD SON. CAN YOU DO IT?
I... I THINK SO.
YOUR ACTING HAD BETTER BE GOOD. *BOTH* OUR LIVES DEPEND ON IT!
WHEN I TELL YOU TO SCRUB THE FLAGSTONES *YOU WILL DO AS YOU ARE TOLD!*
OW! YES, FATHER!
FATHER! YOU'RE HURTING ME!
NOT AS MUCH AS I'M *GOING* TO HURT YOU!
I PROMISE I'LL BE GOOD!
PLEASE, FATHER! YOU'RE *HURTING* ME!

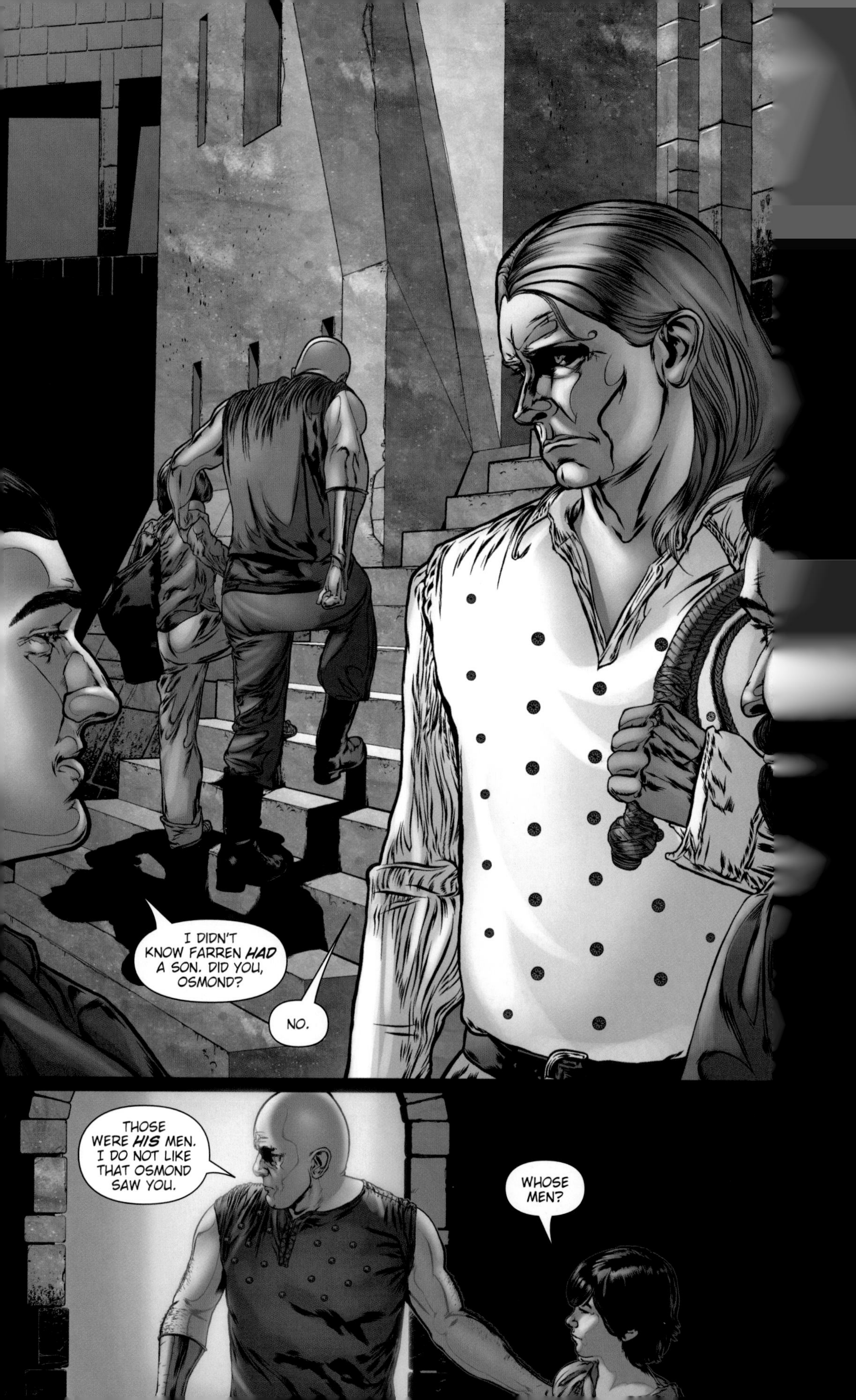
I DIDN'T KNOW FARREN *HAD* A SON. DID YOU, OSMOND?
NO.
THOSE WERE *HIS* MEN. I DO NOT LIKE THAT OSMOND SAW YOU.
WHOSE MEN?

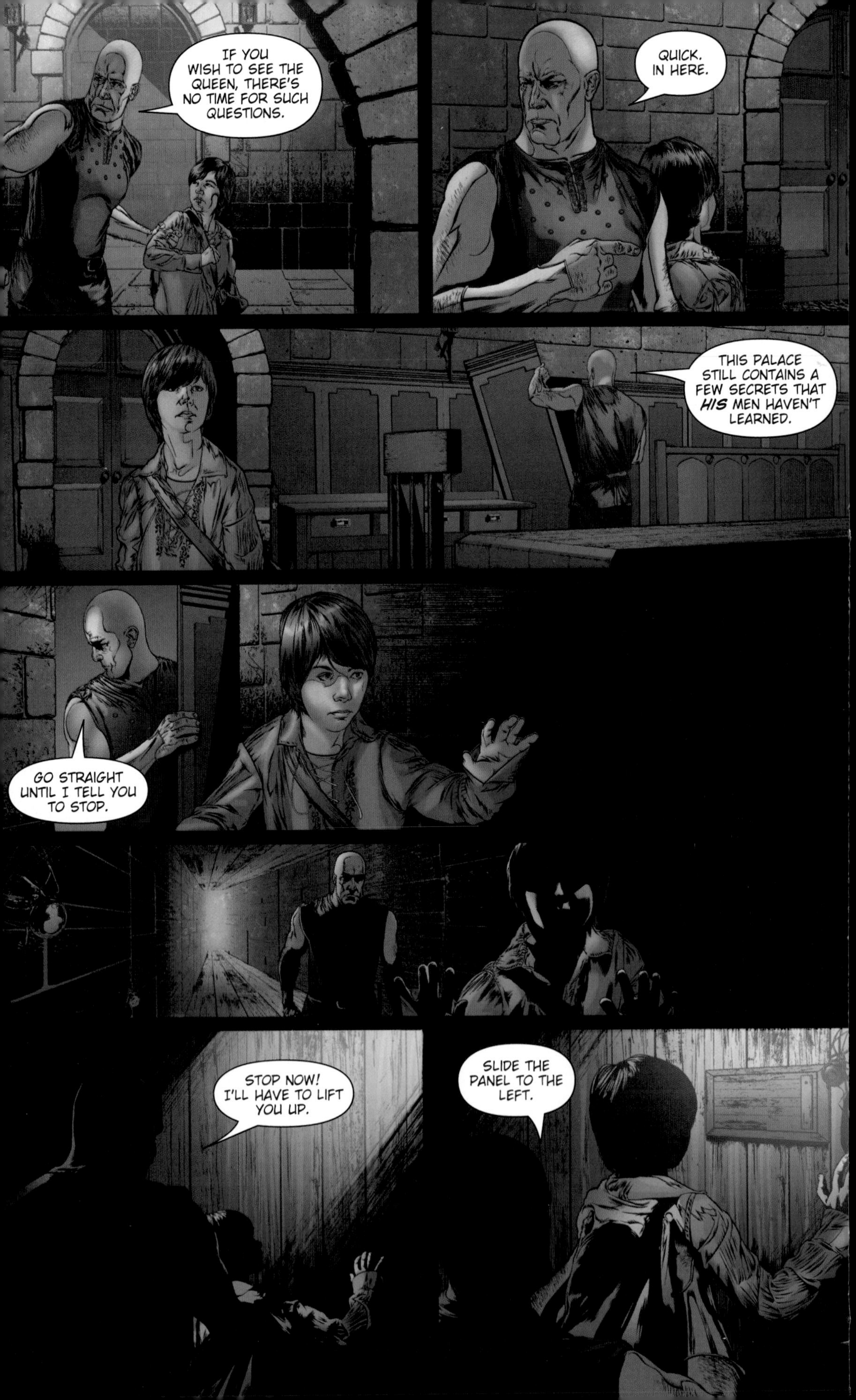
IF YOU WISH TO SEE THE QUEEN, THERE'S NO TIME FOR SUCH QUESTIONS.
QUICK. IN HERE.
THIS PALACE STILL CONTAINS A FEW SECRETS THAT *HIS* MEN HAVEN'T LEARNED.
GO STRAIGHT UNTIL I TELL YOU TO STOP.
STOP NOW! I'LL HAVE TO LIFT YOU UP.
SLIDE THE PANEL TO THE LEFT.

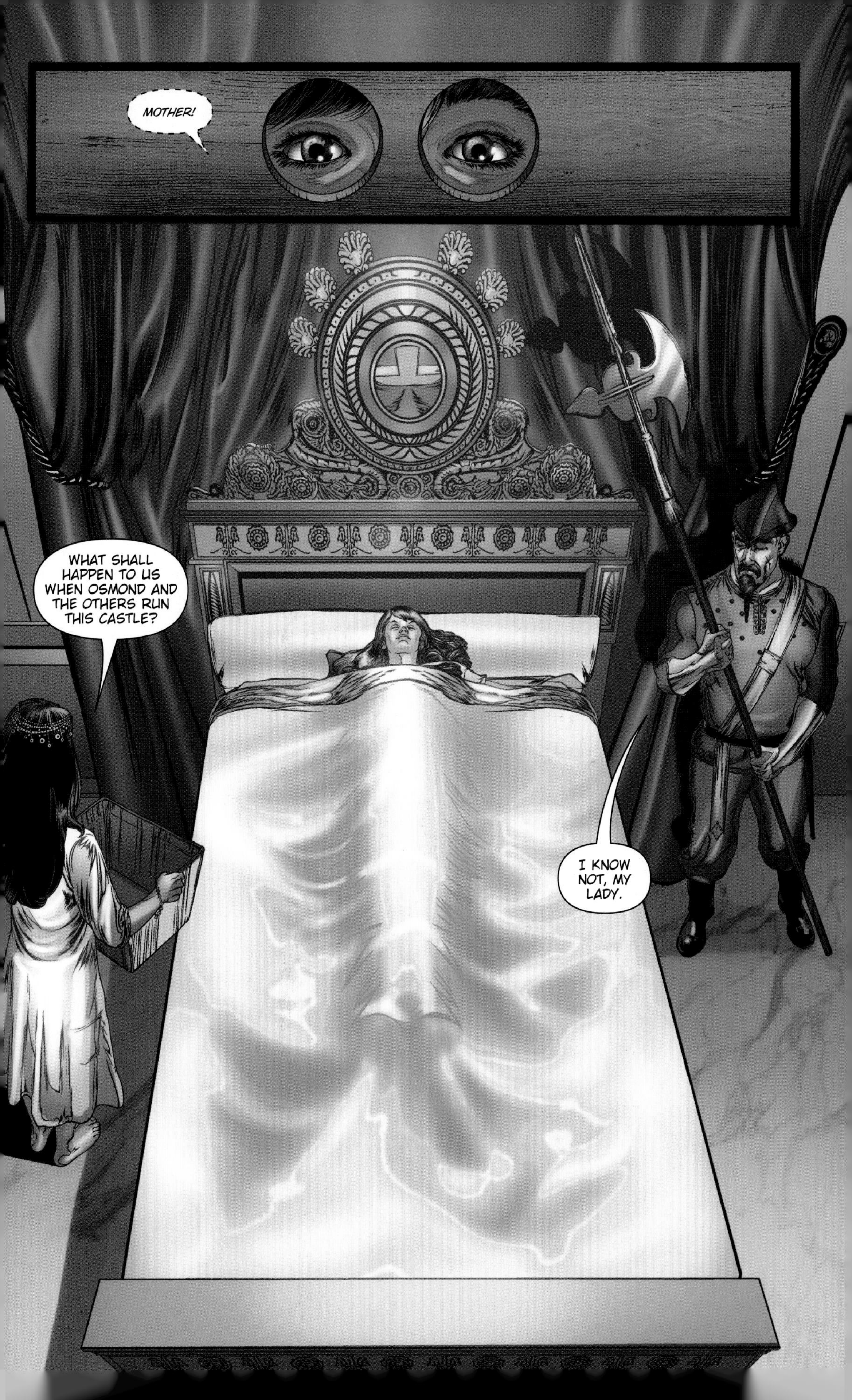
MOTHER!
WHAT SHALL HAPPEN TO US WHEN OSMOND AND THE OTHERS RUN THIS CASTLE?
I KNOW NOT, MY LADY.

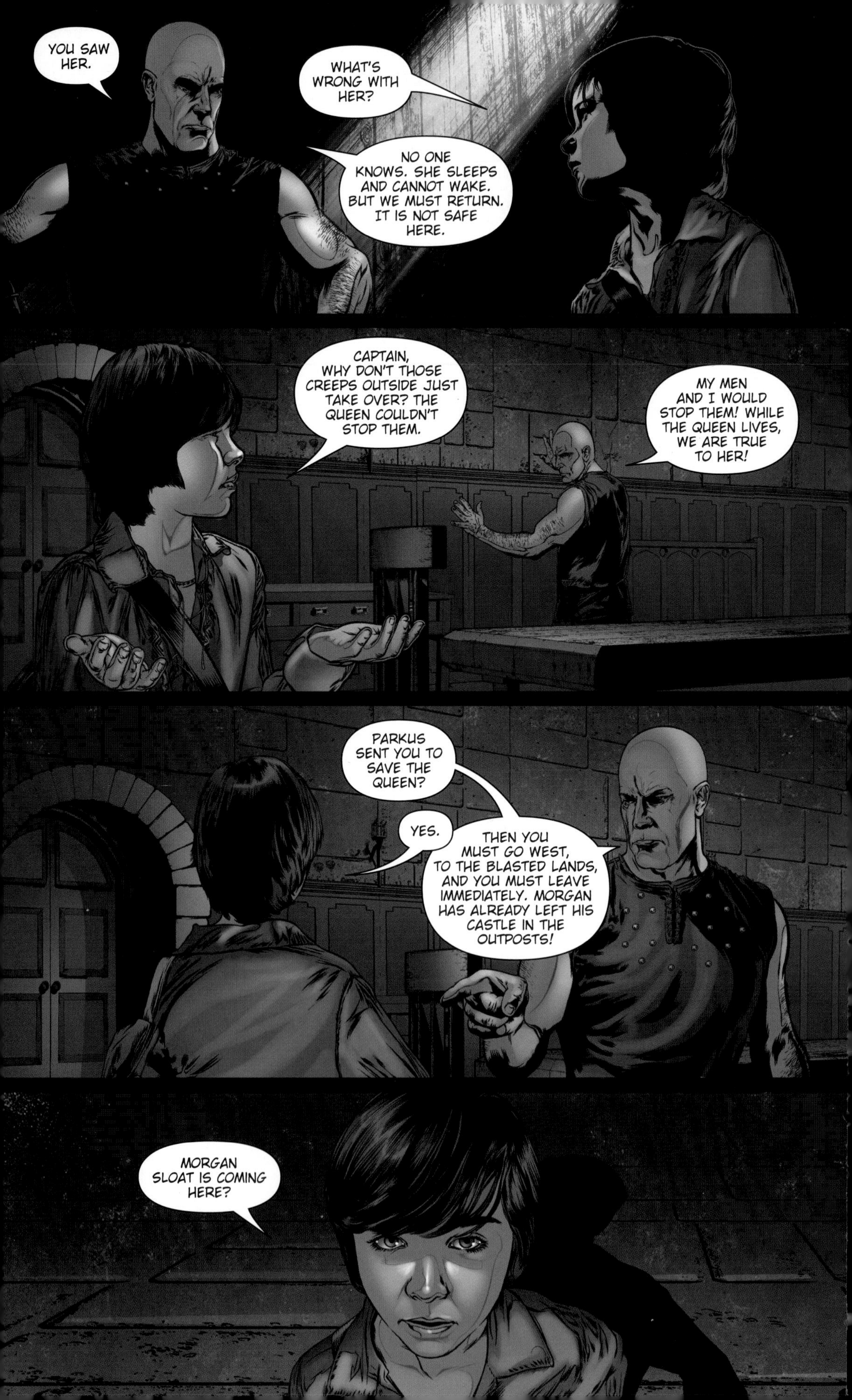
YOU SAW HER.
WHAT'S WRONG WITH HER?
NO ONE KNOWS. SHE SLEEPS AND CANNOT WAKE. BUT WE MUST RETURN. IT IS NOT SAFE HERE.
CAPTAIN, WHY DON'T THOSE CREEPS OUTSIDE JUST TAKE OVER? THE QUEEN COULDN'T STOP THEM.
MY MEN AND I WOULD STOP THEM! WHILE THE QUEEN LIVES, WE ARE TRUE TO HER!
PARKUS SENT YOU TO SAVE THE QUEEN?
YES.
THEN YOU MUST GO WEST, TO THE BLASTED LANDS, AND YOU MUST LEAVE IMMEDIATELY. MORGAN HAS ALREADY LEFT HIS CASTLE IN THE OUTPOSTS!
MORGAN SLOAT IS COMING HERE?

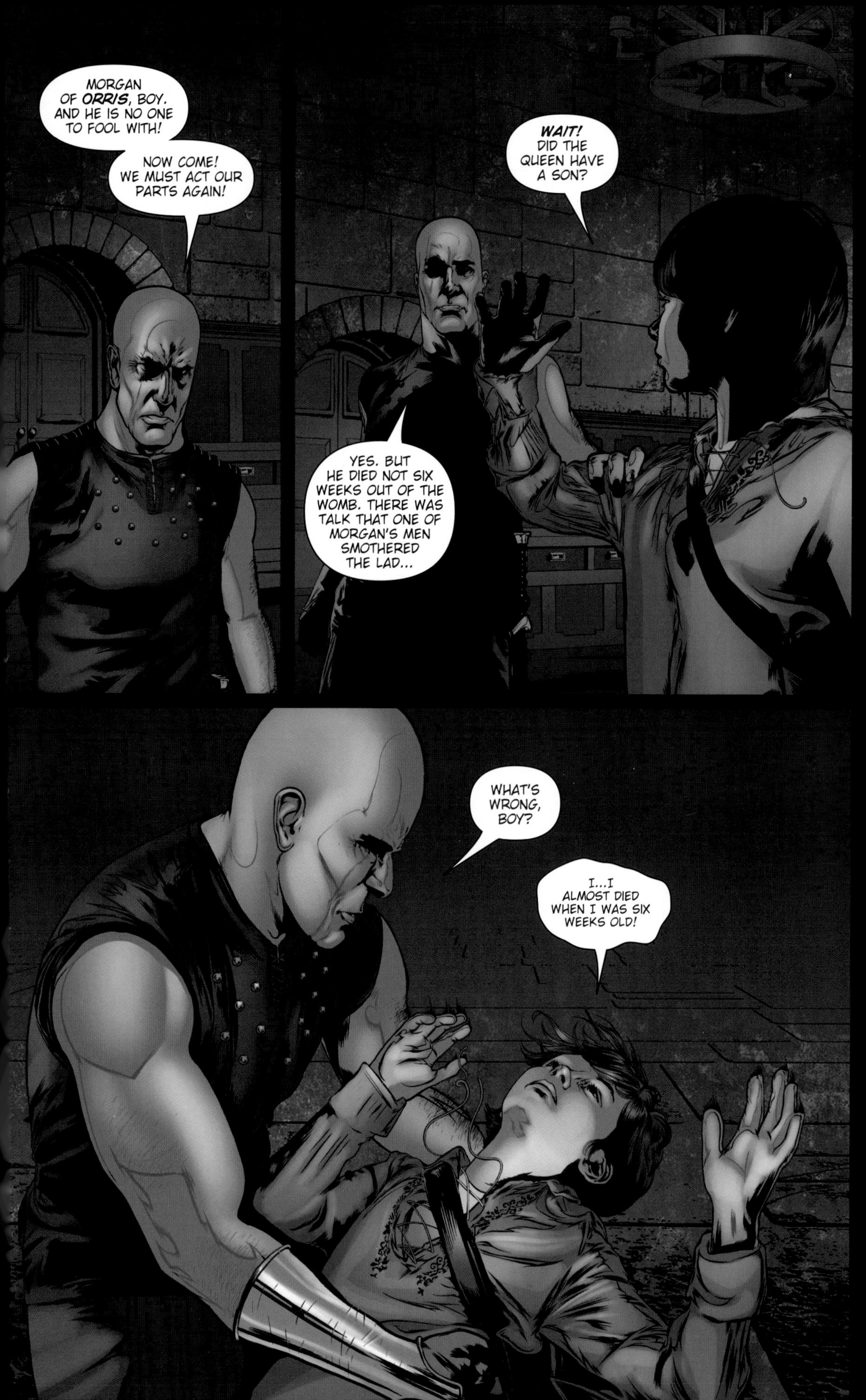
MORGAN OF ORRIS, BOY. AND HE IS NO ONE TO FOOL WITH!
NOW COME! WE MUST ACT OUR PARTS AGAIN!
WAIT! DID THE QUEEN HAVE A SON?
YES. BUT HE DIED NOT SIX WEEKS OUT OF THE WOMB. THERE WAS TALK THAT ONE OF MORGAN'S MEN SMOTHERED THE LAD...
WHAT'S WRONG, BOY?
I...I ALMOST DIED WHEN I WAS SIX WEEKS OLD!

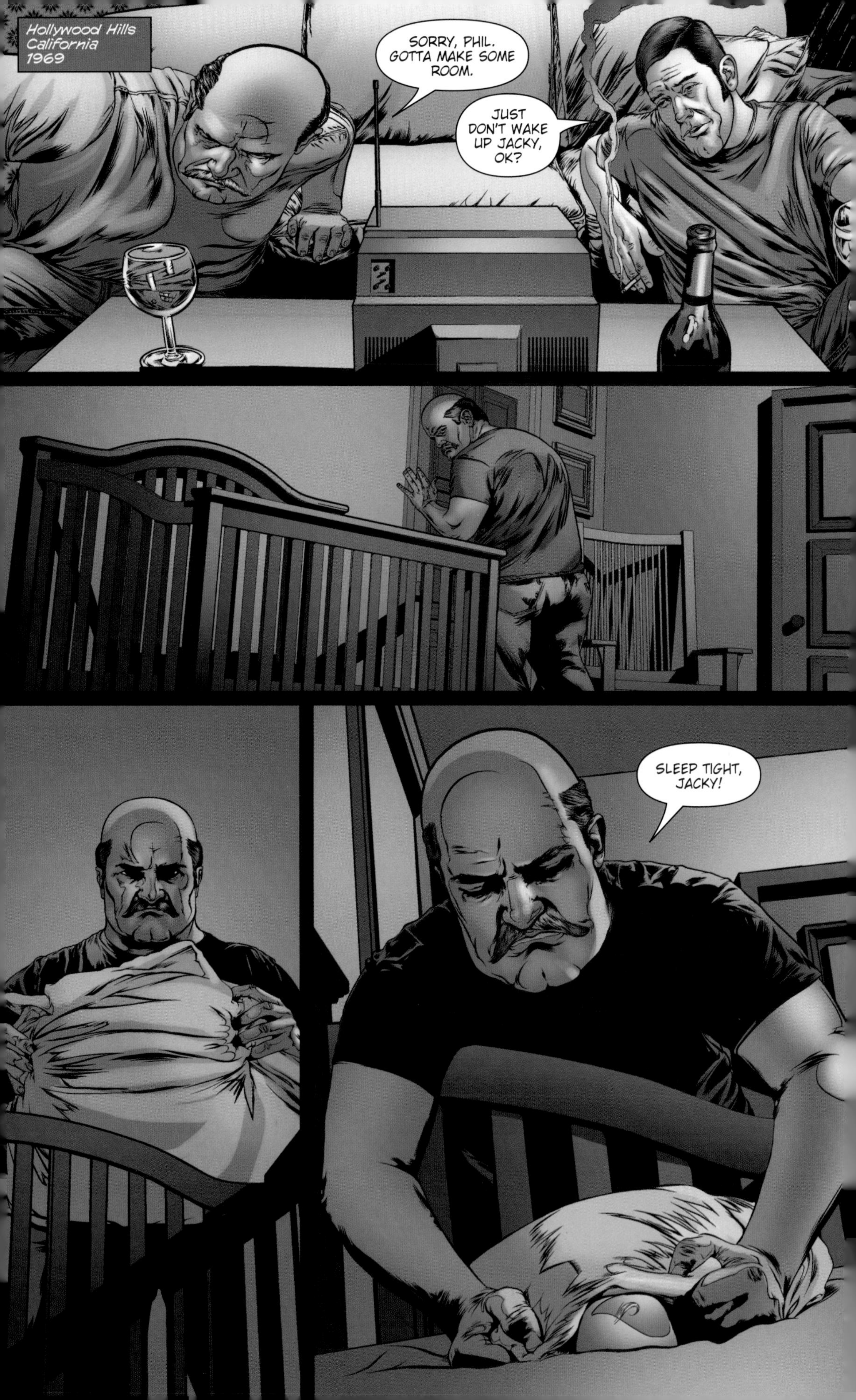
Hollywood Hills
California
1969
SORRY, PHIL. GOTTA MAKE SOME ROOM.
JUST DON'T WAKE UP JACKY, OK?
SLEEP TIGHT, JACKY!

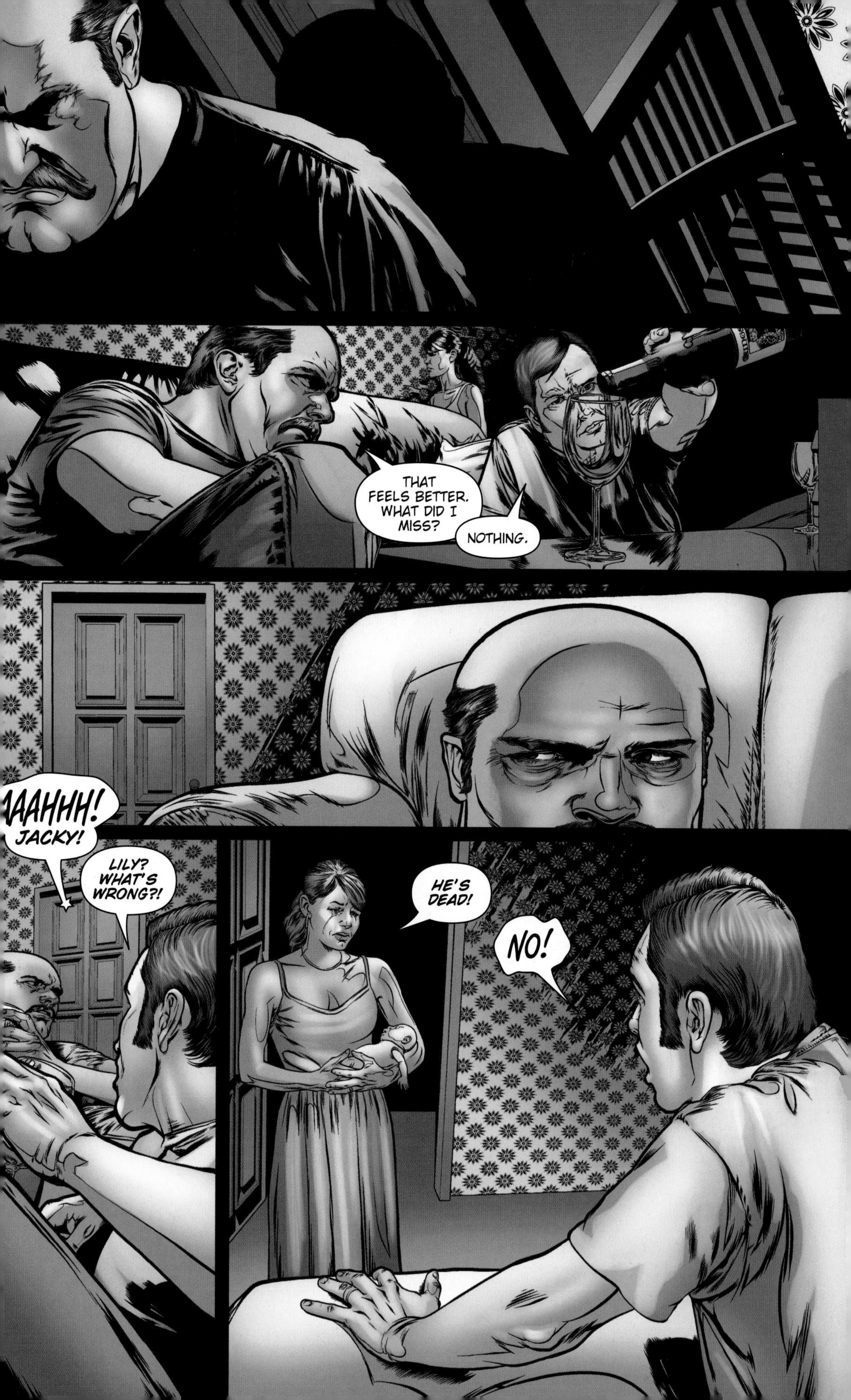
THAT FEELS BETTER. WHAT DID I MISS?
NOTHING.
AAAHHH! JACKY!
LILY? WHAT'S WRONG?!
HE'S DEAD!
NO!

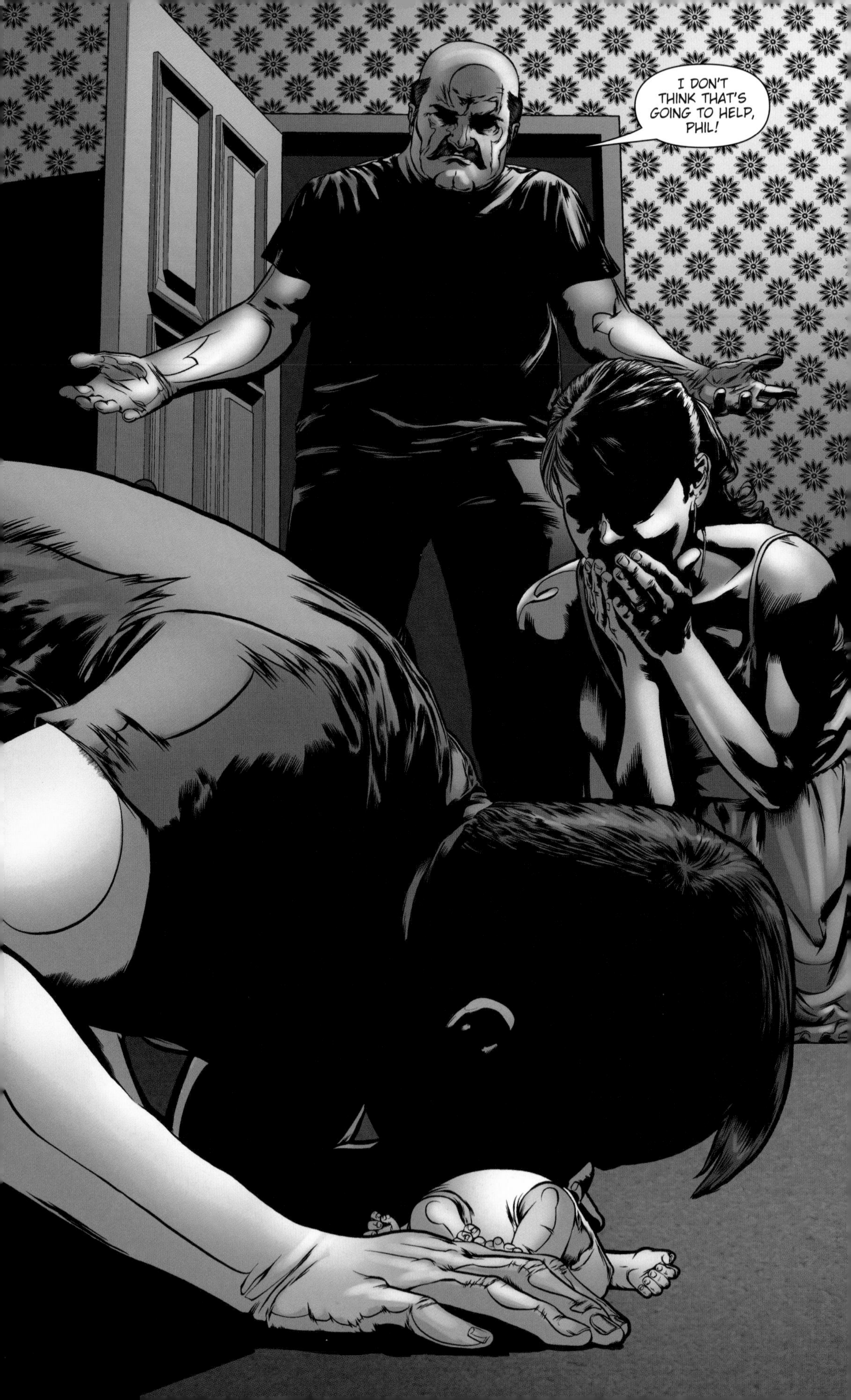
I DON'T THINK THAT'S GOING TO HELP, PHIL!

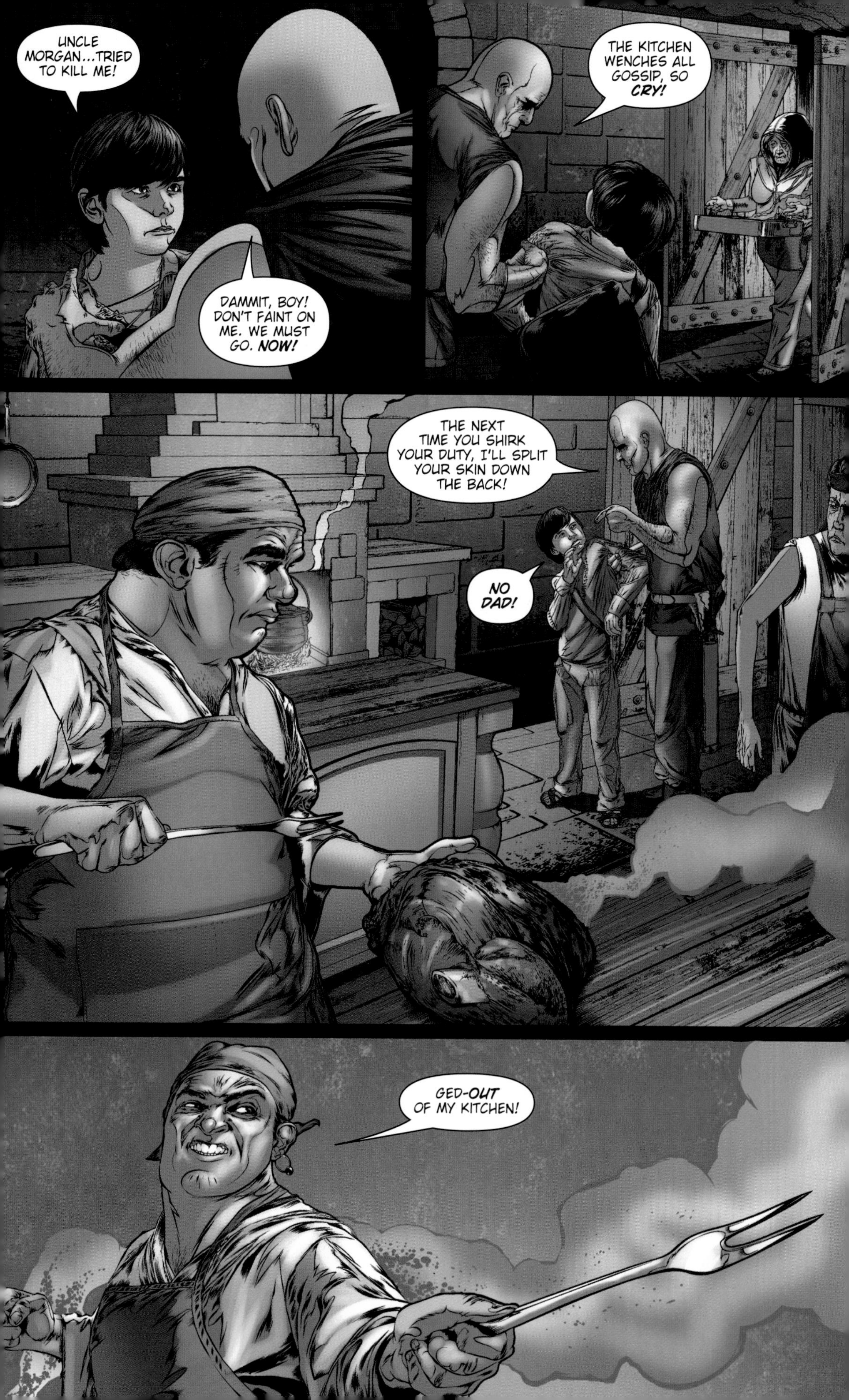
UNCLE MORGAN...TRIED TO KILL ME!
DAMMIT, BOY! DON'T FAINT ON ME. WE MUST GO. NOW!
THE KITCHEN WENCHES ALL GOSSIP, SO CRY!
THE NEXT TIME YOU SHIRK YOUR DUTY, I'LL SPLIT YOUR SKIN DOWN THE BACK!
NO DAD!
GED-OUT OF MY KITCHEN!

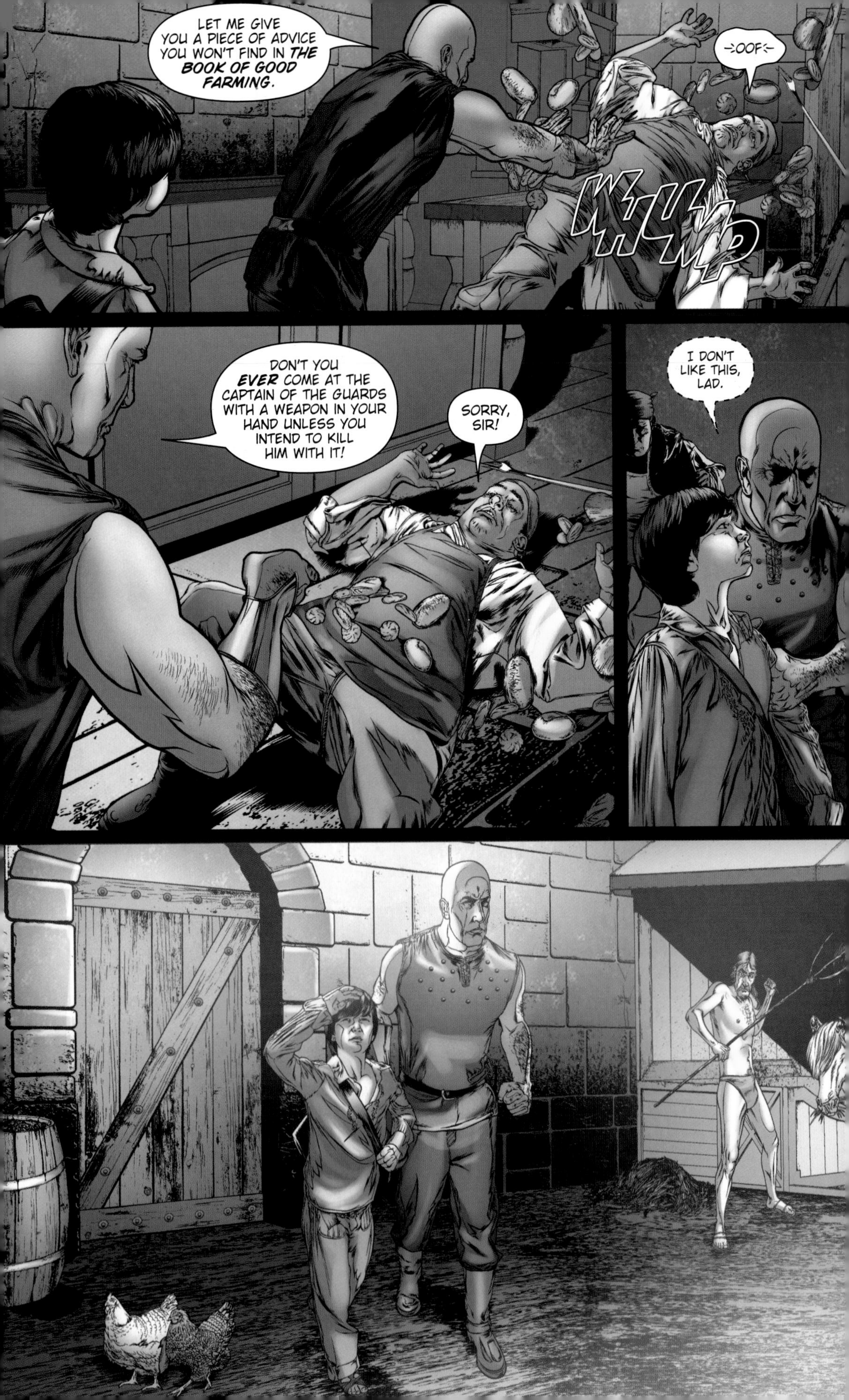
LET ME GIVE YOU A PIECE OF ADVICE YOU WON'T FIND IN ***THE BOOK OF GOOD FARMING***.
-OOF-
WHUMP
DON'T YOU ***EVER*** COME AT THE CAPTAIN OF THE GUARDS WITH A WEAPON IN YOUR HAND UNLESS YOU INTEND TO KILL HIM WITH IT!
SORRY, SIR!
I DON'T LIKE THIS, LAD.

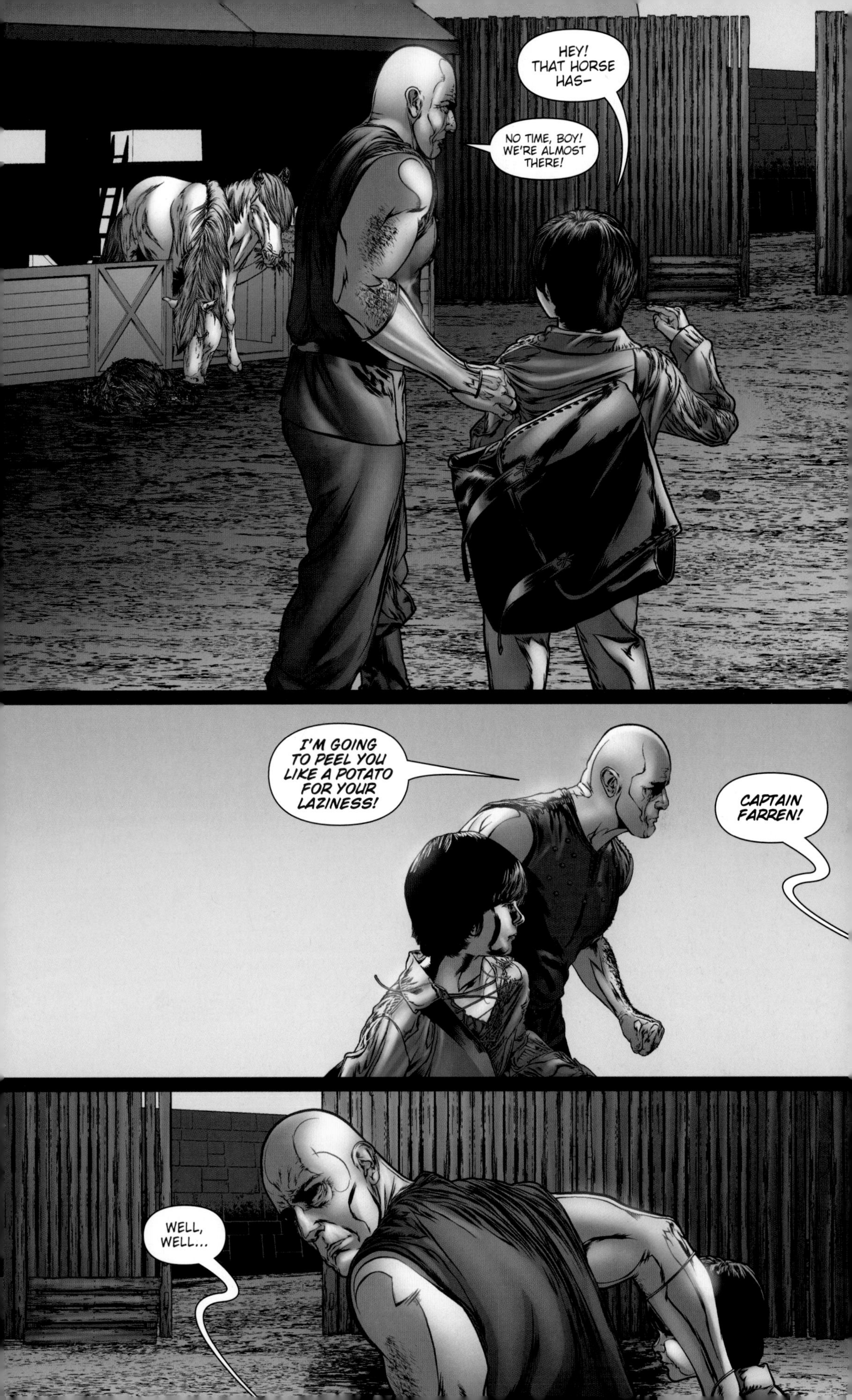
HEY! THAT HORSE HAS–
NO TIME, BOY! WE'RE ALMOST THERE!
I'M GOING TO PEEL YOU LIKE A POTATO FOR YOUR LAZINESS!
CAPTAIN FARREN!
WELL, WELL...

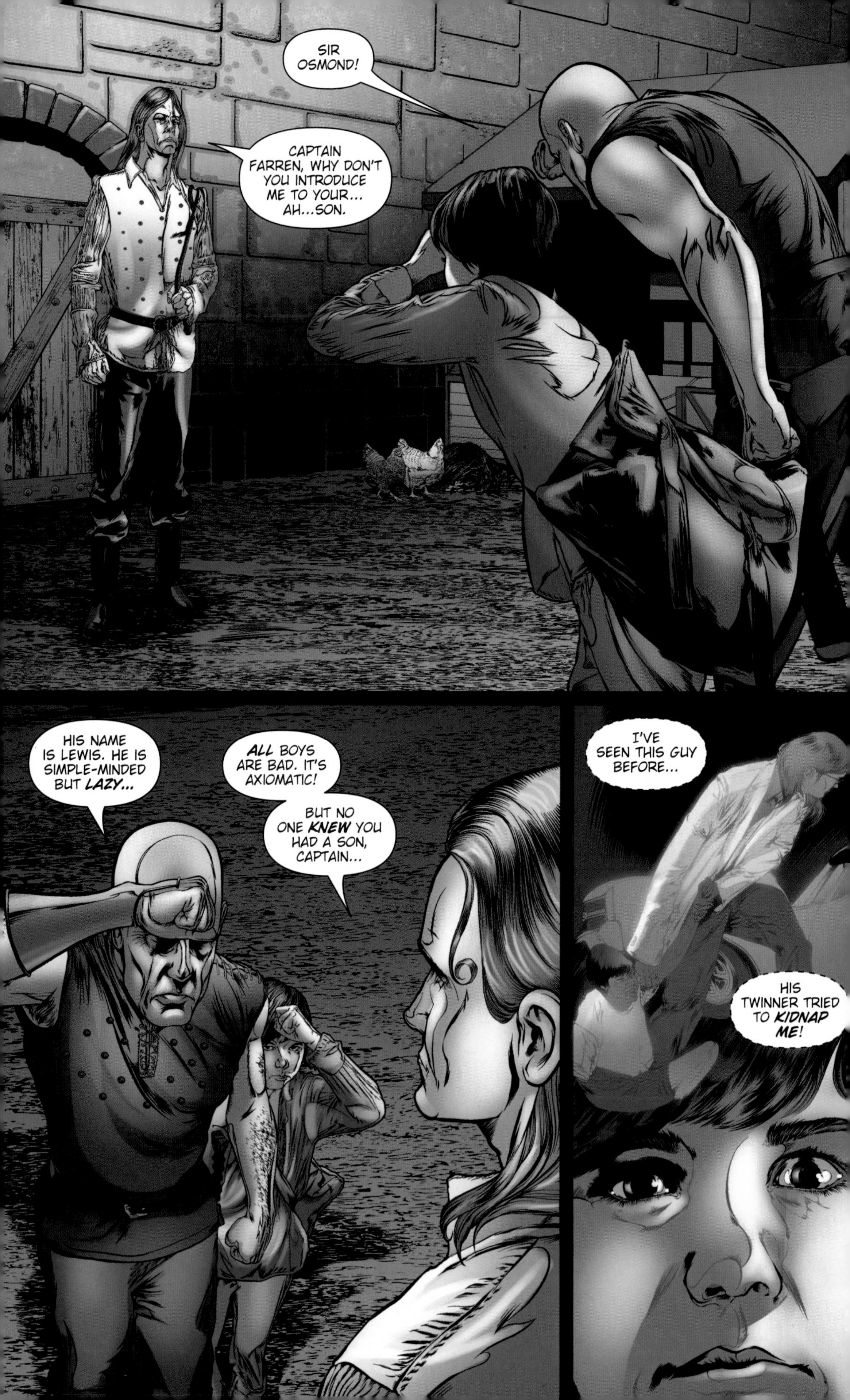
SIR OSMOND!
CAPTAIN FARREN, WHY DON'T YOU INTRODUCE ME TO YOUR... AH...SON.
HIS NAME IS LEWIS. HE IS SIMPLE-MINDED BUT LAZY...
ALL BOYS ARE BAD. IT'S AXIOMATIC!
BUT NO ONE KNEW YOU HAD A SON, CAPTAIN...
I'VE SEEN THIS GUY BEFORE...
HIS TWINNER TRIED TO KIDNAP ME!

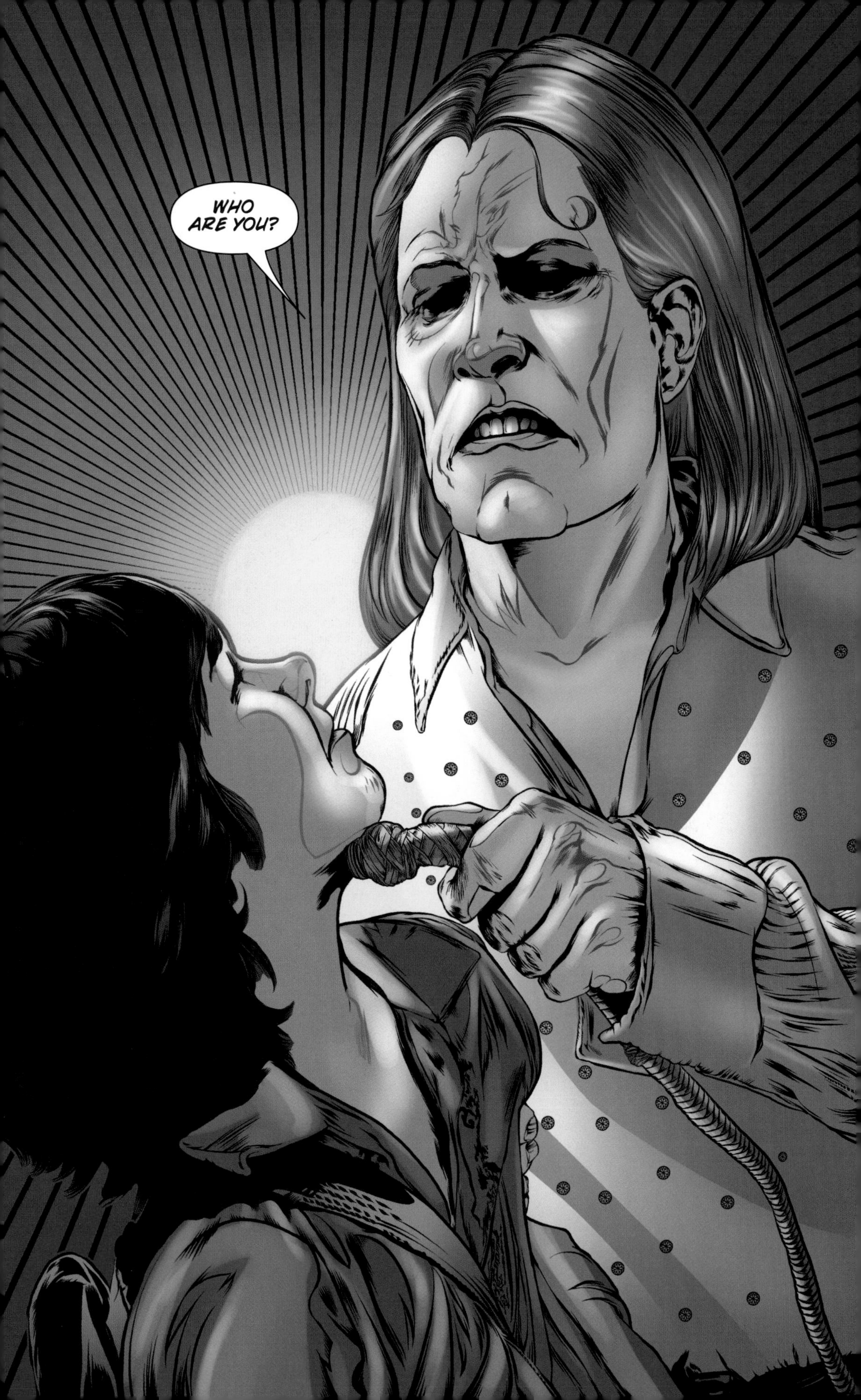
WHO ARE YOU?

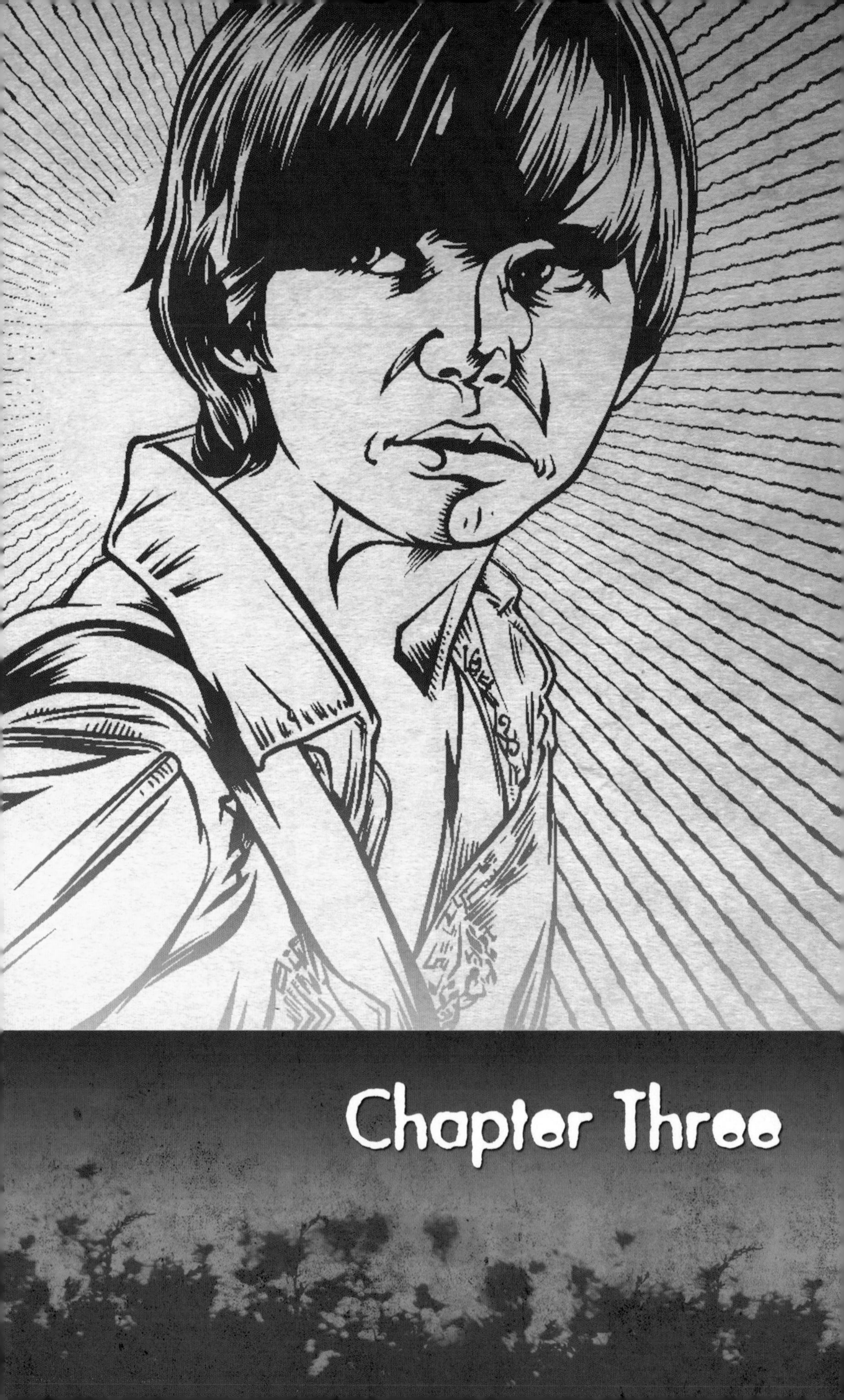

Chapter Three

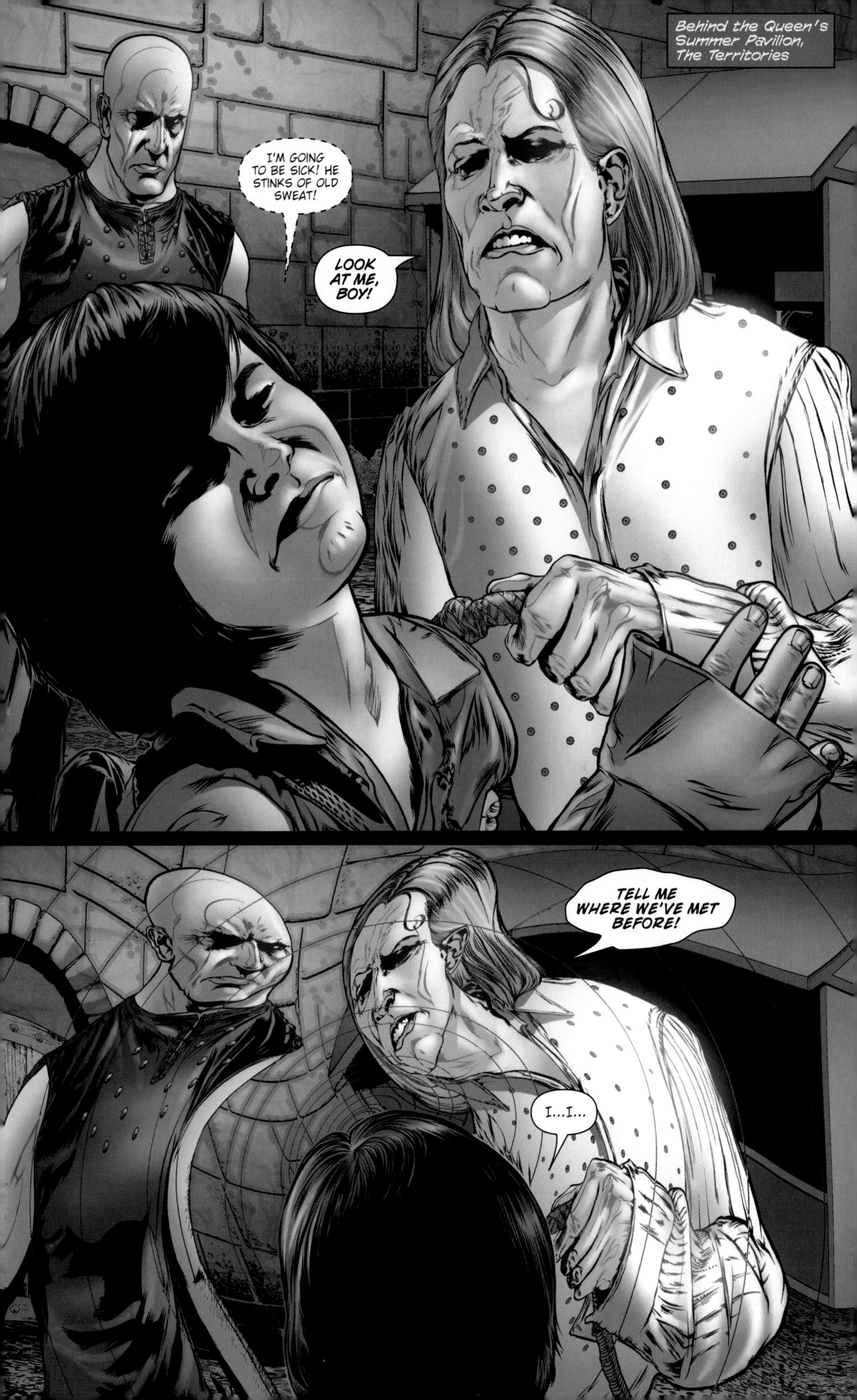
Behind the Queen's Summer Pavilion, The Territories
I'M GOING TO BE SICK! HE STINKS OF OLD SWEAT!
LOOK AT ME, BOY!
TELL ME WHERE WE'VE MET BEFORE!
I...I...

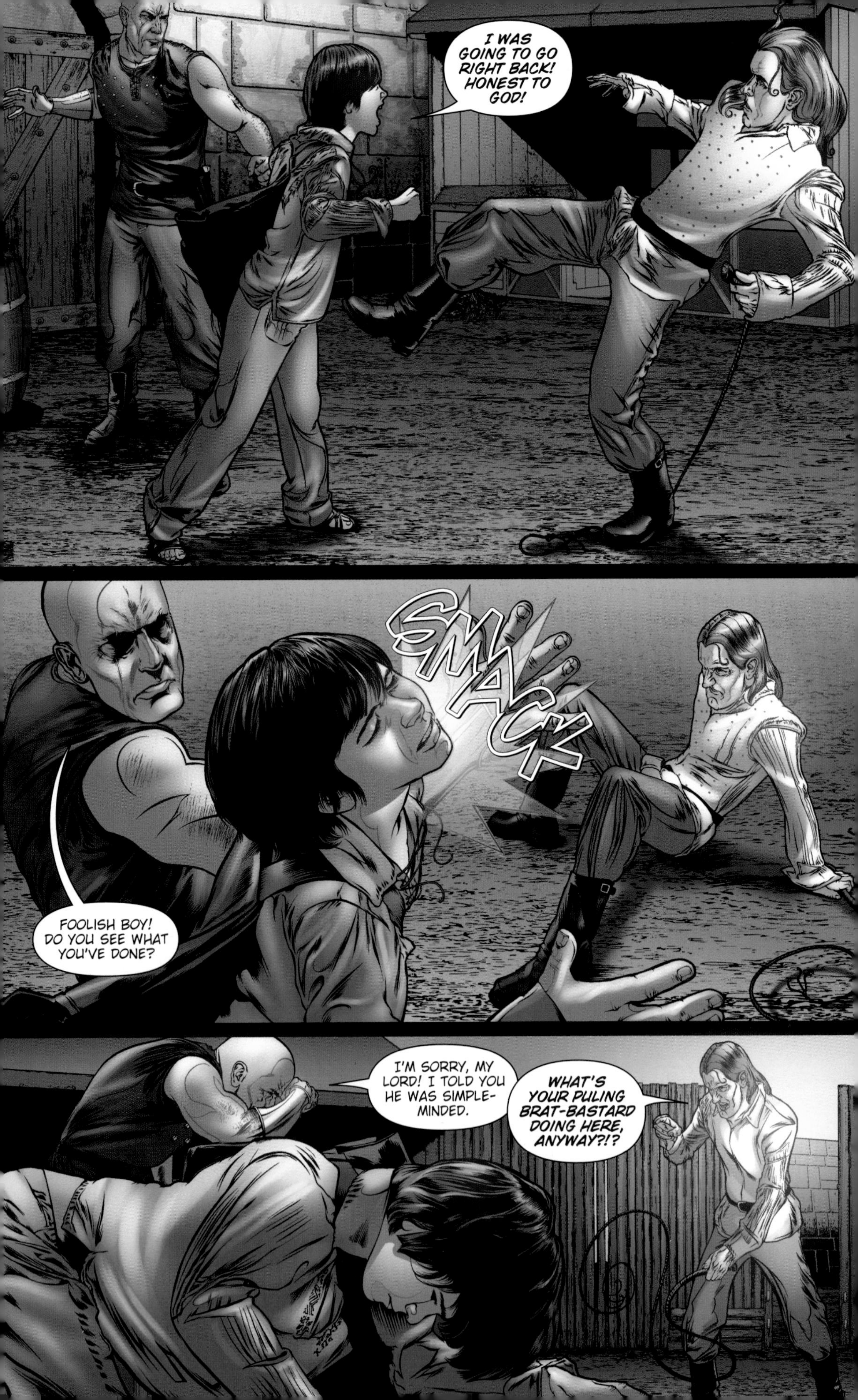
I WAS GOING TO GO RIGHT BACK! HONEST TO GOD!
SMACK
FOOLISH BOY! DO YOU SEE WHAT YOU'VE DONE?
I'M SORRY, MY LORD! I TOLD YOU HE WAS SIMPLE-MINDED.
WHAT'S YOUR PULING BRAT-BASTARD DOING HERE, ANYWAY?!?

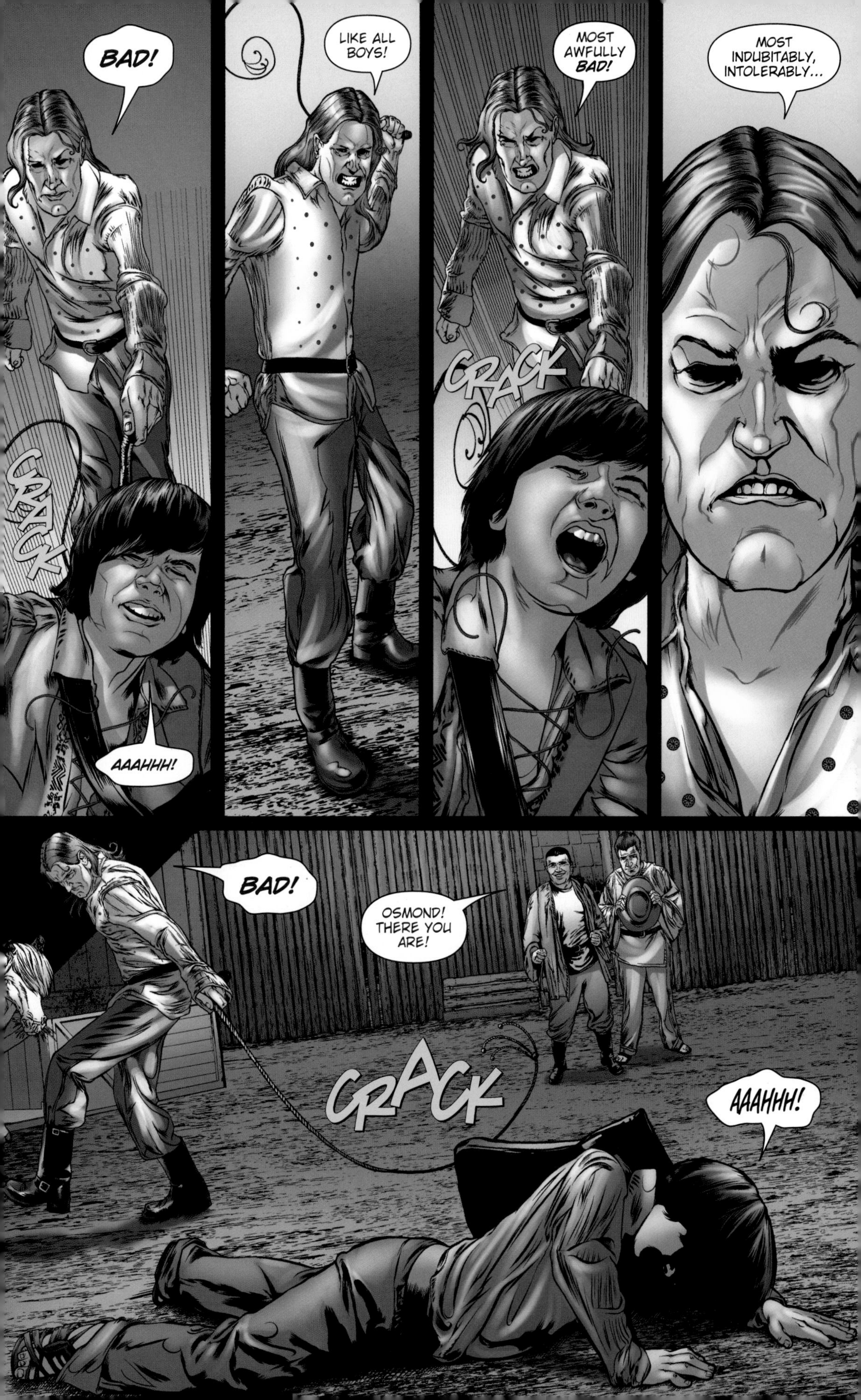
BAD!
CRACK
AAAHHH!
LIKE ALL BOYS!
MOST AWFULLY BAD!
CRACK
MOST INDUBITABLY, INTOLERABLY...
BAD!
OSMOND! THERE YOU ARE!
CRACK
AAAHHH!

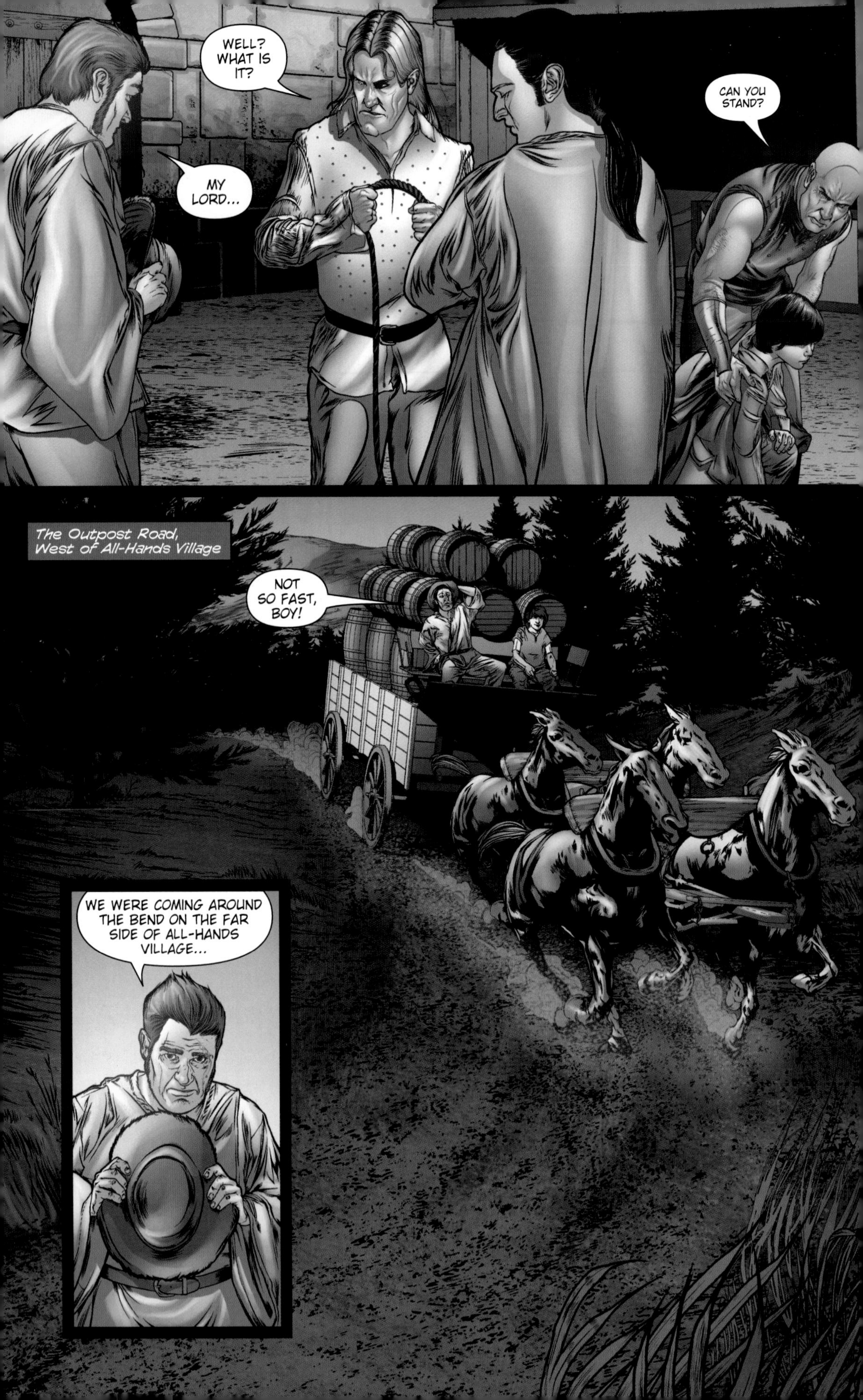
WELL? WHAT IS IT?
MY LORD...
CAN YOU STAND?
The Outpost Road, West of All-Hands Village
NOT SO FAST, BOY!
WE WERE COMING AROUND THE BEND ON THE FAR SIDE OF ALL-HANDS VILLAGE...

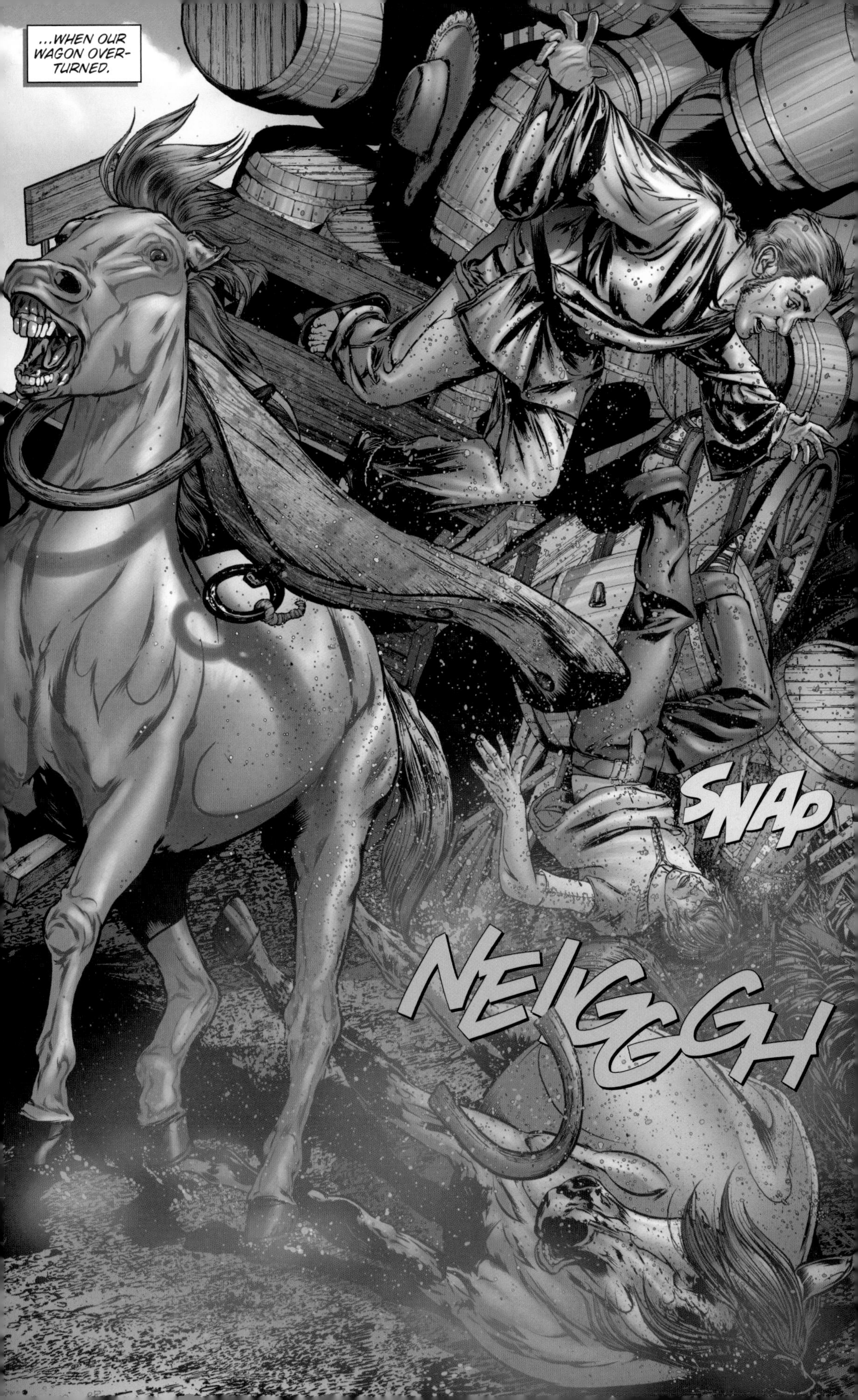
...WHEN OUR WAGON OVER-TURNED.
SNAP
NEIGGGH

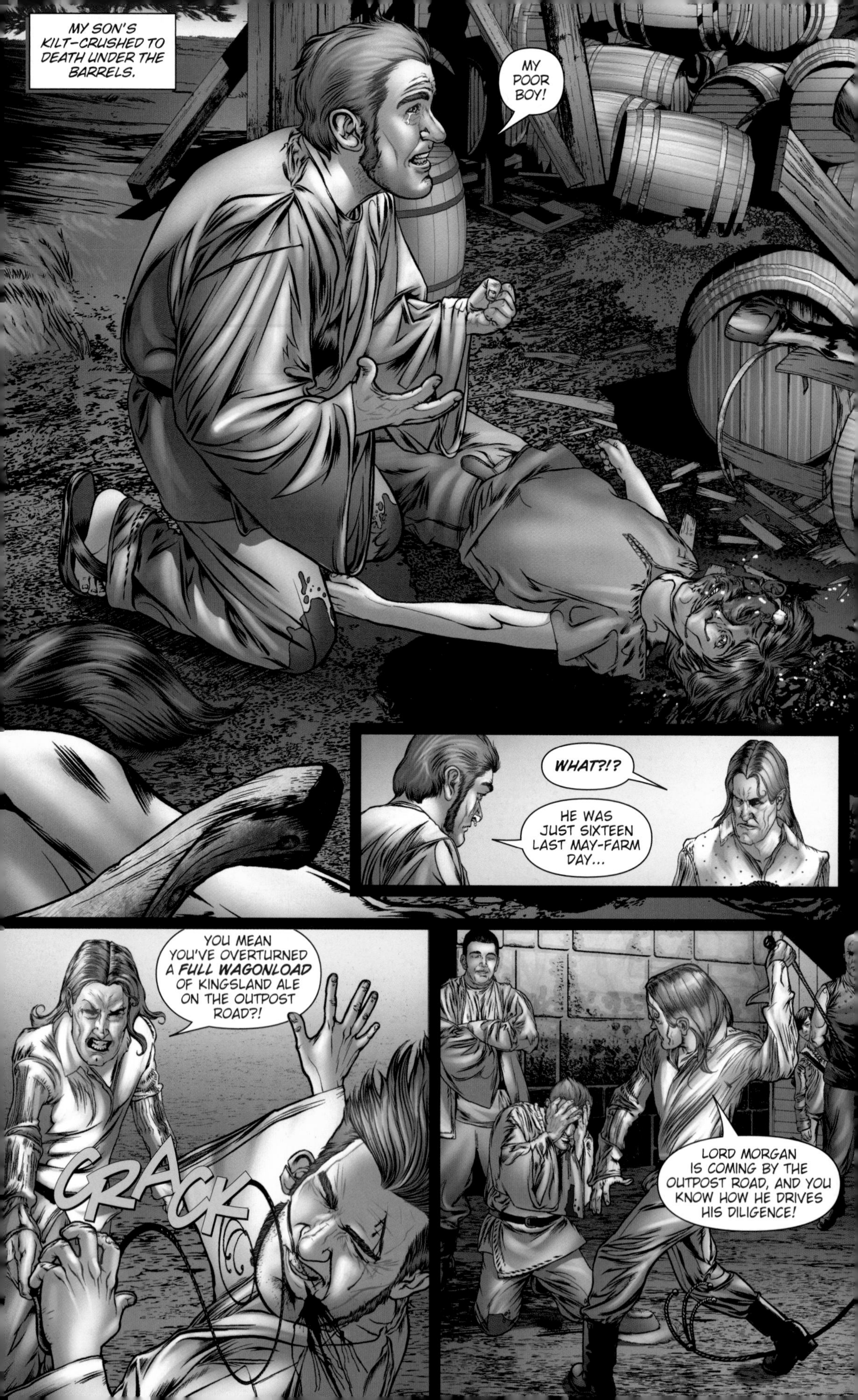
MY SON'S KILT—CRUSHED TO DEATH UNDER THE BARRELS.
MY POOR BOY!
WHAT?!?
HE WAS JUST SIXTEEN LAST MAY-FARM DAY...
YOU MEAN YOU'VE OVERTURNED A *FULL WAGONLOAD* OF KINGSLAND ALE ON THE OUTPOST ROAD?!
CRACK
LORD MORGAN IS COMING BY THE OUTPOST ROAD, AND YOU KNOW HOW HE DRIVES HIS DILIGENCE!

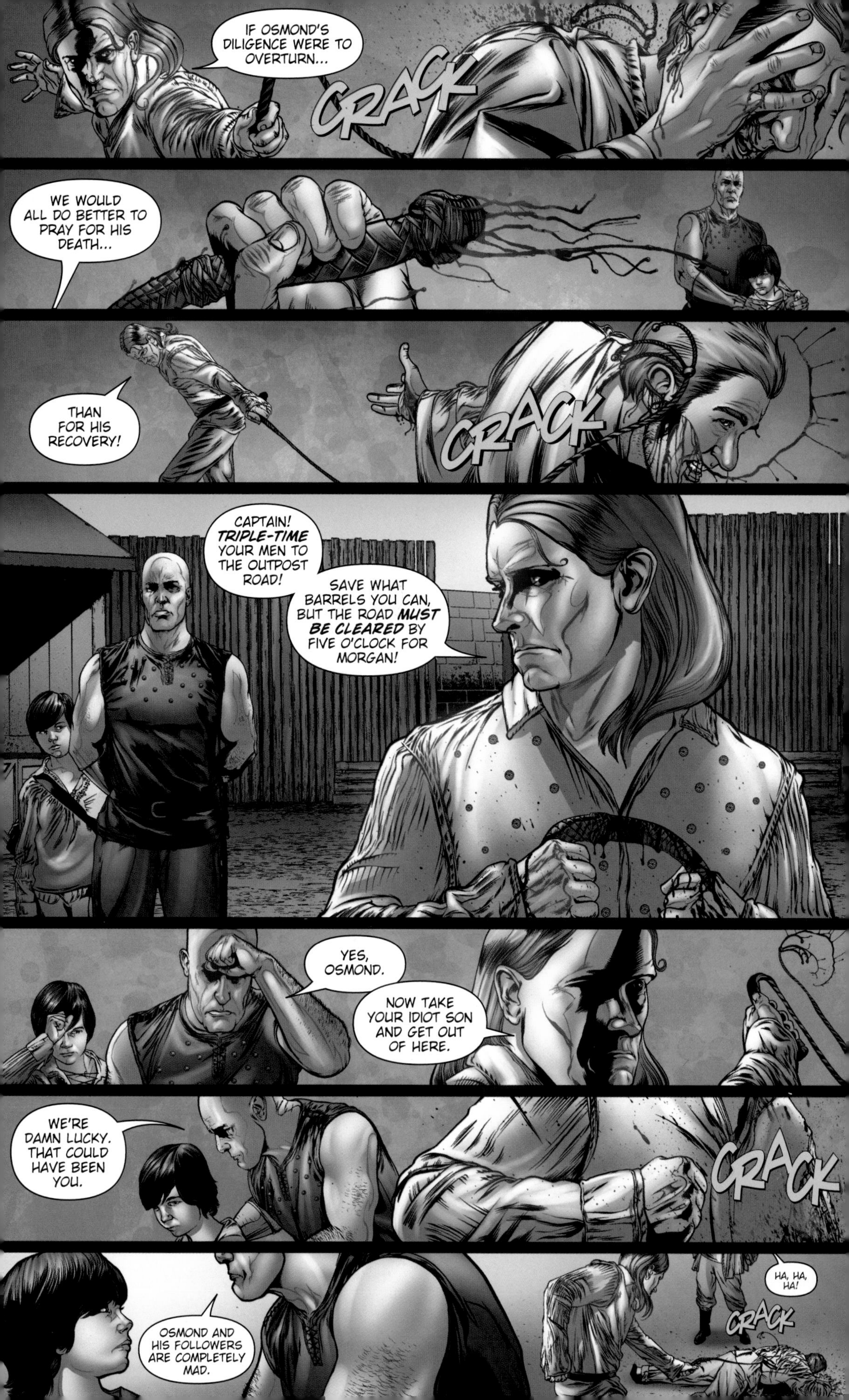
IF OSMOND'S DILIGENCE WERE TO OVERTURN...
CRACK
WE WOULD ALL DO BETTER TO PRAY FOR HIS DEATH...
THAN FOR HIS RECOVERY!
CRACK
CAPTAIN! TRIPLE-TIME YOUR MEN TO THE OUTPOST ROAD!
SAVE WHAT BARRELS YOU CAN, BUT THE ROAD MUST BE CLEARED BY FIVE O'CLOCK FOR MORGAN!
YES, OSMOND.
NOW TAKE YOUR IDIOT SON AND GET OUT OF HERE.
WE'RE DAMN LUCKY. THAT COULD HAVE BEEN YOU.
CRACK
OSMOND AND HIS FOLLOWERS ARE COMPLETELY MAD.
HA, HA, HA!
CRACK

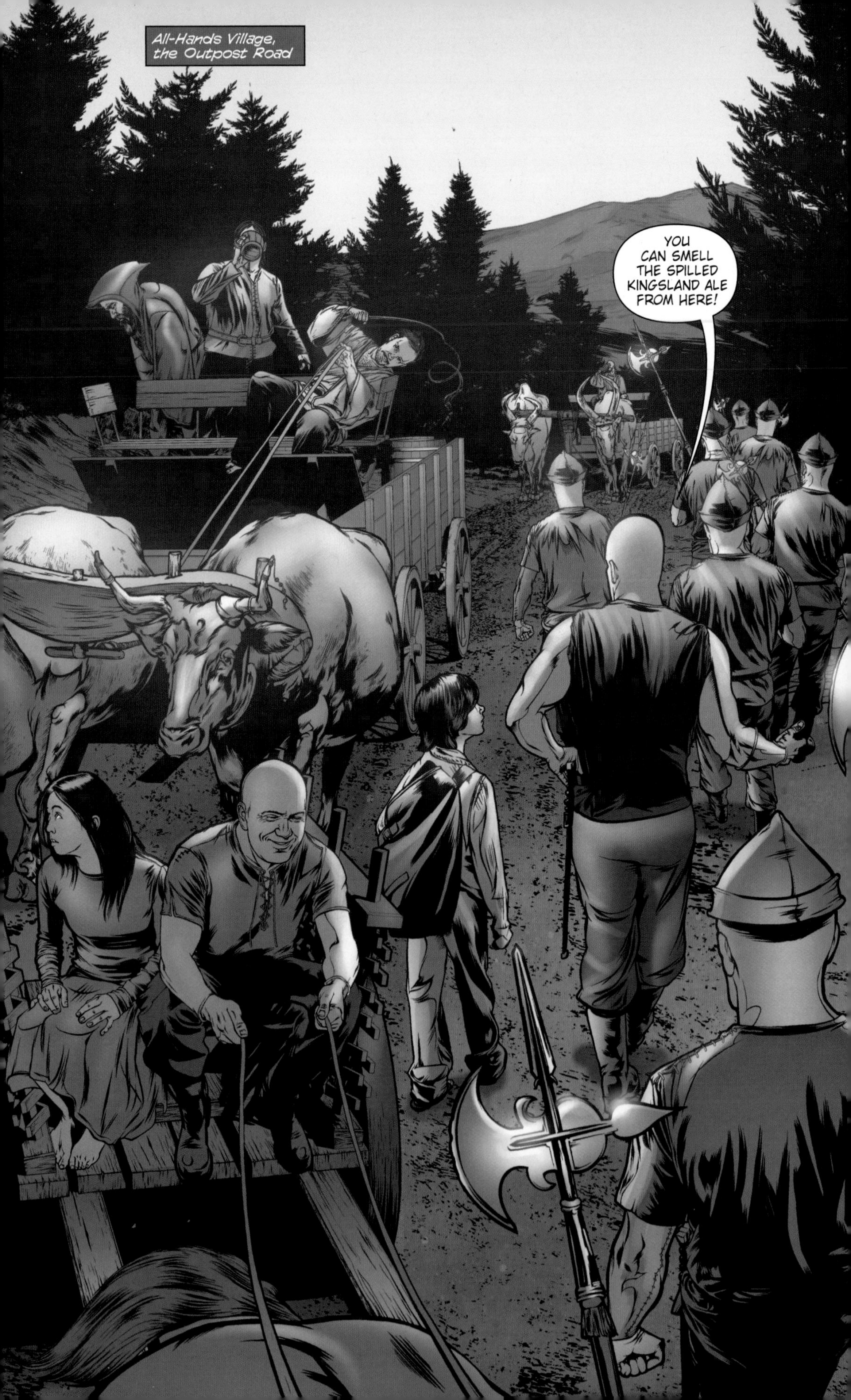
All-Hands Village, the Outpost Road
YOU CAN SMELL THE SPILLED KINGSLAND ALE FROM HERE!

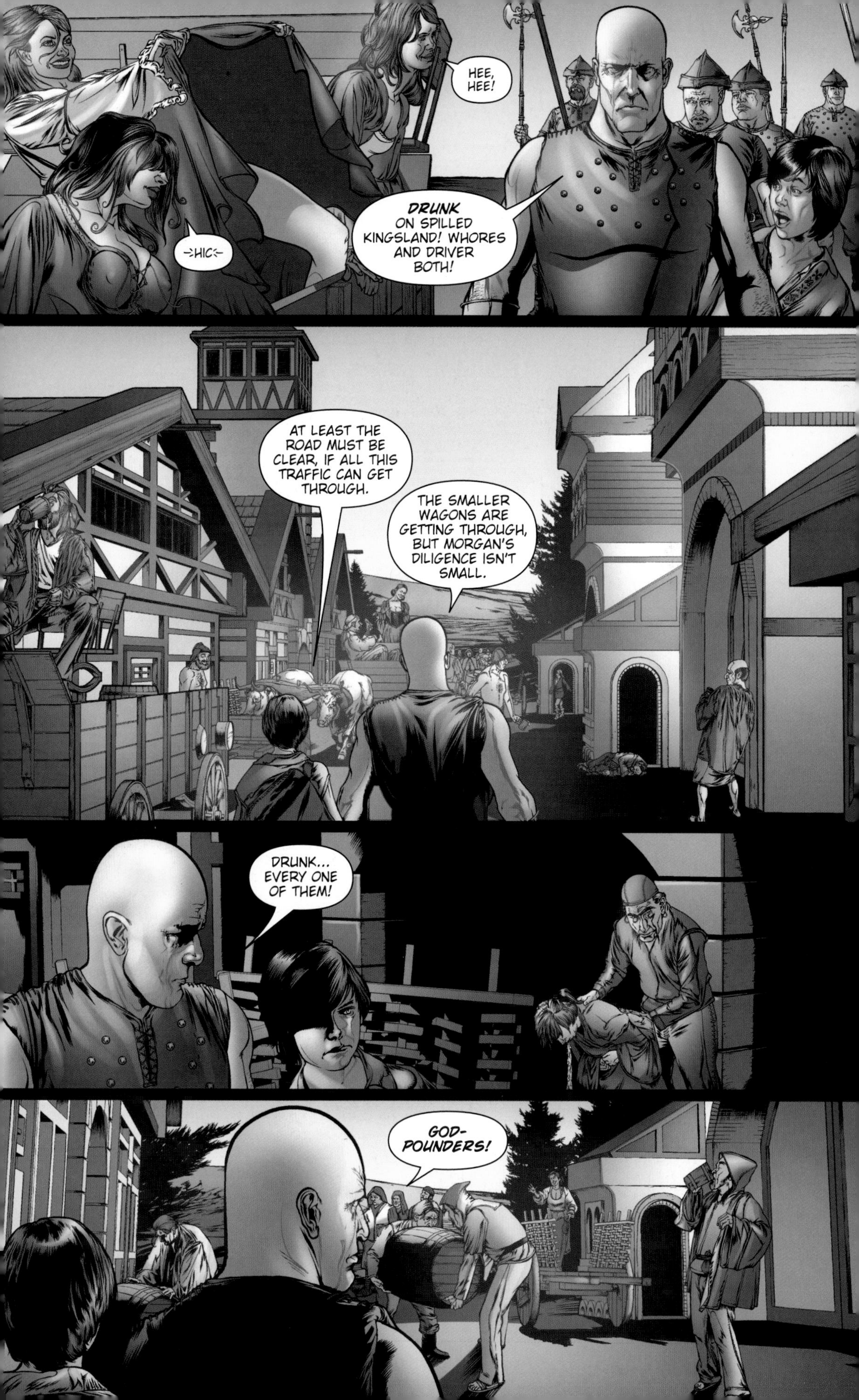
HEE, HEE!
-HIC-
DRUNK ON SPILLED KINGSLAND! WHORES AND DRIVER BOTH!
AT LEAST THE ROAD MUST BE CLEAR, IF ALL THIS TRAFFIC CAN GET THROUGH.
THE SMALLER WAGONS ARE GETTING THROUGH, BUT MORGAN'S DILIGENCE ISN'T SMALL.
DRUNK... EVERY ONE OF THEM!
GOD-POUNDERS!

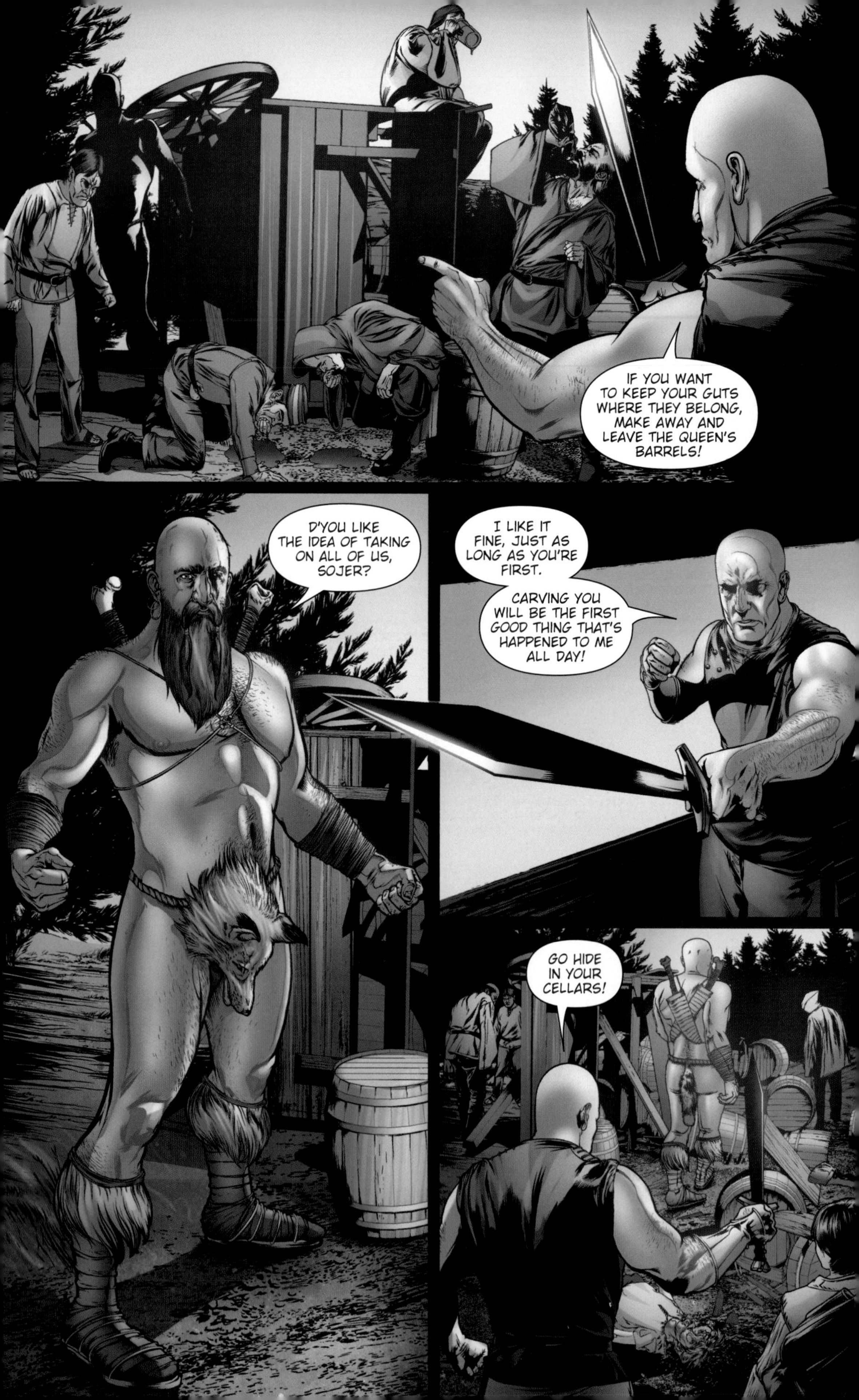
IF YOU WANT TO KEEP YOUR GUTS WHERE THEY BELONG, MAKE AWAY AND LEAVE THE QUEEN'S BARRELS!
D'YOU LIKE THE IDEA OF TAKING ON ALL OF US, SOJER?
I LIKE IT FINE, JUST AS LONG AS YOU'RE FIRST.
CARVING YOU WILL BE THE FIRST GOOD THING THAT'S HAPPENED TO ME ALL DAY!
GO HIDE IN YOUR CELLARS!

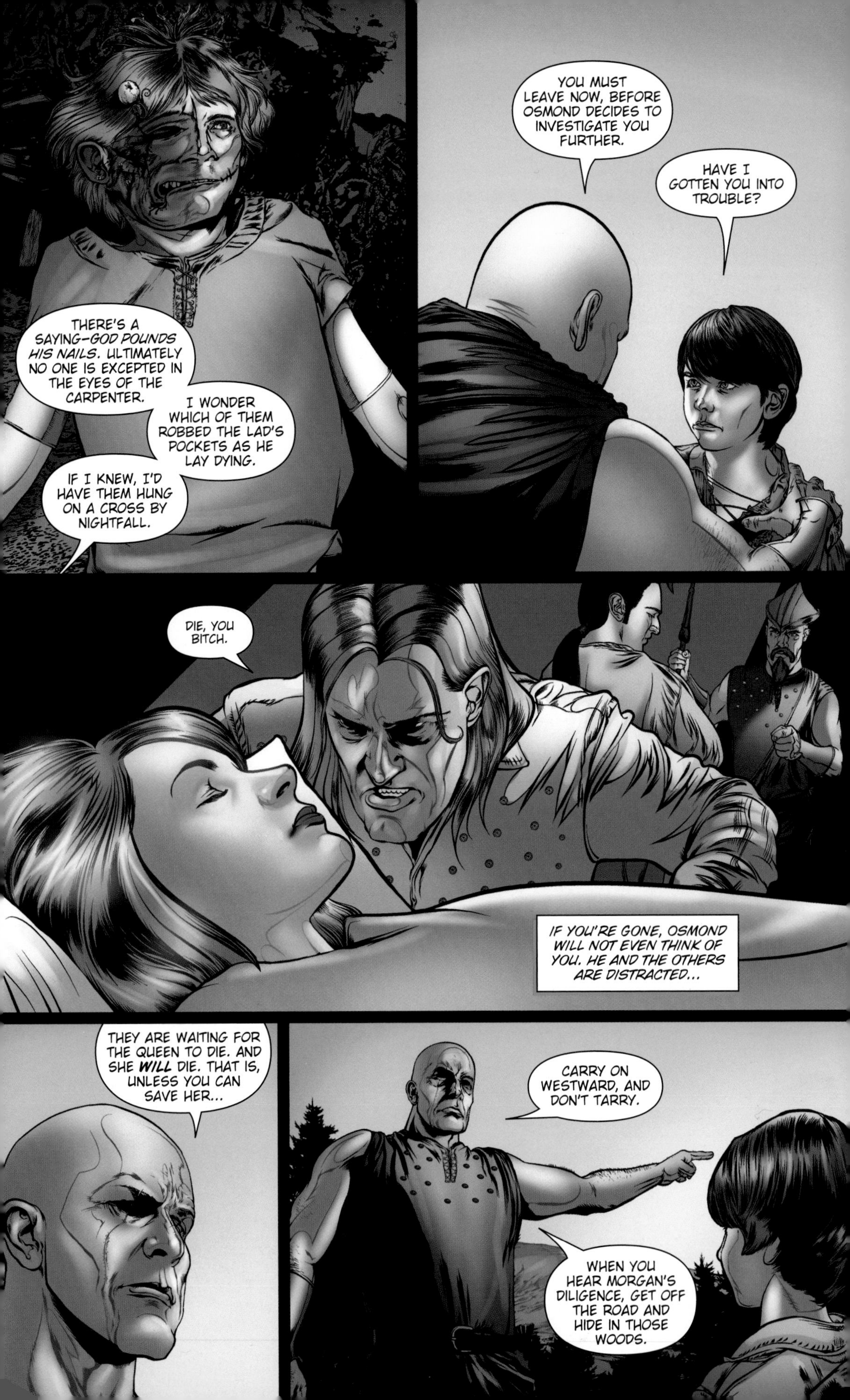
THERE'S A SAYING—GOD POUNDS HIS NAILS. ULTIMATELY NO ONE IS EXCEPTED IN THE EYES OF THE CARPENTER.
I WONDER WHICH OF THEM ROBBED THE LAD'S POCKETS AS HE LAY DYING.
IF I KNEW, I'D HAVE THEM HUNG ON A CROSS BY NIGHTFALL.
YOU MUST LEAVE NOW, BEFORE OSMOND DECIDES TO INVESTIGATE YOU FURTHER.
HAVE I GOTTEN YOU INTO TROUBLE?
DIE, YOU BITCH.
IF YOU'RE GONE, OSMOND WILL NOT EVEN THINK OF YOU. HE AND THE OTHERS ARE DISTRACTED...
THEY ARE WAITING FOR THE QUEEN TO DIE. AND SHE WILL DIE. THAT IS, UNLESS YOU CAN SAVE HER...
CARRY ON WESTWARD, AND DON'T TARRY.
WHEN YOU HEAR MORGAN'S DILIGENCE, GET OFF THE ROAD AND HIDE IN THOSE WOODS.

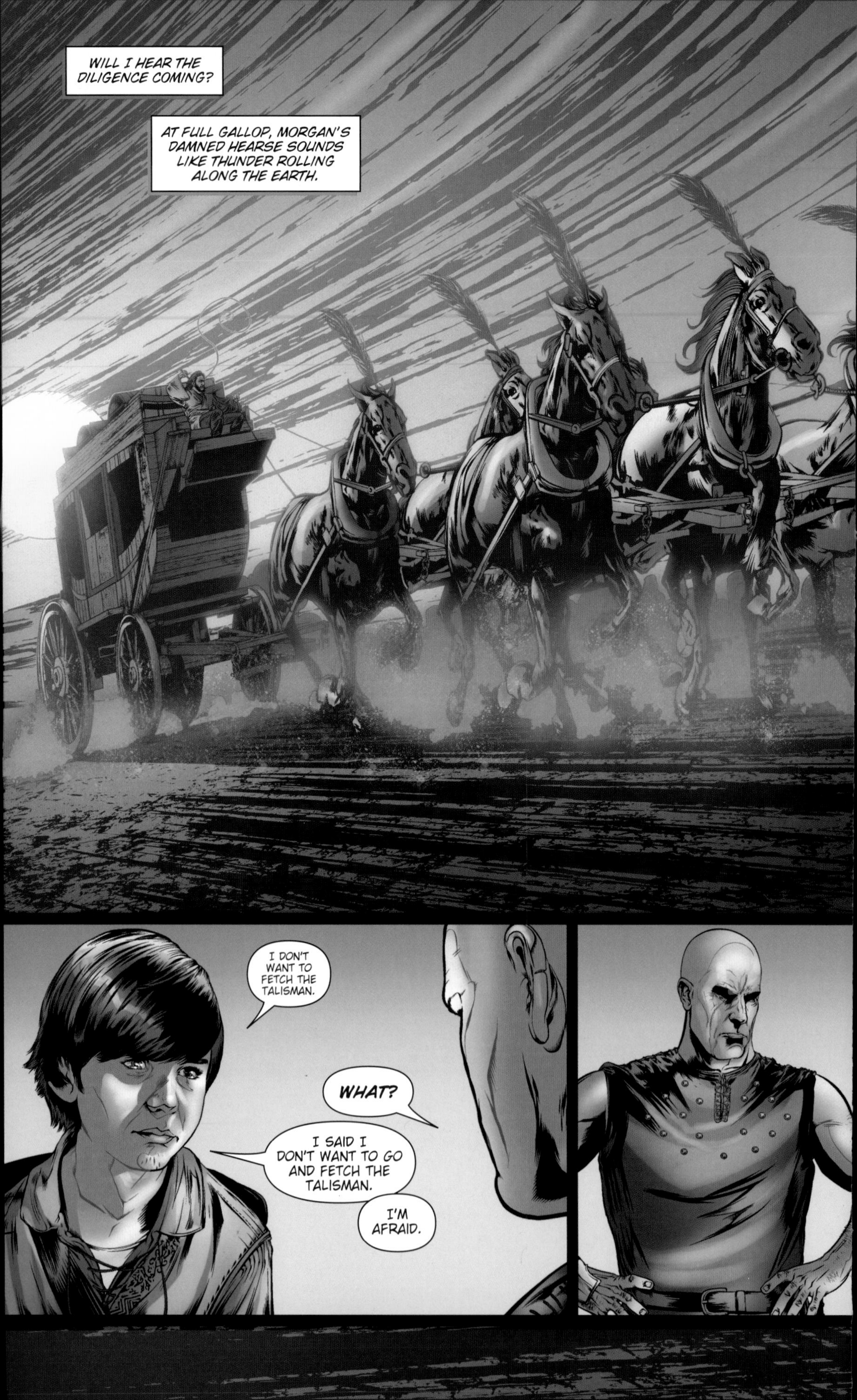
WILL I HEAR THE DILIGENCE COMING?
AT FULL GALLOP, MORGAN'S DAMNED HEARSE SOUNDS LIKE THUNDER ROLLING ALONG THE EARTH.
I DON'T WANT TO FETCH THE TALISMAN.
WHAT?
I SAID I DON'T WANT TO GO AND FETCH THE TALISMAN.
I'M AFRAID.

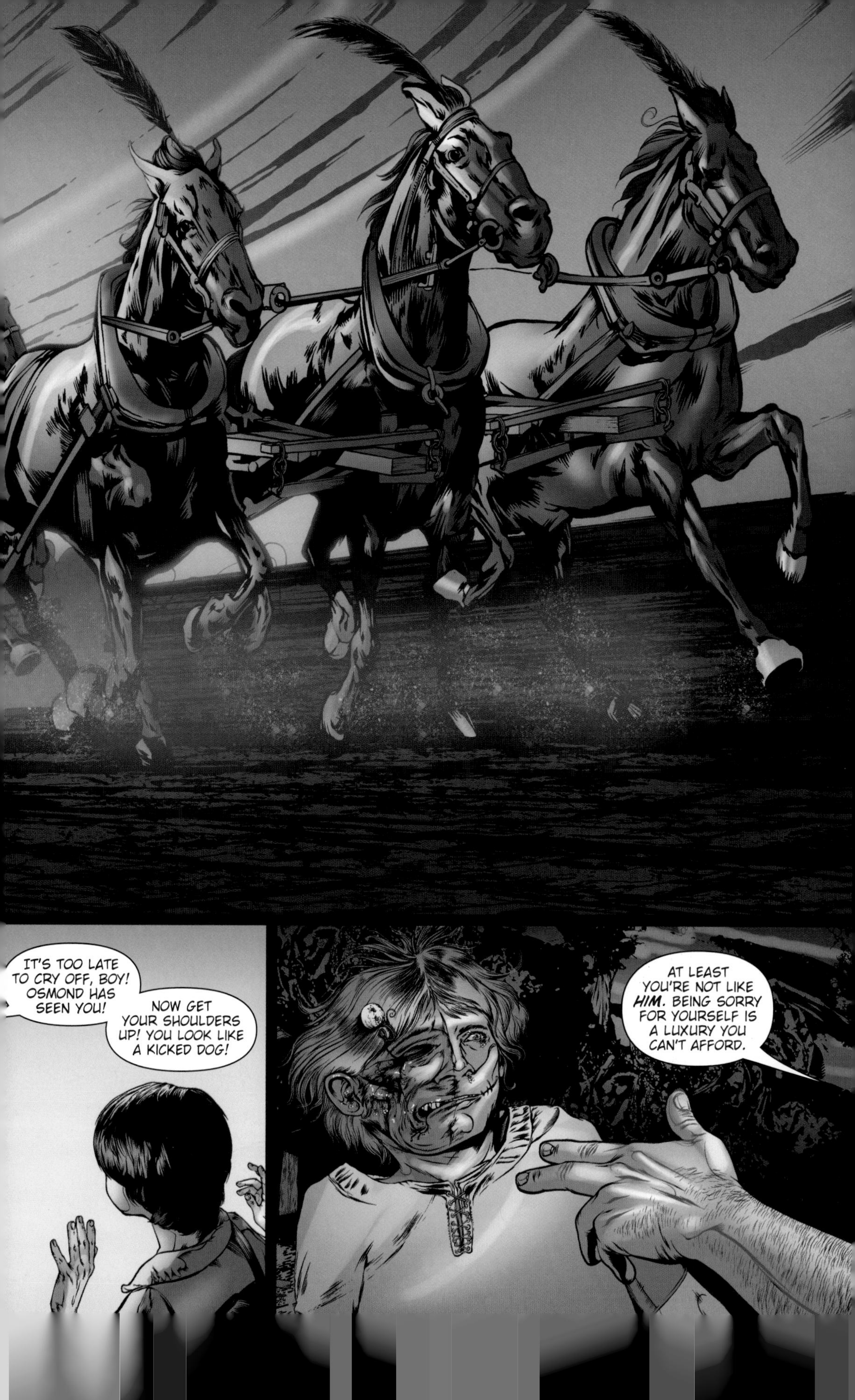
IT'S TOO LATE TO CRY OFF, BOY! OSMOND HAS SEEN YOU!
NOW GET YOUR SHOULDERS UP! YOU LOOK LIKE A KICKED DOG!
AT LEAST YOU'RE NOT LIKE **HIM.** BEING SORRY FOR YOURSELF IS A LUXURY YOU CAN'T AFFORD.

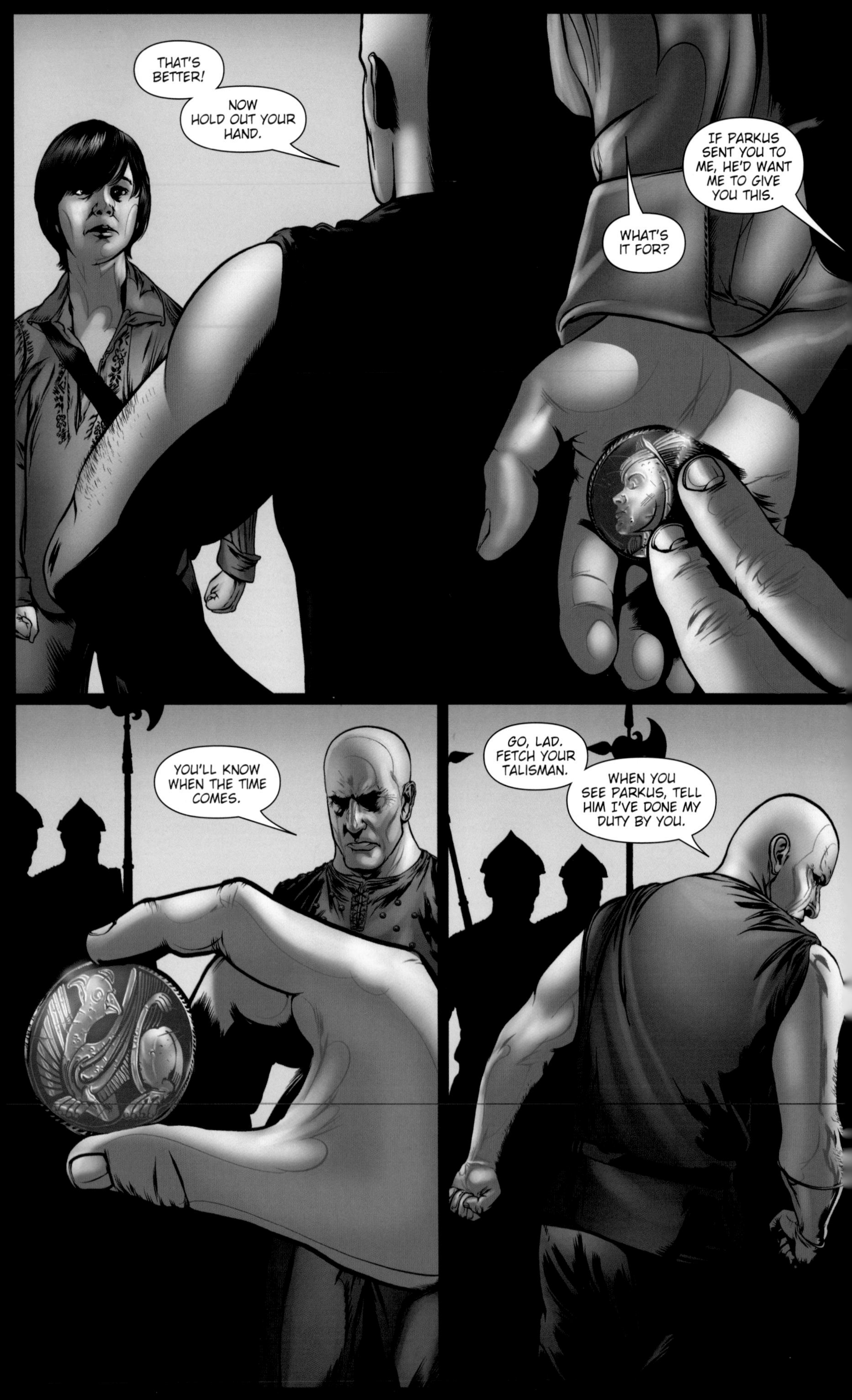
THAT'S BETTER!
NOW HOLD OUT YOUR HAND.
IF PARKUS SENT YOU TO ME, HE'D WANT ME TO GIVE YOU THIS.
WHAT'S IT FOR?
YOU'LL KNOW WHEN THE TIME COMES.
GO, LAD. FETCH YOUR TALISMAN.
WHEN YOU SEE PARKUS, TELL HIM I'VE DONE MY DUTY BY YOU.

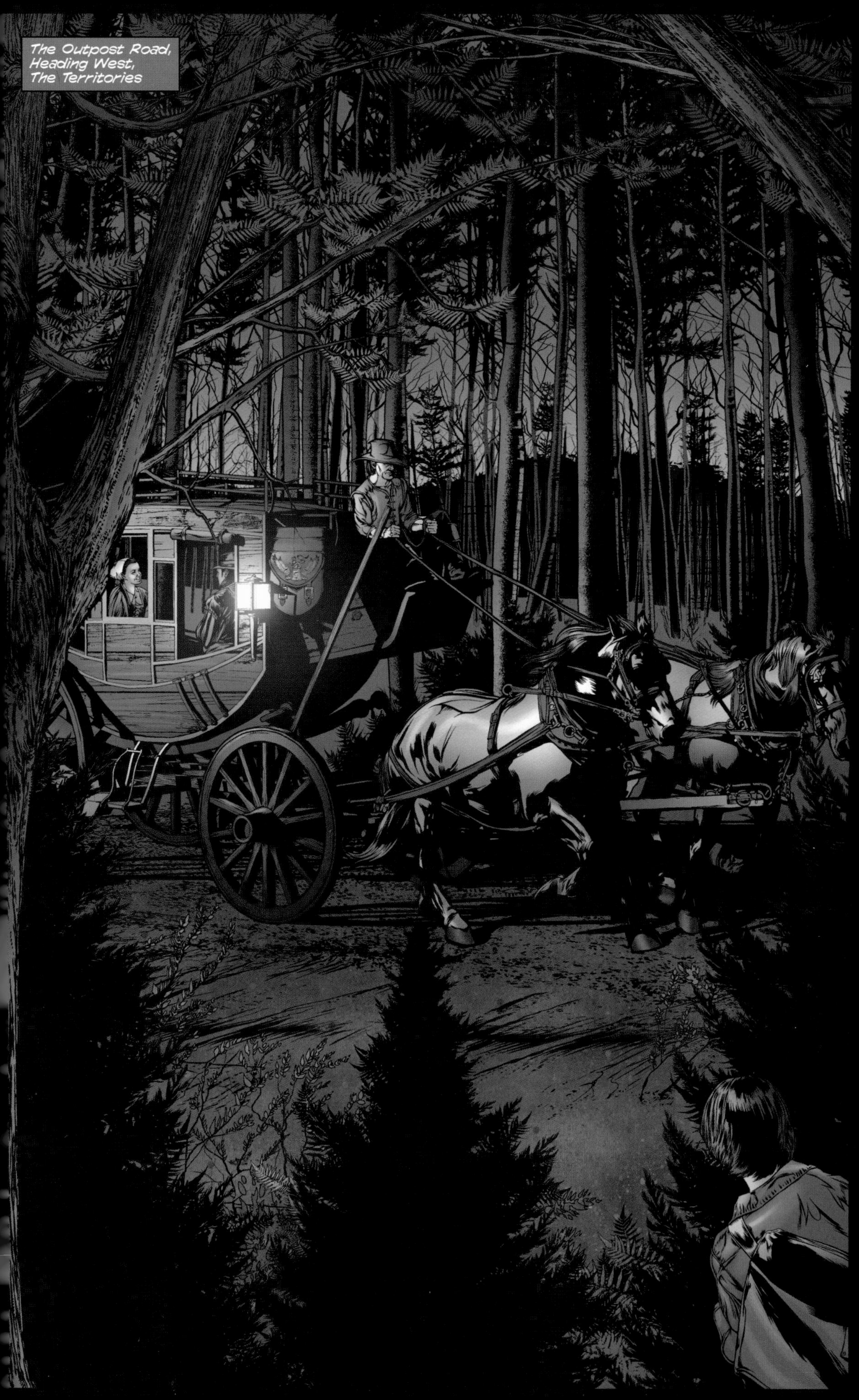
The Outpost Road,
Heading West,
The Territories

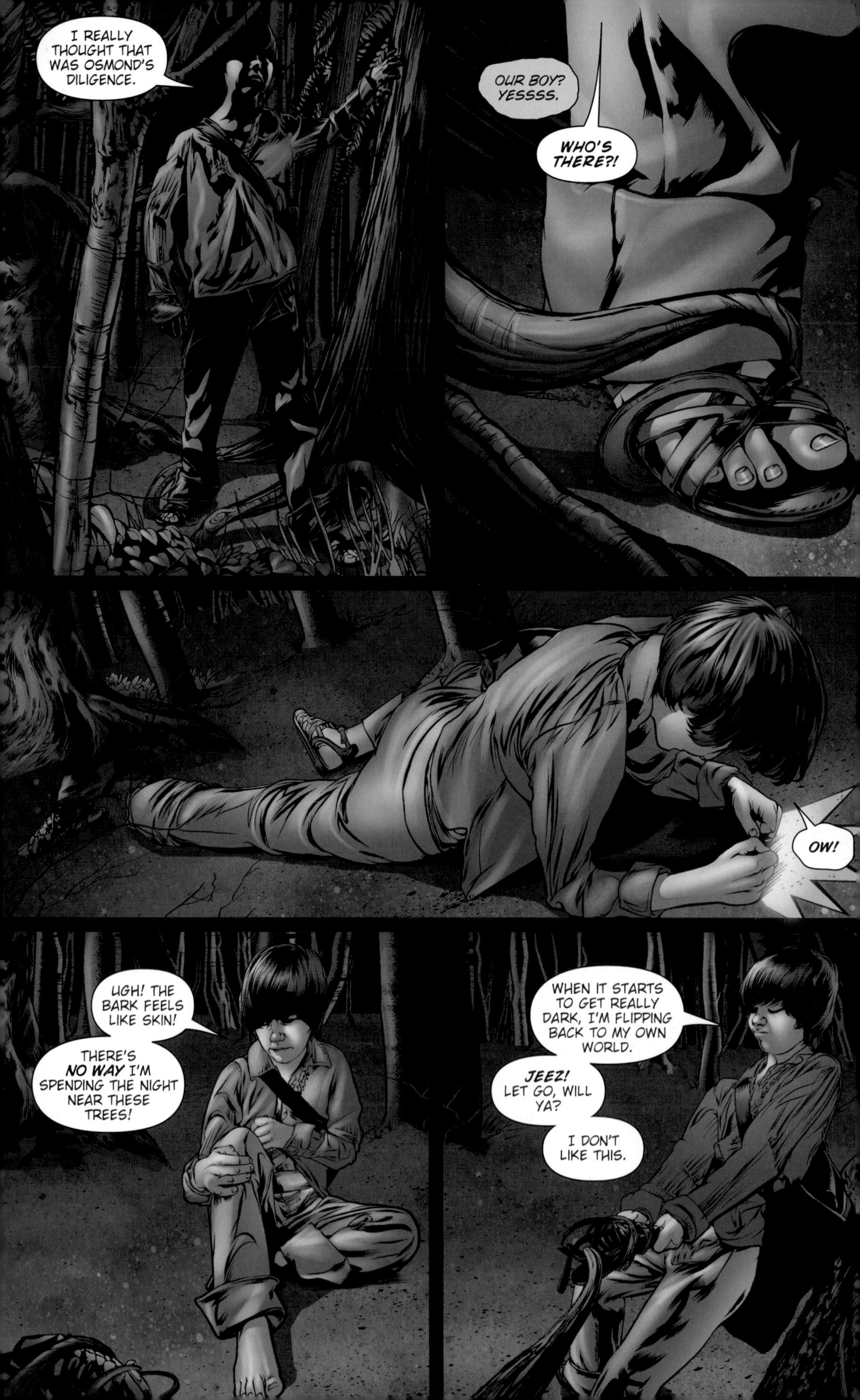
I REALLY THOUGHT THAT WAS OSMOND'S DILIGENCE.
OUR BOY? YESSSS.
WHO'S THERE?!
OW!
UGH! THE BARK FEELS LIKE SKIN!
THERE'S NO WAY I'M SPENDING THE NIGHT NEAR THESE TREES!
WHEN IT STARTS TO GET REALLY DARK, I'M FLIPPING BACK TO MY OWN WORLD.
JEEZ! LET GO, WILL YA?
I DON'T LIKE THIS.

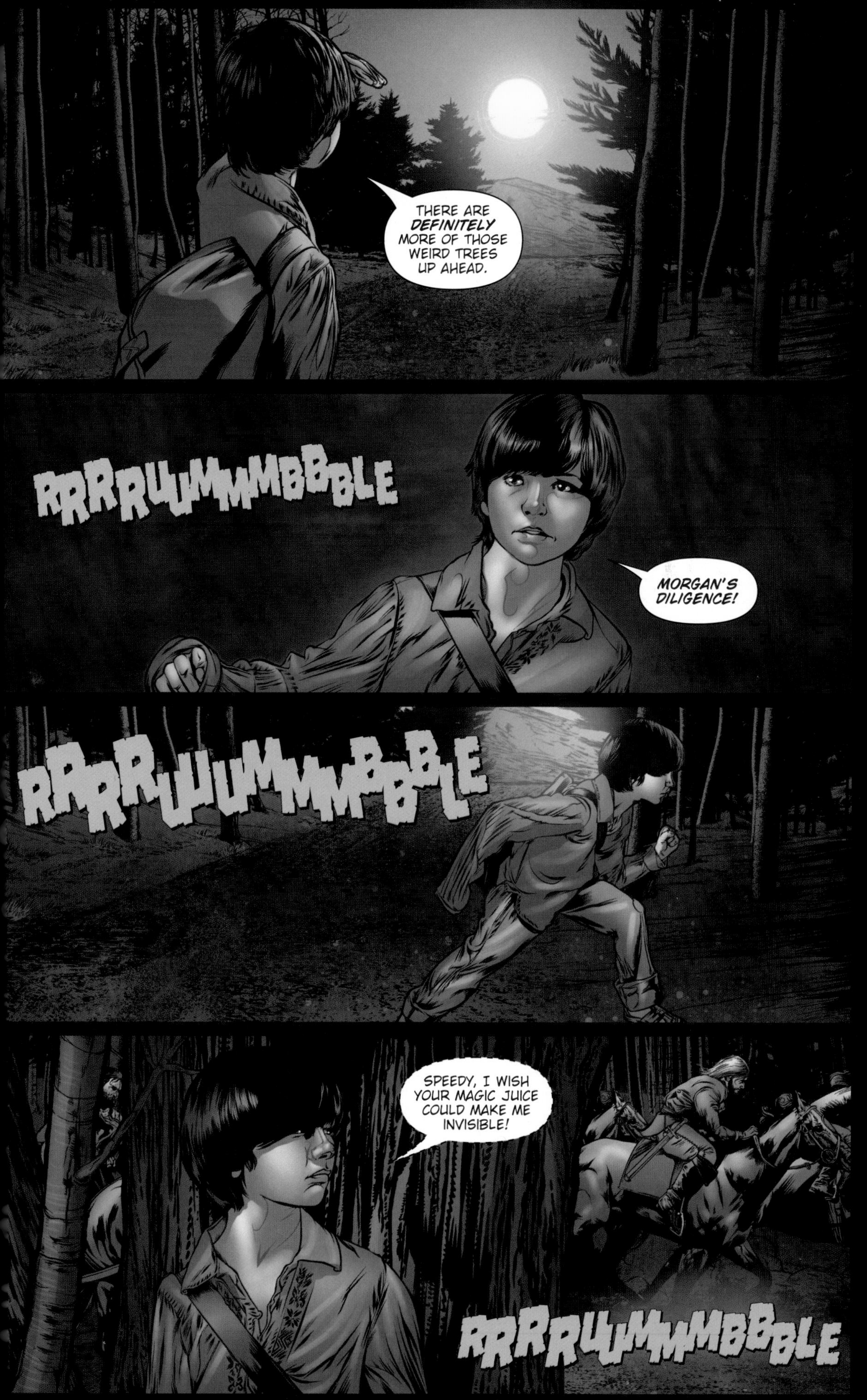
THERE ARE *DEFINITELY* MORE OF THOSE WEIRD TREES UP AHEAD.
RRRRUUMMMBBBLE
MORGAN'S DILIGENCE!
RRRRUUUMMMBBBLE
SPEEDY, I WISH YOUR MAGIC JUICE COULD MAKE ME INVISIBLE!
RRRRUUMMMBBBLE

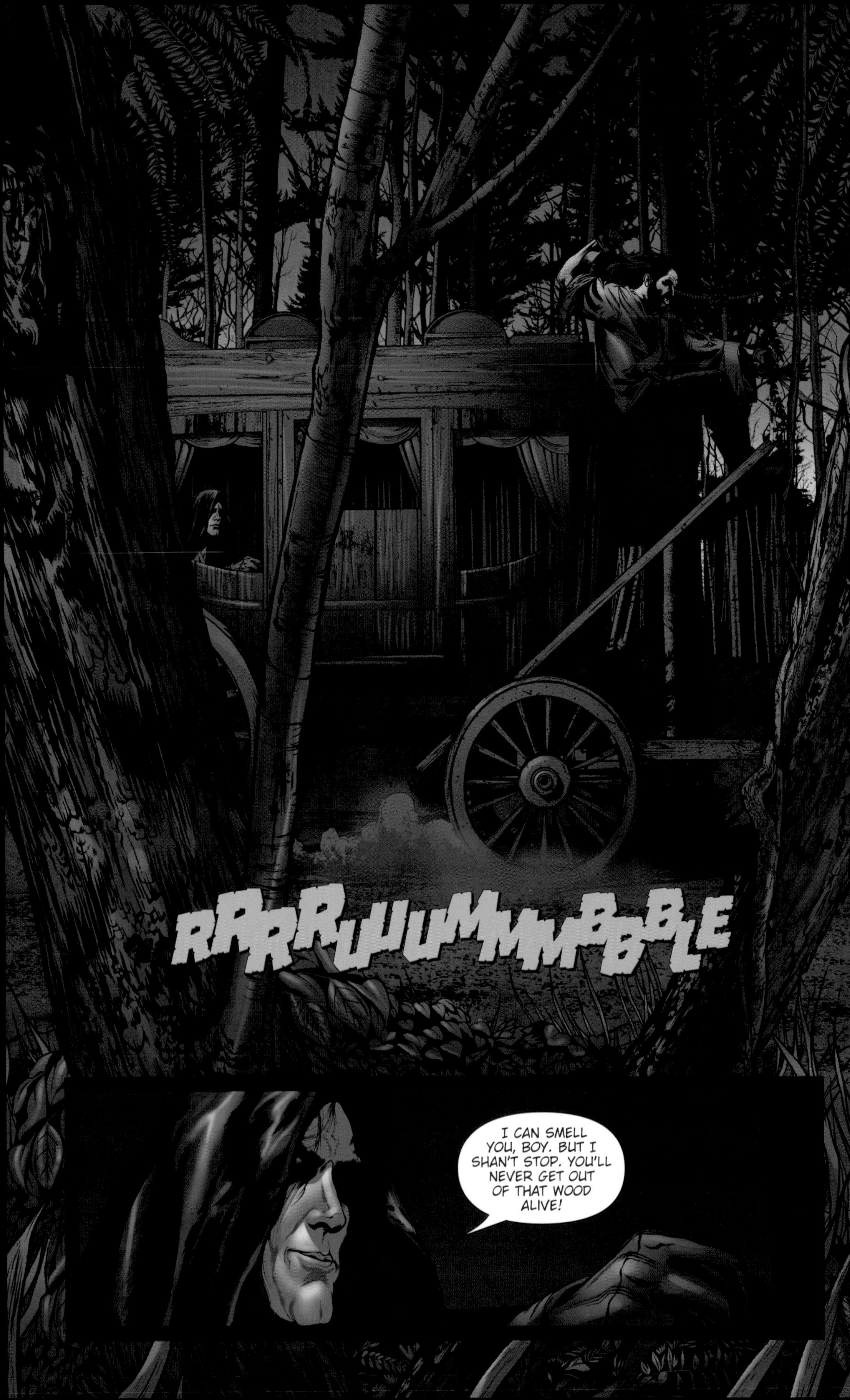
RRRRUUUMMMMBBBLE
I CAN SMELL YOU, BOY. BUT I SHAN'T STOP. YOU'LL NEVER GET OUT OF THAT WOOD ALIVE!

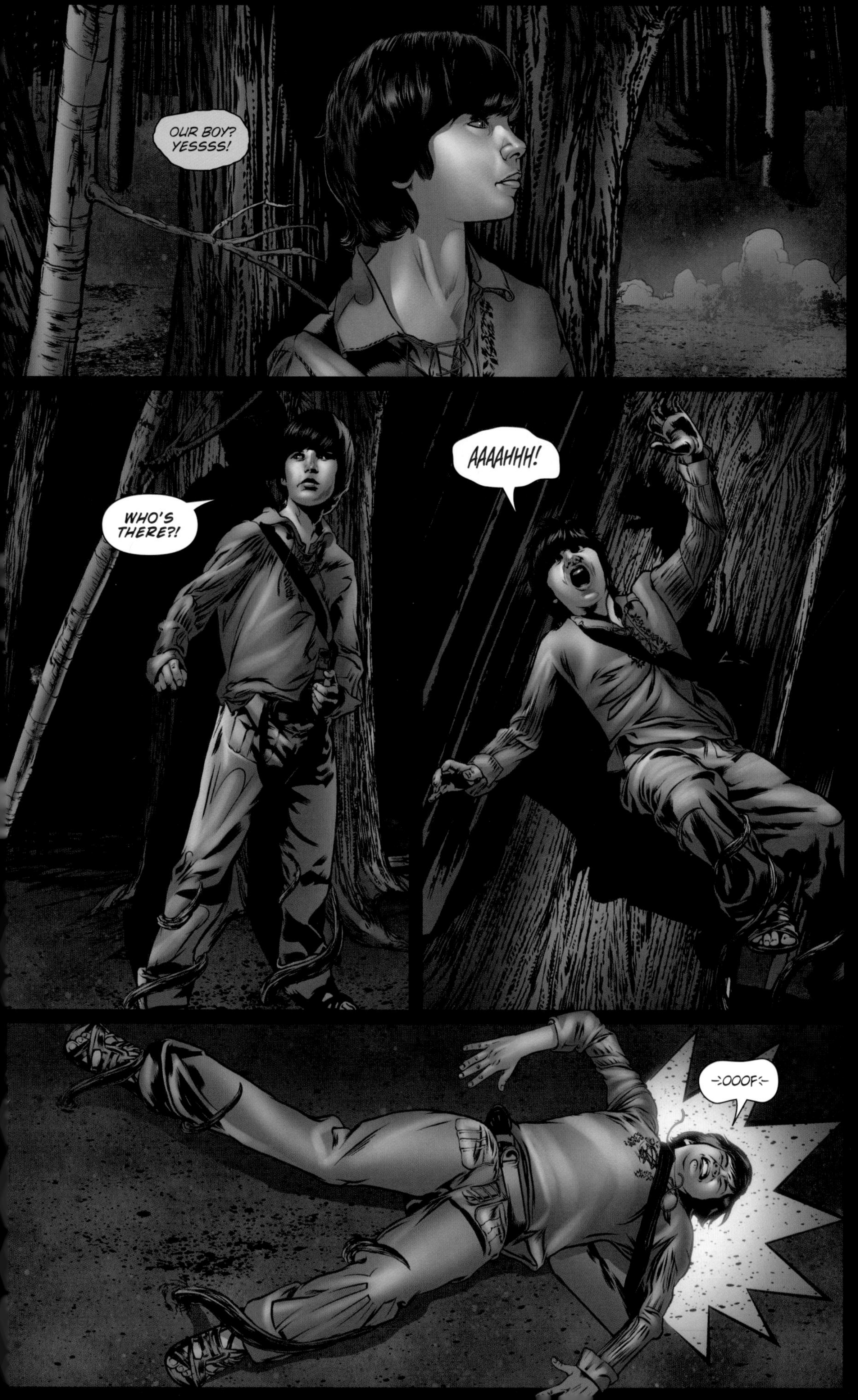
OUR BOY? YESSSS!
WHO'S THERE?!
AAAAHHH!
OOOF

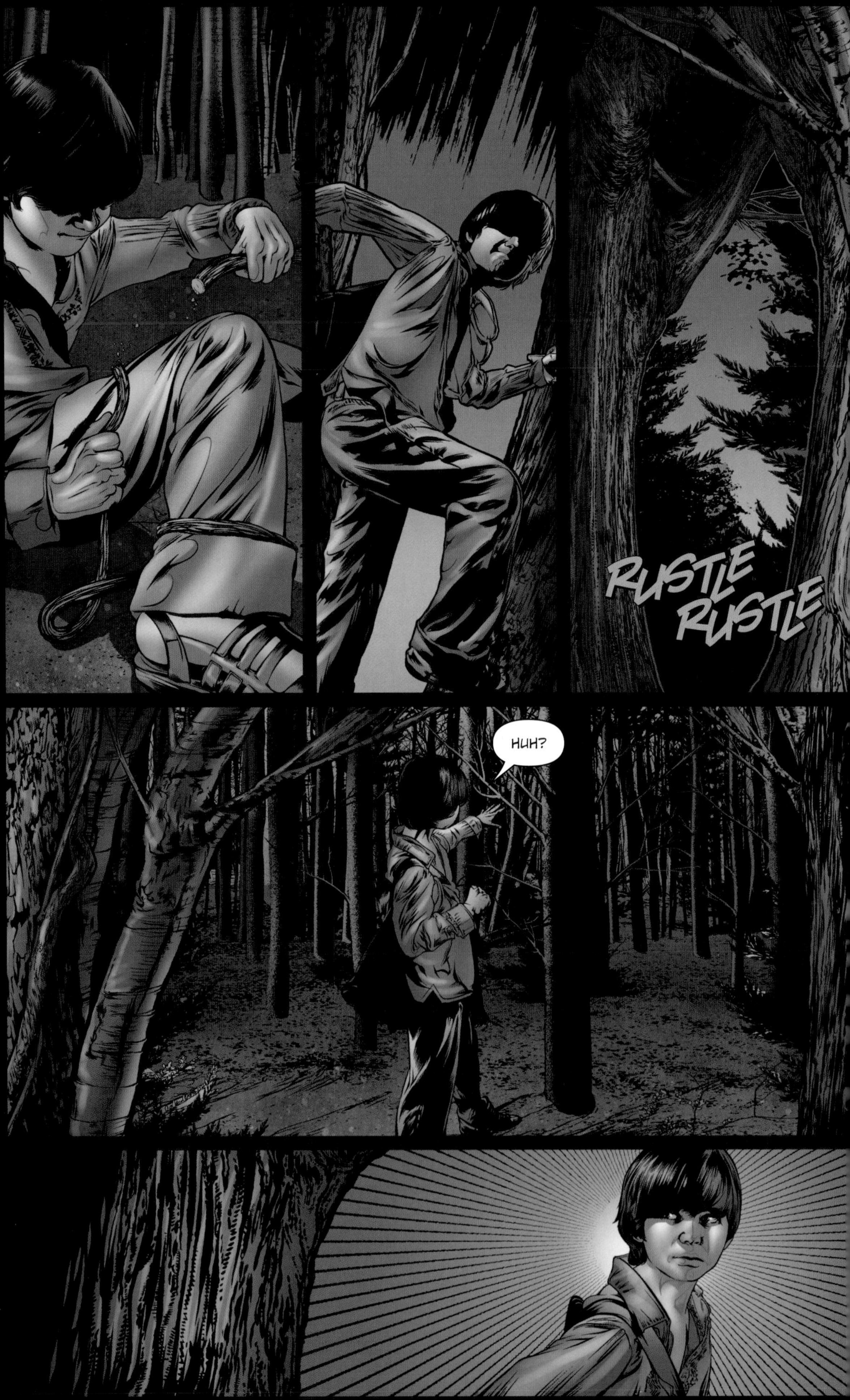
RUSTLE
RUSTLE
HUH?

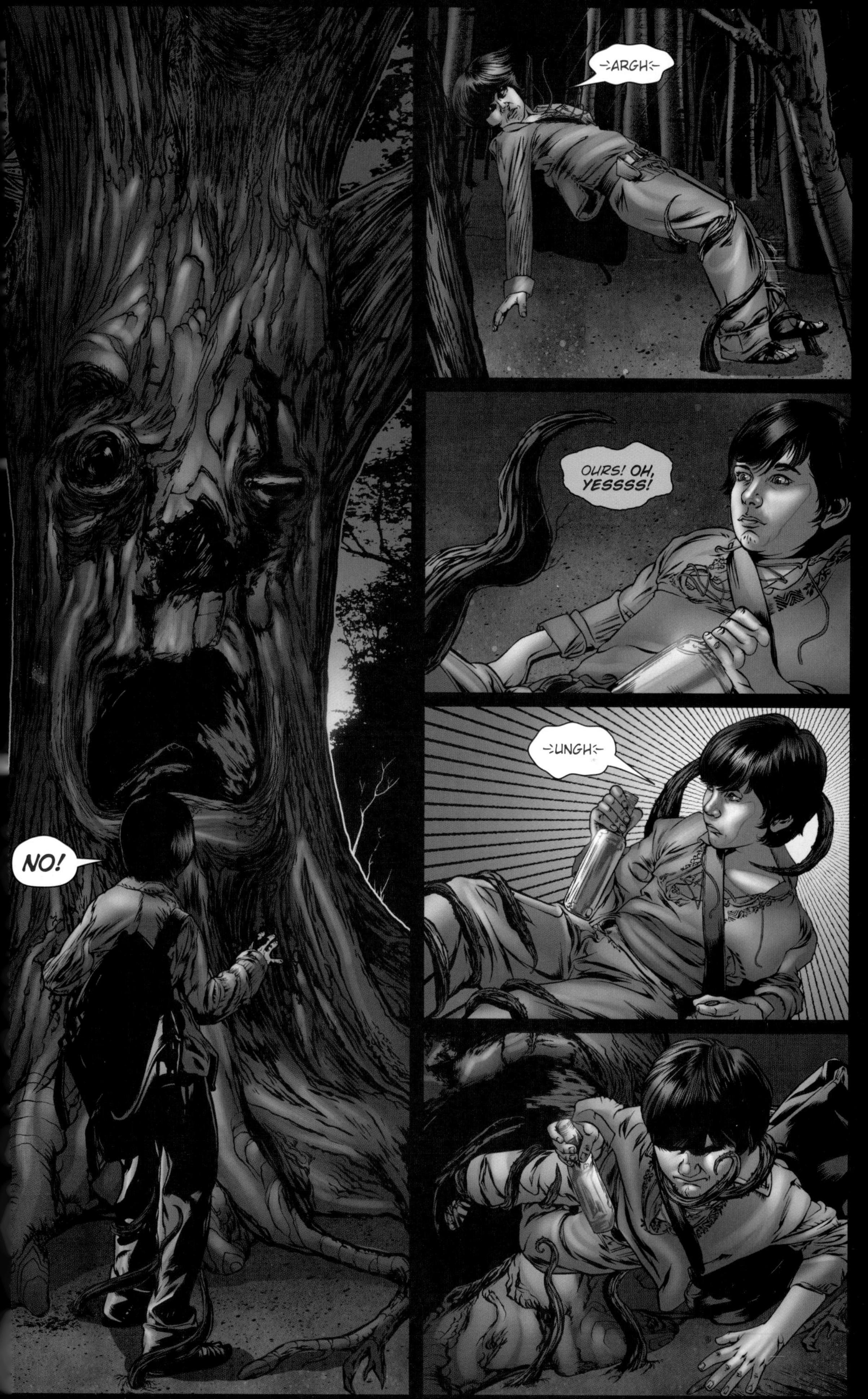
NO!
ARGH
OURS! OH, YESSSS!
UNGH

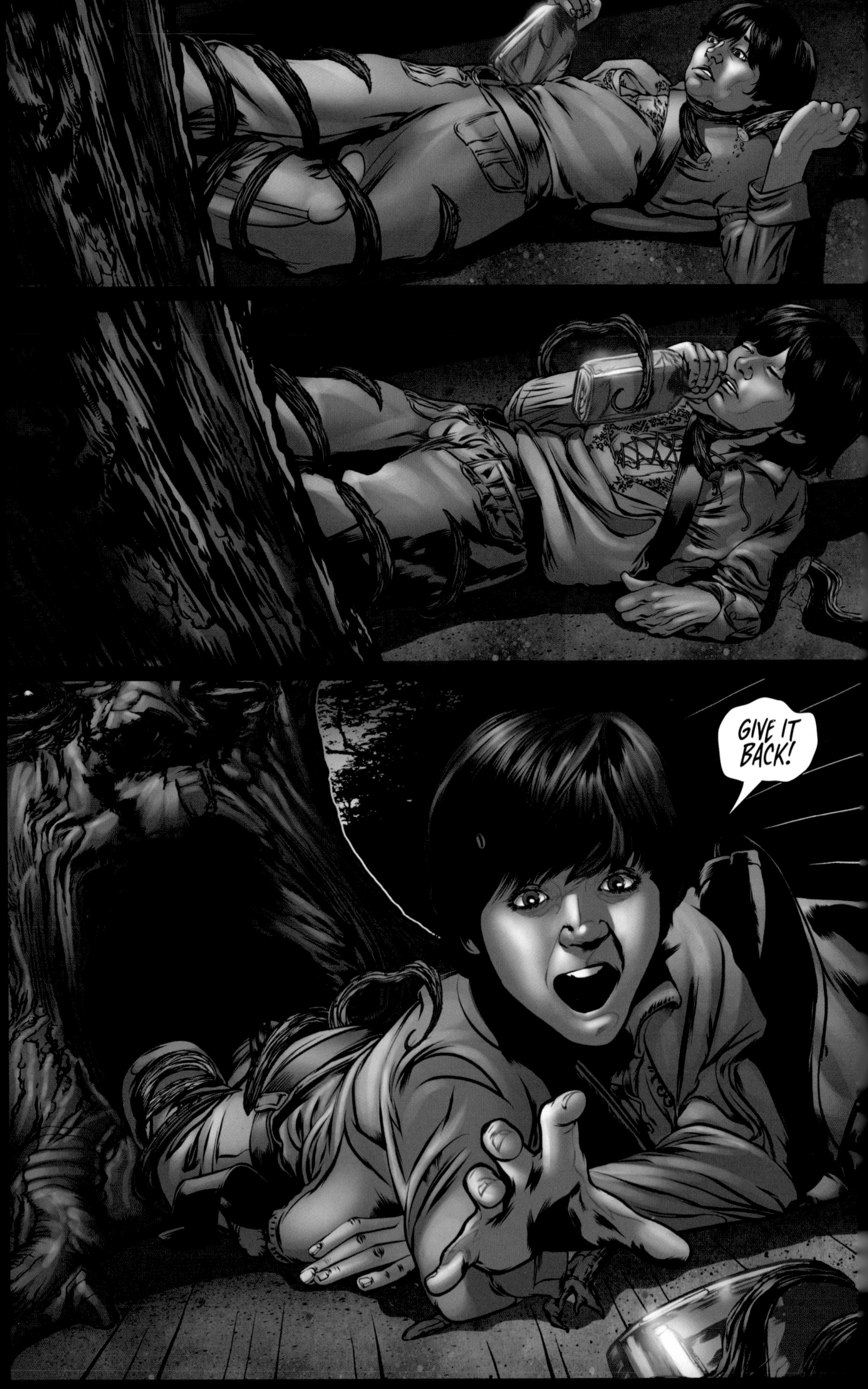
GIVE IT BACK!

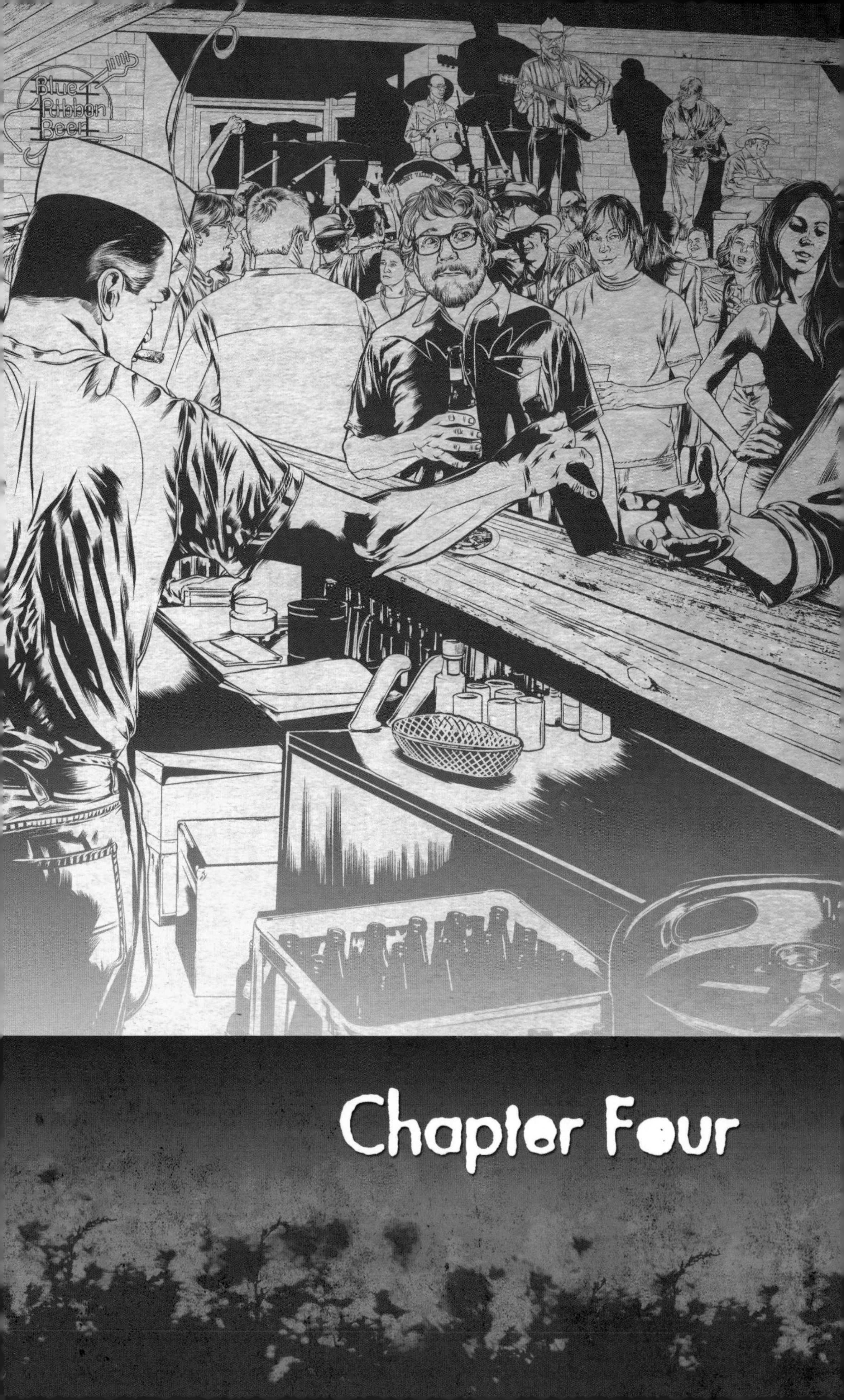
Blue Ribbon Beer

Chapter Four

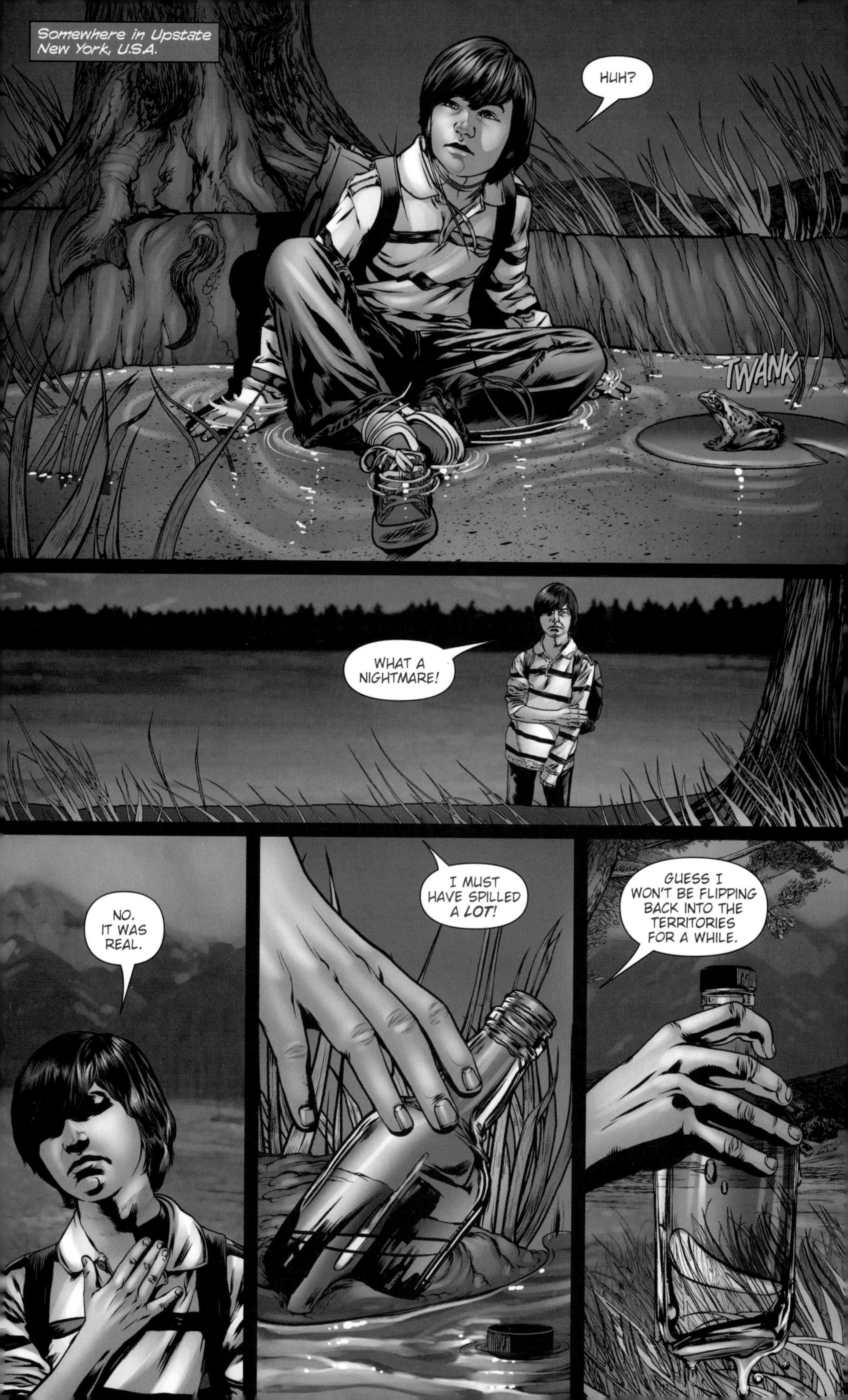

Somewhere in Upstate New York, U.S.A.
HUH?
TWANK
WHAT A NIGHTMARE!
NO. IT WAS REAL.
I MUST HAVE SPILLED A *LOT*!
GUESS I WON'T BE FLIPPING BACK INTO THE TERRITORIES FOR A WHILE.

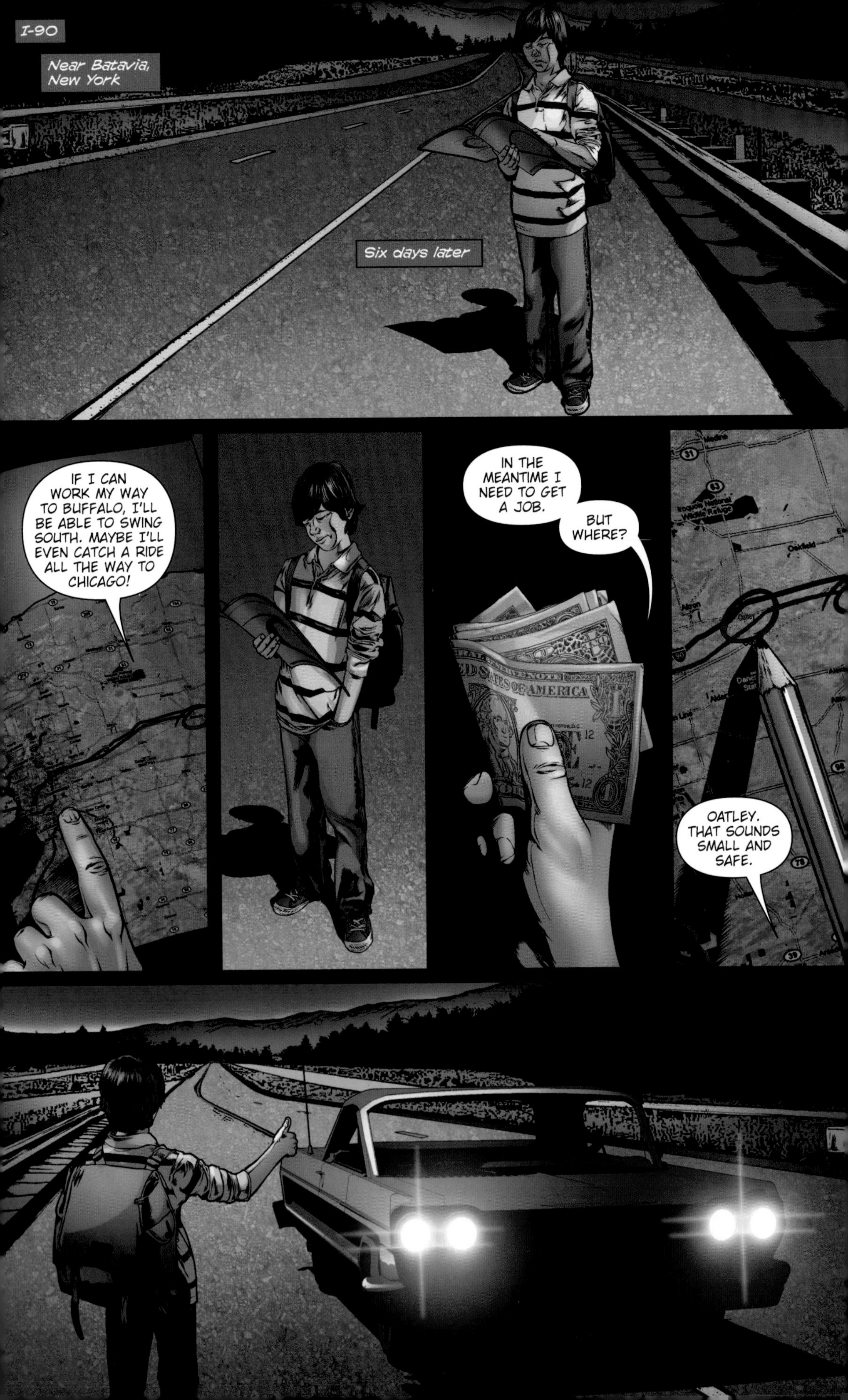
I-90
Near Batavia, New York
Six days later
IF I CAN WORK MY WAY TO BUFFALO, I'LL BE ABLE TO SWING SOUTH. MAYBE I'LL EVEN CATCH A RIDE ALL THE WAY TO CHICAGO!
IN THE MEANTIME I NEED TO GET A JOB.
BUT WHERE?
OATLEY. THAT SOUNDS SMALL AND SAFE.

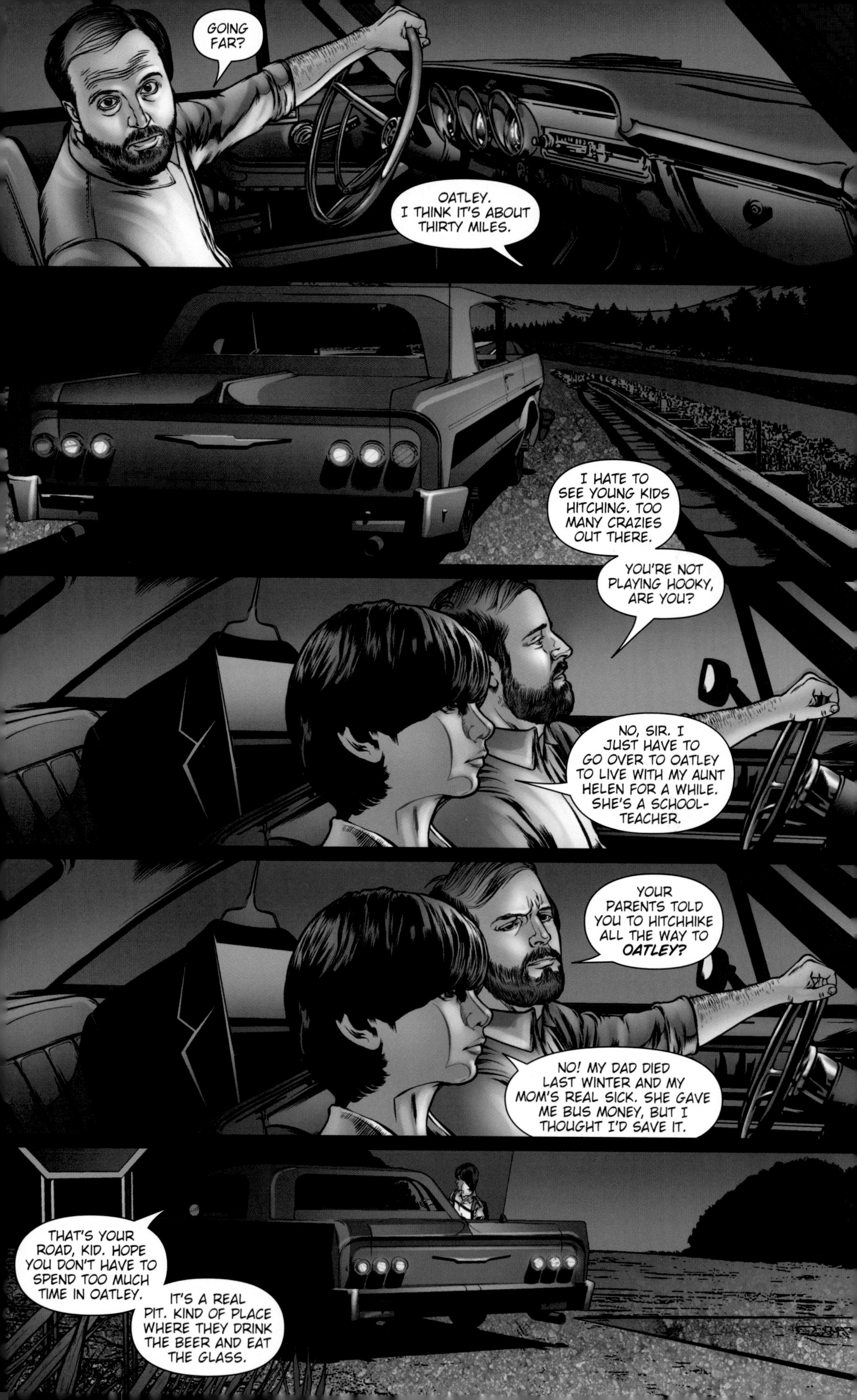
GOING FAR?
OATLEY. I THINK IT'S ABOUT THIRTY MILES.
I HATE TO SEE YOUNG KIDS HITCHING. TOO MANY CRAZIES OUT THERE.
YOU'RE NOT PLAYING HOOKY, ARE YOU?
NO, SIR. I JUST HAVE TO GO OVER TO OATLEY TO LIVE WITH MY AUNT HELEN FOR A WHILE. SHE'S A SCHOOL-TEACHER.
YOUR PARENTS TOLD YOU TO HITCHHIKE ALL THE WAY TO ***OATLEY?***
NO! MY DAD DIED LAST WINTER AND MY MOM'S REAL SICK. SHE GAVE ME BUS MONEY, BUT I THOUGHT I'D SAVE IT.
THAT'S YOUR ROAD, KID. HOPE YOU DON'T HAVE TO SPEND TOO MUCH TIME IN OATLEY.
IT'S A REAL PIT. KIND OF PLACE WHERE THEY DRINK THE BEER AND EAT THE GLASS.

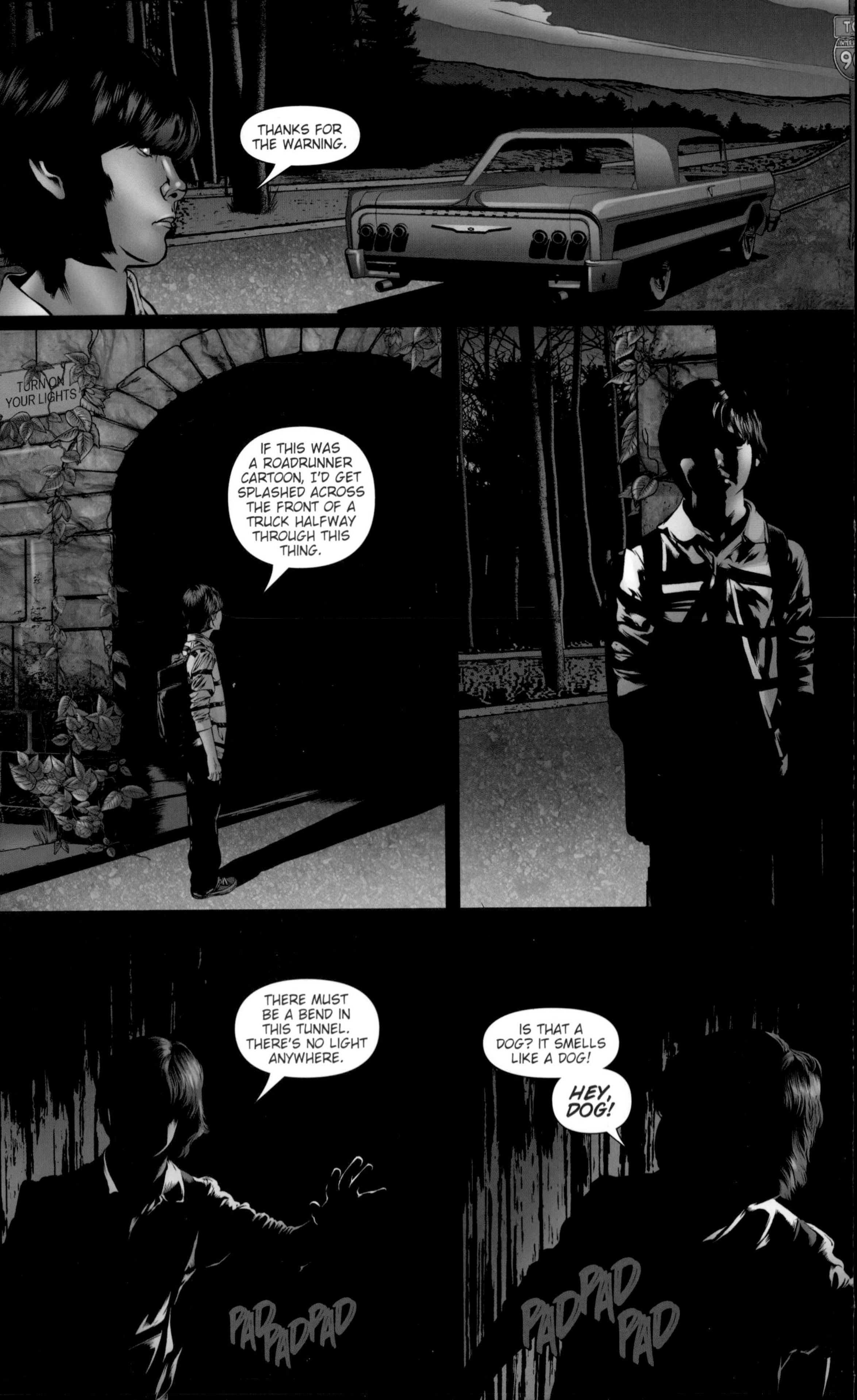
THANKS FOR THE WARNING.
TURN ON YOUR LIGHTS
IF THIS WAS A ROADRUNNER CARTOON, I'D GET SPLASHED ACROSS THE FRONT OF A TRUCK HALFWAY THROUGH THIS THING.
THERE MUST BE A BEND IN THIS TUNNEL. THERE'S NO LIGHT ANYWHERE.
PAD PAD PAD
IS THAT A DOG? IT SMELLS LIKE A DOG!
HEY, DOG!
PAD PAD PAD

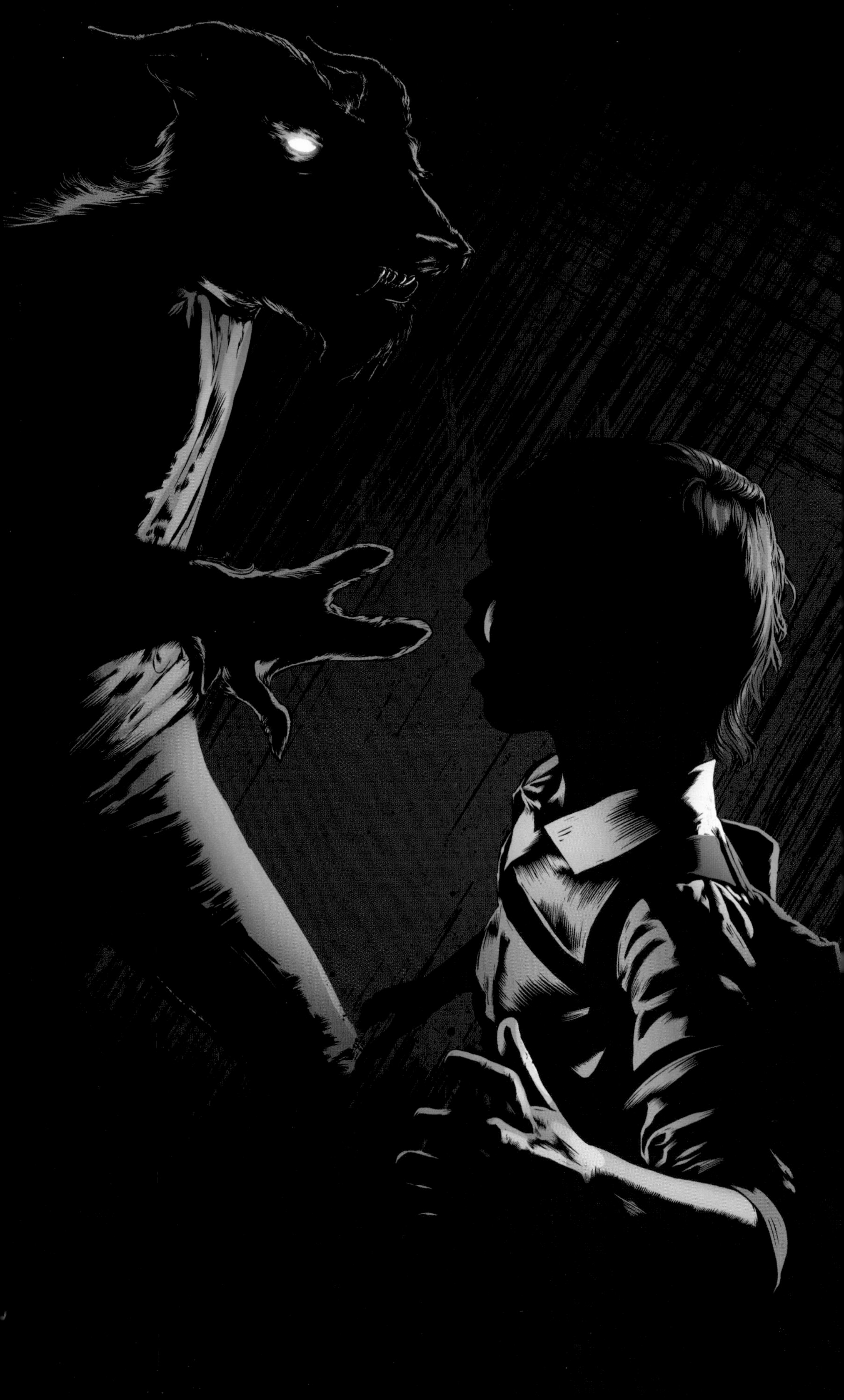

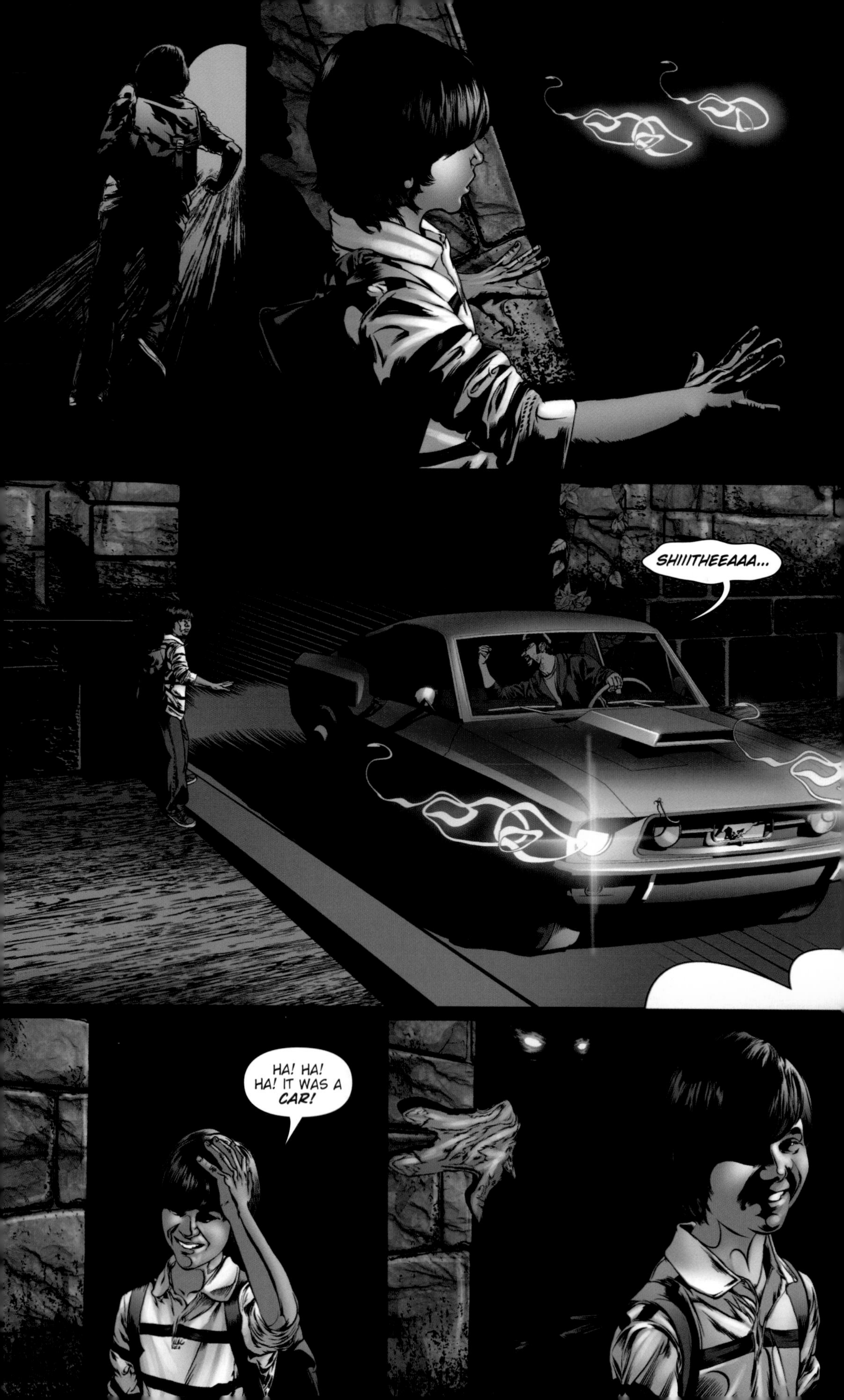
SHIIITHEEAAA...
HA! HA! HA! IT WAS A CAR!

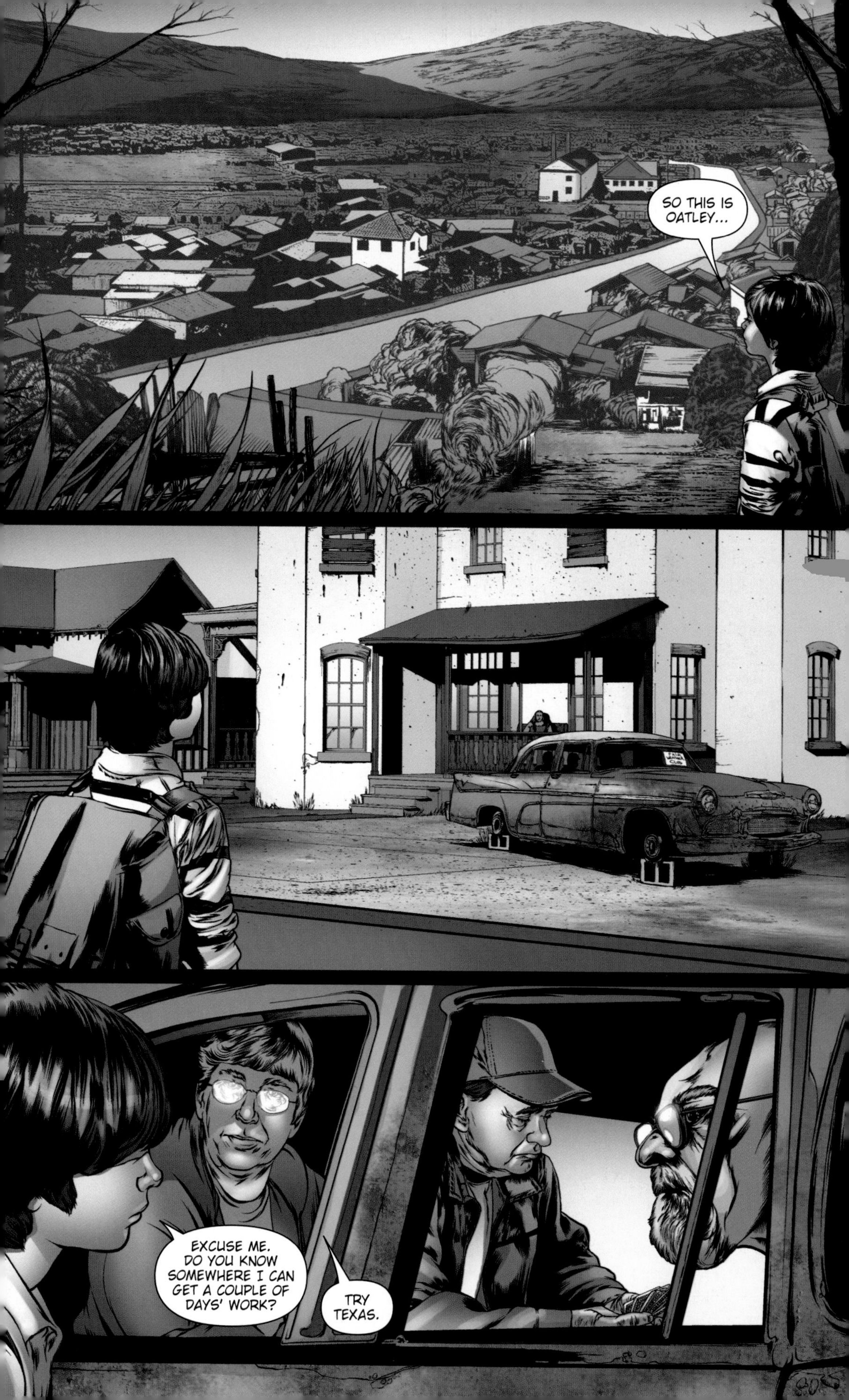
SO THIS IS OATLEY...
EXCUSE ME. DO YOU KNOW SOMEWHERE I CAN GET A COUPLE OF DAYS' WORK?
TRY TEXAS.

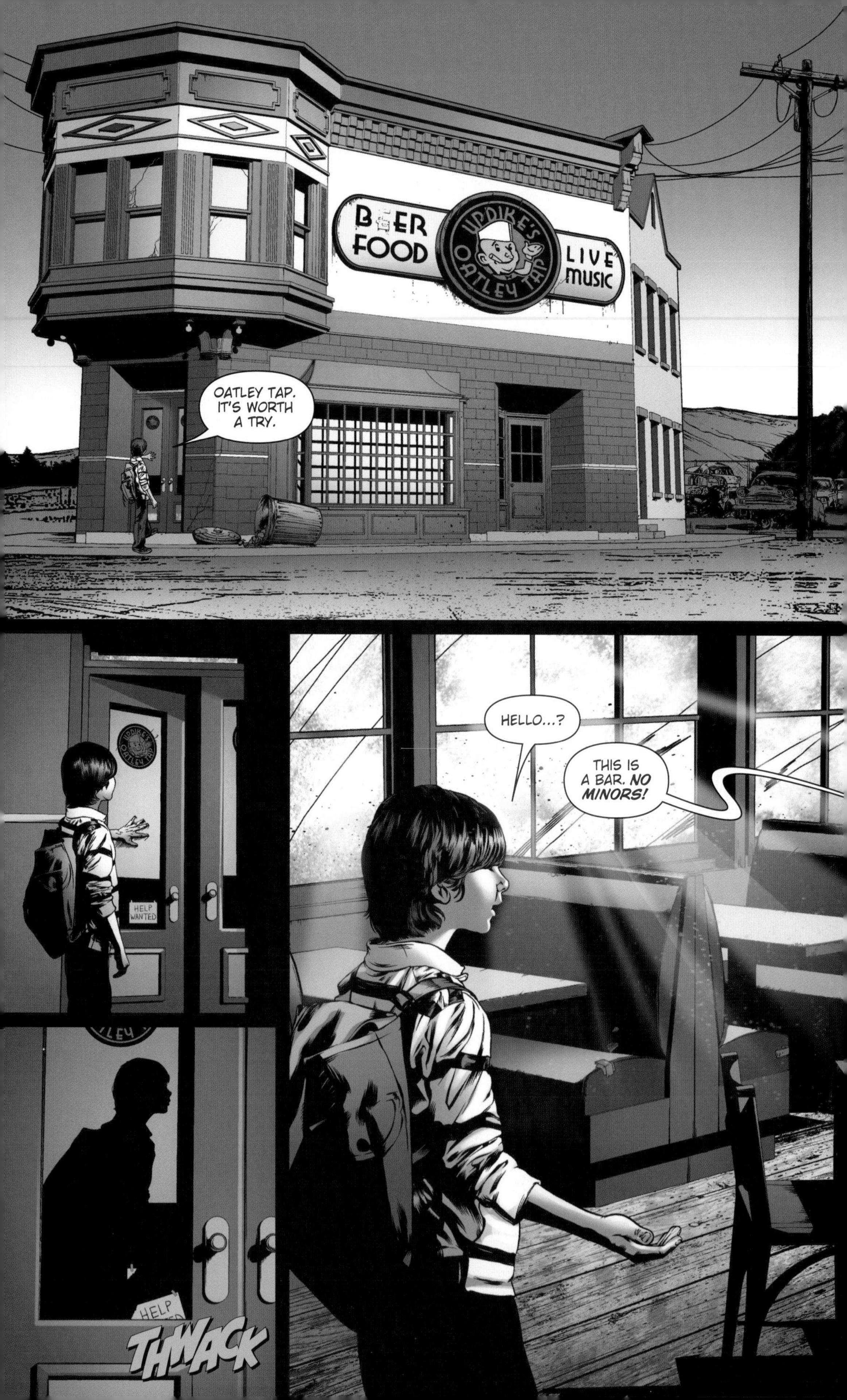
BEER
FOOD
UPDIKE'S OATLEY TAP
LIVE MUSIC
OATLEY TAP. IT'S WORTH A TRY.
UPDIKE'S OATLEY TAP
HELP WANTED
HELP
THWACK
HELLO...?
THIS IS A BAR. *NO MINORS!*

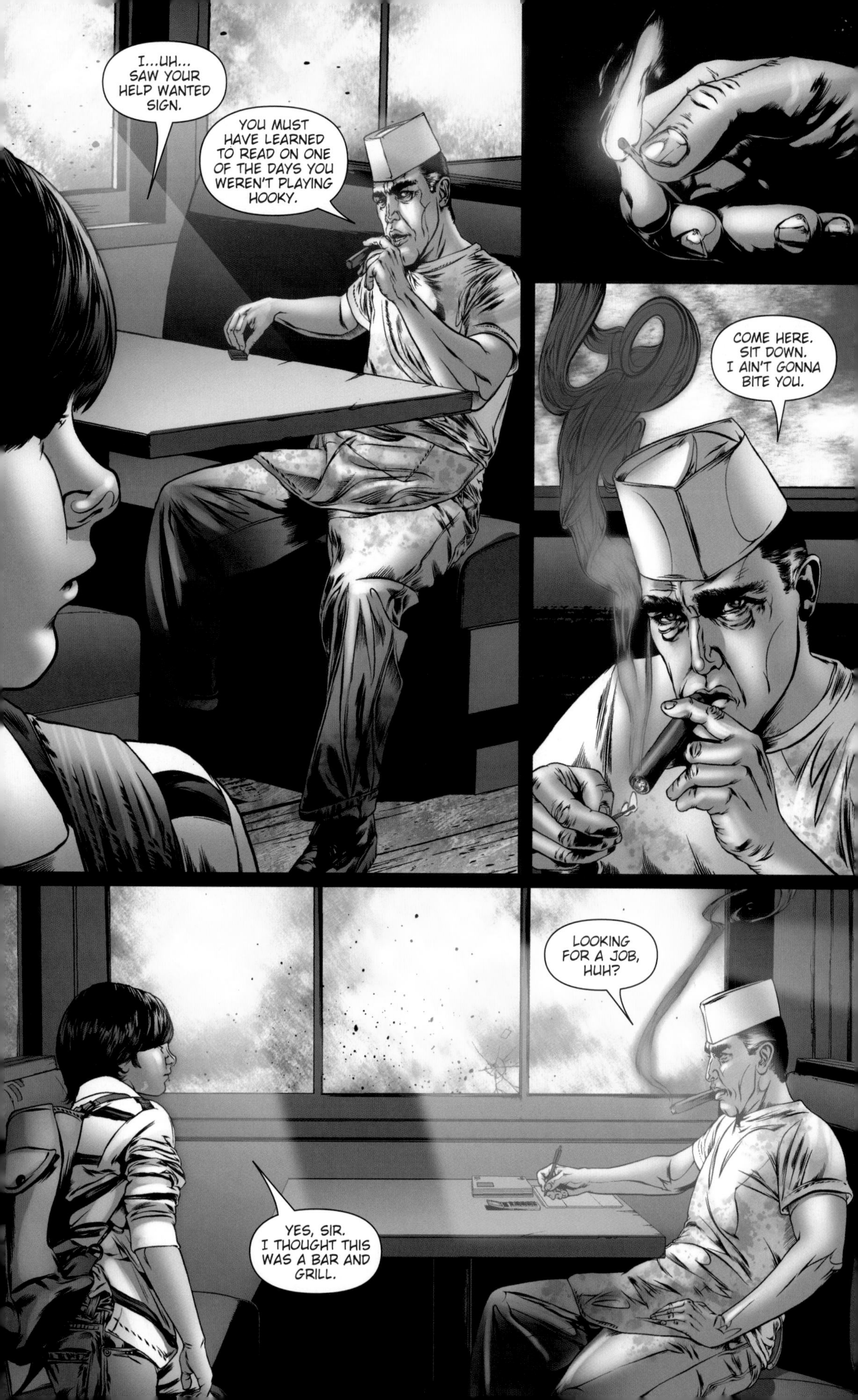
I...UH... SAW YOUR HELP WANTED SIGN.
YOU MUST HAVE LEARNED TO READ ON ONE OF THE DAYS YOU WEREN'T PLAYING HOOKY.
COME HERE. SIT DOWN. I AIN'T GONNA BITE YOU.
LOOKING FOR A JOB, HUH?
YES, SIR. I THOUGHT THIS WAS A BAR AND GRILL.

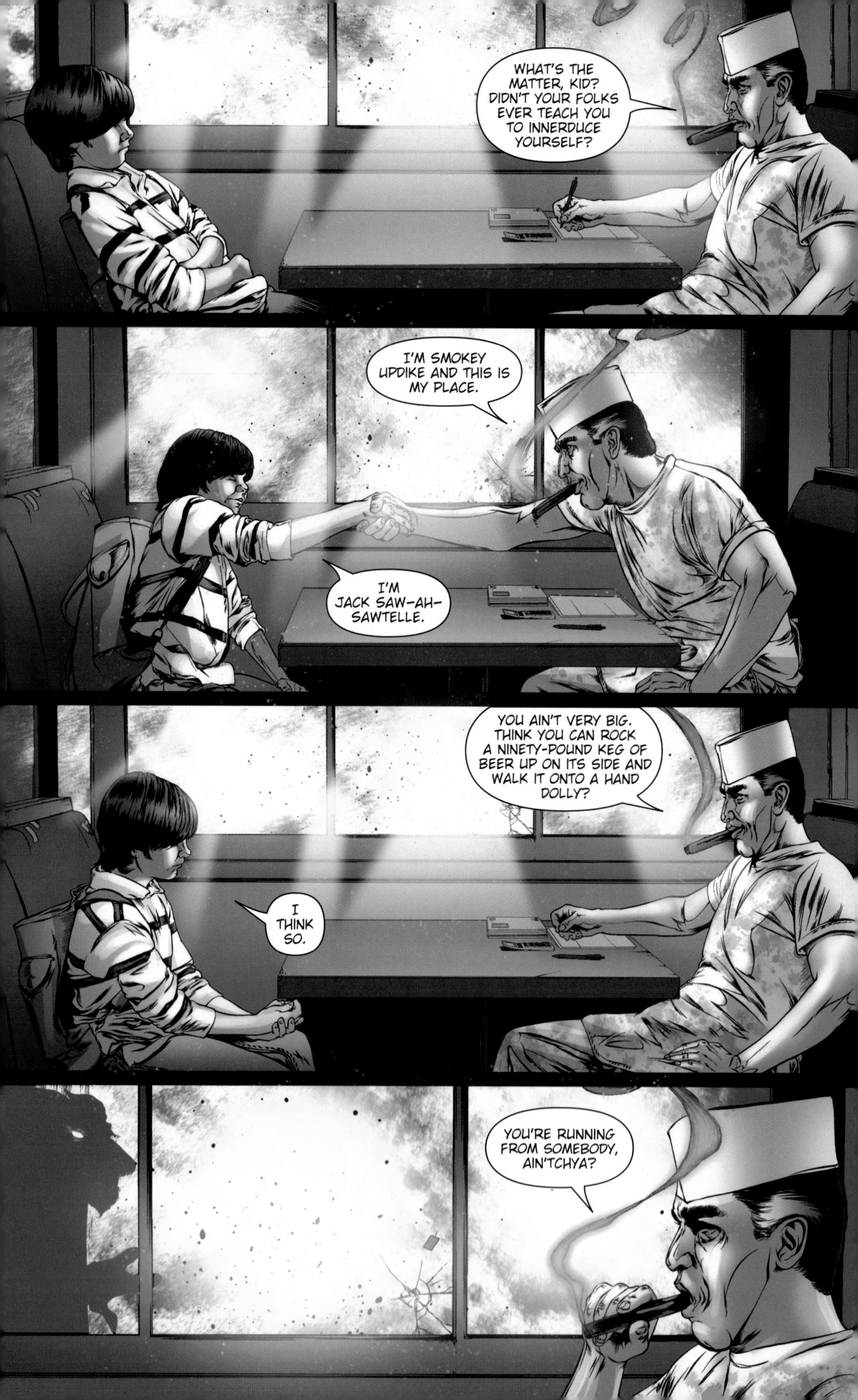
WHAT'S THE MATTER, KID? DIDN'T YOUR FOLKS EVER TEACH YOU TO INNERDUCE YOURSELF?
I'M SMOKEY UPDIKE AND THIS IS MY PLACE.
I'M JACK SAW-AH-SAWTELLE.
YOU AIN'T VERY BIG. THINK YOU CAN ROCK A NINETY-POUND KEG OF BEER UP ON ITS SIDE AND WALK IT ONTO A HAND DOLLY?
I THINK SO.
YOU'RE RUNNING FROM SOMEBODY, AIN'TCHYA?

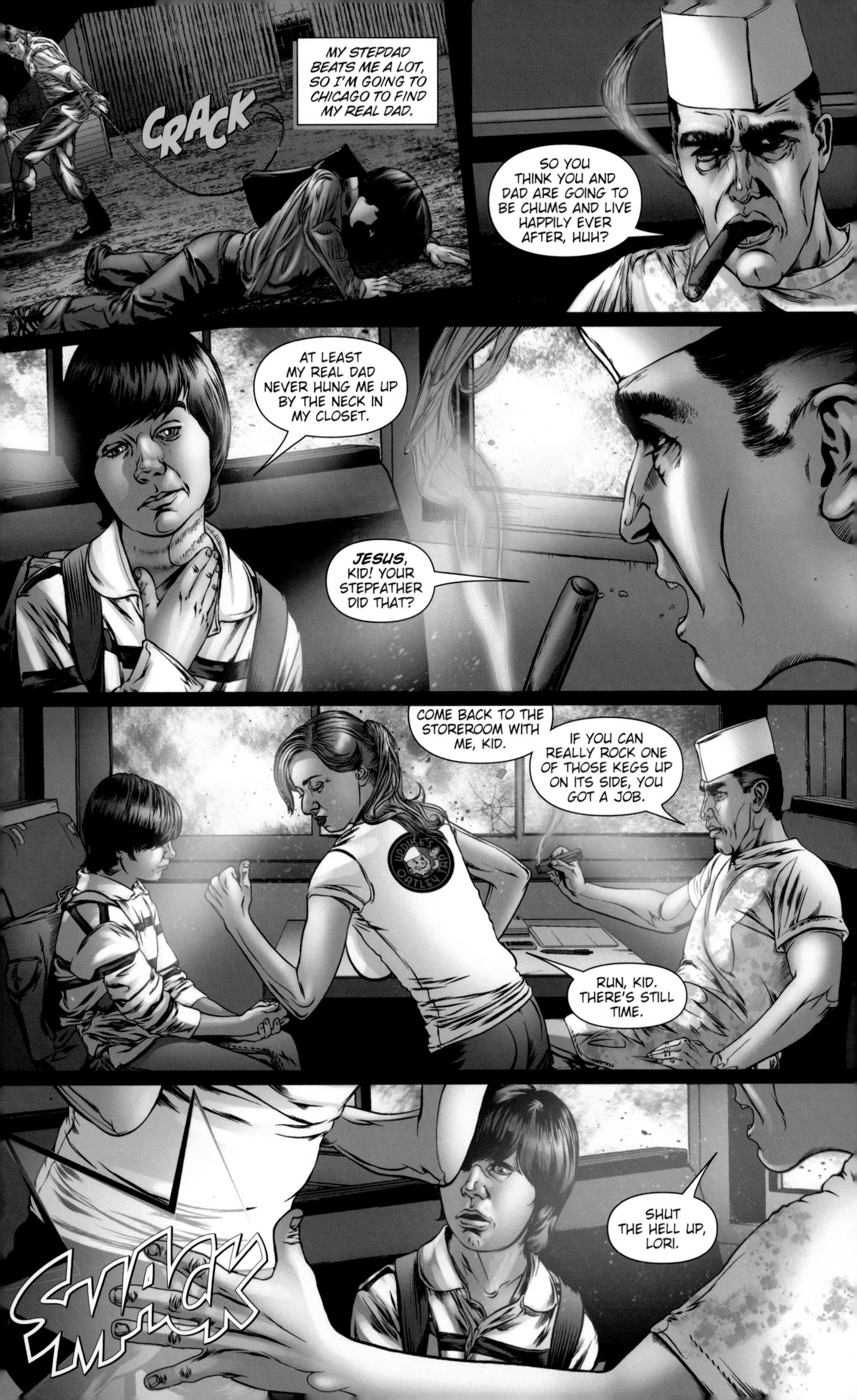

MY STEPDAD BEATS ME A LOT, SO I'M GOING TO CHICAGO TO FIND MY REAL DAD.
CRACK
SO YOU THINK YOU AND DAD ARE GOING TO BE CHUMS AND LIVE HAPPILY EVER AFTER, HUH?
AT LEAST MY REAL DAD NEVER HUNG ME UP BY THE NECK IN MY CLOSET.
JESUS, KID! YOUR STEPFATHER DID THAT?
COME BACK TO THE STOREROOM WITH ME, KID.
IF YOU CAN REALLY ROCK ONE OF THOSE KEGS UP ON ITS SIDE, YOU GOT A JOB.
RUN, KID. THERE'S STILL TIME.
SHUT THE HELL UP, LORI.

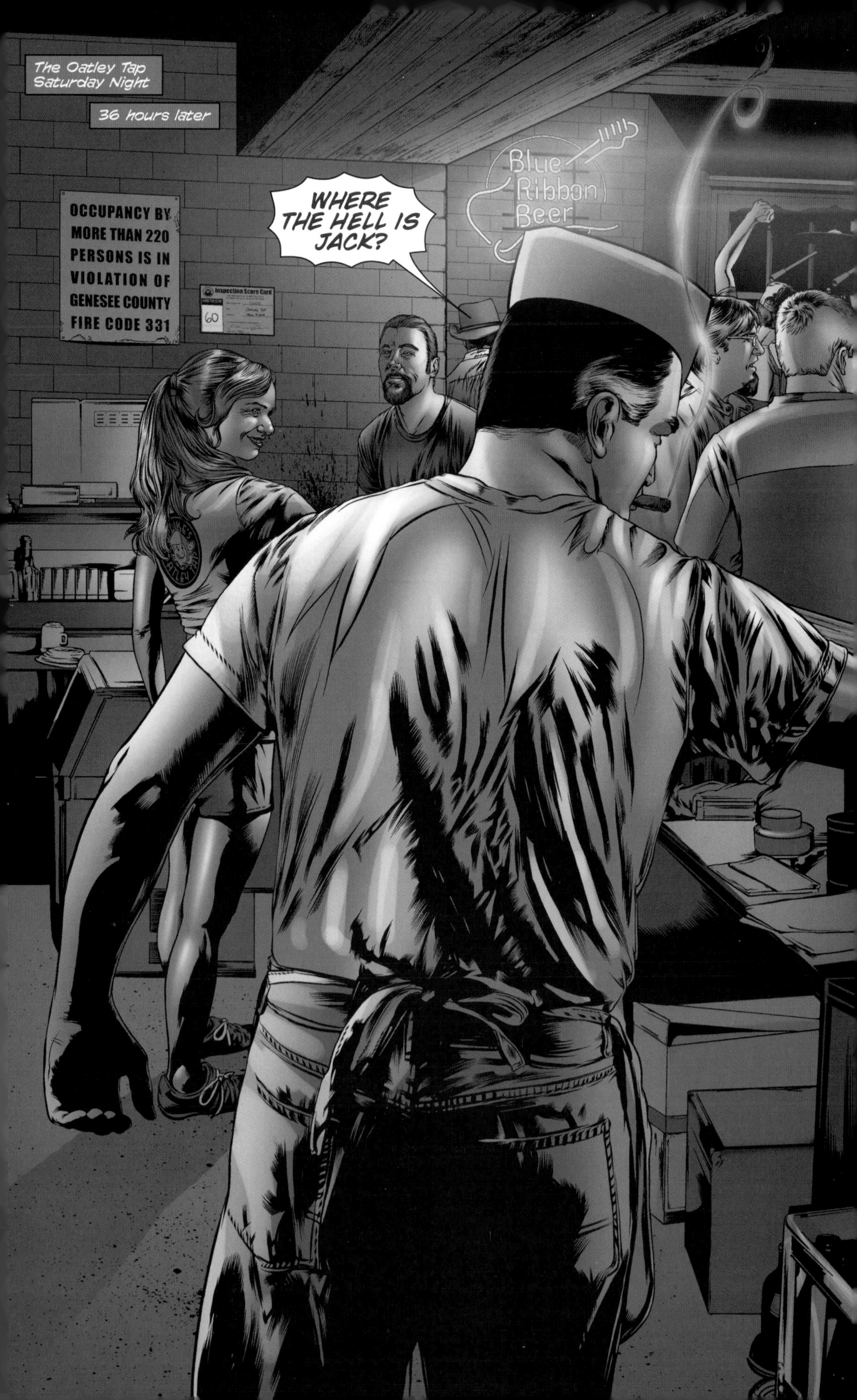
The Oatley Tap
Saturday Night
36 hours later
OCCUPANCY BY MORE THAN 220 PERSONS IS IN VIOLATION OF GENESEE COUNTY FIRE CODE 331
Inspection Score Card
60
Blue Ribbon Beer
WHERE THE HELL IS JACK?

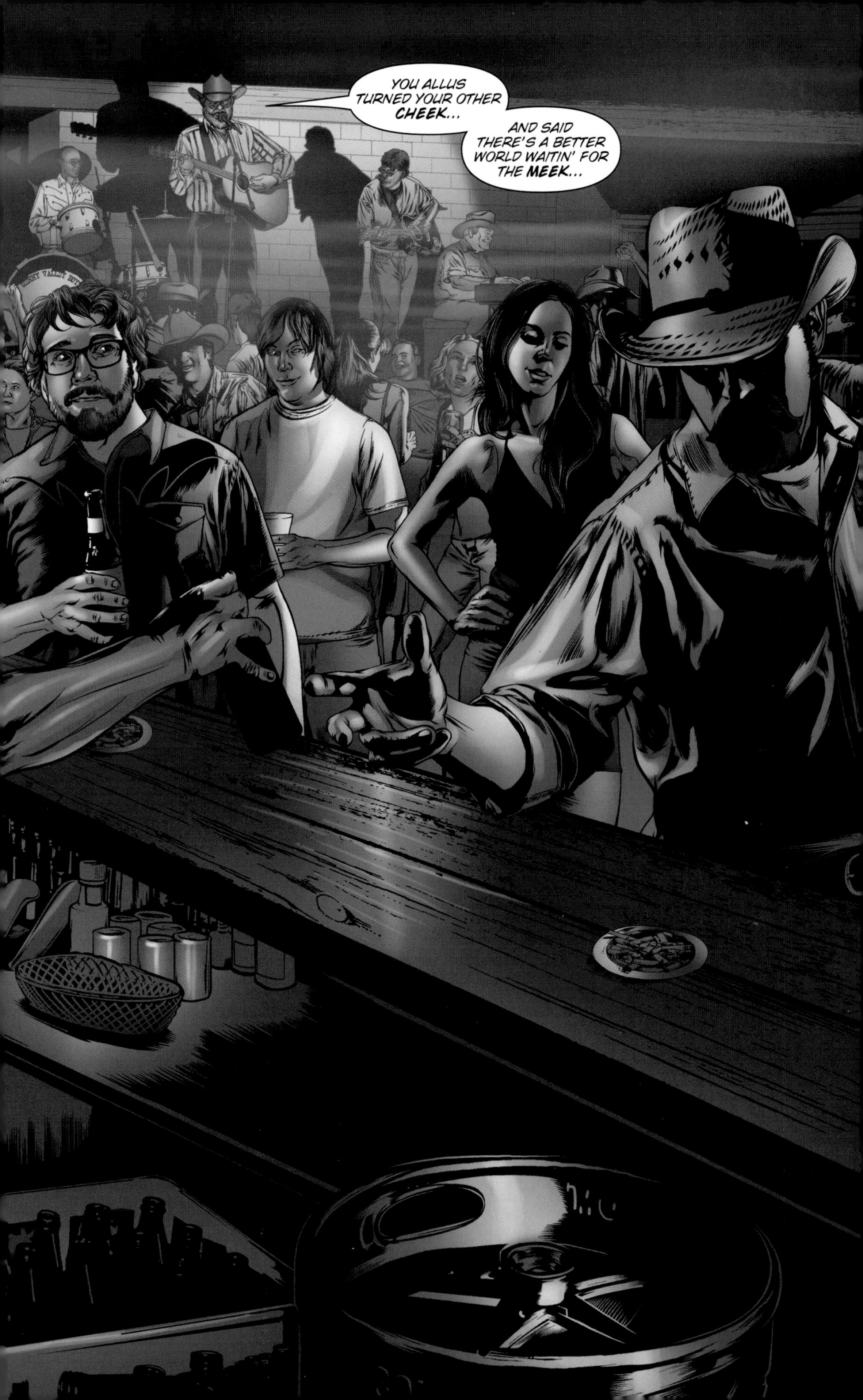
YOU ALLUS TURNED YOUR OTHER **CHEEK**...
AND SAID THERE'S A BETTER WORLD WAITIN' FOR THE **MEEK**...

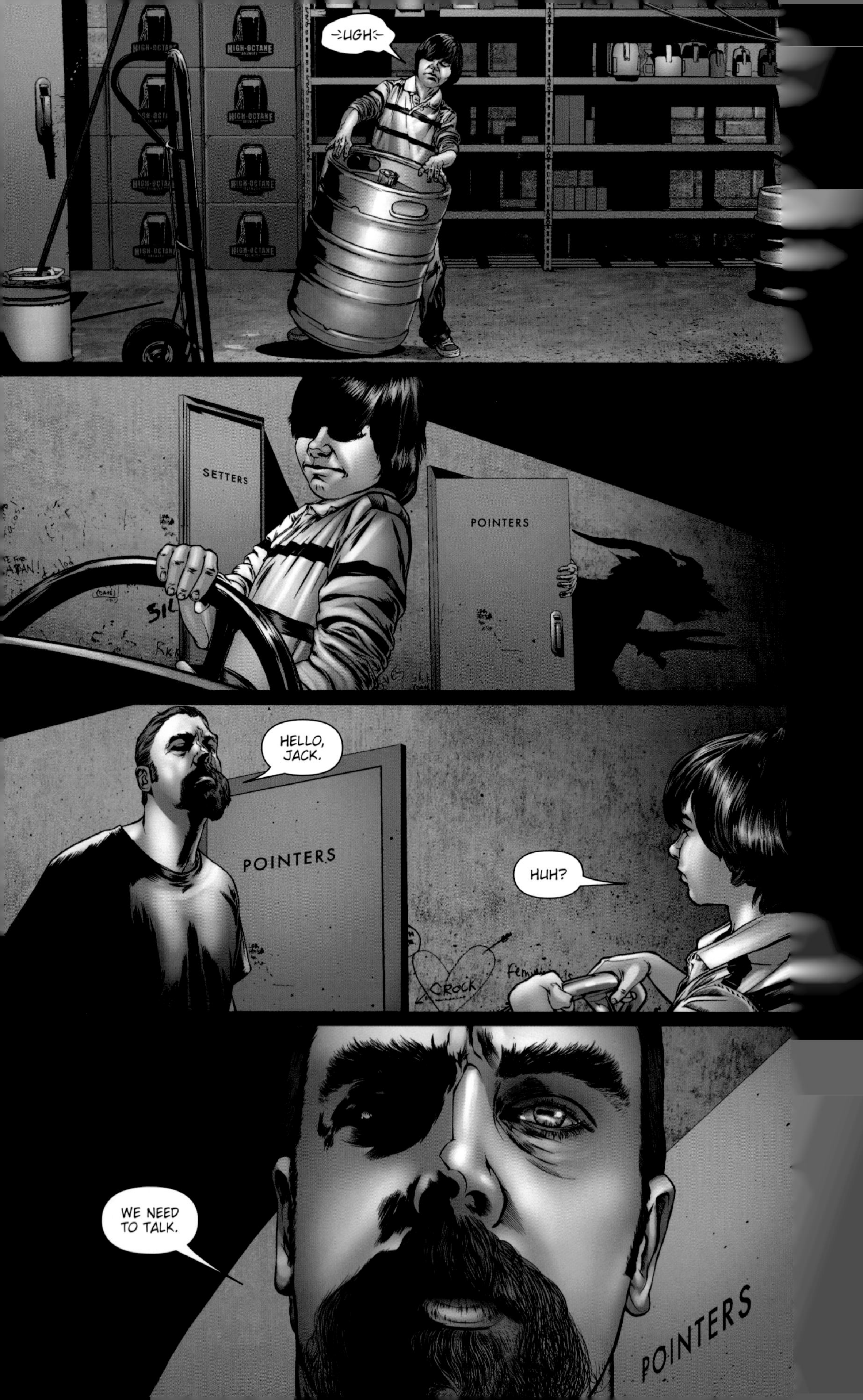
UGH
HIGH-OCTANE
SETTERS
POINTERS
HELLO, JACK.
POINTERS
HUH?
WE NEED TO TALK.
POINTERS

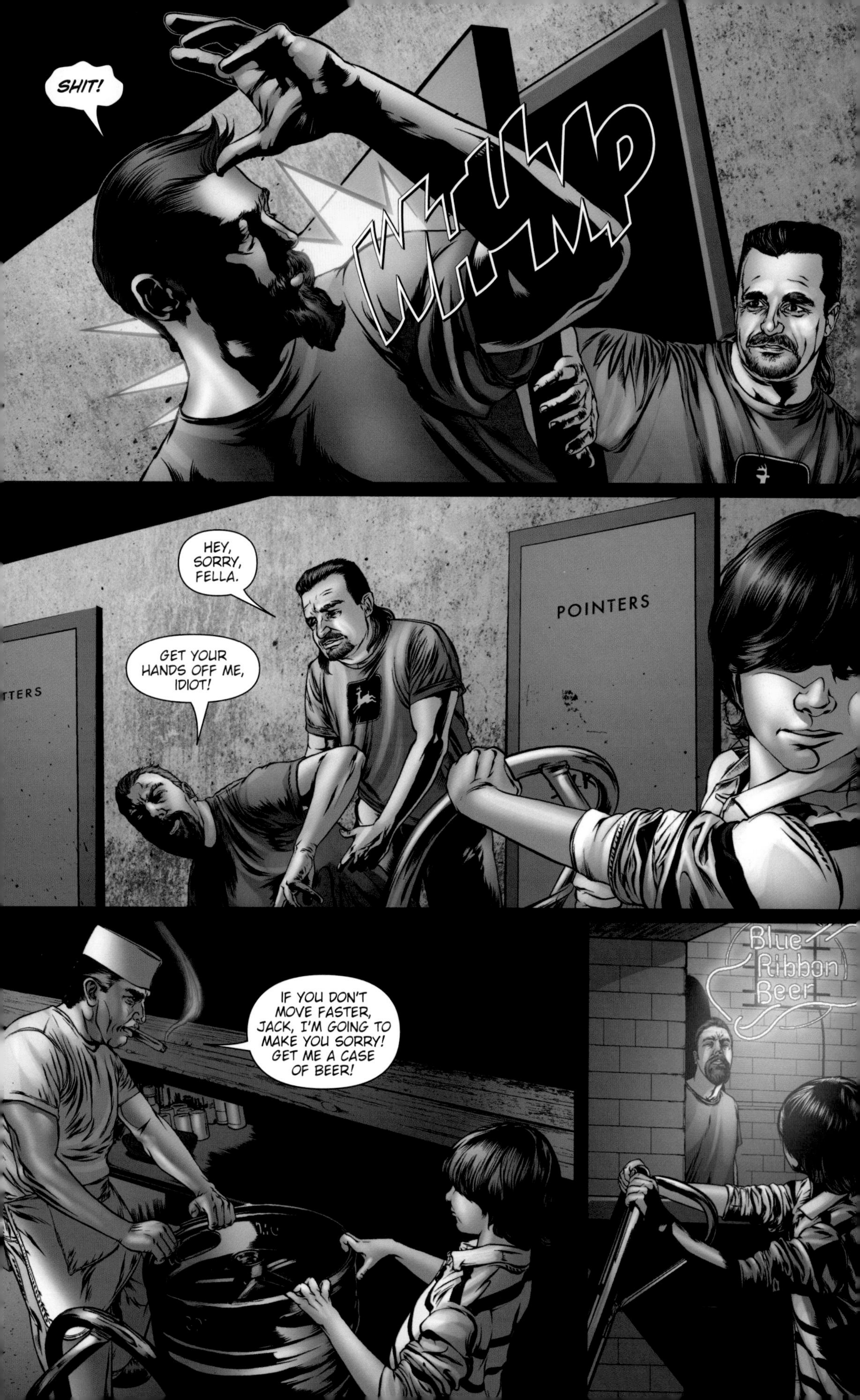
SHIT!
WHUMP
HEY, SORRY, FELLA.
GET YOUR HANDS OFF ME, IDIOT!
POINTERS
IF YOU DON'T MOVE FASTER, JACK, I'M GOING TO MAKE YOU SORRY! GET ME A CASE OF BEER!
Blue Ribbon Beer

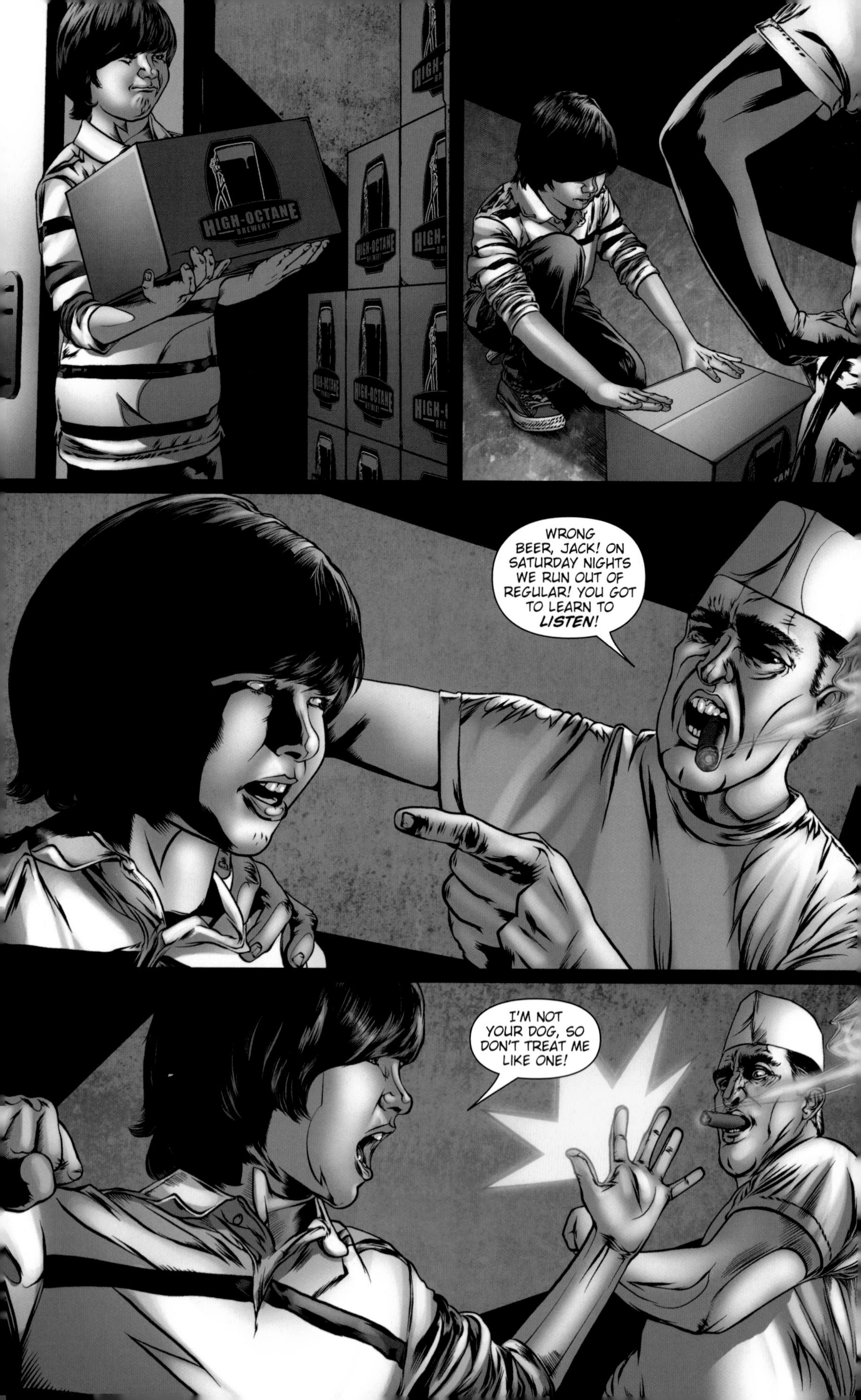
HIGH-OCTANE BREWERY
WRONG BEER, JACK! ON SATURDAY NIGHTS WE RUN OUT OF REGULAR! YOU GOT TO LEARN TO LISTEN!
I'M NOT YOUR DOG, SO DON'T TREAT ME LIKE ONE!

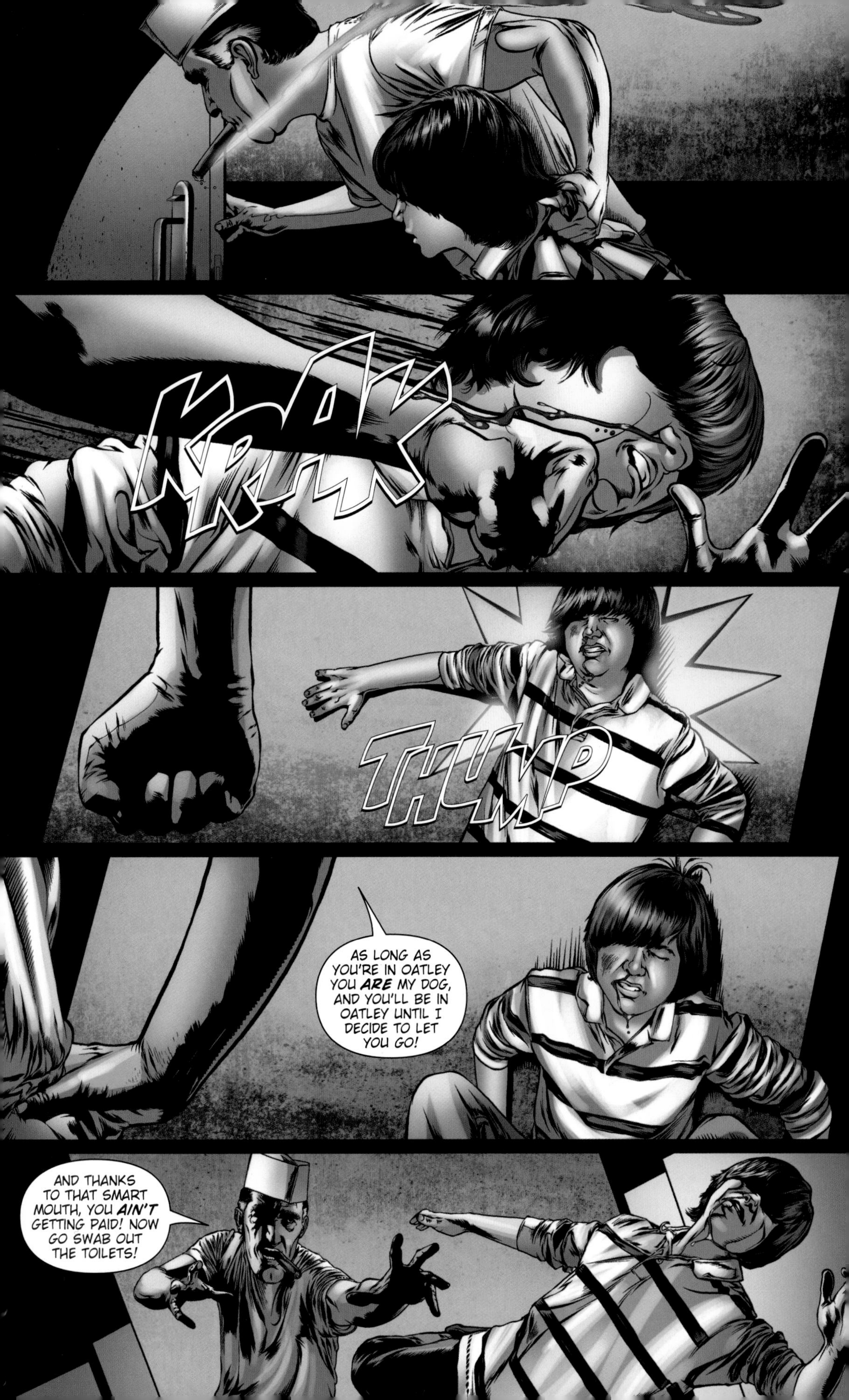
KRAK
THUMP
AS LONG AS YOU'RE IN OATLEY YOU ARE MY DOG, AND YOU'LL BE IN OATLEY UNTIL I DECIDE TO LET YOU GO!
AND THANKS TO THAT SMART MOUTH, YOU AIN'T GETTING PAID! NOW GO SWAB OUT THE TOILETS!

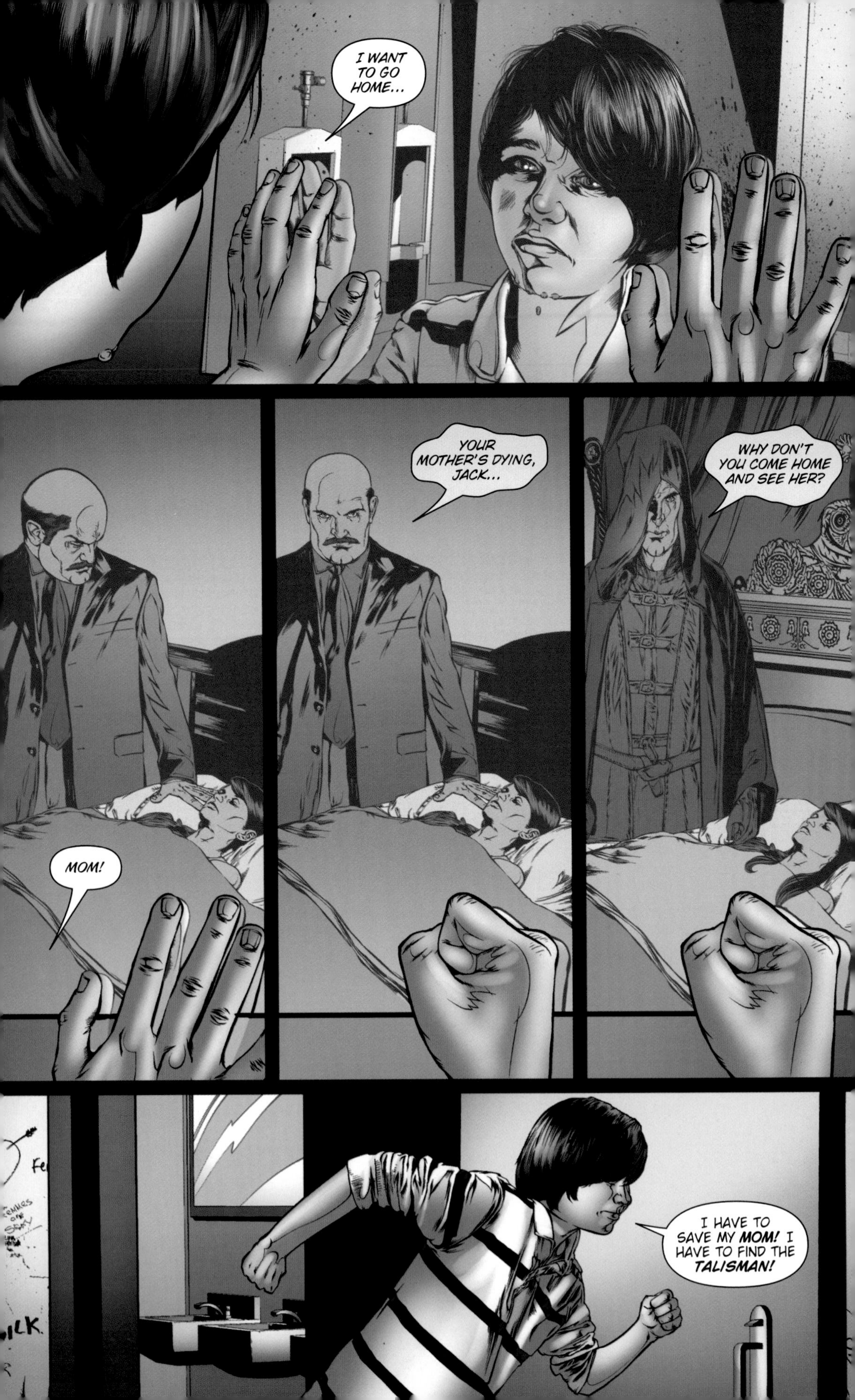

I WANT TO GO HOME...
YOUR MOTHER'S DYING, JACK...
WHY DON'T YOU COME HOME AND SEE HER?
MOM!
I HAVE TO SAVE MY **MOM!** I HAVE TO FIND THE ***TALISMAN!***

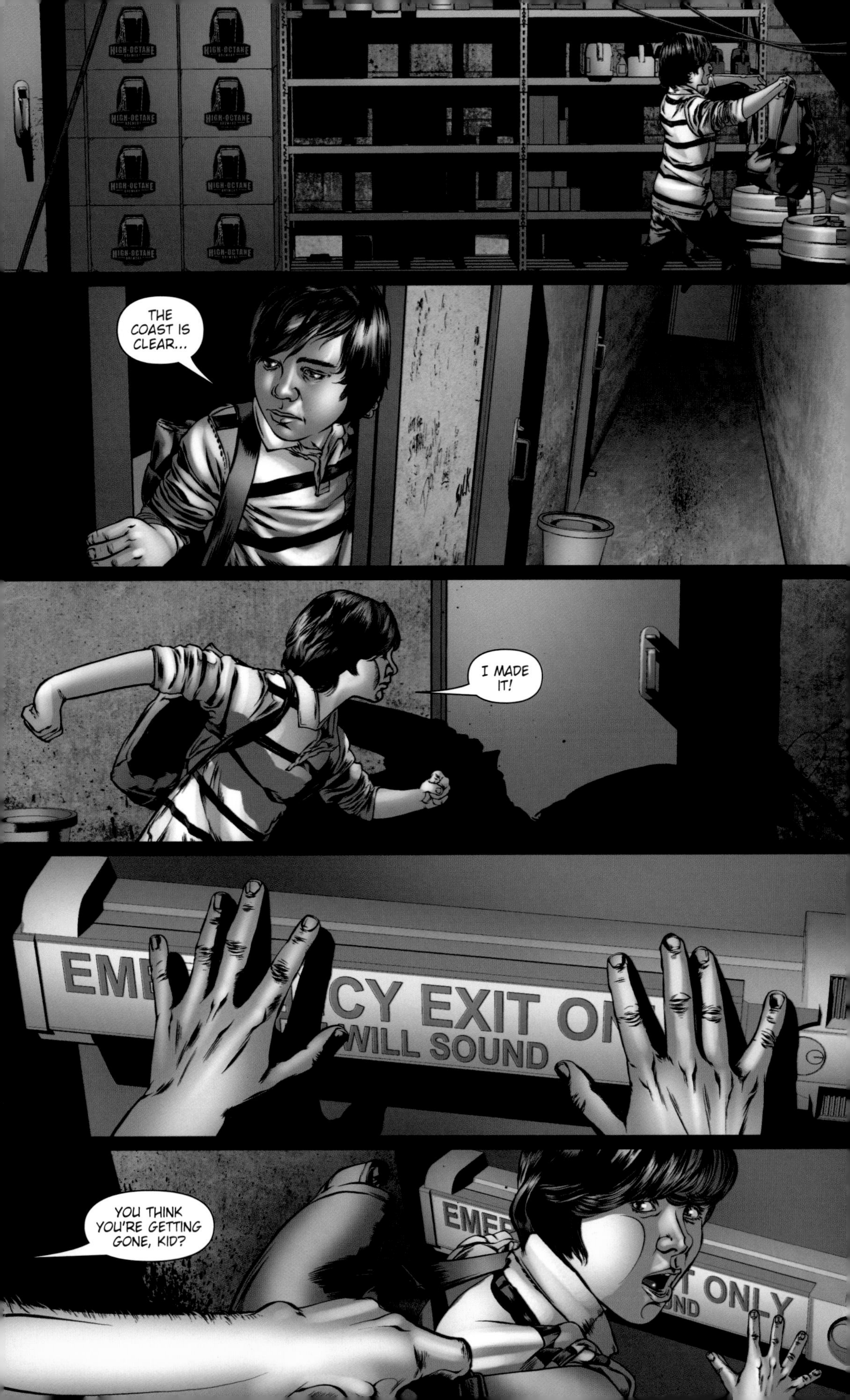
THE COAST IS CLEAR...
I MADE IT!
YOU THINK YOU'RE GETTING GONE, KID?

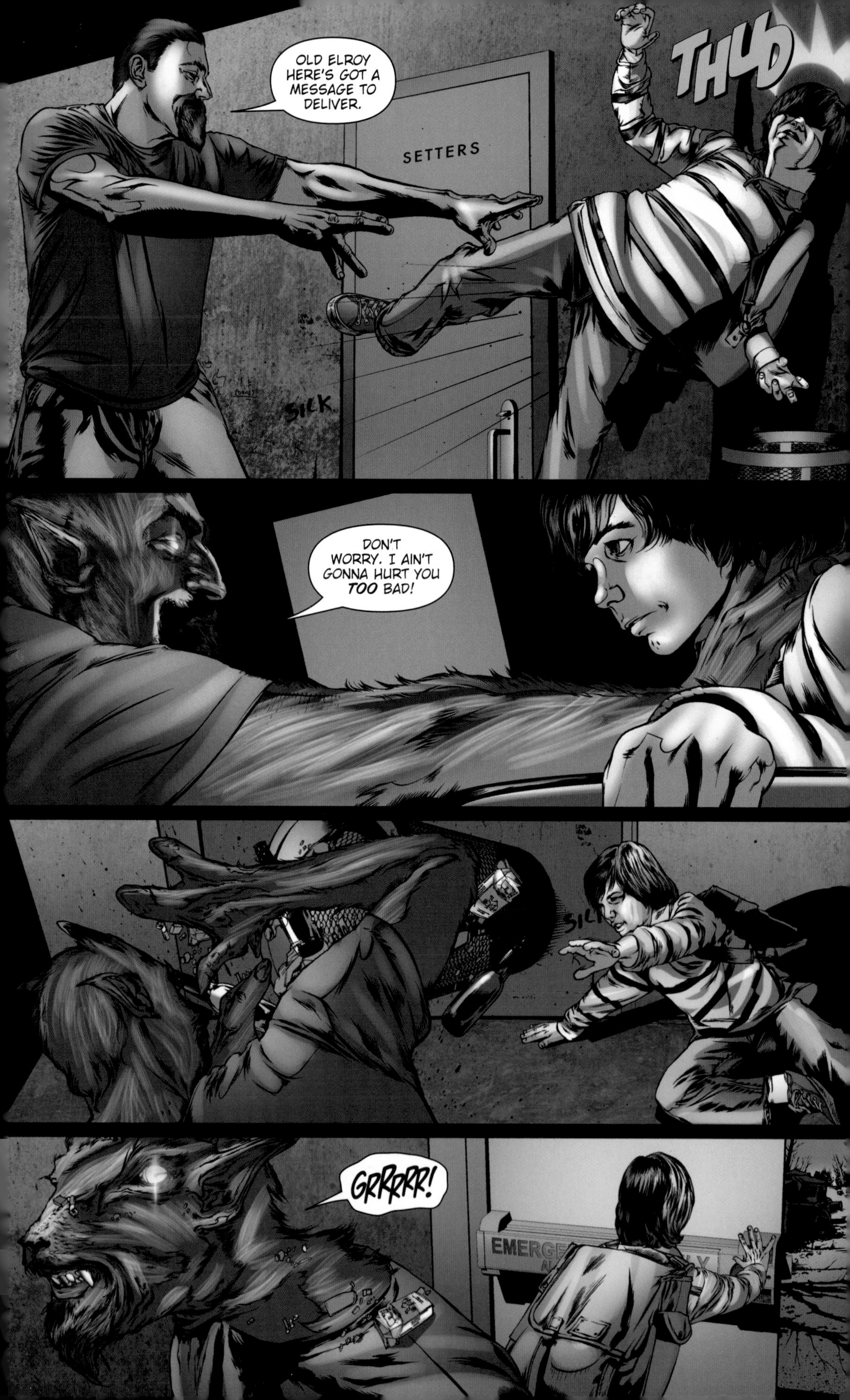
OLD ELROY HERE'S GOT A MESSAGE TO DELIVER.
THUD
SETTERS
SICK
DON'T WORRY. I AIN'T GONNA HURT YOU *TOO* BAD!
GRRRRR!

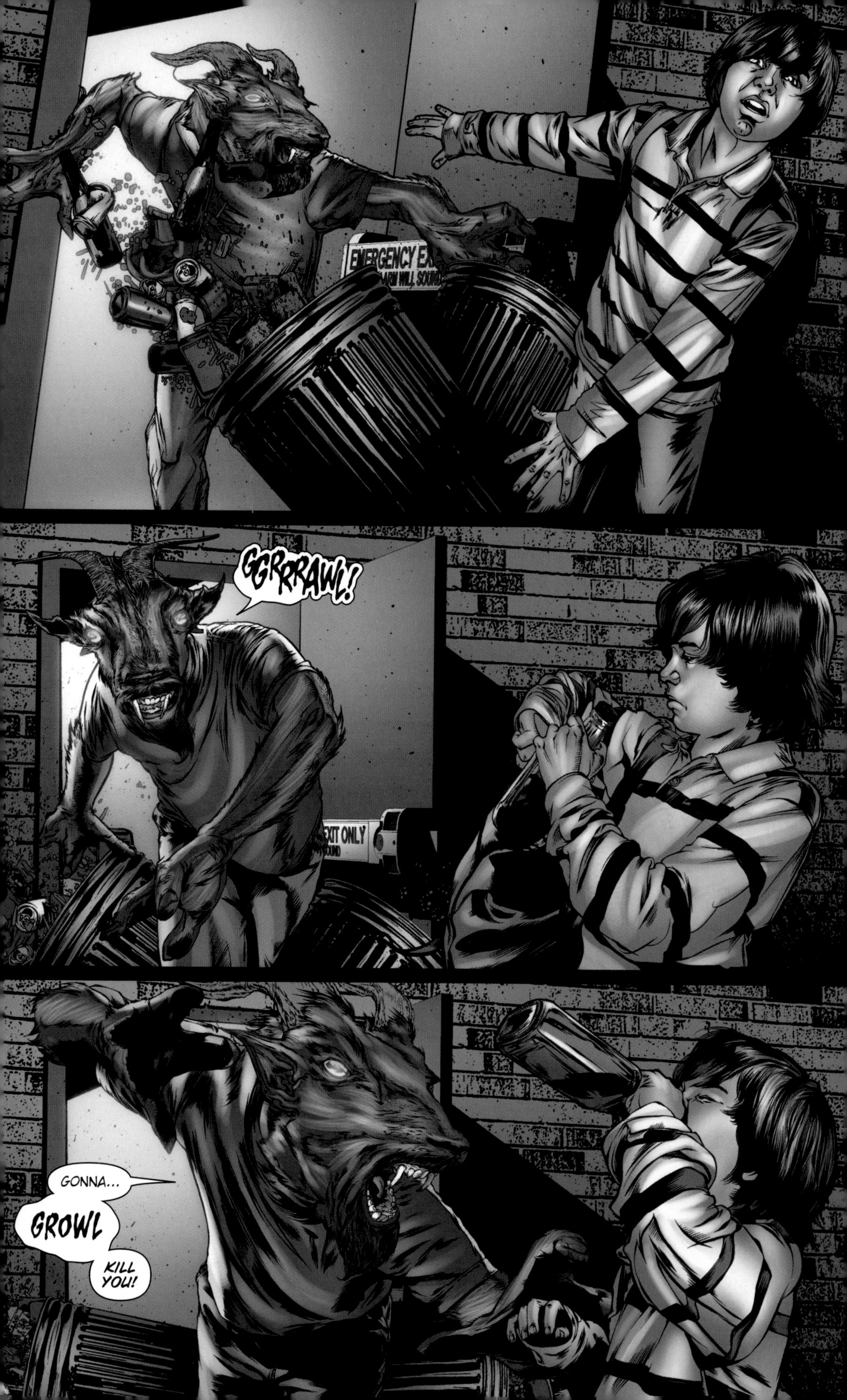
EMERGENCY EX
GGRRRAWL!
EXIT ONLY
GONNA...
GROWL
KILL YOU!

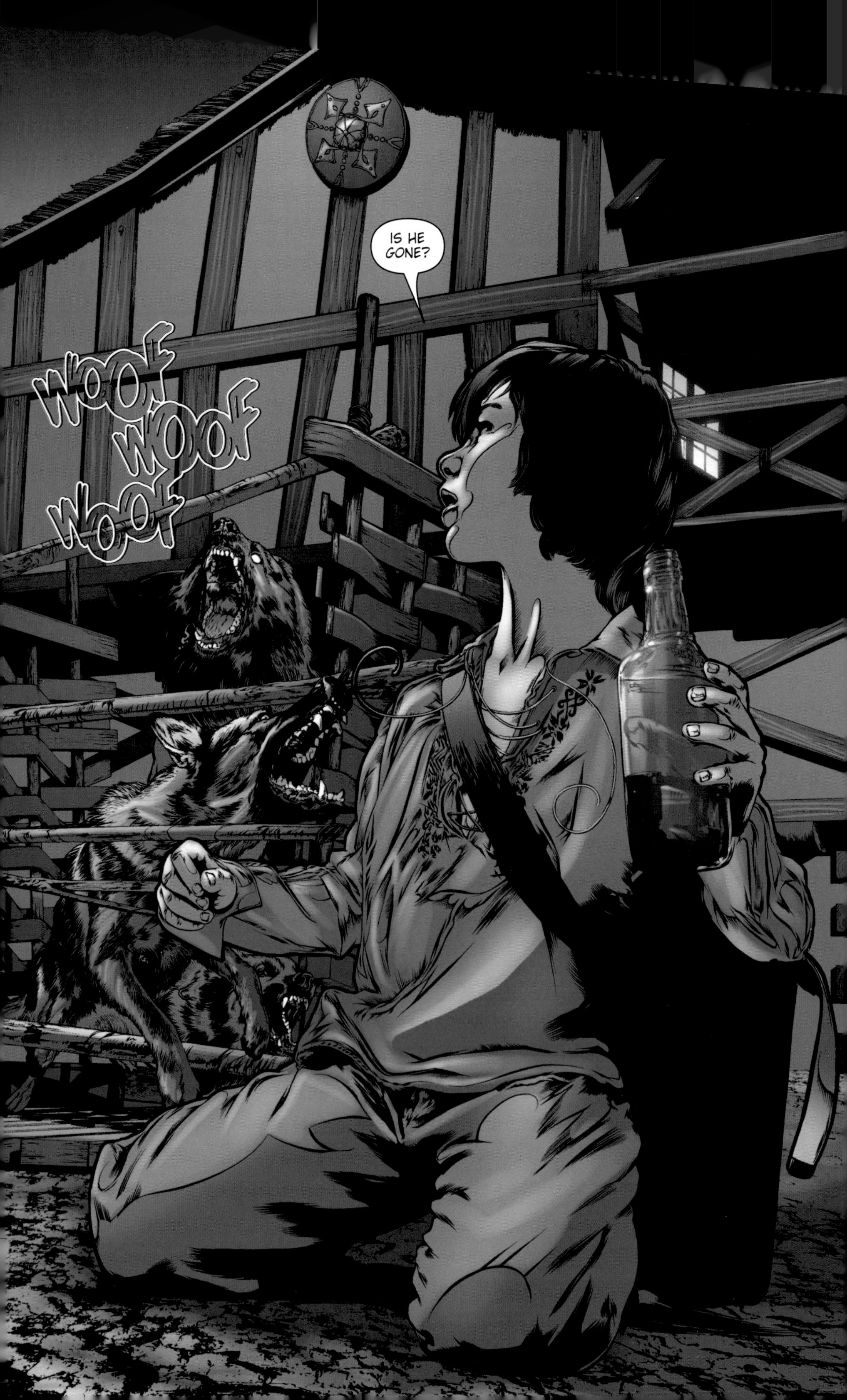
IS HE GONE?
WOOF WOOF WOOF

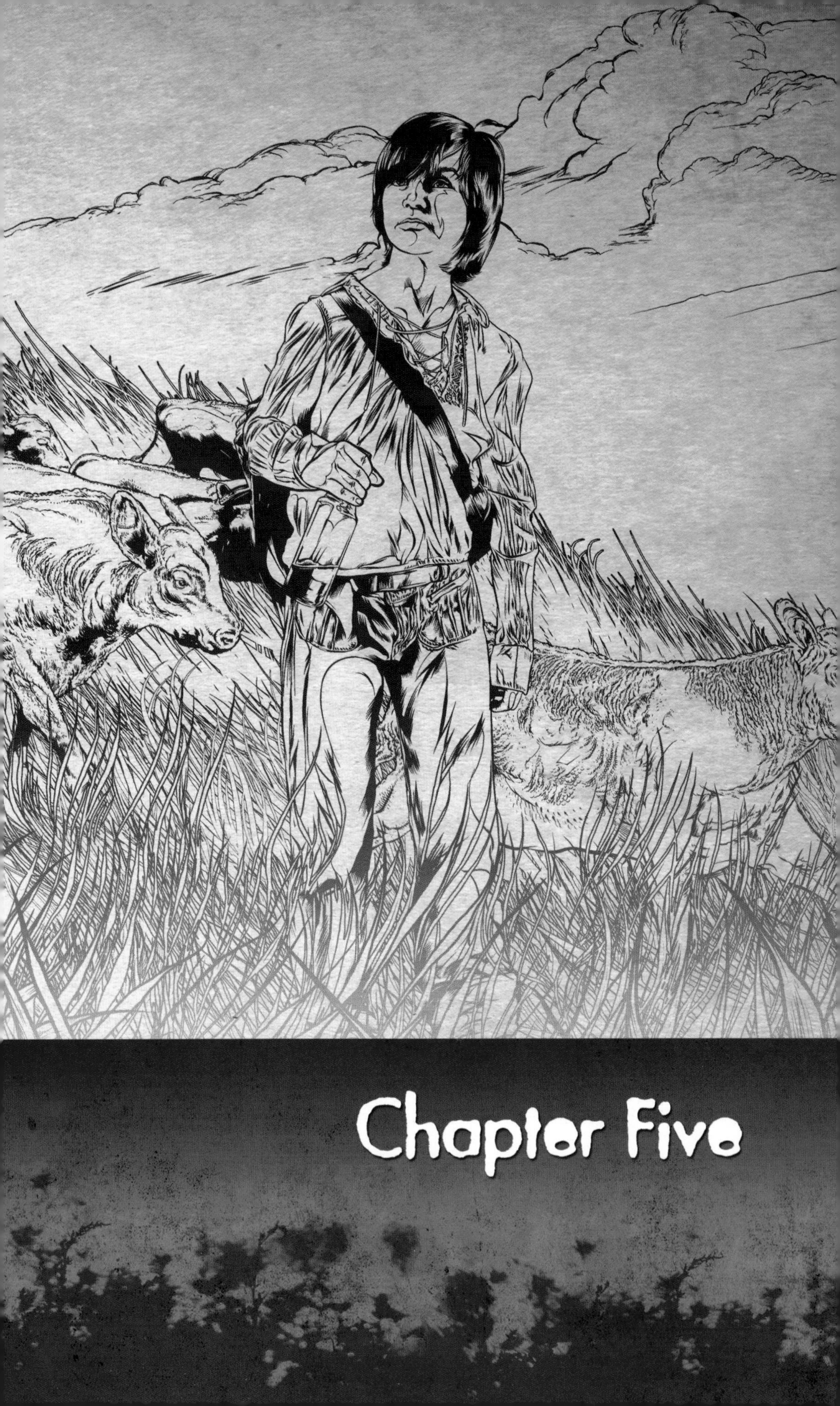

Chapter Five

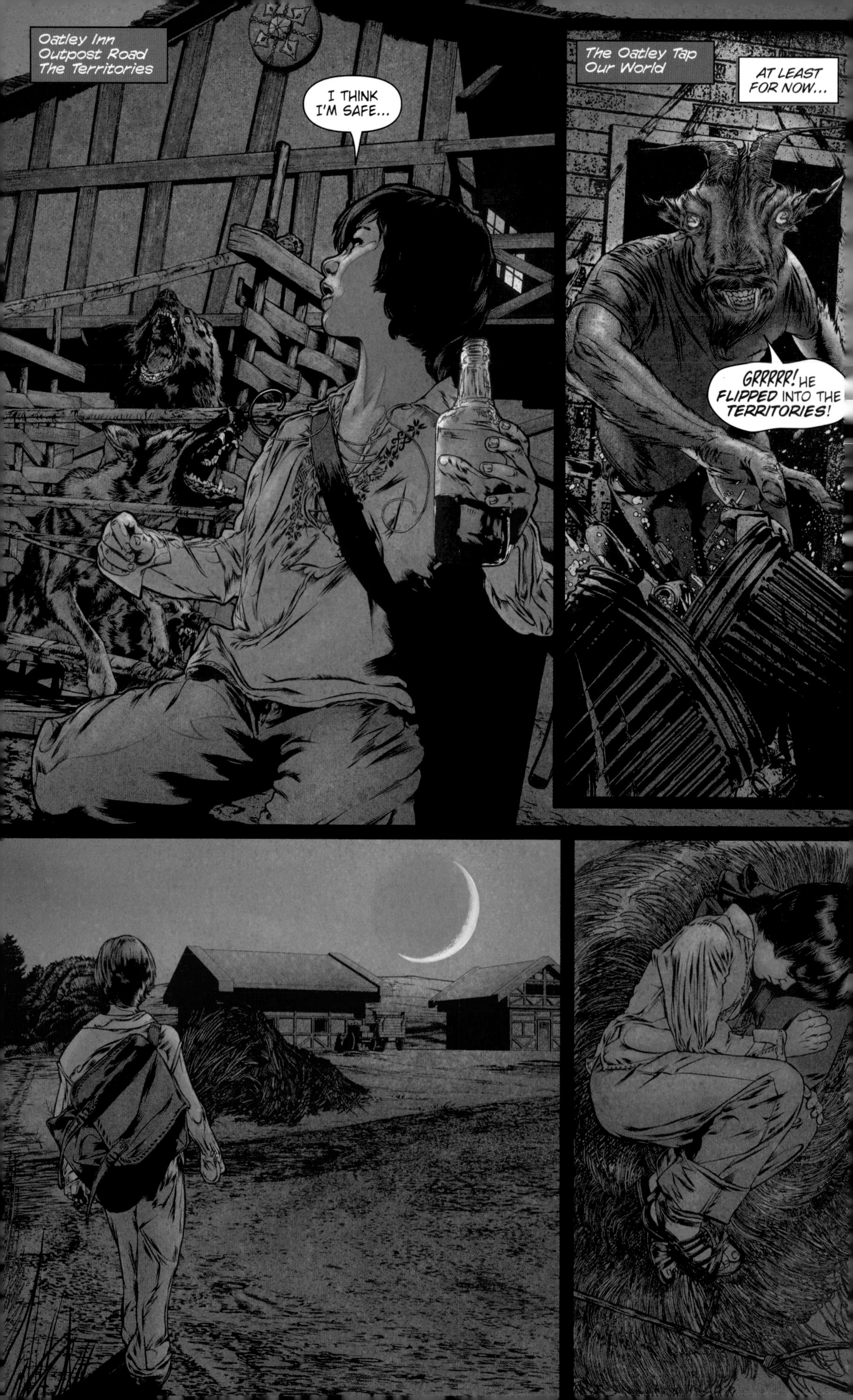
Oatley Inn
Outpost Road
The Territories
I THINK I'M SAFE...
The Oatley Tap
Our World
AT LEAST FOR NOW...
GRRRRR! HE FLIPPED INTO THE TERRITORIES!

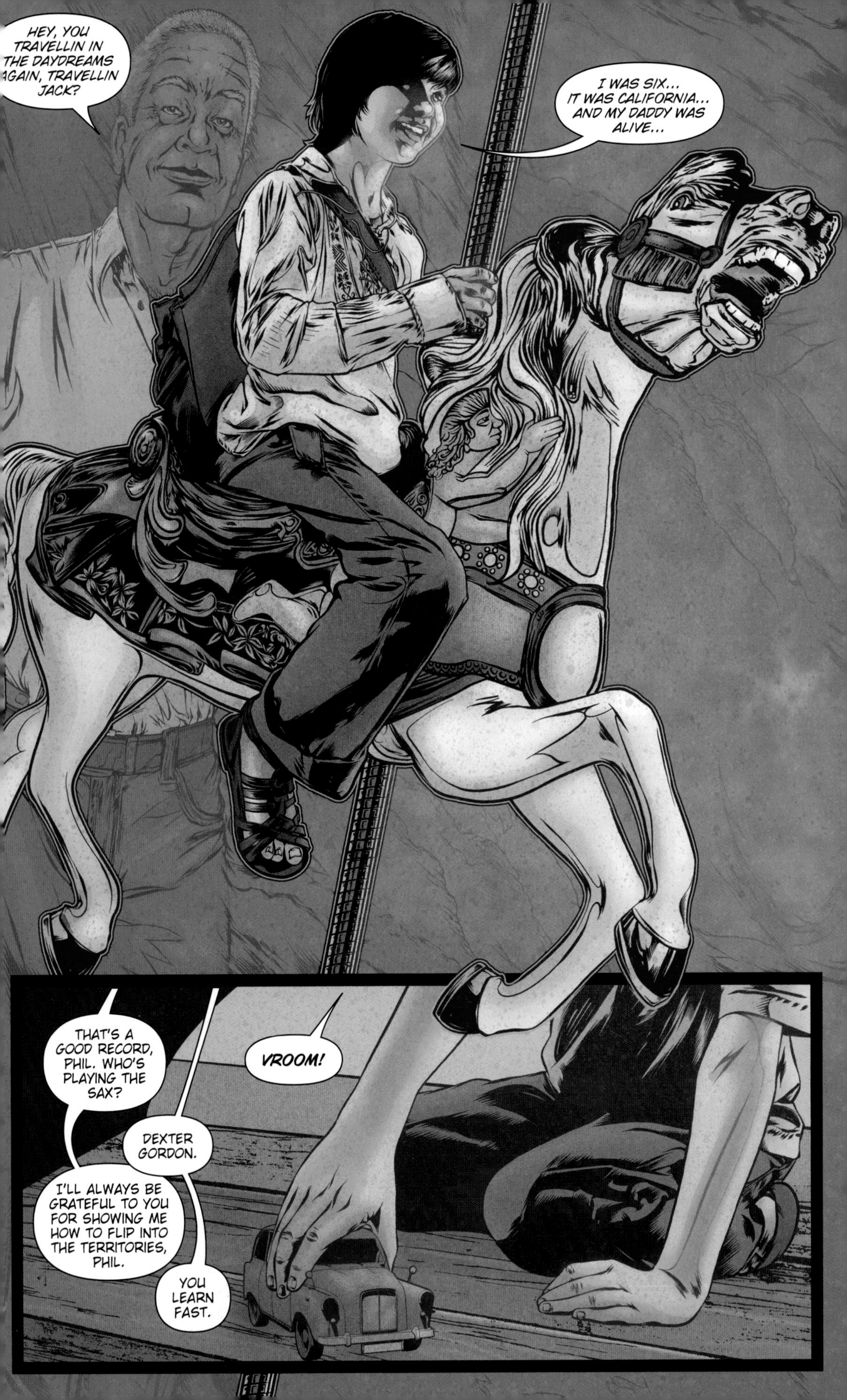
HEY, YOU TRAVELLIN IN THE DAYDREAMS AGAIN, TRAVELLIN JACK?
I WAS SIX... IT WAS CALIFORNIA... AND MY DADDY WAS ALIVE...
THAT'S A GOOD RECORD, PHIL. WHO'S PLAYING THE SAX?
VROOM!
DEXTER GORDON.
I'LL ALWAYS BE GRATEFUL TO YOU FOR SHOWING ME HOW TO FLIP INTO THE TERRITORIES, PHIL.
YOU LEARN FAST.

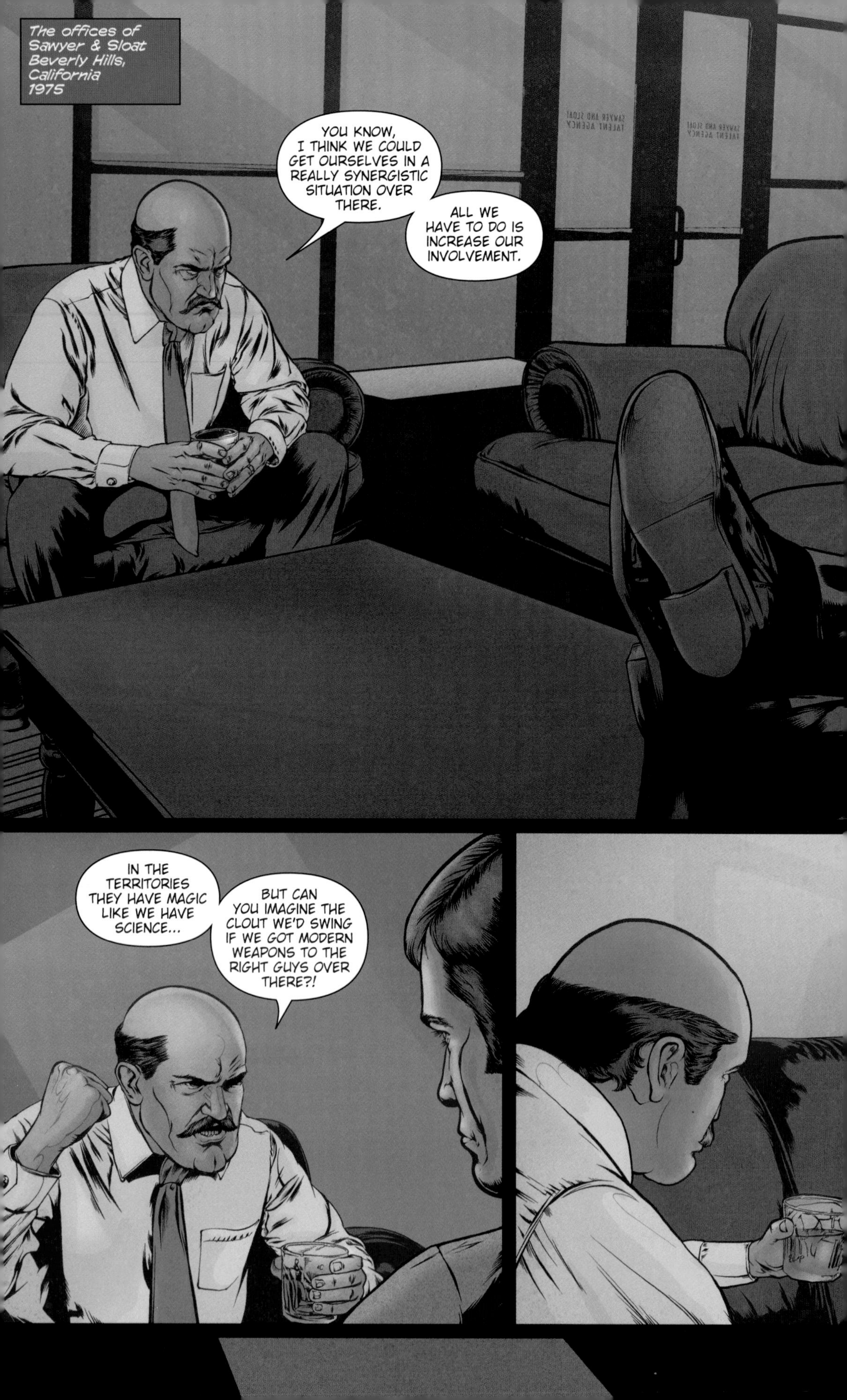
The offices of Sawyer & Sloat Beverly Hills, California 1975
YOU KNOW, I THINK WE COULD GET OURSELVES IN A REALLY SYNERGISTIC SITUATION OVER THERE.
ALL WE HAVE TO DO IS INCREASE OUR INVOLVEMENT.
IN THE TERRITORIES THEY HAVE MAGIC LIKE WE HAVE SCIENCE...
BUT CAN YOU IMAGINE THE CLOUT WE'D SWING IF WE GOT MODERN WEAPONS TO THE RIGHT GUYS OVER THERE?!

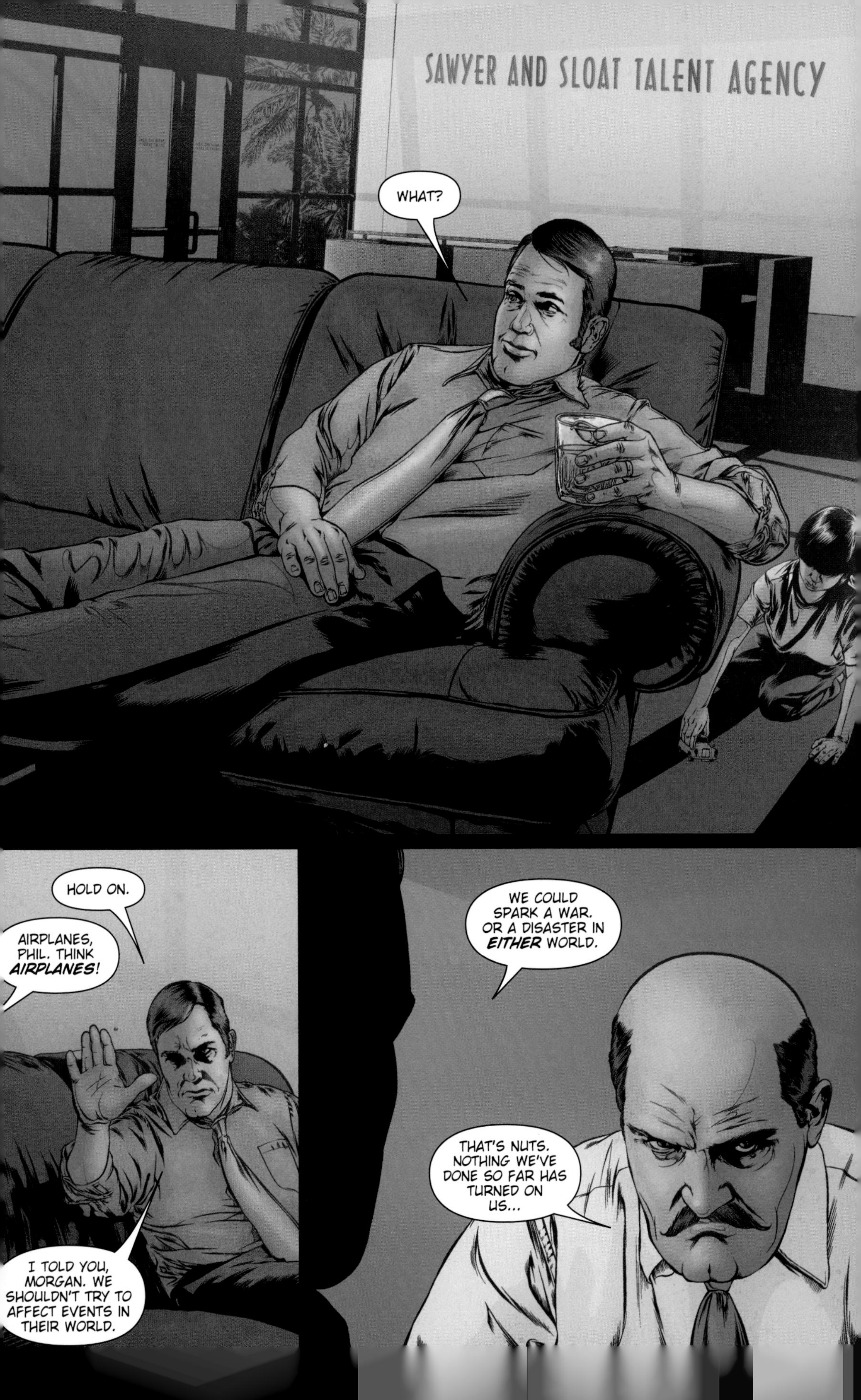
SAWYER AND SLOAT TALENT AGENCY
WHAT?
HOLD ON.
AIRPLANES, PHIL. THINK *AIRPLANES*!
I TOLD YOU, MORGAN. WE SHOULDN'T TRY TO AFFECT EVENTS IN THEIR WORLD.
WE COULD SPARK A WAR. OR A DISASTER IN *EITHER* WORLD.
THAT'S NUTS. NOTHING WE'VE DONE SO FAR HAS TURNED ON US...

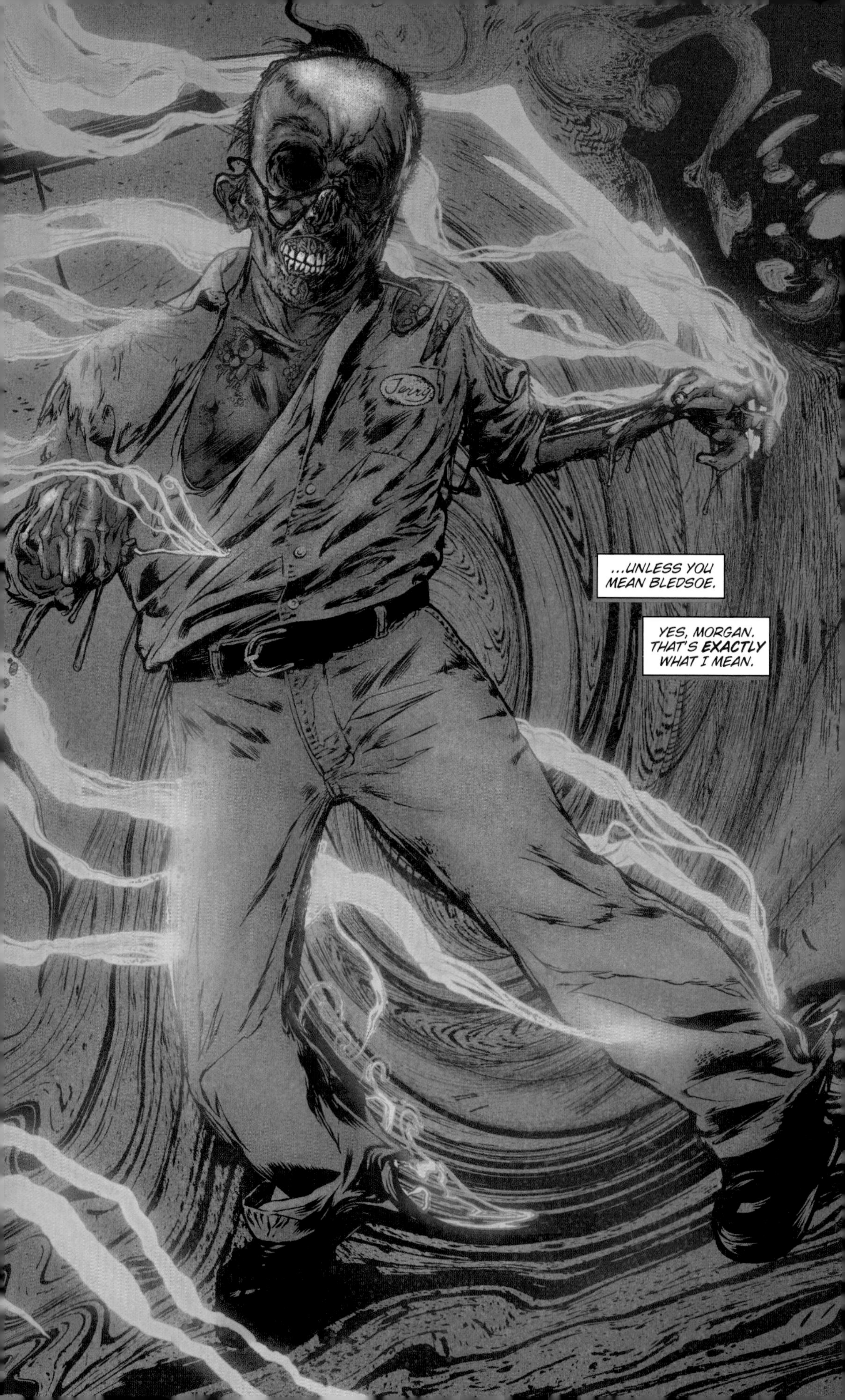
Jerry
...UNLESS YOU MEAN BLEDSOE.
YES, MORGAN. THAT'S **EXACTLY** WHAT I MEAN.

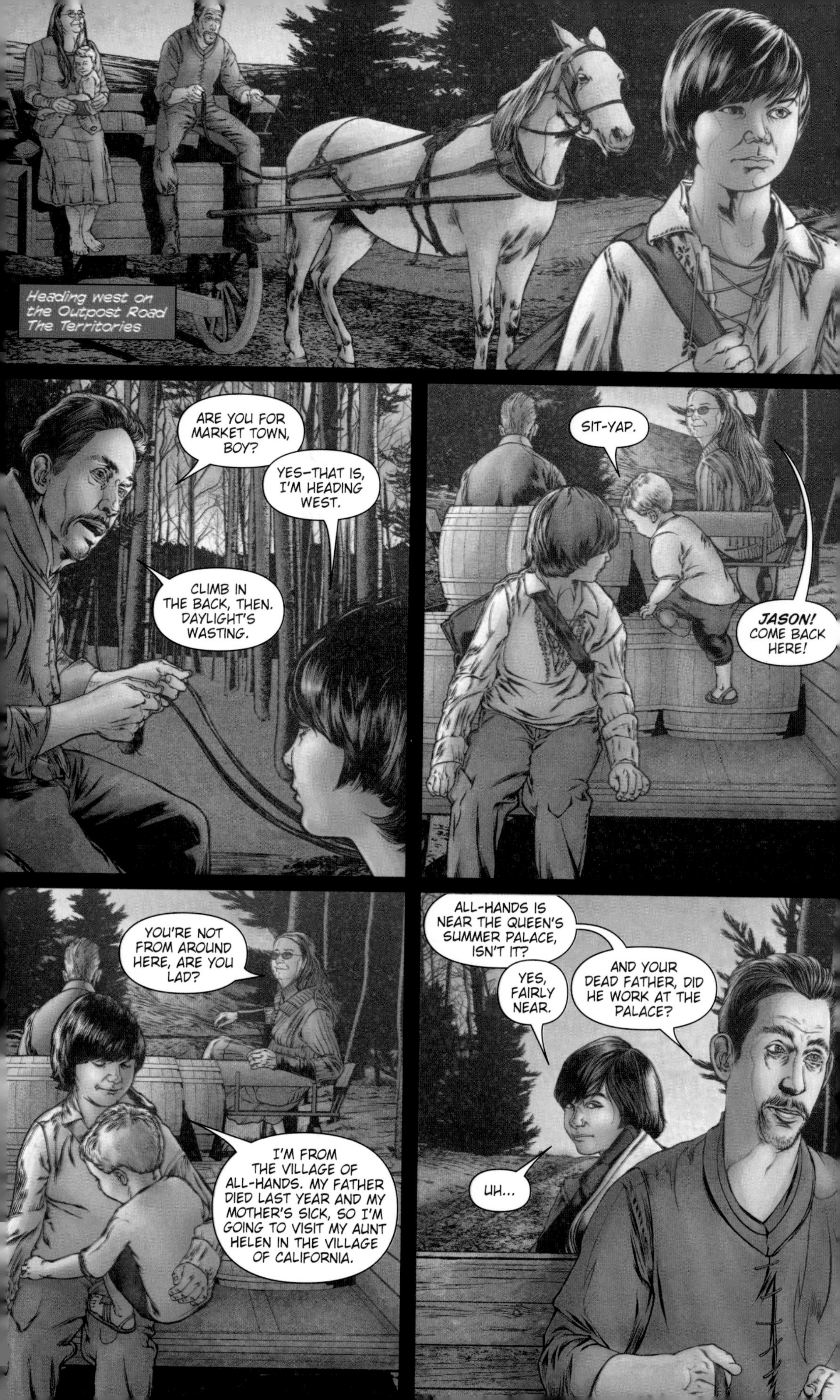

Heading west on the Outpost Road The Territories
ARE YOU FOR MARKET TOWN, BOY?
YES—THAT IS, I'M HEADING WEST.
CLIMB IN THE BACK, THEN. DAYLIGHT'S WASTING.
SIT-YAP.
JASON! COME BACK HERE!
YOU'RE NOT FROM AROUND HERE, ARE YOU LAD?
I'M FROM THE VILLAGE OF ALL-HANDS. MY FATHER DIED LAST YEAR AND MY MOTHER'S SICK, SO I'M GOING TO VISIT MY AUNT HELEN IN THE VILLAGE OF CALIFORNIA.
ALL-HANDS IS NEAR THE QUEEN'S SUMMER PALACE, ISN'T IT?
YES, FAIRLY NEAR.
AND YOUR DEAD FATHER, DID HE WORK AT THE PALACE?
UH...

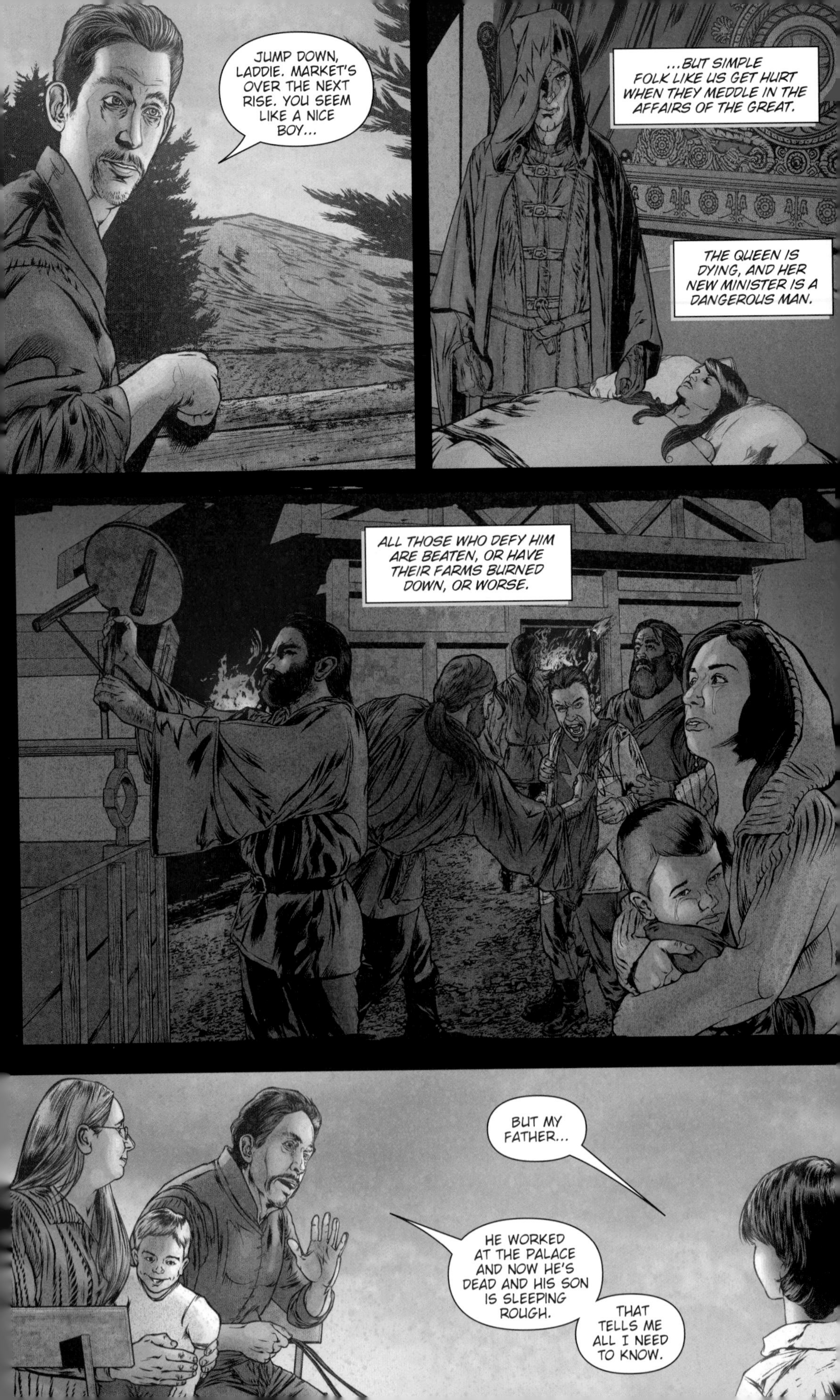
JUMP DOWN, LADDIE. MARKET'S OVER THE NEXT RISE. YOU SEEM LIKE A NICE BOY...
...BUT SIMPLE FOLK LIKE US GET HURT WHEN THEY MEDDLE IN THE AFFAIRS OF THE GREAT.
THE QUEEN IS DYING, AND HER NEW MINISTER IS A DANGEROUS MAN.
ALL THOSE WHO DEFY HIM ARE BEATEN, OR HAVE THEIR FARMS BURNED DOWN, OR WORSE.
BUT MY FATHER...
HE WORKED AT THE PALACE AND NOW HE'S DEAD AND HIS SON IS SLEEPING ROUGH.
THAT TELLS ME ALL I NEED TO KNOW.

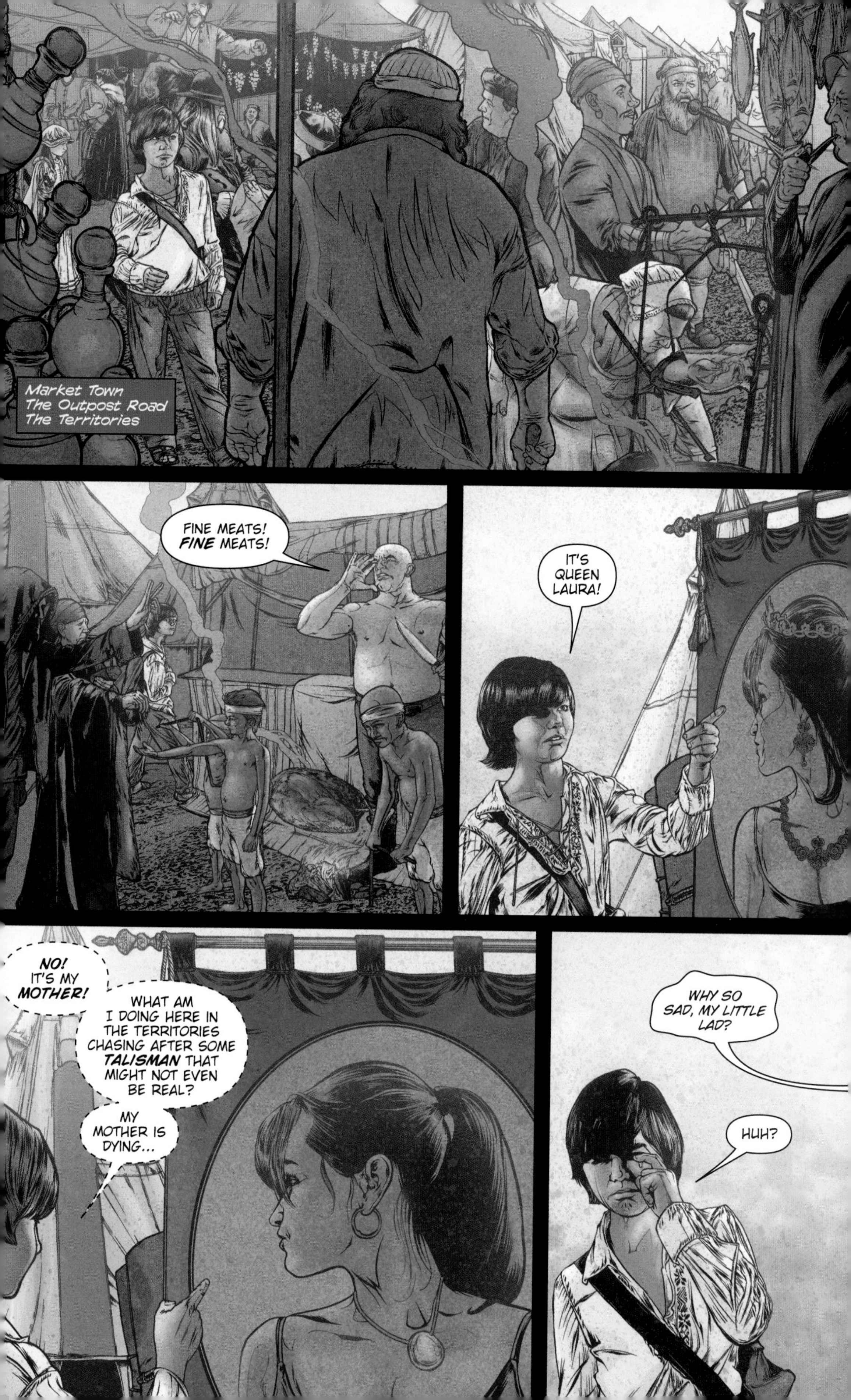
Market Town
The Outpost Road
The Territories
FINE MEATS! FINE MEATS!
IT'S QUEEN LAURA!
NO! IT'S MY MOTHER!
WHAT AM I DOING HERE IN THE TERRITORIES CHASING AFTER SOME TALISMAN THAT MIGHT NOT EVEN BE REAL?
MY MOTHER IS DYING...
WHY SO SAD, MY LITTLE LAD?
HUH?

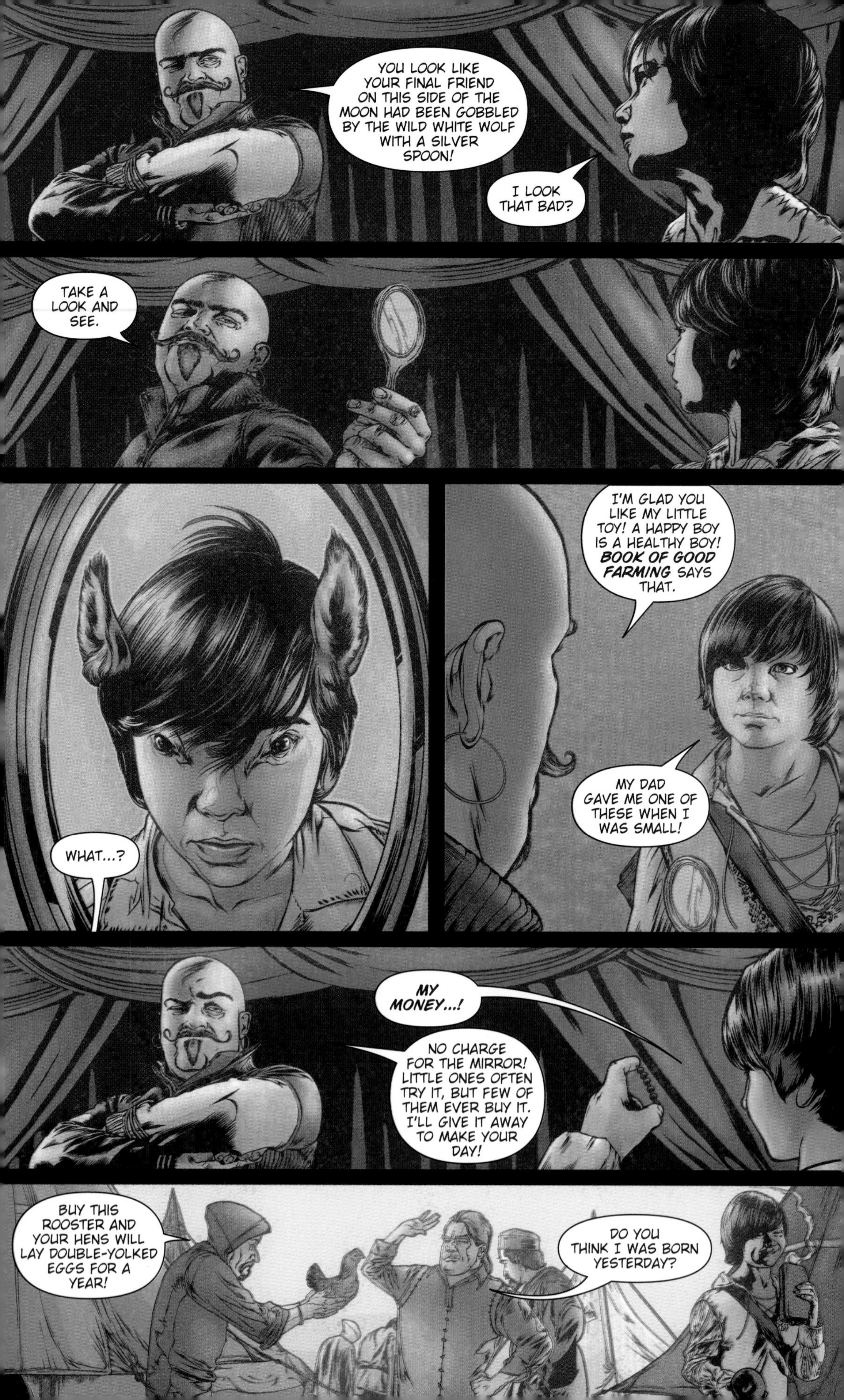

YOU LOOK LIKE YOUR FINAL FRIEND ON THIS SIDE OF THE MOON HAD BEEN GOBBLED BY THE WILD WHITE WOLF WITH A SILVER SPOON!
I LOOK THAT BAD?
TAKE A LOOK AND SEE.
WHAT...?
I'M GLAD YOU LIKE MY LITTLE TOY! A HAPPY BOY IS A HEALTHY BOY! **BOOK OF GOOD FARMING** SAYS THAT.
MY DAD GAVE ME ONE OF THESE WHEN I WAS SMALL!
MY MONEY...!
NO CHARGE FOR THE MIRROR! LITTLE ONES OFTEN TRY IT, BUT FEW OF THEM EVER BUY IT. I'LL GIVE IT AWAY TO MAKE YOUR DAY!
BUY THIS ROOSTER AND YOUR HENS WILL LAY DOUBLE-YOLKED EGGS FOR A YEAR!
DO YOU THINK I WAS BORN YESTERDAY?

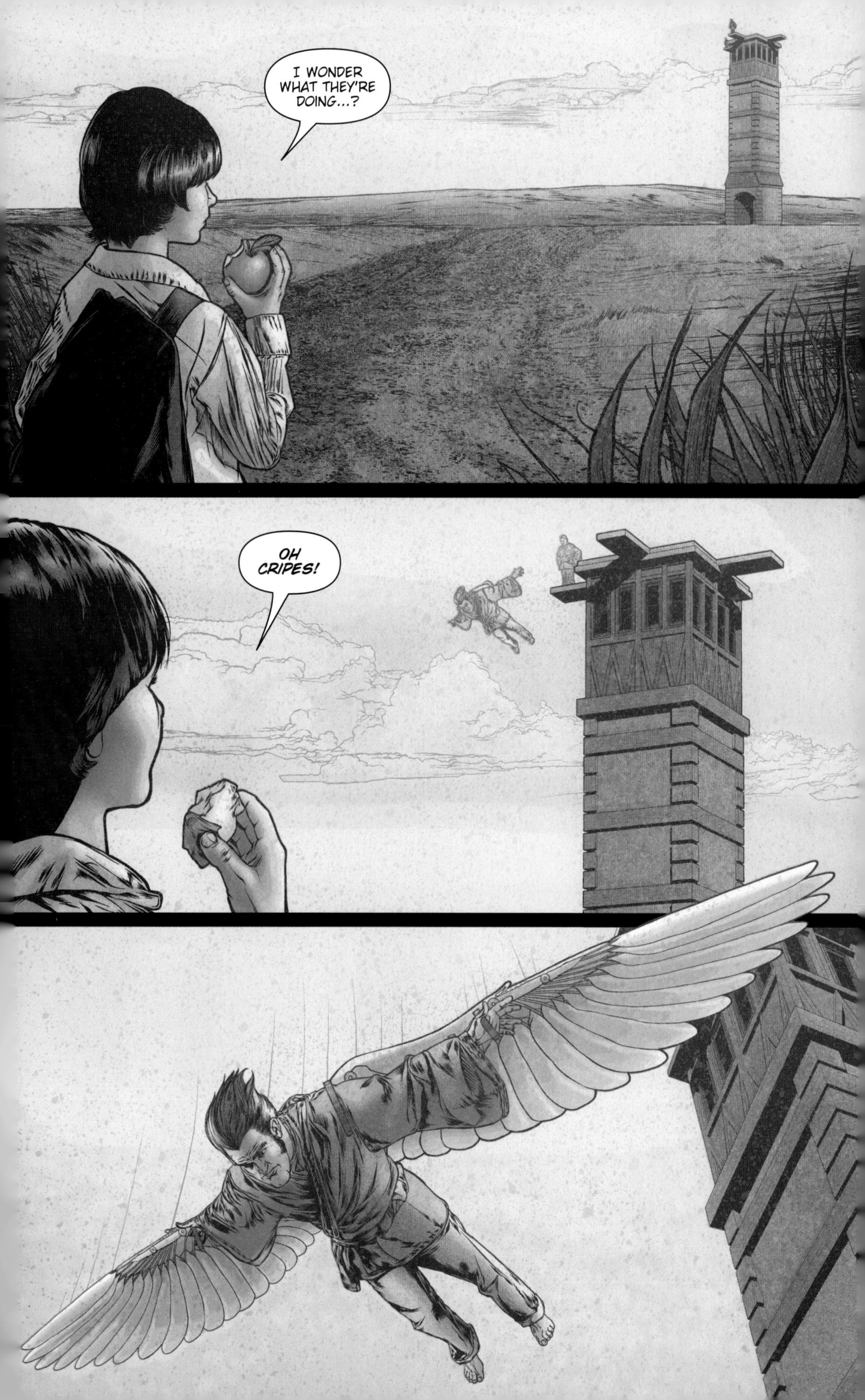
I WONDER WHAT THEY'RE DOING...?
OH CRIPES!

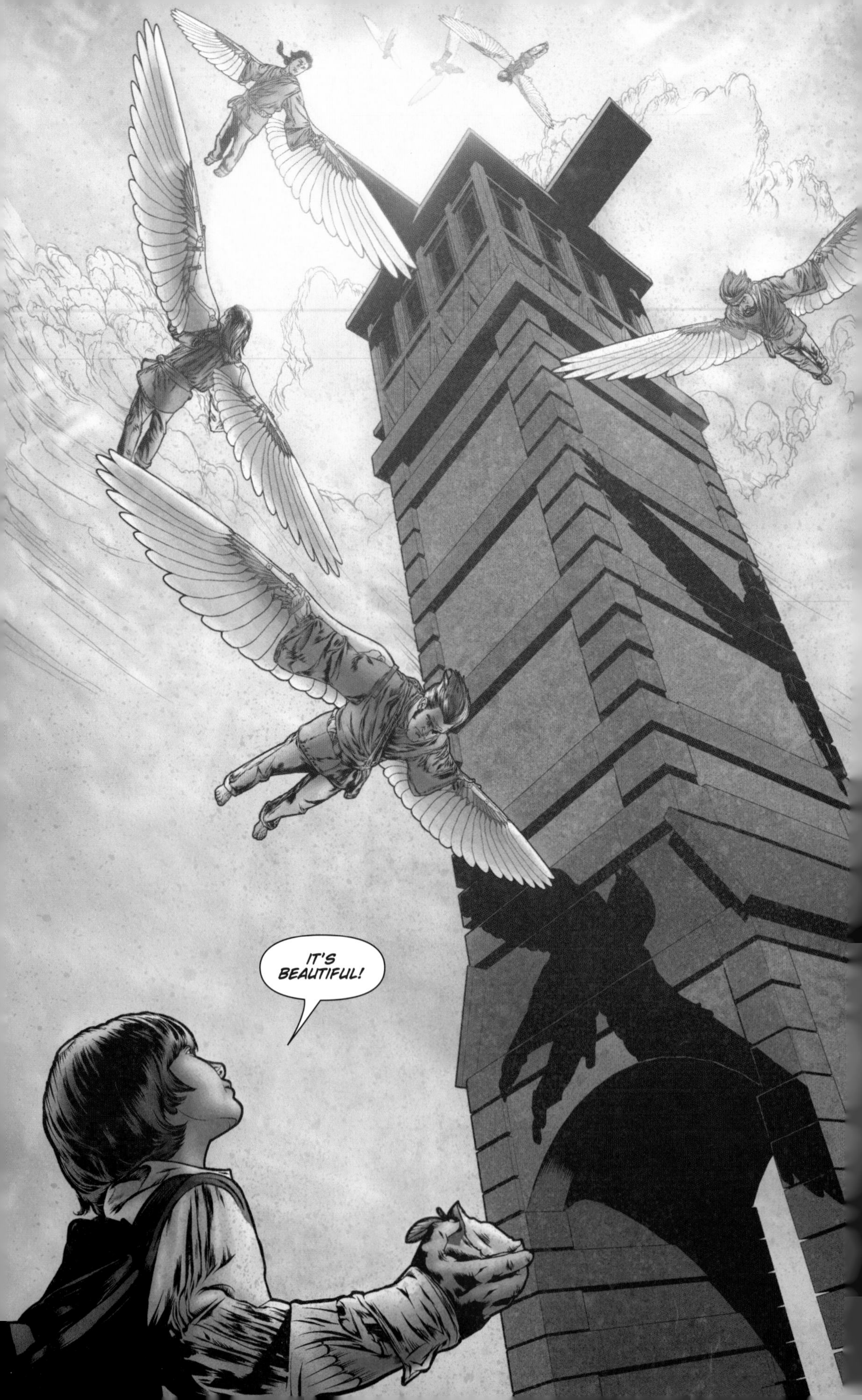
IT'S
BEAUTIFUL!

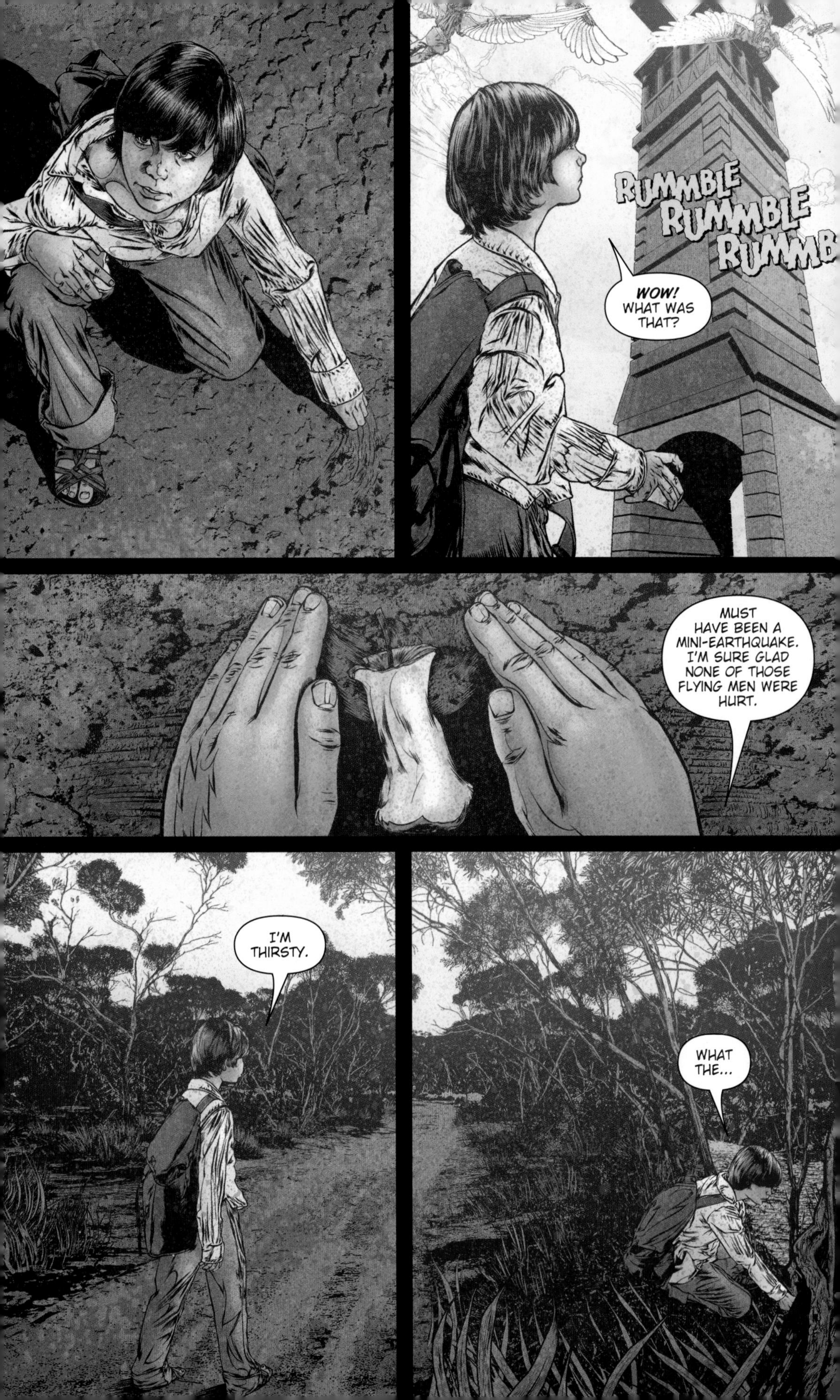
RUMMBLE RUMMBLE RUMMB
WOW! WHAT WAS THAT?
MUST HAVE BEEN A MINI-EARTHQUAKE. I'M SURE GLAD NONE OF THOSE FLYING MEN WERE HURT.
I'M THIRSTY.
WHAT THE...

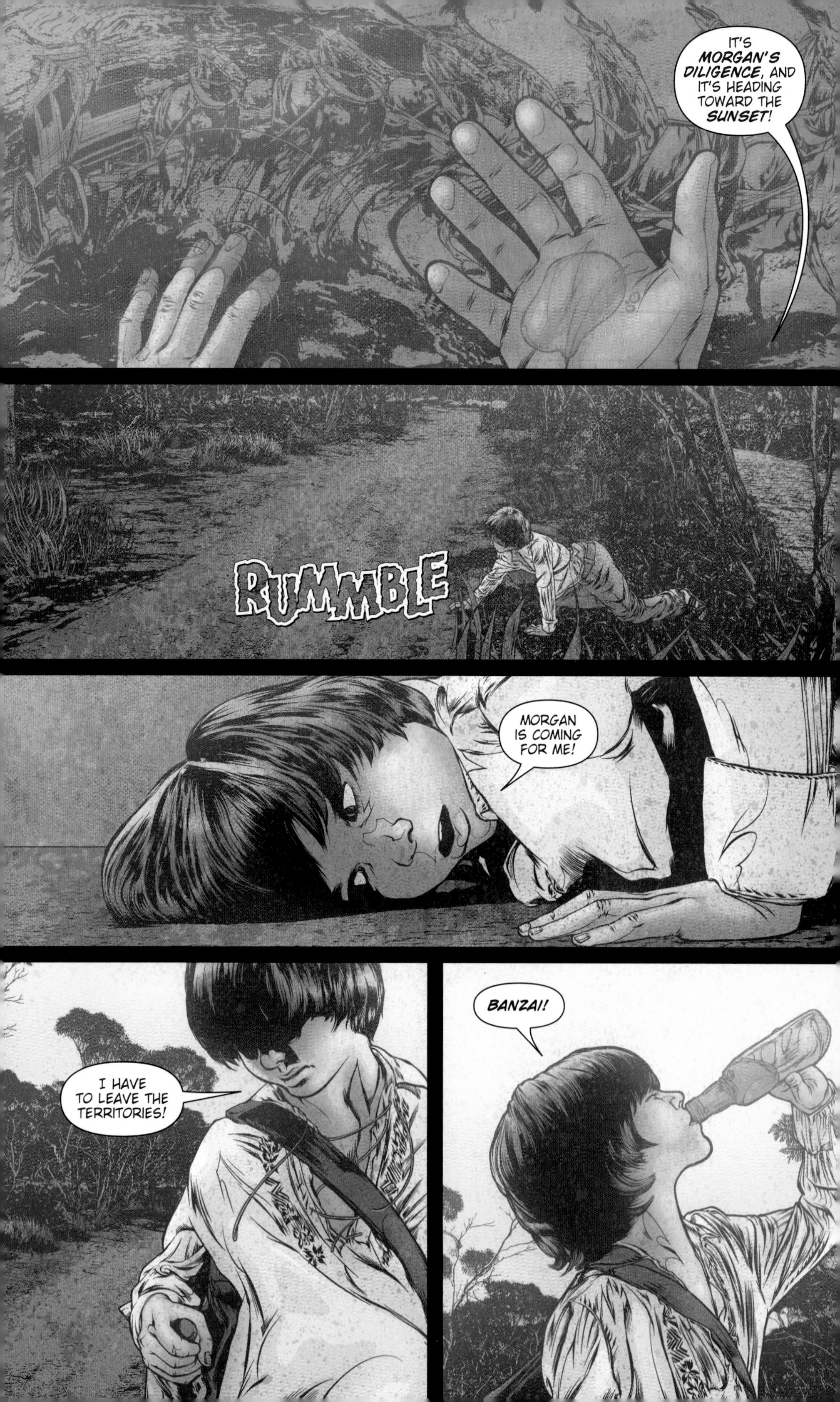
IT'S MORGAN'S DILIGENCE, AND IT'S HEADING TOWARD THE SUNSET!
RUMMBLE
MORGAN IS COMING FOR ME!
I HAVE TO LEAVE THE TERRITORIES!
BANZAI!

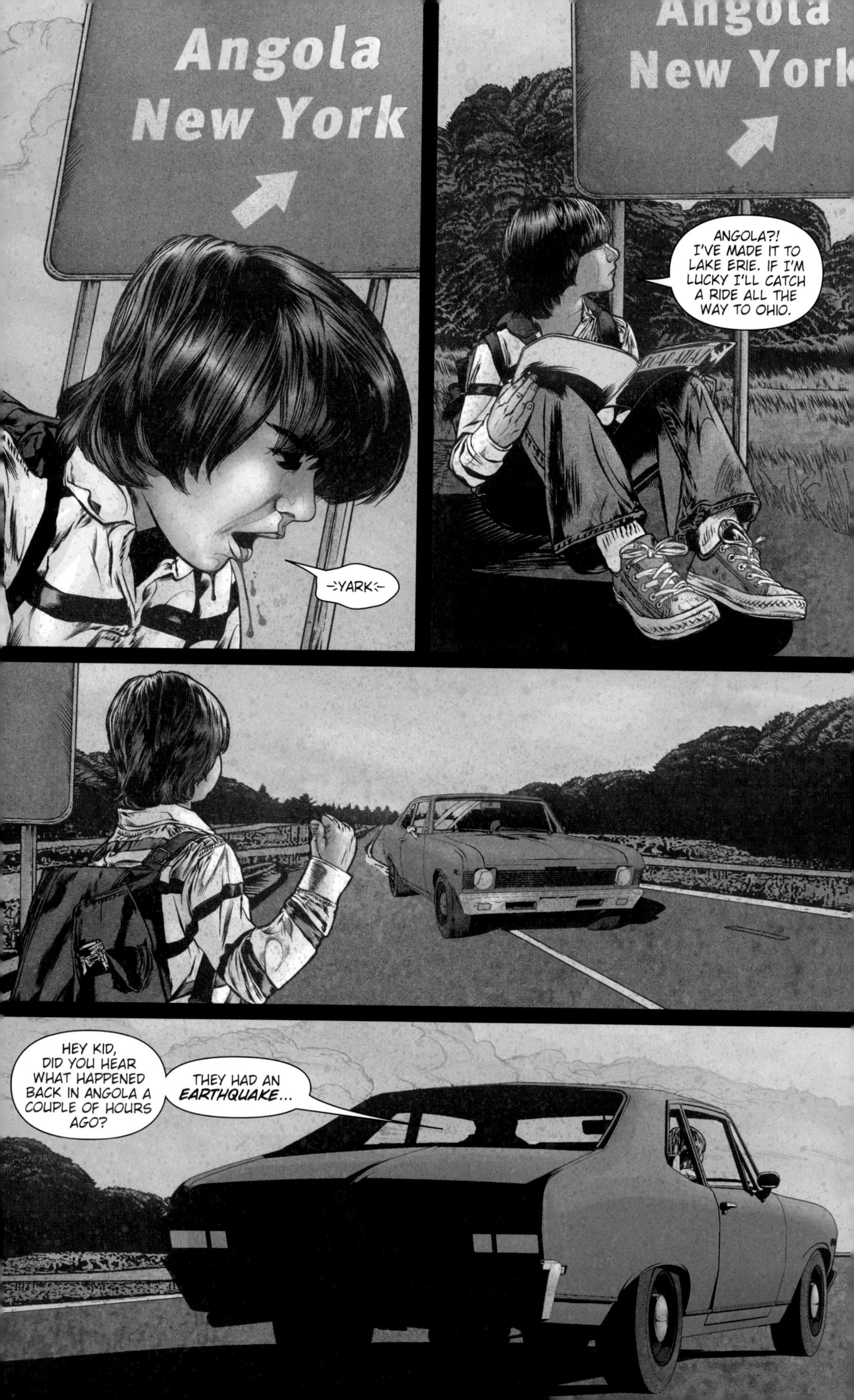
Angola
New York
-YARK-
Angola
New York
ANGOLA?! I'VE MADE IT TO LAKE ERIE. IF I'M LUCKY I'LL CATCH A RIDE ALL THE WAY TO OHIO.
HEY KID, DID YOU HEAR WHAT HAPPENED BACK IN ANGOLA A COUPLE OF HOURS AGO?
THEY HAD AN *EARTHQUAKE*...

Freak Earthquake Kills Five Workers

Work on the Rainbird Towers was tragically halted yesterday as an unprecedented earth tre
collapsed the structure of the building, burying many construction workers beneath the rub

as
cle
by
ter,
was
they
d my
. This
ed my
t years
ughter.
s on my
ppeared,
er back.

cle dated
12, 1982.

at they had
es and Don
as well. For
they were 36
harles Mercer
they were 56
Gary was an
rinder machine
ifications were
ject an image of
ns qualified and
e for accident.

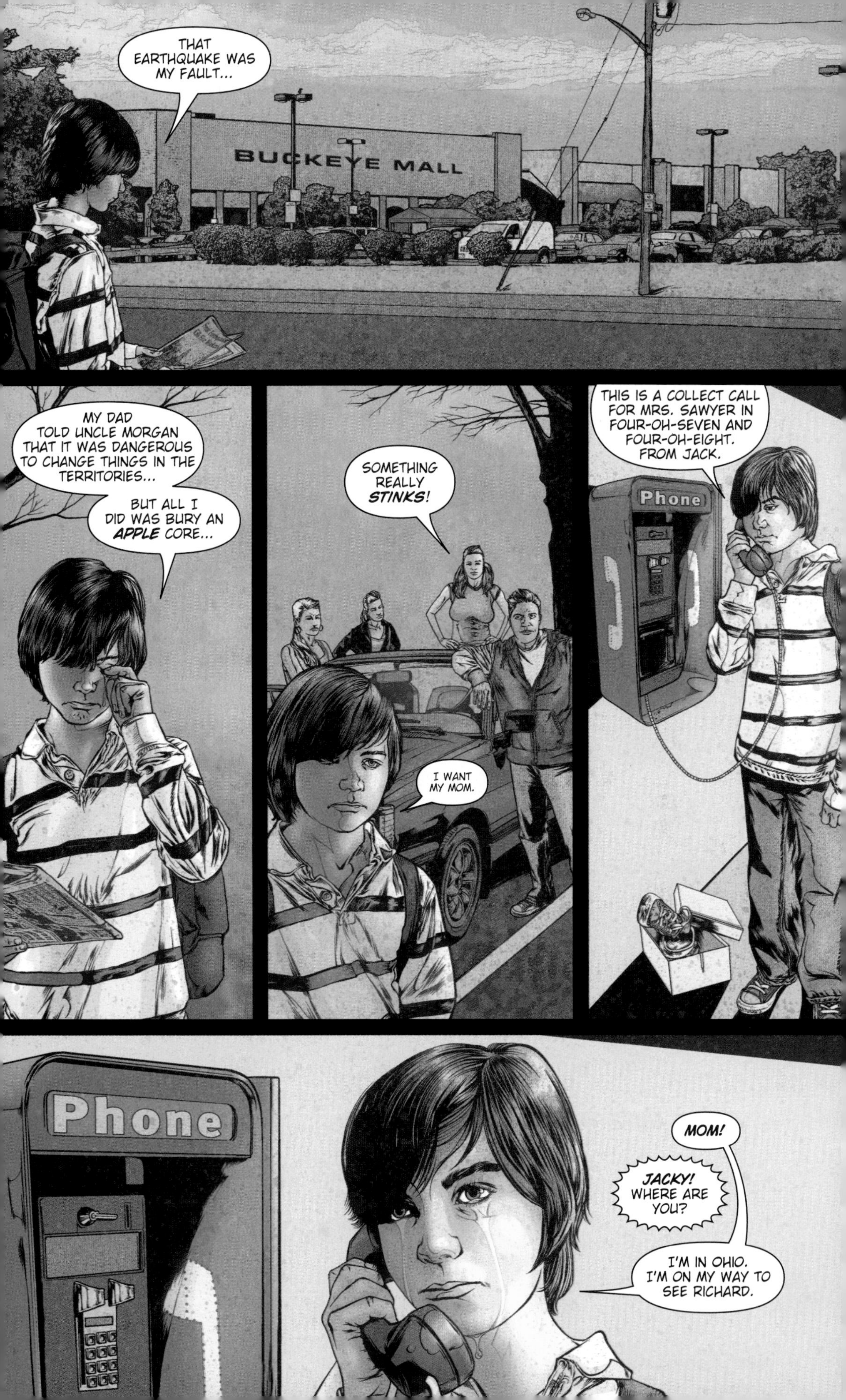
THAT EARTHQUAKE WAS MY FAULT...
BUCKEYE MALL
MY DAD TOLD UNCLE MORGAN THAT IT WAS DANGEROUS TO CHANGE THINGS IN THE TERRITORIES...
BUT ALL I DID WAS BURY AN *APPLE* CORE...
SOMETHING REALLY *STINKS*!
I WANT MY MOM.
THIS IS A COLLECT CALL FOR MRS. SAWYER IN FOUR-OH-SEVEN AND FOUR-OH-EIGHT. FROM JACK.
Phone
Phone
MOM!
JACKY! WHERE ARE YOU?
I'M IN OHIO. I'M ON MY WAY TO SEE RICHARD.

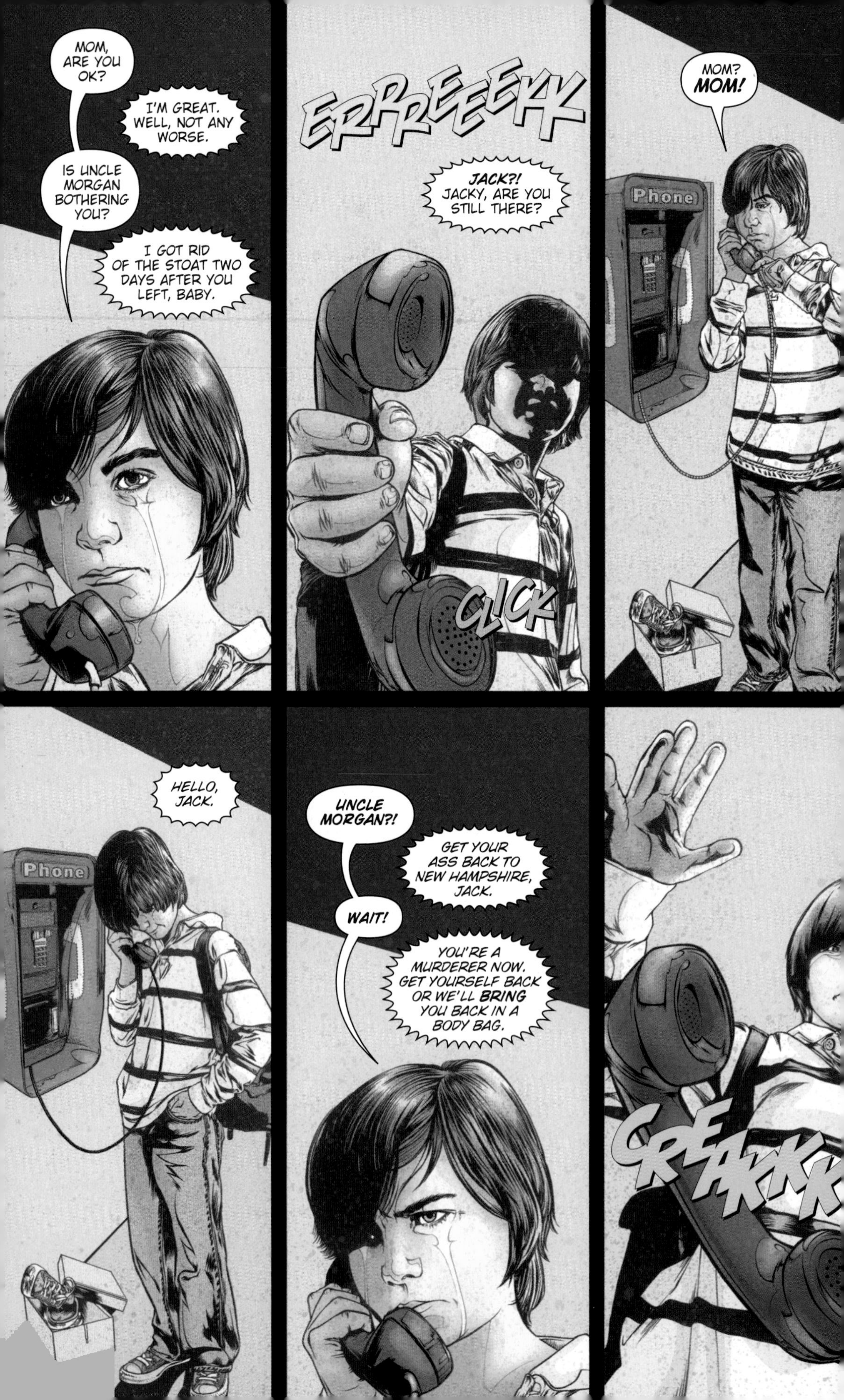
MOM, ARE YOU OK?
I'M GREAT. WELL, NOT ANY WORSE.
IS UNCLE MORGAN BOTHERING YOU?
I GOT RID OF THE STOAT TWO DAYS AFTER YOU LEFT, BABY.
ERRREEEKK
JACK?! JACKY, ARE YOU STILL THERE?
CLICK
MOM? MOM!
Phone
HELLO, JACK.
Phone
UNCLE MORGAN?!
GET YOUR ASS BACK TO NEW HAMPSHIRE, JACK.
WAIT!
YOU'RE A MURDERER NOW. GET YOURSELF BACK OR WE'LL BRING YOU BACK IN A BODY BAG.
CREAKKK

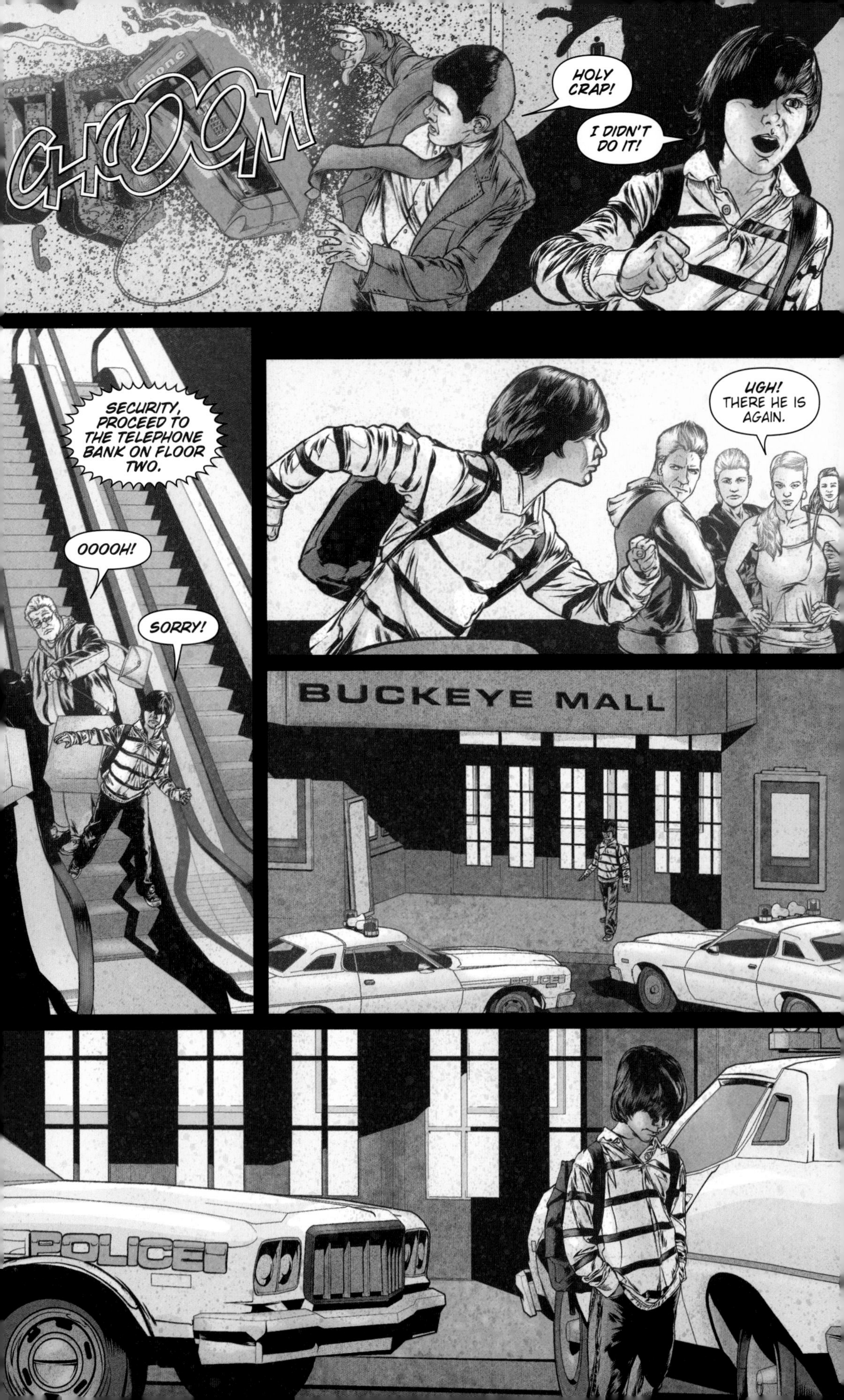
HOLY CRAP!
I DIDN'T DO IT!
SECURITY, PROCEED TO THE TELEPHONE BANK ON FLOOR TWO.
OOOOH!
SORRY!
UGH! THERE HE IS AGAIN.
BUCKEYE MALL
POLICE
POLICE

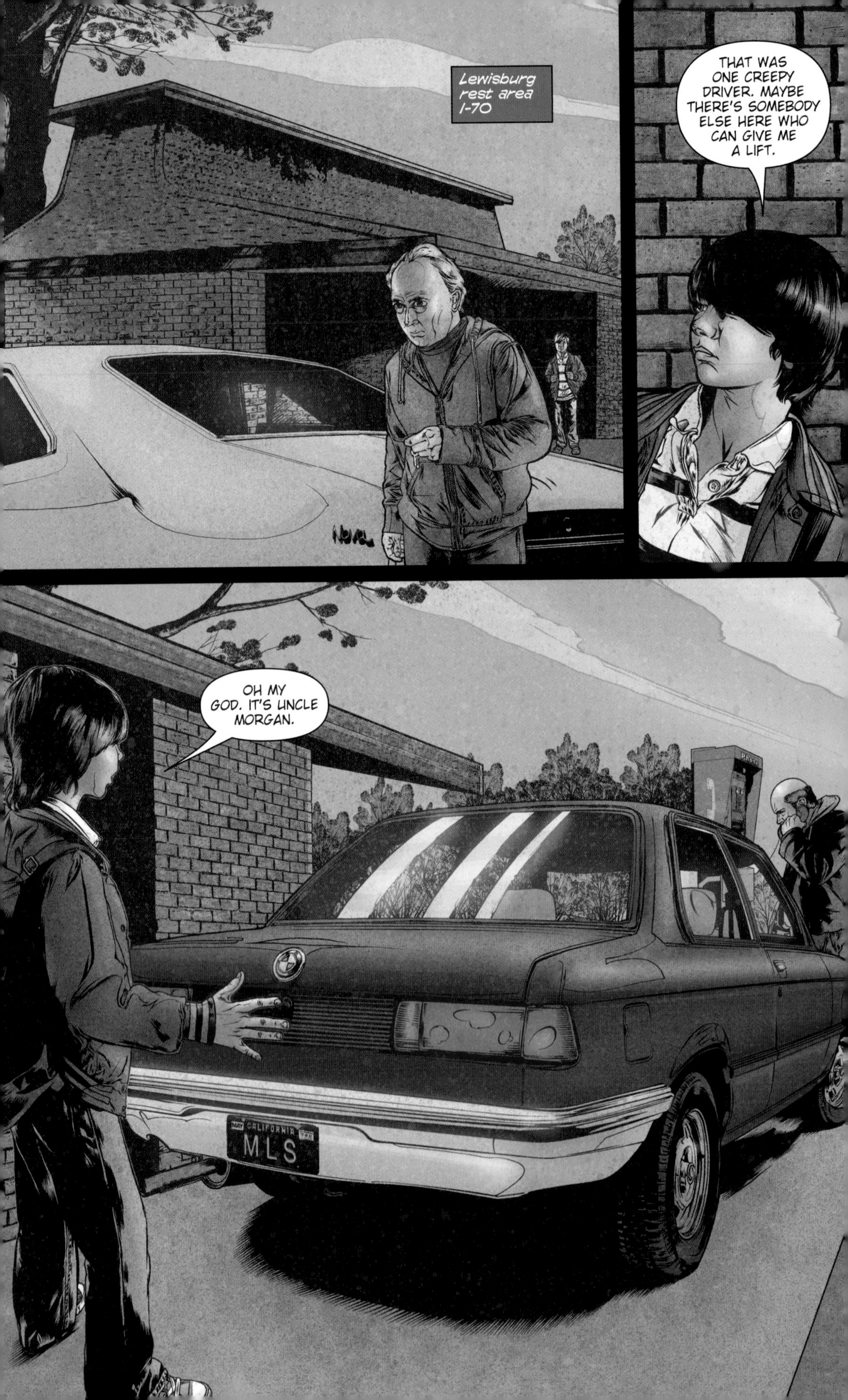
Lewisburg rest area I-70
THAT WAS ONE CREEPY DRIVER. MAYBE THERE'S SOMEBODY ELSE HERE WHO CAN GIVE ME A LIFT.
OH MY GOD. IT'S UNCLE MORGAN.
MAY CALIFORNIA
MLS

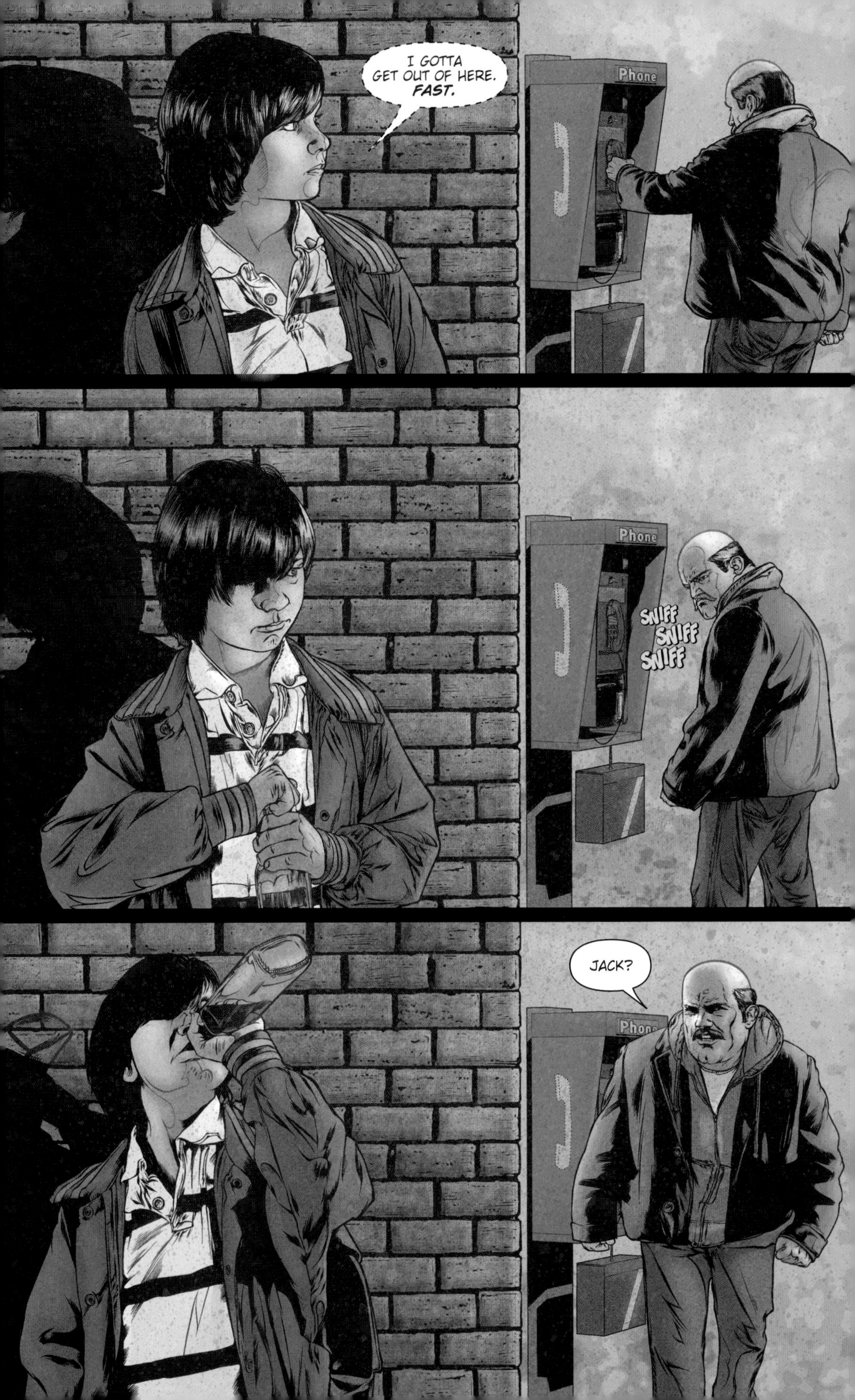
I GOTTA GET OUT OF HERE. FAST.
Phone
Phone
SNIFF SNIFF SNIFF
JACK?
Phone

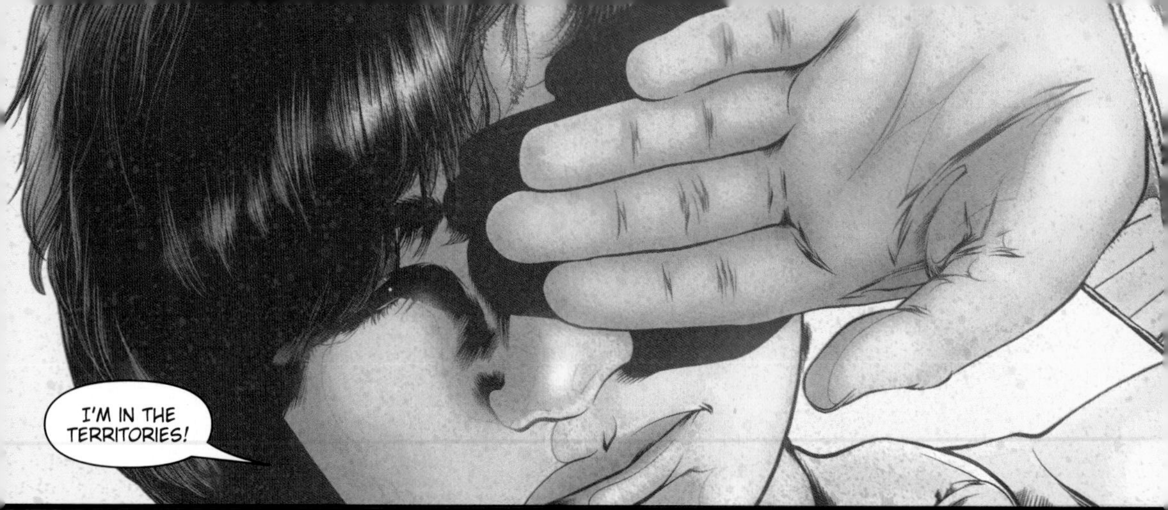
I'M IN THE TERRITORIES!

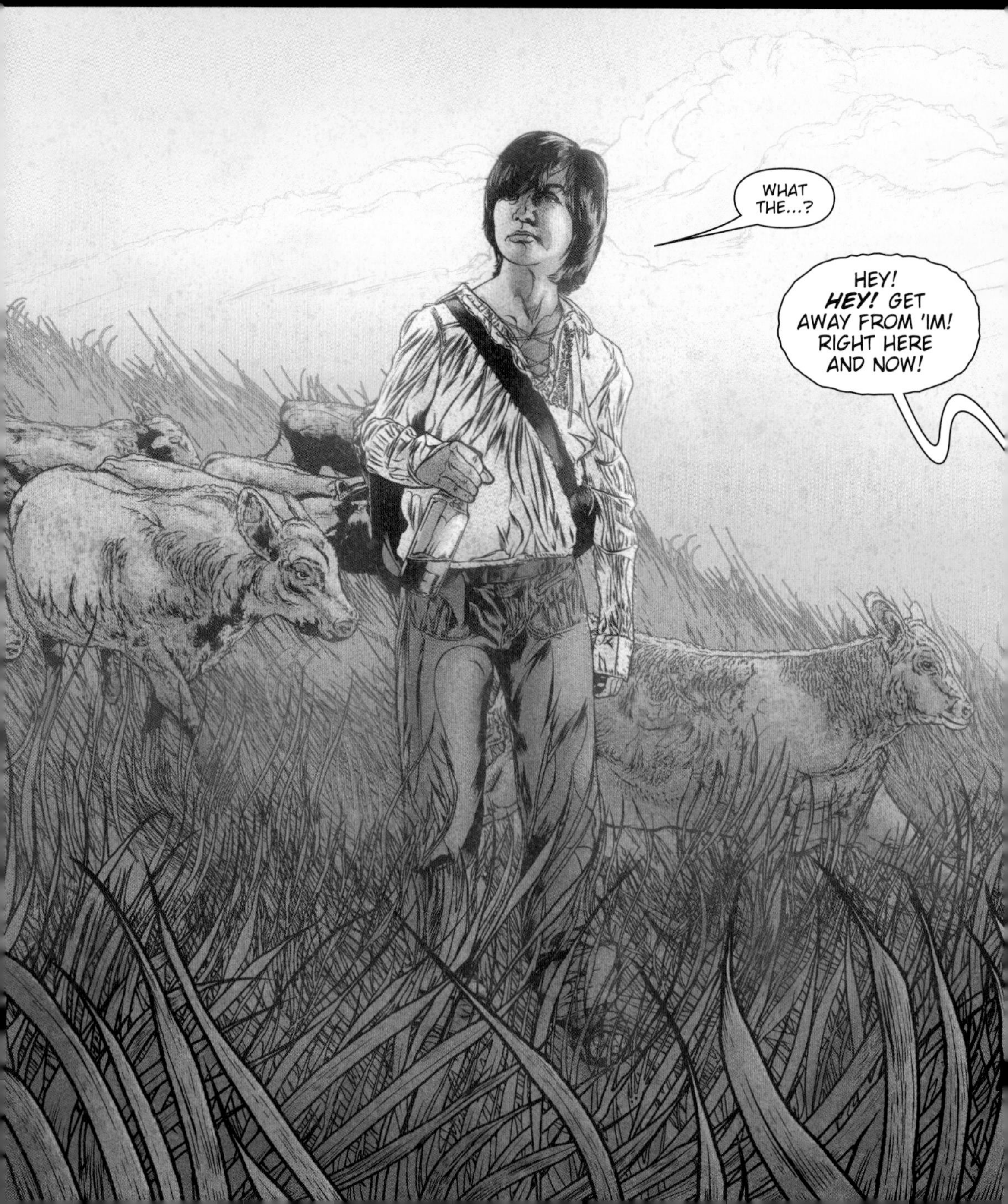
WHAT THE...?
HEY! **HEY!** GET AWAY FROM 'IM! RIGHT HERE AND NOW!

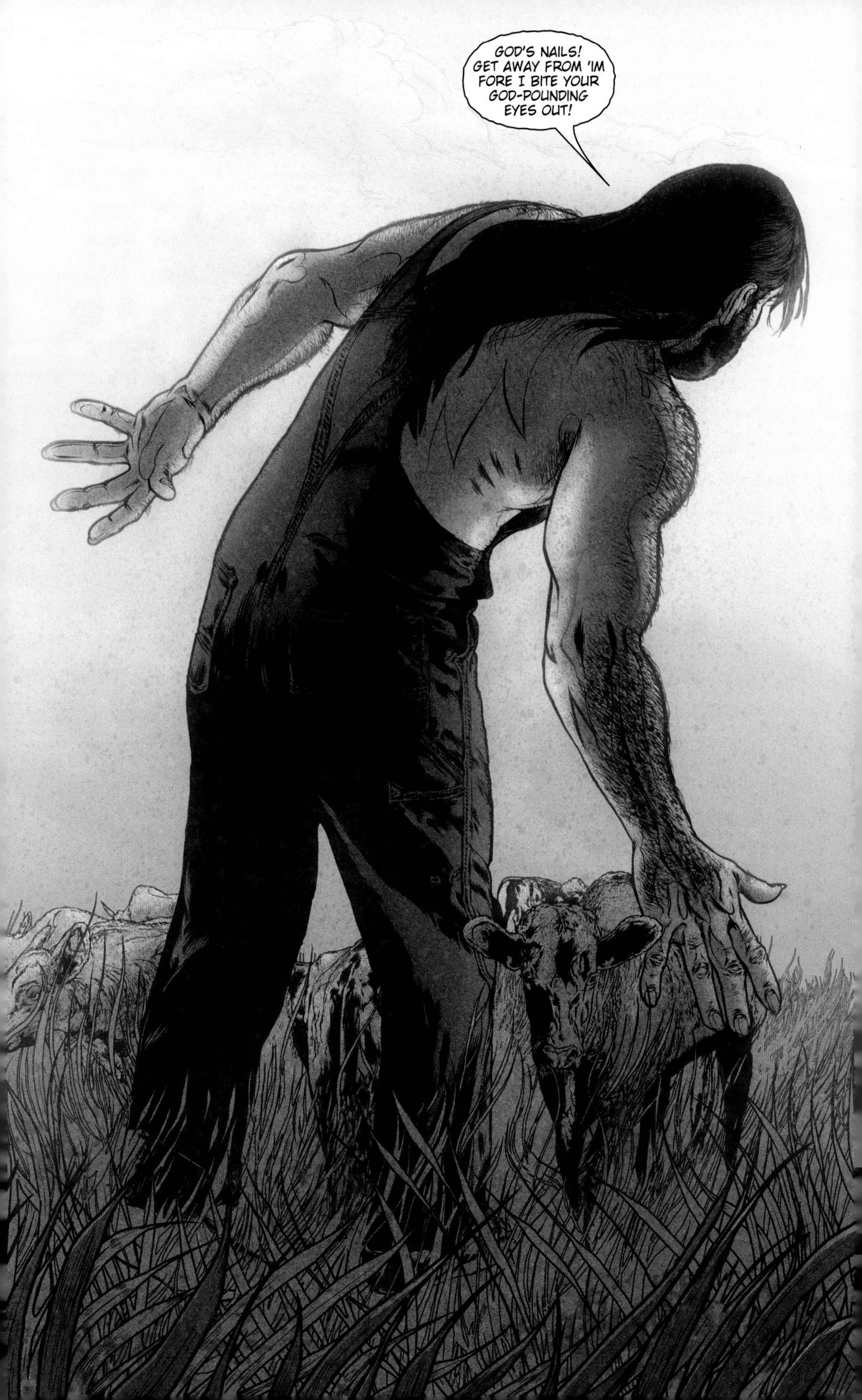
GOD'S NAILS! GET AWAY FROM 'IM FORE I BITE YOUR GOD-POUNDING EYES OUT!

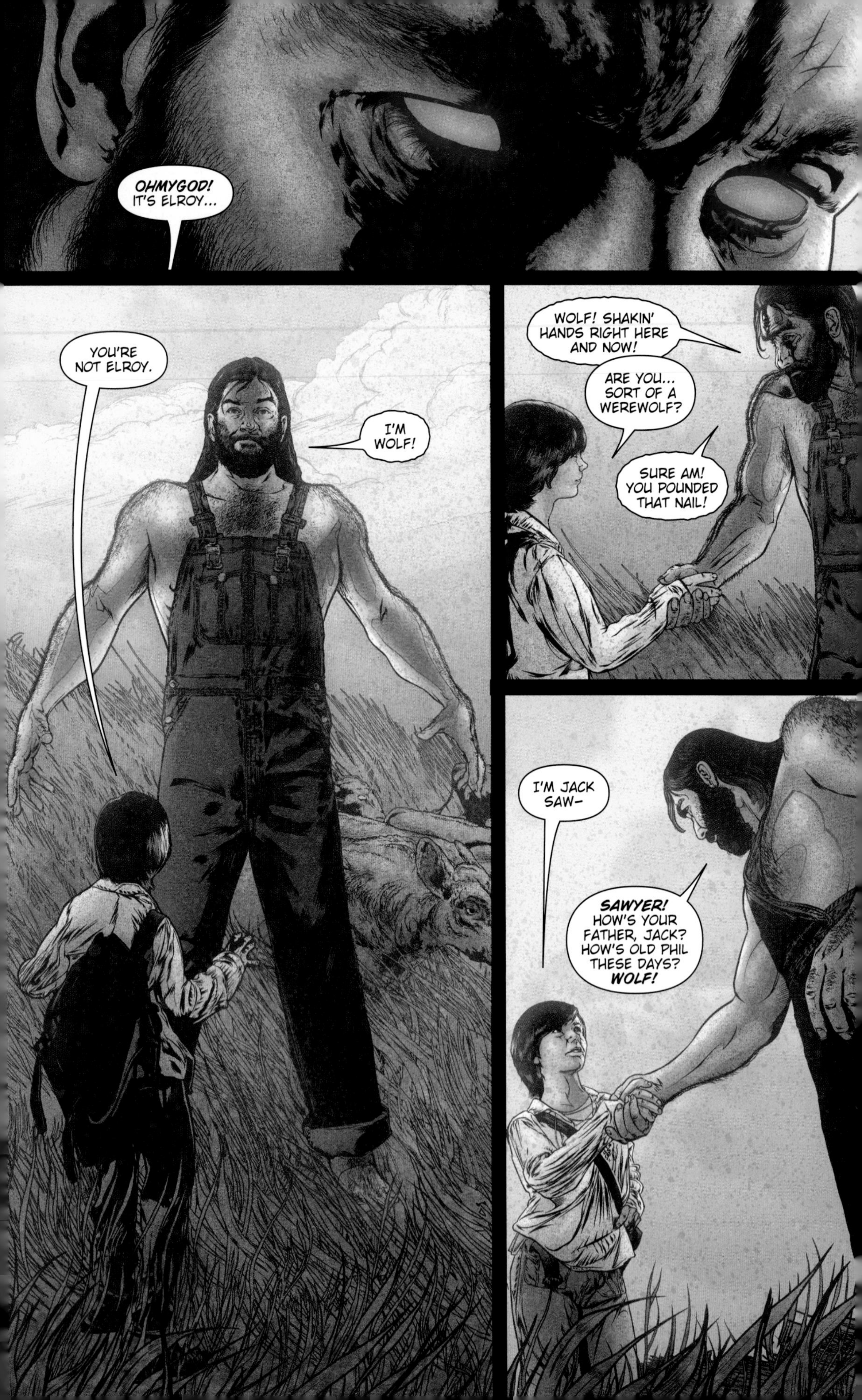

OHMYGOD! IT'S ELROY...
YOU'RE NOT ELROY.
I'M WOLF!
WOLF! SHAKIN' HANDS RIGHT HERE AND NOW!
ARE YOU... SORT OF A WEREWOLF?
SURE AM! YOU POUNDED THAT NAIL!
I'M JACK SAW-
SAWYER! HOW'S YOUR FATHER, JACK? HOW'S OLD PHIL THESE DAYS? WOLF!

A [Brief] Interview with Stephen King and Peter Straub

Did you read comics growing up? What were your favorites?

Peter Straub: As a kid, I loved comics. They taught me to read. Among my favorites were *Superman, Captain Marvel, Batman, The Hawkeyes* (I think—about a group of proto-fascist airmen who yelled "Hawkaaa!" whenever they went into battle), *Mary Jane, Henry, Nancy, Pogo, Li'l Abner,* and many others.

Stephen King: Oh, come on—EVERY-THING! But my favorite, by a country mile, was Plastic Man and his pal, Woozy Winks. I dug Plaz's dark glasses! Peter probably means the Blackhawks. The really cool violence-oriented one was *Combat Casey.*

Are either of you artwork lovers, and have you created your own artwork?

PS: I buy a good many paintings and graphics, and I like to make elaborate collages.

SK: If I drew a cat, you wouldn't know what it was.

Have you read any comics or graphic novels recently, or do you have any on your reading wish lists?

PS: Let's see . . . I reread *Watchmen* after I saw a DVD of the movie, and I've been reading a five-part Batman tale, *Gotham Central,* which focuses mainly on the Gotham police force. And I try to keep up with John Constantine.

SK: I've been reading *Scalped* and *North-landers.* I've also been reading my son Joe's *Lock and Key* series.

Who would you rather be drawn by: Jack Kirby or Will Eisner?

PS: Will Eisner.

SK: Kirby.

Betty or Veronica?

PS: Veronica, no contest.

SK: Betty. Can I say "both"?

Cover Gallery

The chapters of this volume
originally appeared as individual comic
books with cover art by award-winning
Italian artist Massimo Carnevale.

Here is his cover art for
the six issues.

Issue #0

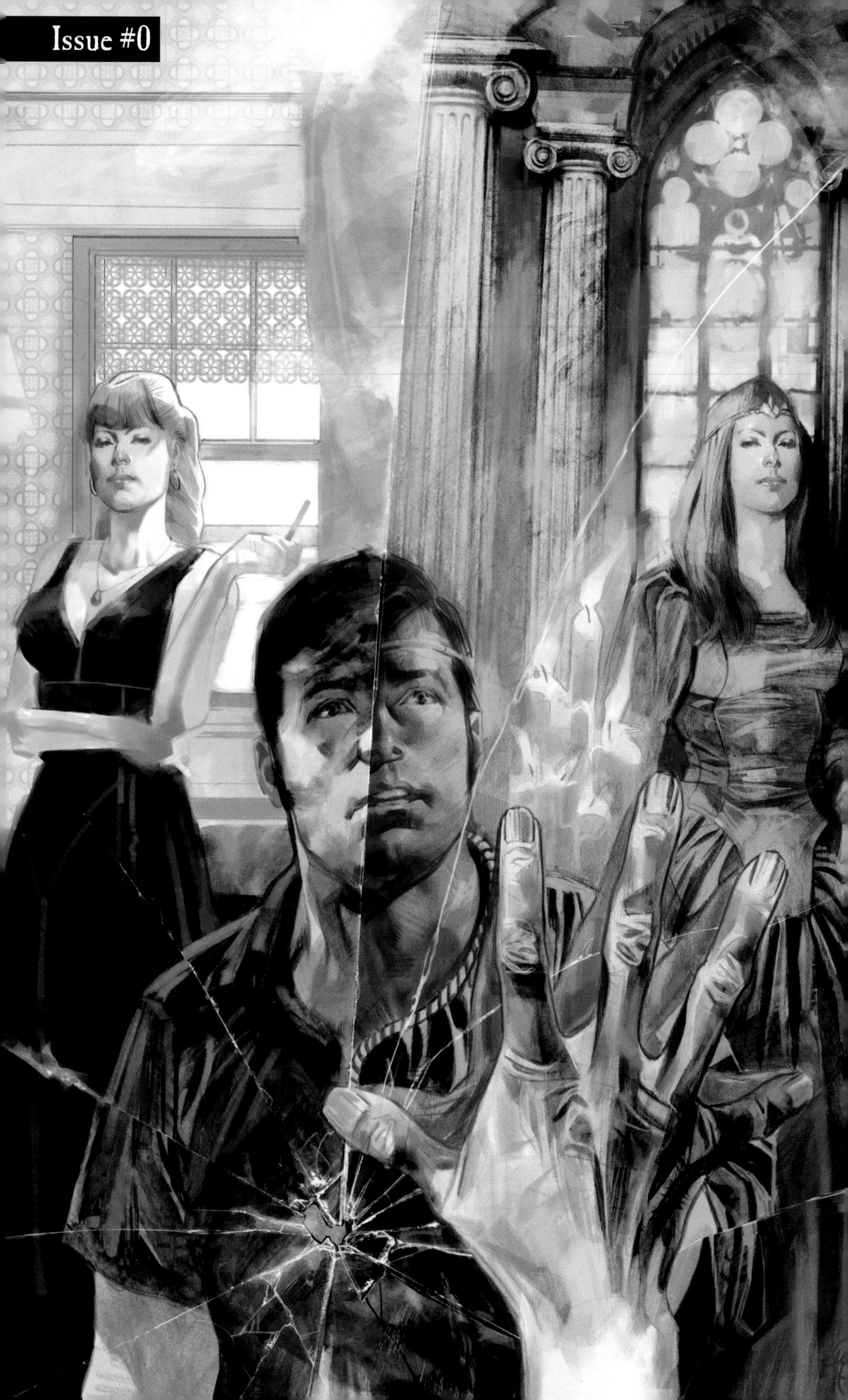

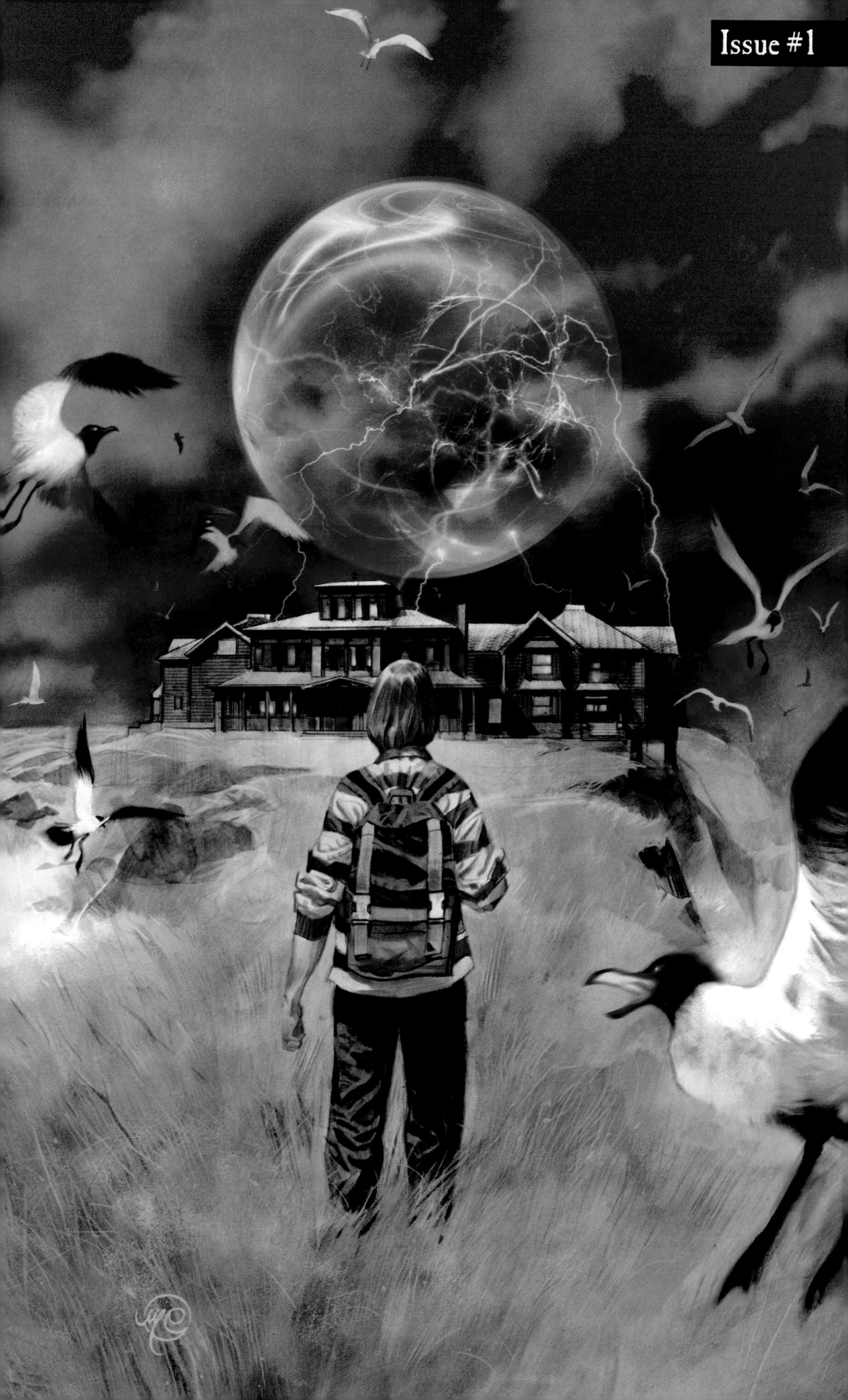
Issue #1

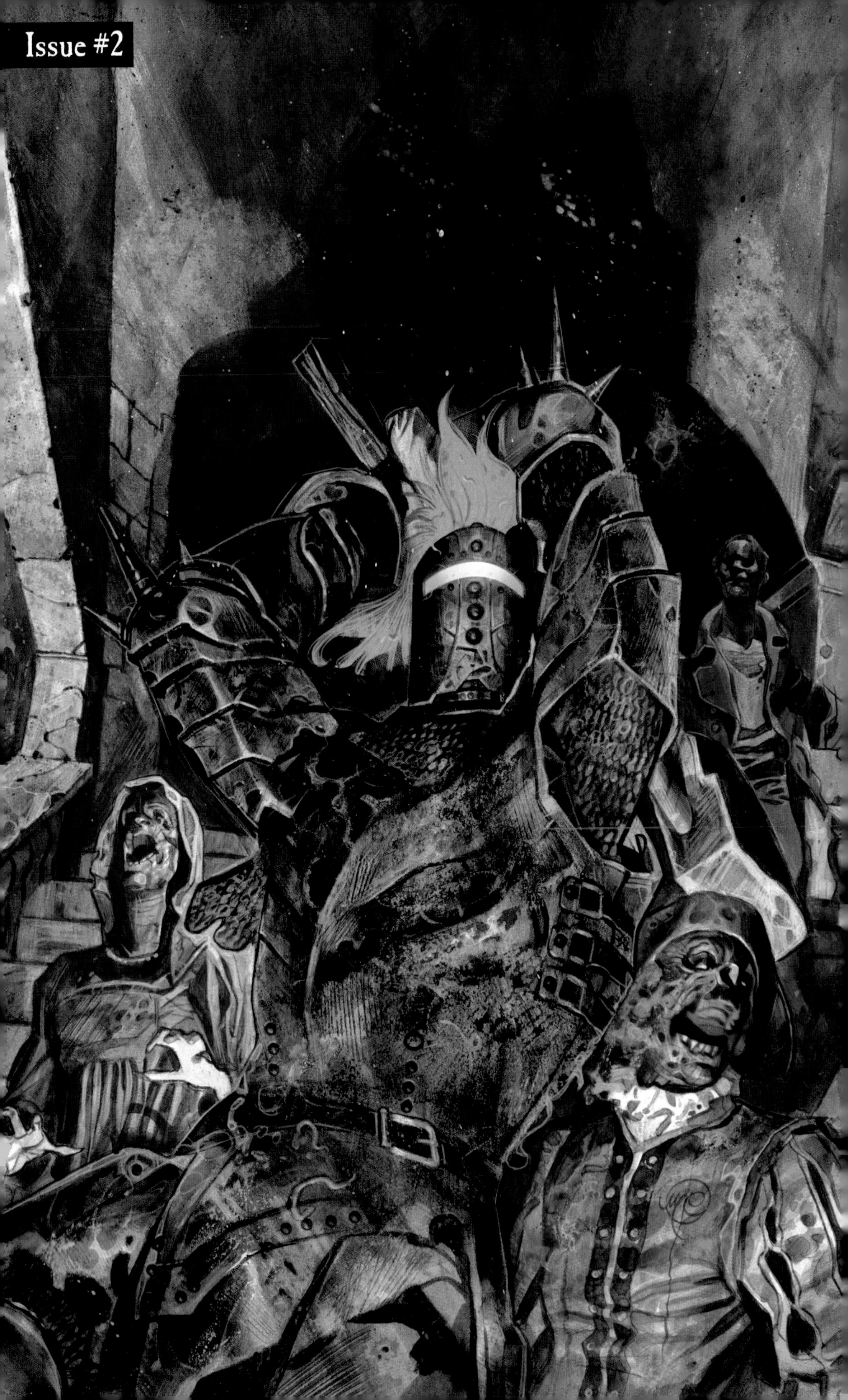
Issue #2

Issue #3

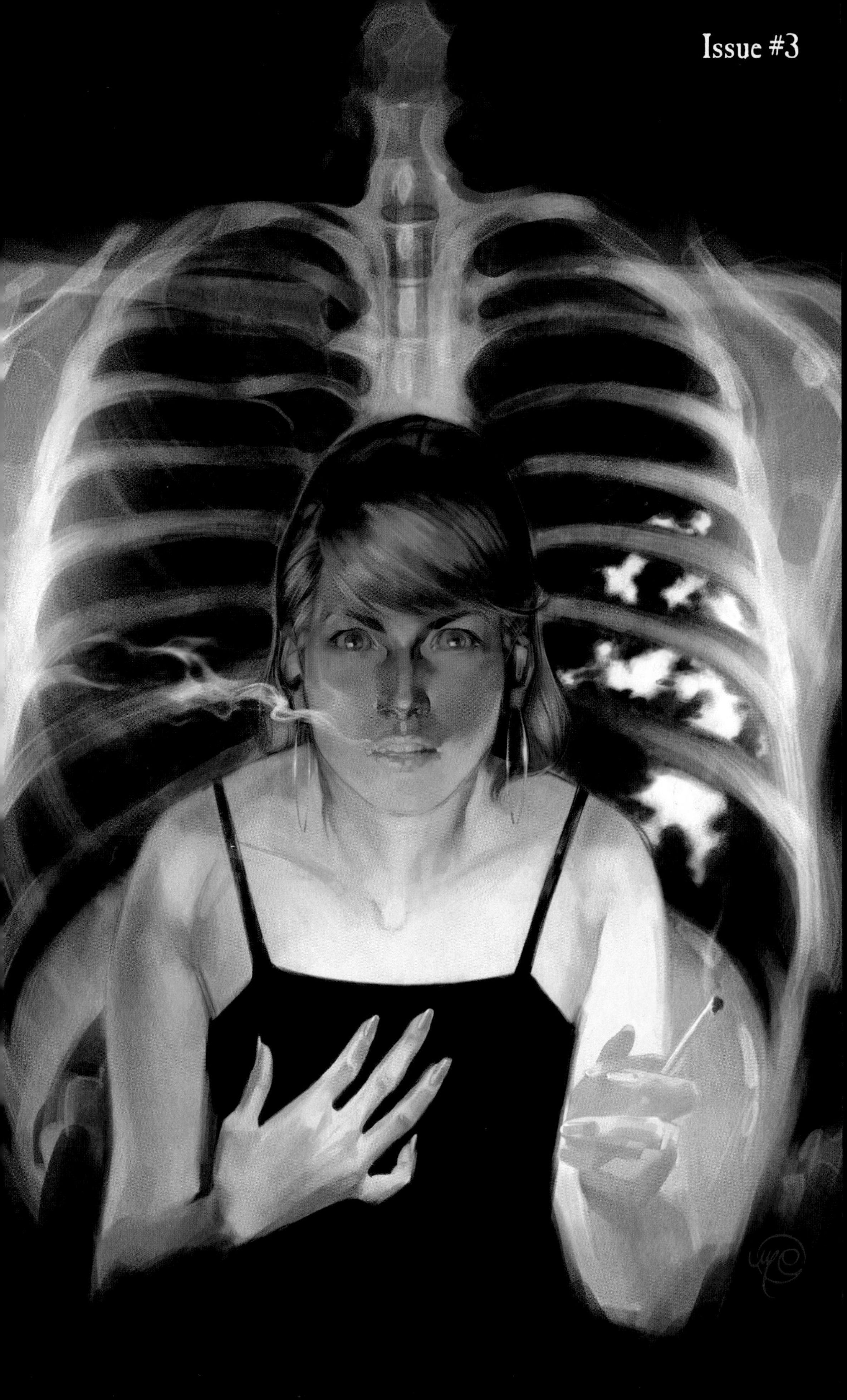

Issue #4

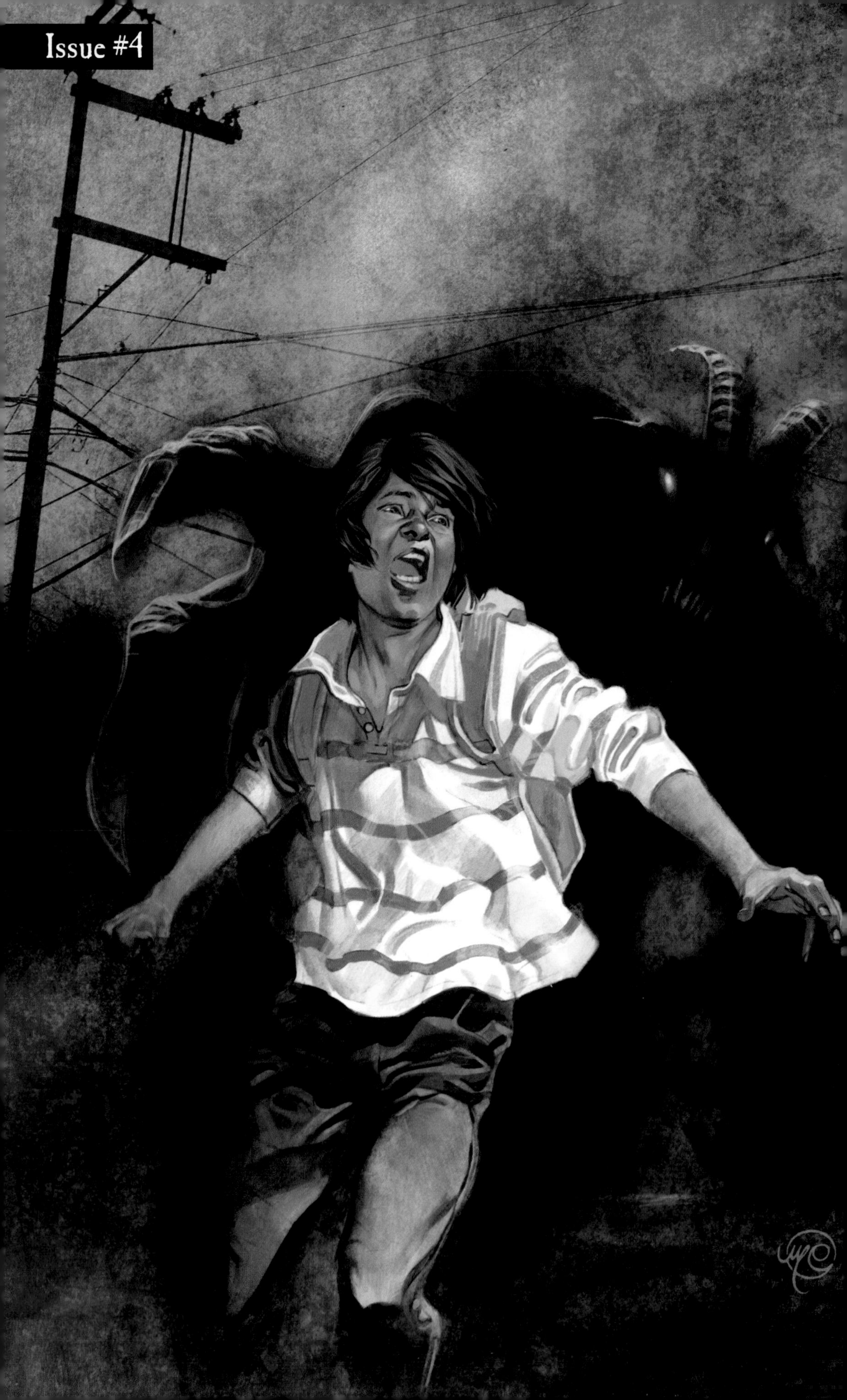

Issue #5

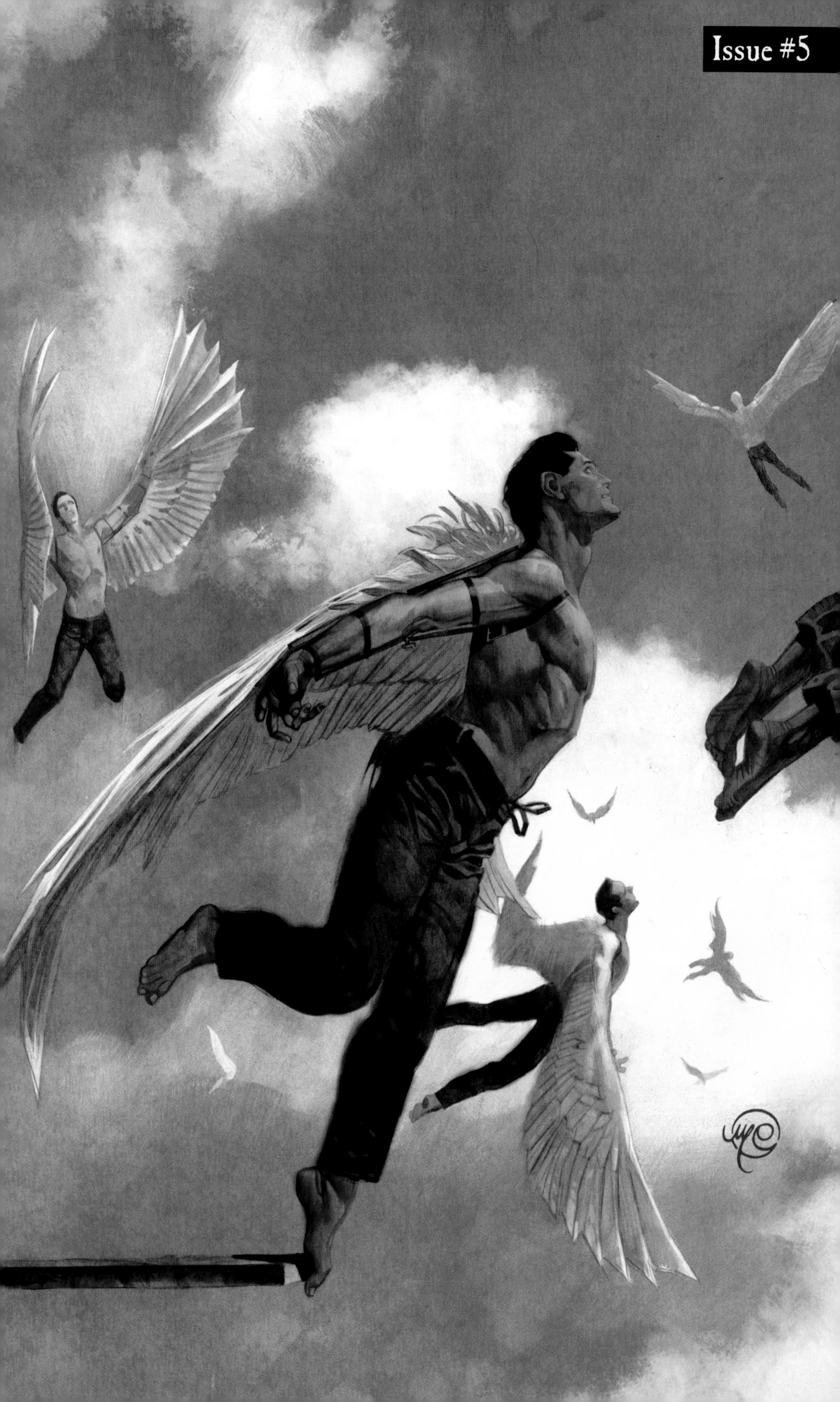

Sketchbook

Every reader will have a different mental picture of the characters in *The Talisman*, and what appears in this book may not be what many fans had envisioned. The novel's original authors can be the only real authority on the issue, and as artist Tony Shasteen began to work on the look of each character in the story, he had the task of creating visual representations that were acceptable to Stephen King and Peter Straub.

Adaptor Robin Furth spent many hours pulling together details sprinkled throughout the novel to create composite descriptions of each character. Working from her notes, Shasteen submitted first-round sketches for approval. King and Straub approved several characters right away: Morgan of Orris and his Twinner, Morgan Sloat; Speedy; and Queen Laura got a quick go-ahead. Others took more time.

Tony's first version of Wolf was delightful but not as close to the book as it needed to be.

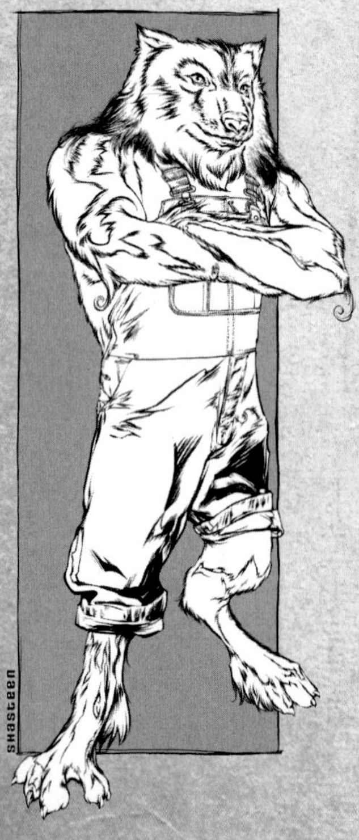
SHASTEEN

First-round sketch—
too wolflike

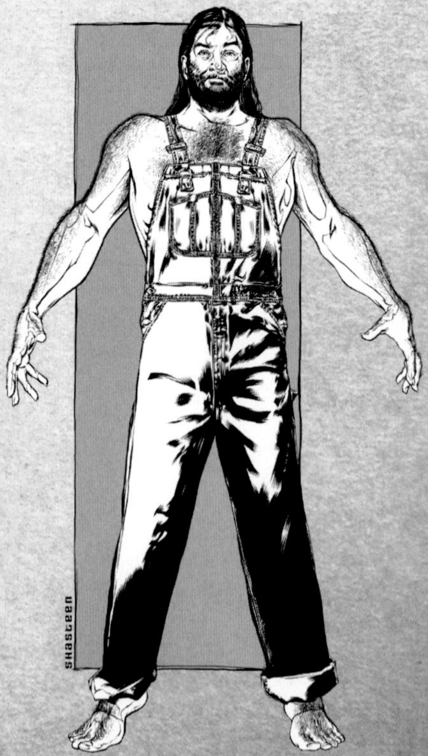
SHASTEEN

Approved version

Jack's mother, Laura, also went through several drafts. But of all the characters, Jack and his father, Phil, were the toughest to capture.

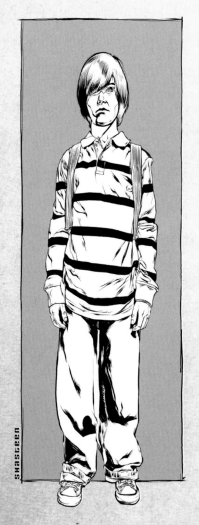

Jack, original version

Phil, original version

"We had Huckleberry Finn in mind. Or Everyboy," Stephen King responded to the initial sketch of Jack. "Think of an unremarkably handsome kid of twelve or thirteen, give him clear, curious eyes and a nice grin . . . and I think you're home. Oh, and a few muscles. Kid's gotta work in a bar, after all." Both authors said Phil looked too much like a model, mid '70s style.

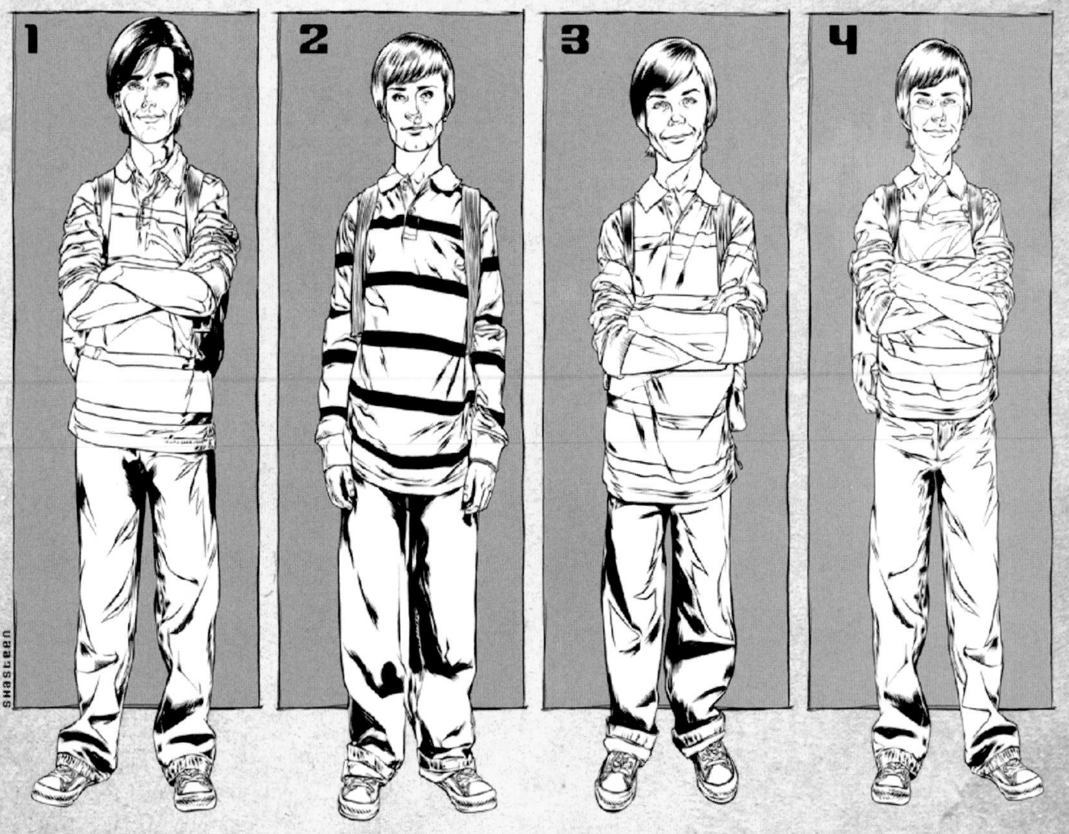
1
2
3
4

Tony decided to create a range of looks for King and Straub to choose from.

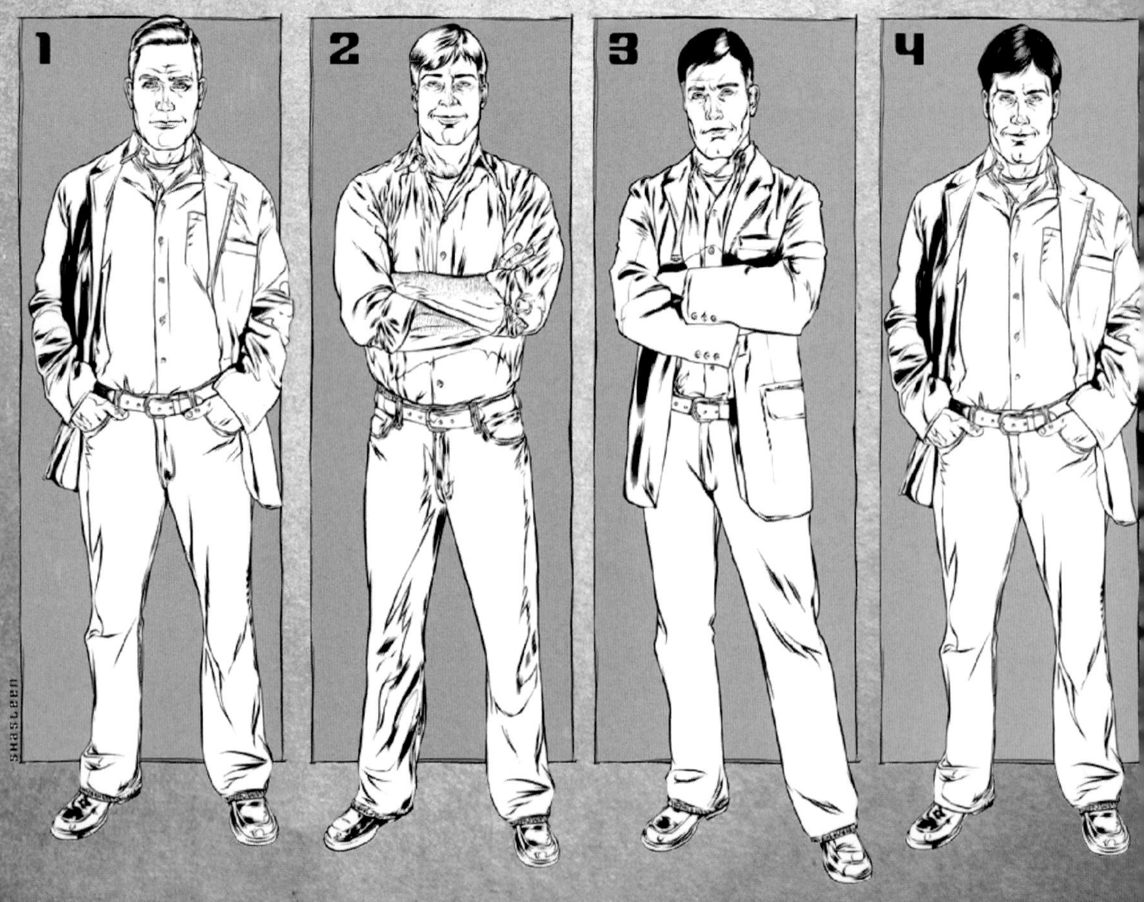
1
2
3
4

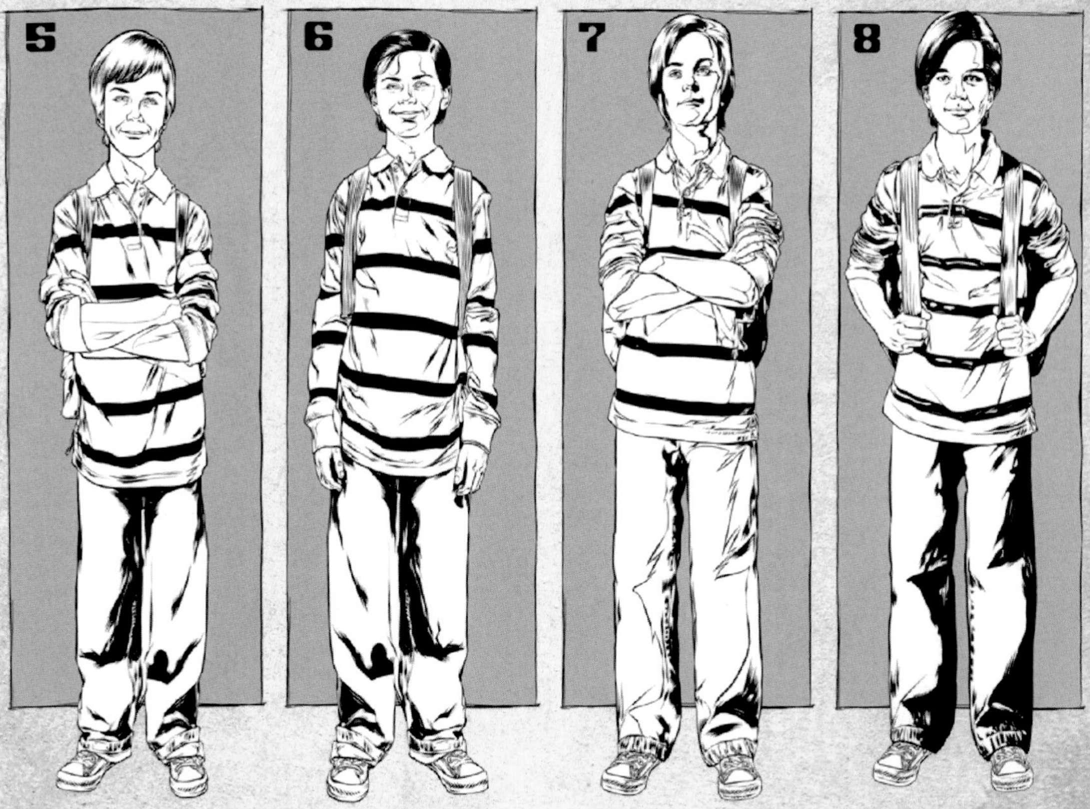
5
6
7
8

For Jack, the authors went for a composite of sketch #8 with the hairstyle from sketch #5.

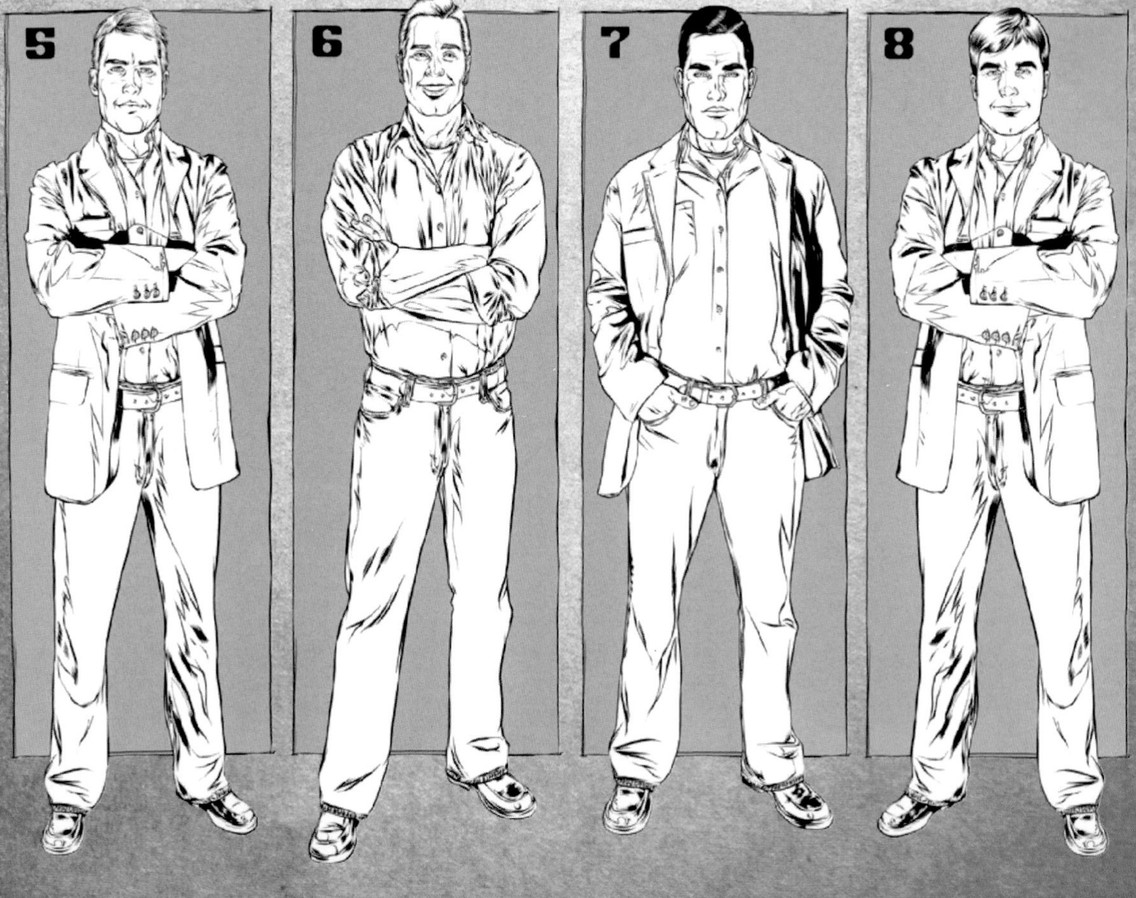
5
6
7
8

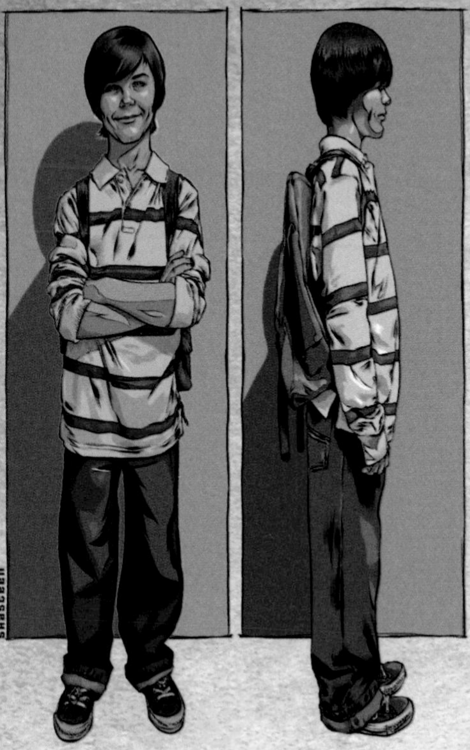
SHASTEEN

Jack, final version

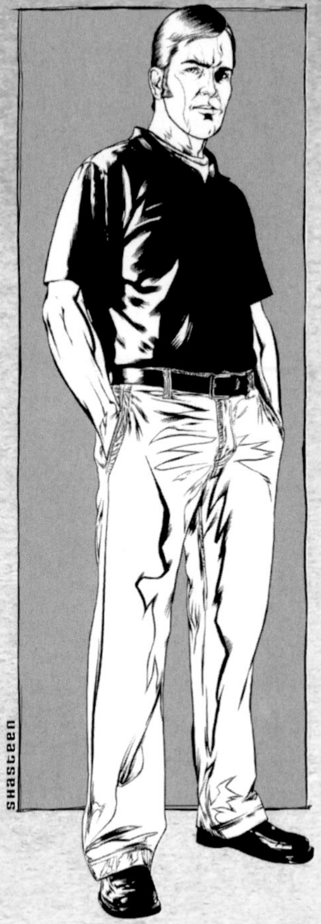
SHASTEEN

Phil, final version

Visit Stephen King's official website:
www.stephenking.com

Visit Peter Straub's official website:
www.peterstraub.net